Madame Seraphine

By

Caroline Nesbitt

ISBN 979-8-3507-4134-6

Epona Books, P.O. Box 52,
North Sandwich, New Hampshire 03259

I.

"It is the stars, the stars above us, govern our conditions"

- William Shakespeare, *King Lear,* III.3

On this April day that was to herald a sea change in the lives of a great many people, the weather was more remarkable for a cold and driving rain than for the fragrant, floriferous affair beloved of poets, musicians, and writers of romantic novels. It was a piercing, incessant rain. It had gone on for days, turning London's streets to a slimy stew of mud, cobble, shit, ash, soot, garbage, and offal too disgusting to name. Thames, its banks thawed and warmed by frequent soaking, stank. But then, Thames always stank. Those with business near the water, or those forced by circumstance to cross it by bridge or boat, gagged and held lavender-scented handkerchiefs or oranges stuffed with cloves to their nostrils to make it bearable. The rivermen who ran passengers and goods up and down from embankment to soggy landing, and the mudlarks who trolled through the undefinable sludge of animal and human life thrown onto Thames' banks by floodwaters that roared through the city from the north and west, were made of sterner stuff. There were livings to be made on the river, and rich pickings in the mangled, fetid rot left behind when the tide went out and the waters regained their normal level.

But the Fates do not require blossom to do their work; or fragrance, or even a particularly fine climatic moment. They require only a certain confluence of star, planet, season, politics, and opportunity; spiced with a large dollop of human error. And whimsy, of course. Whatever have the Fates brought to pass that was not in some way influenced by whimsy?

So, it was a raw, wet day in April, in the year 1793. It was a day on which two ships arrived at two of England's teeming and noisome ports. One was a large trading vessel from the Colonies that cruised to a weary halt with the help of several large rowboats manned by burly dockers just as dawn struggled to light a sodden world. On its deck amongst the bustle of the crew, two young men stood, shrouded in cloaks against the raw dawn, and stared dispassionately at the immense size and clamor of London's congested docks. Each thought separately of the other ports they had seen in the last decade - small, large, tropical, colonial, ancient and crumbling, new and rough; every port with its own character, its languages, its smells. Each drew separate comparisons and came to separate conclusions about the landing they were about to make. Each turned without a word to go below decks and prepare for this latest docking.

The other vessel was a small, swift packet, fresh from the coast of Italy, that settled to rest in Southampton like a tern seeking refuge from the storm. From it there issued a great quantity of luggage overseen by a fussy, self-important man named Tibbs, who bullied the overburdened porters tirelessly. Last to disembark was an older man, his lean physique ravaged less by the rigors of the journey than by a lifetime of loose living, who stood for several silent moments on the dock and looked about him as if trying to make a marriage of memory and present circumstance, before being unctuously ushered toward a private parlor in the warmth of the whitewashed inn that sat alluringly just across the cobbled way.

It was a day on which Mr. Tristan Neville decided that a circuitous walk along the green edge of the Park - at an hour of the morning his man Hubbard would have declared as barely Christian, had he known of it - was just the thing to clear his head of an alcoholic haze incurred from a very long night in St. James. The night should have been worth the pain of a heroic hangover. The cards had favored him, and he came away plumper in the pocket than he had been for some weeks. Yet the winnings left him restless, and aware of something lacking in his pleasant and predictable world, that the momentary thrill of risking all on a throw of the dice, then winning against the odds, could no longer assuage. So he walked, and observed the quiet stirrings of the gardeners, and the sweeps, and the shopkeepers and stall holders as they set about creating another day in the prosperous city that existed for the pleasure of those like himself.

It was a day on which Miss Angel Hathaway walked along the same green edge of the Park even though it was not precisely on her way to work, simply because the air there was mild and fresh, and offered space for quiet reflection before a long day putting needle and thread to fabric in the small shop where she worked; and also because her great, hairy, brindled lurcher Brutus needed a good walk. While Brutus was certainly a good enough protector for any young woman, appearances dictated that Miss Hathaway was also attended by Jacob Freeman, an imposing African gentleman whose battered face illustrated a past life of unspeakable hardship.

Inevitably, Brutus growled low in his throat, his attention caught by movement in the misting rain. Inevitably, Angel looked up sharply as the disheveled figure of Tristan Neville emerged from the fog. Her green eyes met his blue ones, she blushed and imperfectly hid a smirk at the stale smells of tobacco and wine that emanated from him, he wished the trio a good morning and a tip of the hat while suddenly wondering why on God's green earth he was walking abroad in such a disgraceful state, and the moment passed.

It was a day on which Mme. Seraphine Hathaway, the celebrated French *emigré* actress and sharer in The Swan Theatre, was implored to run an errand for her cousin-in-law and fellow sharer, Charles Pearce. It would not do, Mr. Pearce maintained, for him to make an appearance at Mme. Simard's dress shop on such a frivolous errand, when so much was at stake in preparing for the imminent opening of Mr. Shakespeare's *Romeo and Juliet*. Seraphine acidly retorted that her cousin's real reason for not picking up his own damned parcel was that he already owed Mme. Simard so much money that the thought of an unpleasant confrontation made him weak in the knees.

And it was a day on which a small notice in the *Morning Post & Daily Advertiser* launched several groups of heretofore complacent females into a state of stunning emotional turmoil.

The notice said simply that on such and such a day in such and such a month in the year of our Lord 1793, The Hon. Edward Badgeley (heir to the title, goods, and considerable

revenues of Torrington Manor) and Lady Henrietta Attenborough
(daughter of Lord Henry & Lady Abigail Attenborough, who were
of ancient and respected lineage if not precisely wealthy in this age
of risky ventures in places like the West Indies) would be joined in
holy matrimony in keeping with the traditions of both august
families from time immemorial. Or at least, as several wags had it,
since the time something more than a century or so earlier when
the Badgeleys and Attenboroughs had had the good sense to ally
themselves with Charles II on his return to England after the final
overthrow of the Cromwellian regime.

But that was all in the past. In this new and modern age of
enlightened thought, social upheaval, and treasonous zeal, the
American Colonies had won their freedom from the Crown, and
struggled toward nationhood. Revolutionary France offered
amnesty - coupled with a dire threat of being accused of treason
for refusing it - to those who had fled the 1789 Revolution, while
shock waves from the recent deaths of Louis XVI and his family
reverberated around the Polite world, and political strife between
Jacobins and Robespierre's Girondists led to the social collapse
and mass executions that would later be known only as The
Terror.

England, however, settled and thrice-blessed England, was for
the moment at peace with itself. 'Farmer' George III had
maintained his regal return to sanity for three full years and
delayed the hopes of the floridly handsome Prince Regent, whose
ascendancy would come to name an age. In The City, the Ports,
and the Government, the wheels of industry and trade flourished.
And behind the ornate doors of the wealthy, well-connected
matriarchs of every stripe continued to ply their own political
Trade, peddling well-bred daughters to the highest bidder on the
Marriage Mart.

Thus it was that in a large and comfortable Georgian house in
Grosvenor Square, the titled but poverty-stricken Lady Damson
threw the *Morning Post & Daily Advertiser* into the fire with a very
unladylike oath, boxed her languidly beautiful daughter's ears so

that they rang and caused said daughter to shriek and weep, and announced that this horrifying and unlooked-for marriage announcement was all Amelia's fault for not *trying* hard enough to ensnare young Badgeley's affections when she had felt *assured* that an offer should have been forthcoming to so lovely and eligible a young lady, and *now* what were they to do but to find her another swain with enough scratch to pull them out of the debt incurred by the late Sir Horace Damson at the gaming tables? 'And O, *why oh why* must we come to such a pass, and Jasper with nothing left to inherit of his entitlement unless you marry well? We shall end in the *streets*, begging for our bread, I have no doubt!'

'Jasper! Jasper! *Jasper!* Always *Jasper!* What about *my* entitlement, mama? What about *my* happiness?'

'You keep a civil tongue in your head, miss!' ordered her mama, 'and Do What You Must to Save Your Family!' But Amelia stamped her foot in a towering rage that was easily the match of her parent's, and swore through angry tears that she would *never* marry Benjamin Dorset who looked like a barge, *never, never, never.* So her mother boxed Amelia's ears again and sent the girl howling from the room.

In the cramped dressing room of The Swan Theatre in Covent Garden, far from the comforts of Grosvenor Square, young Bridie Murphy echoed these passions and lay screaming, writhing, and drumming her heels on the dressing room floor in a fit of strong hysterics brought about after her friend (and, it must be said, chief rival) Doll Bridger had read the *Morning Post & Daily Advertiser's* simple passage aloud, thinking it would be of interest to Bridie, whose ability to read was not great.

'*No! No! No! It ain't true, it's me he loves, memememe me the wicked bastard, the cheating cur, I'll eat his heart I will, I love him and he loves mememe!*' Bridie screamed shrilly, writhing in agony on a surface that was, at the very least, grimy, until her hair and petticoat were so besmirched with bits of sawdust, pebbles, scraps of paper, dirt, and shreds of fabric that she no longer looked like the favored opera dancer of a small but thriving theatrical company and pampered mistress of a young man of wealth and title, but rather more like the half-starved Irish ragamuffin that had arrived at the Swan's stage door two years prior. Her hysteria was watched with interest by Doll and several other members of the dancing corps, none of whom made any effort to quiet the distressed girl.

'*What the hell is going on in here?*' roared a stentorian voice, immediately accompanied by the large presence of Charles Pearce in the doorway. The other girls scattered back to their places at the long dressing counter, all but Doll, who stood her ground cheekily and said smugly, 'I just told her about the bit in *The Morning Post & Daily Advertiser*, Mr. Pearce, sir, so I did. Thought she ought to know, like.'

'Know *what*, for gawd'sake?'

'About her young Mr. Badgeley as is, sir, who's to be a-marryin' of a lady name of...'

'*No! No! No!*' shrieked Bridie sobbing with fresh fervor on the floor.

'Oh, Lord,' muttered Mr. Pearce, and backed hurriedly into the hall, bellowing '*Mrs. Hathaway! Madame Seraphine*, you are needed in the dressing room *immediately*!' at the top of his theatrical lungs. The care of hysterical young females was not - most definitely *not* - a part of what he accepted as an Actor-Manager's job. Seeing Seraphine coming quickly down the stairs from the stage, a question ready on her lips, he jerked a thumb toward the dressing room, from which emanated a new crescendo of wails. 'Trouble,' he said succinctly, bolted to his office, and shut the door.

'*Qu'est-ce que c'est*' – began that lady, steaming into the room with as much sail as a small, neat figure could manage. She came to a halt in the doorway, observed Bridie, listened to Doll's round-eyed confession, noted the smirk under the air of concern, and brusquely ordered, 'Back to your mending, Doll. And you others, *vite, vite*, rehearsal is in ten minutes and there will be a fine if you are late, *je vous assure*!'

Then she dragged the wailing Bridie to her feet, slapped her smartly on each cheek - which caused the girl to gasp, choke, and stop wailing - and sat her firmly in a chair. '*Maintenant, fille la plus stupide*' she ordered her. 'Stop this mad blubbering at once. *Qu'est-ce que tu fait, alors?*'

'He-he-he-' Bridie hiccuped. 'It's a *lie*. He-he loves *me, me*. He cannot marry that-that- he *promised* he was mine if I was his, he *said...*'

'*Ah, que tu est bête!* You stupid, stupid girl!' Madame said callously. 'What exactly did you expect, eh? Did you think that young Badgeley would marry you, a girl like you? *Regardez vous-meme!* How many times have I told you - *all* of you - 'she glared at the whole room - 'that these men will say anything, *anything* to take what they want from you. And they will abandon you, *oui, bien sur*, they will. Without a thought, or a penny. Do you not understand this? *Hein?*'

Now Bridie's grief turned from hysterics to tears of deep shuddering sorrow, because she had known in her heart that it was true, that Ned Badgeley would never marry her. But she had hoped, and fooled herself, and accepted his gifts, his passionate words, his kisses, his body taking possession of hers behind the curtain on the darkened stage, hidden in the stairwells, even God help her, in the alley, against the rough, damp stone of the theatre wall. And now it was over. And she was ruined.

'Bridie,' said Mrs. Hathaway, more gently now. She took the girl's chin in her hand and looked into her eyes - oh! Heartbreakingly blue, like cornflowers, like a washed sky - and asked, 'Did he put a child in your belly, Bridie? Are you keeping anything from me that I should know?"

Bridie's eyes widened, and she blushed deeply. 'Sure, I don't know, ma'am. I could not say, yet awhile.'

'*Bien.* All may yet be well.' She patted the girl's cheek. 'But,' she added, as a calculating gleam began to kindle in Bridie's eyes, 'do not - do not for *a moment*, do you hear, think that if you are with child that Badgeley will marry you after all. *Au contraire*, like all his kind, he will say the father is some other man. No, do not speak! I tell you, *moi meme*, that is what he will say. *Eh bien.* Clean yourself and get onstage. You must not disgrace yourself so, like a common *putain* but be proud, and unconcerned. *Oui? C'est vrai.* The world is full of handsome young men, after all. And one day, one will be yours. But - *écoutez-moi bien* - such a one will *not* have an ancient title, and live in a grand house, eh?'

Then, making her way to the tiny office that Mr. Pearce and Mrs. Hathaway shared to run the business that was The Swan Theatre, Seraphine flung herself onto the sofa that sat perpendicular to the desk behind which sat her husband's cousin, and released a very long diatribe in very rapid and explicit French that left Mr. Pearce blinking in utter bewilderment.

'My dear Sera,' he protested, as she looked at him as if awaiting his response. '*En Anglais, s'il vous plait.* I cannot follow your thoughts at all.'

'*Merde!*' swore Seraphine irritably. 'It does not bear repeating.' And then with a deep breath, asked rhetorically, 'Why is it, do you suppose, that the vastly wealthy persist in marrying one another? It would do so much more good in the world if they would marry where their hearts - or their cocks - lead them instead. It would serve to,' she waved her hands around vaguely, 'make more wealth to go around to more people. The world would be a happier place. And there would be fewer hysterical young girls rolling about the floors and making rehearsal late.'

'But then they would no longer be rich, my dear,' said Mr. Pearce reasonably.

'*Pas du tout.* They would still have far more wealth than you or I can dream of.'

'Speak for yourself,' said Mr. Pearce, peering over the rims of his spectacles at her from behind a pile of papers, prompt books, and bills that threatened to drown both the desk and the man. 'I can dream of a great deal of wealth.'

'It would be better for the general health of the population, as well,' she continued, as if he hadn't spoken. 'Mental and physical.'

'You're sounding perilously republican again, my dear. Pray you, do not come over all Bluestocking on us, it'll be the ruin of the Swan.'

'Perhaps I should go to the American colonies, then,' sighed Seraphine. 'And begin anew.'

'I sincerely hope you will not, my dear. I have it on the best authority that they are quite barbaric, you know,' he said. Then added anxiously. 'O Sera, do promise me you won't do anything so foolish as go to the Colonies. There is such a deal of dangerous water to be crossed before one arrives.'

'Do not fear it, my dear. How should I leave The Swan? Nearly every *sou* I possessed when I arrived is wrapped up in it. Though,' she added thoughtfully, 'I could return to France. That is not so very much water to cross, after all. And they have handsomely promised amnesty to *les gens comme moi* if we should go back and help to build their brave new world.'

'Seraphine!' exclaimed her partner in alarm. 'You cannot be serious! Listen to me, I beg of you. It would be madness - madness! - to return. What are their promises but the lures of Robespierre? You would be arrested for treason and sent to the guillotine the moment you set foot on French earth. He has made it clear that all emigrés are considered traitors.'

'Unless they return home.'

'Sera, if you think for a single moment...'

'I cannot help myself,' Seraphine interrupted in exasperation. 'When I see the misery of Bridie and a hundred - no, a *thousand* like her, led on by the empty promises of young men of wealth and little conscience. They think these gullible young girls nothing better than whores. When *en effet* they are trying by every means possible to earn their way in this world - a man's world, with a man's laws and a man's morals. It makes me so very angry I could put my fingers around the throats of these young men *et les etrangler, comme ca.*' She curled her fingers with a grimace of rage and demonstrated.

'Very melodramatic, my dear,' said Pearce nervously, noting the strength in those hands and the murderous expression in his leading lady's eyes. 'I've no doubt you could. But it isn't at all the thing, you know. Only lead you to the gallows, in the end. And I'm quite certain that the lot of young females is quite as bad in France. I say,' he brightened suddenly, 'Here's an idea, Sera. You could write it down - the whole sad story of the young girl abandoned, the young man damned... hint at the characters without mentioning names... and we'll present it as 'written by a lady'. People love a good *roman a clef*. What do you say?'

Seraphine eyed him warily. 'Perhaps I shall. It is after all, not such an unusual story.' She lapsed into a musing silence for a moment, then shook herself and sighed. 'Charles, it does not solve the immediate problem of Bridie Murphy, or her damaged heart, or her ruined virtue.'

'I cannot think why I should spend a single moment worrying about an opera dancer,' maintained Mr. Pearce. 'She is beautiful enough to find another well born lover, surely. And if she has any wit at all, she'll find a way to keep the next one. Why, look at Kitty El...' he limped to a halt and blinked rapidly in the face of Seraphine's glare.

'Right,' he amended himself, putting down his quill and steepling ink-stained fingers in thought. 'Then we shall have to find Bridie a swain who will make an honest woman of her. Doubtless there will be money involved. I don't suppose her parents...' she glanced at Seraphine, '...er. No. I thought not.'

'She can still dance, if she is not with child. That is a very good dowry for a young couple, a woman with such a line of work. *Mon Dieu*, will you *listen* to us!' she threw her hands up. 'We could be trying to sell a milk cow!'

'Damme if I will take this any farther!' swore the beleaguered manager, slamming his palm on the surface of the desk, sending a plume of dust into the air and a cascade of papers to the floor. 'Can the chit still perform tonight? Will she collapse in hysterics in the middle of her song? Shall we put Doll Bridger in her place?'

'Only if you want to meet the very definition of *le mort passionale*. I should not hazard it, *moi-meme*. I must go back to the rehearsal. But you know - I believe I *will* write that play.' She dimpled prettily, rose with a flourish, and exited.

'You won't forget that errand!' Pearce called after her, and received nothing in response but a ripple of ironic laughter.

*****

On yet another street, in a modish dress shop not so far distant from Bond Street as to make its location shabby-genteel, whose proprietor (so the gold-edged calligraphy on the sign above the door stated) was one *Mme. Simard*, the noise rivaled that of The Swan, but this was the noise of unfettered jubilation.

'My dears!' Madame herself crowed, bursting through the front door of her own establishment, shaking rain from the paper that she waved in ecstasy, and quite forgetting about the French accent and air of mystery that she usually took great care to cultivate, 'My dearest dearie-dears, we are made women! Young Lady Henrietta Attenborough is to be married to *The* Hon. Edward Badgeley, *as* ever was, him who is to be the 5th Earl Torrington, and I have *just* been closeted with Lady Attenborough *herself*, *in* her front parlour, *and* the long and short of it is: we are to have the dressing of Lady Henrietta for the wedding!'

This caused shrieks of joy followed by complete pandemonium in the small shop, as Madame, her chief assistant Angel, and the apprentices Maria and Elsie hugged one another, laughed in joy, and danced a jig all over the shop and into the little workshop behind it, where they adorned themselves and each other giddily with bits of lace and scraps of cloth every color of the rainbow until the back of the shop looked like the site of some springtime pagan fertility rite.

All this song and physical merriment sent Madame into a paroxysm of painful coughing, and she sat heavily on a stool to catch her breath while Angel - darling Angel - rushed to her side full of solicitous concern. She patted the girl's face and waved her away. 'Now then,' she said somewhat breathlessly, when she had regained her composure and the other girls had collapsed panting against the work table and the bright bolts of sprigged muslin that had just come in to make up the newest spring fashions carefully copied by Angel and Madame herself from the latest Paris patterns. 'We must Plan.'

And she outlined the ideas that had been talked about by herself and the redoubtable Lady Attenborough. 'For you know, she is ever a nip-farthing, and that of course is why she has come to us, my girls. For we can pass off workmanship as good as any in London, for far less. The *ton* may say she smells of trade, and it is true that Attenborough married her to save his estates, but *she* has never forgot where she came from, nor never forgot old Madame Simard who made her dresses *before* she was Milady, and Henrietta is her only daughter. So I have here in my purse a *generous* downpayment *in* good faith with which to achieve the materials - O! Such materials! And it will be a commission as will make us famous!' She allowed herself an in-drawn breath to think starry-eyed of shimmery silks, and lace as airy as a snowflake, and her eyes shone so that for a moment, the years rolled away and she looked like a young and hopeful lass again.

Then she gathered the girls around her at the table and briskly laid out the details of how they would proceed. As she sketched and talked, Angel took detailed notes and wrote neat figures next to them, for she had a good clear fist for writing and could figure accurately. Oh yes, Madame thought with satisfaction, it had been a fortunate day when Angel Hathaway had entered into her service. For the girl was as beautiful as she was clever, and she was quiet and steady and good humored. With Madame's clients she was forthright without presuming, respectful without fawning, and comported herself with a nicely modulated voice and pleasing manners, even in the presence of members of the Quality. *And* her French-accented English was *real*, which lent a certain urbanity to everything she said. The girl was a blessing, that's what it was, arriving at Madame's time of greatest need. For Madame's highest aspiration had been to have the dressing of Milady and her friends, and not just those self-important mamas and their marriageable daughters whose fortunes came from Coal or Slaves or even, save the mark, Rubbish, and who had appalling taste that had to be carefully guided into the realm of artistic decency.

But up to now the aristocratic clients Madame desired had proven far more overpowering than she had anticipated. For one thing, they looked at a person of Madame's station as if she were invisible and existed only to serve. For another, they seemed oblivious to the need to pay, as if the simple honor of dressing them ought to be enough for any *modiste*. And how then was Madame to pay for her expensive address, for her beautiful materials? She knew people who had been ruined by the unpaid bills run up by aristocratic ladies. Good, hardworking people who died paupers while their entitled clients danced on to the next victim.

No. Her first unnerving brushes with the *ton* had taught her that she was better to stay with the dressing of the likes of Mrs. Toomey or Miss Johnson in their fine new houses in Mayfair, rather than risk debt-ridden Lady This or Countess That from Grosvenor. She did greatly desire to maintain her lease at the toney shop she had worked so hard to achieve, no matter who her customers were.

But Madame did still yearn to dress those entitled ladies. O, she did. They looked so lovely in beautiful clothes, did those ladies. They had such exquisite taste and style, and would be such spectacular vehicles for her more delicious creations. O she had surely earned this much. O, she had labored so hard and so long for it. O, it was so elusive.

And then as an answer to her prayers, came Angel. Angel could, with a winning smile, persuade even the most notably indebted ladies to loosen their purse strings out of a desire to be seen wearing a frothy confection lovingly created just for them by Madame's clever hands. She could charm a blackbird out of its song, could Angel, almost as if she were born to the manor herself. A skill learned, no doubt, from being raised in the theatre; for how else came the girl by such pretty manners, when her mother was, after all, only an actress, if a successful and shrewd actress, with some blunt of her own stashed away.

Madame Simard herself - Molly Boggs by birth - owed much to the theatre, truth be known. She had been born and grew up in a noisome warren of tenements along dark, dingy, gin-soaked, shit-stinking Bankside. All Molly Boggs knew of France was what she gleaned from the sailors who got drunk in the neighborhood's taverns and fucked the neighborhood's whores, or that she had learned from the histories of Mr. Shakespeare, with which she had become familiar while hanging about Drury Lane and Covent Garden from the time she was a small child, goggle-eyed with the pageant and the stories and - most of all - the sumptuous clothes worn onstage by the actors.

It had been Molly's mother's job to clean those clothes, and to repair them. And because they were so often the cast-offs of aristocratic patrons, the clothes had been of rich materials - brocades and velvets and silks, among the best - that Molly would never otherwise have been close enough to touch. There were also the beautiful costumes owned by the leading actors themselves, built over the years specifically for each one's line of business: black for Hamlet, an assortment of ermines and other furs for royal figures, elaborate head dresses and plumes for anything smacking of the oriental, uniforms suggesting anything in the military mode, purest white for Juliet, deep ruby for noble ladies. She learned from them a reverence for the feel and heft and scent of lush fabrics, and how to judge good cloth from that which was second rate, no matter how cleverly disguised. She learned how to tease out stains, brush out imperfections, make repairs so fine that after a time the needlework of her small fingers surpassed that of her mother. In the space of a very few years she was employed in her own right as a seamstress to the actors and actresses of the stage, and did so well that her mother, aged beyond her time with poverty, care, and the hard work of raising nearly a dozen children without the aid of any of their mostly anonymous fathers, had been able to cease working quite so hard and let Molly support the family.

Even without a pattern, Molly found she could take a length of fabric and create something beautiful with it. 'The cloth, see, it speaks to me, like,' she would say when asked about this rare talent. And she would go about fashioning something graceful. Soon enough she found herself not only repairing costumes, but creating fashionable clothing for the rising stars of the theatres to wear when out in Society, and then, as word got round that she was reasonable and reliable, her pool of clients spread to that class of people in London that aspired to make more of themselves than their birth might dictate, and who were finding the odd and varied careers by which to raise their standards by dint of cleverness, hard work, and a callous disregard to the welfare of those they left behind. They were both men and women. They were builders, trash pickers, and carters, scriveners, gamblers, and haberdashers, knackers, watermen, shop keepers, and entrepreneurs with an eye to filling a need and turning a profit. With their new clothes, and new money both legitimate and illegal, they moved into new neighborhoods, married above themselves, sent their children to school, became solid members of an emerging middle class, and learned to modulate speech patterns that might no longer betray any knowledge of Bow Bells, Seven Dials, or the filthiest of riverside hovels.

A clientele of this sort had another benefit that in Molly's eyes far outweighed any lack of gentility or taste. They knew the value of money, and expected to lay down the blunt for her services instead of living on tic as the *ton* were wont to do. She liked to see the color of money before goods changed hands, did young Molly Boggs.

So Molly, along with this rising class of ambitious and often ruthless people, saved every penny not immediately required for the support of her family, and hid it from the rest of her siblings, who thought they deserved to share in the profits of her hard work, for they were her own blood, see. She moved into a tiny shop near Covent Garden, took her ailing mother with her, built her trade, and continued to thrive. During that early Revolutionary time there were many well-bred but impoverished Loyalist colonials and French emigrés about. Growing up hard by both river and theatre, Molly developed a quick ear for dialect, and could imitate both her betters and the locals with such skewering and hilarious accuracy that she was the life and soul of many a boisterous evening at the local.

It was in this way that she attracted the attention of one Jonas River, a young man who owned a boat and ran a successful business running travelers, revelers, swains, sweethearts, and those with pressing business affairs across to Southwark and up and down the river to Westminster or Richmond or Lincoln's Fields or wherever else those with the means to travel made their way by water. He had a great future, did Jonas. Like Molly, he was hardworking of habit, drank as much ale as was needful to quench his thirst or to celebrate good fortune but no more, and avoided the horrifyingly addictive nature of the cheap and plentiful blue ruin that so often began as a way to alleviate suffering and ended only in compounding it. He had a dream, Jonas did, to make something of himself in life, and he liked the look of Molly, who had the same ambition. He set about courting her.

At first Molly was reluctant. Jonas River was black, son of a runaway slave named Sarah and one Harry River, himself of indeterminate lineage. His mother died of childbed fever when Jonas's sister was born. The sister survived, pale enough to Pass, and as quickly as biology allowed, married a sailor and moved away.

But Jonas stayed. And when it became clear to Molly that - unlike many - he was not the sort of man to stop working as soon as he put his shoes under her bed and commence a life of drinking away her own earnings, she changed her mind about him. They planned to marry, in time. When Jonas went to the Colonies to make his fortune on the giant rivers he had heard stories about, Molly waited patiently to be sent for, in expectation and with a growing belly.

A year passed with no word. At first, Molly did not fear, for Jonas could not write, and any message must needs come her way memorized by a returning citizen, or from the fist of a clerk who for a modest fee wrote letters for those who could not. But the child was born, and a second year went by, and then a third was underway. And in the end all she ever heard of Jonas River again came at the end of a long and difficult winter, in the form of a fifth-hand message from a returning Londoner who found Molly hard at work with chilblained fingers in her little shop, a small runny-nosed child at her knee.

The message said that Jonas had taken ill of a fierce fever and died somewhere in the wild place called Virginia. So very sorry he was, then, the messenger said. Sorry for the news. For the friend-of-a-friend had sworn that Jonas had truly loved her to the last, and wanted Molly to know that he would never have abandoned their dream. That he died with her name on his lips.

Whether this broke Molly's heart or not is a matter of conjecture. She had loved Jonas truly in the flesh, but three years of waiting and hoping for a word had reduced that love to something illusory, existing solely in mind, and then only when there was time for such thoughts. Her mother had died in the interim, leaving Molly with her own son to raise, hers and Jonas', as well as the running of a growing business. Most nights, Molly fell into bed and a dead and dreamless sleep until the first cock crow sent her back to the double work of child and needlework, needlework and child. And yet, after she received the news of Jonas' death, her friends noted that Molly worked harder and faster than ever before; as if with every stitch and every hem she could sew his memory into a safe pocket, never to be looked upon again.

Her son's name was Jack. She apprenticed him as soon as he was of an age to a thriving cabinetmaker so that he should have a career of his own in time, and never have to worry about where the next meal would come from; for London was growing fast, and there was always plenty of work for craftsmen. She stayed in touch with him for as long as it took to make sure that his master was a just one who neither starved nor beat his 'prentices, nor kept them from what time and learning were rightfully theirs. Then she recommended to Jack over his tears and hers that he should forget all about her, and that was the very best she could do for him as a mother, or so she thought.

It's sad but all too true that one's friends, family, and neighbors in any small community will not support one's desire and hard work in bettering oneself. On the contrary, those who should be our chiefest supporters are more often our worst detractors. Molly's accused her of putting on airs, of getting above herself. Neighbors thought her snobbish and sneered at her. Several of her siblings thought it 'only fair' that they share in her earnings, and she suffered cruelly at the rough hands of two brothers who tried to beat the whereabouts of her money out of her. Molly had the sense to understand that this was nothing more than envy, and also fear. Because if nobody aspires to be better, if nobody succeeds in doing something that nobody else has tried to do, then nobody has to examine their souls and find themselves lacking. Change is hard, and requires hard and single-minded determination. Staying in the same sodden neighborhood, in the same dead-end lives as the generations before, may be depressing. But it is known, understood, and therefore in some way comfortable.

So Molly moved upward again to her present location without informing her remaining family, her neighbors, or even her son of her intentions. She changed her name to Madame Simard, complete with accent and a thrilling if entirely fictitious story of escape from a hideously brutal husband in France, arriving in London with nothing but the clothes she stood in. She took on an apprentice of her own, and kept working.

In the long run, it was probably better that she hadn't told Jack of the change she was making in her life. If she had, it would have gone hard with her to hear from his aggrieved employer about how the boy had taken a notion and bolted, and when last heard of had signed aboard a ship making for the New World, where he would doubtless (in the opinion of his former master) suffer his father's fate. 'These dreamers be all alike,' the man grumbled, and since there was no finding Molly Boggs to give her the information or exact payment, that was the end of it.

Far better, yes, that Molly be spared that. Far better that she believe in her soul that someday she would walk into a cabinetmaker's shop and find her son - grown, handsome, perhaps even with a family of his own - in charge.

The decade and more of hard work that had passed since Molly Boggs had made her move left her with a flinty demeanor that apprentices found terrifying and some gently born would-be customers found impertinent. Yet every single day, when she came downstairs to open the shutters, set her girls to sweeping the walkway in front of the shop, dusting the counters, and rearranging all of the exhibits the better to entice passersby, she knew a thrill of joy and an abiding sense of contentment at what she had achieved.

And now. Now, she had been allowed access to Lady Attenborough's front parlour - *the front parlour* - having entered through the *front door* and divested herself of outer clothing to a very starchy butler, instead of going through the side entrance like a domestic servant or a coster. Really, it was the culmination of a life's dream. She could have died happy at that moment, on that front step.

Well. Not yet, perhaps. Because there was the actual creation of the beautiful dresses to be seen to. Maybe then would she feel that all her hard work, all her desires, would be complete, and *then* she could die happy.

Except that she could not die on command in this way, at the pinnacle of her art. The morning after this success there would be

another project, another commission, another client, another
mountain to climb, more unrelenting labor.

Molly, always a sharp bargainer, always a scrapper, always with
an eye on the main chance, had to admit to herself that she was
getting tired. These years had been hard, and often lean. Her eyes
were beginning to trouble her, and her fingers - stiffened from
years of hard work and many long, chilblained winters - were not
as clever as they once were. And she coughed. Sometimes it was
hard to take in enough air. Sometimes there was a spot of blood.

Sometimes she longed to be simple Molly Boggs again,
chatting and laughing by a cheery fire with her mates and a pint of
bitter before falling into a deep and well deserved sleep. She
wanted nothing more than to enjoy the fruits of her long labor.

But if not herself, who would find the customers? Who woo
them? Who sell them gilt-edged mental portraits of themselves
attired in Mme Simard's finest creations? Who, in short, would
take the daily business over, and allow Madame to stay in
residence, clucking, chiding, cooing, bullying, and needed? For
even though it was a thriving business with a good reputation, it
was a business in a changing world, a competitive world, that
needed a proprietress cleverer by half than ever Molly could be.
Somebody who could read fluently, and speak real French without
fear of a fraud being uncovered, and understand the ever-
changing whims of fashion. Who figured well enough not to be
cheated by the many tradesmen that came and went monthly, with
bolts of cloth that may or may not be the proper quality; that may
or may not be the same in the center as they were on the outside;
that may or may not be dyed correctly and in the requisite shades
to become Madame's clientele.

On the rare occasions that she allowed herself to look into
the future - a future with no family to call on, no home other than
the shop, not much money saved for a comfortable old age - she
didn't see a happy ending.

So Angel Hathaway *was* an angel, to her.

And with Angel by her side, she began to hope that this largest and most wonderful of commissions would see to her partial retirement.

*****

A chance conversation with the French emigré Seraphine Hathaway had brought about the addition of Angel to the staff *chez Madame Simard*.

On the day in question - which had been warm and surprisingly lovely, that particular June - Mrs. Hathaway had entered the shop like a fresh breeze, wafting tantalizing early summer smells of new hay and roses. This must have been a measure of the scent being worn by the lady, Madame had surmised, since the smells emanating even from this part of London tended more toward shit and mud. The lady startled Madame further with a breezy disposition and - *bon dieu* - an elusive but unmistakable French lilt to her pleasingly nuanced voice. The lady was also dressed charmingly in a deep primrose gown in the 'rustic' style made popular by poor Marie Antoinette on the eve of the French Revolution. There was nothing rustic about the materials, however, which fluttered with lace and petticoats, topped by an attractive flat brimmed chip hat adorned with ribbons of rose and green that pointed up the brilliant hazel of the lady's clear eyes and the auburn sheen of her simply dressed hair.

Mrs. Hathaway had come into the shop to order a new redingote in the French style, so simple as to be almost severe, owing more to a man's riding habit than a woman's garment in construction. The art was in a double breasted wide-collared bodice, cut to make the most of female shapeliness, with materials that ranged from superfine wool to silk brocade, adding an expanse of lace at the throat and a hint at the sleeves, and open from the waist to show a skirt of contrasting material. It was Mrs. Hathaway's intent, she said, to own a garment in which she could walk properly in the Park without catching her death of cold in this barbaric climate. Furthermore, she intended this garment to be made of rifle green in the bodice, with a paler shade on cuffs and collar, and a skirt 'of figured sarsnet, *je pense,* the color of old gold to show less of the mud than a prettier ivory, *'n'est-ce pas? Enfin,'* she announced, 'I will add a single ostrich feather to last season's cap, and none the wiser. *Qu-est-ce que vous pensez-la?'*

Madame was impressed.

As she measured and pinned, the ladies chatted easily, and it was during this conversation that Madame discovered two other interesting pieces of information. The first was that, far from being Quality as the dressmaker had supposed, Mrs. Hathaway was an actress. And not just a walking actress, either, but the leading lady known as Mme. Seraphine, who had taken London by storm *and* become a sharer in Mr. Charles Pearce's honored company, The Swan.

Madame was, of course, familiar with The Swan, and with Mr. Pearce, who, it transpired, had been instrumental in Mrs. Hathaway's visit to Mme. Simard's. But try as she might, she could not place Mrs. Hathaway in that company's roster. 'Doubtless,' she said, 'you arrived *apres de ma temps a cette companie.'*

'C'est vrai,' Mrs. Hathaway agreed. 'For I am but lately arrived from France, you see, another piece of driftwood on the revolutionary tide.'

'Ca c'est bien,' mumbled Madame, and hoped that her accent would hold good through the pins that currently crowded her mouth. She glanced up at Mrs. Hathaway's eyes and saw an ironic light in them. She hoped that Mr. Pearce - would he dare? - had not spilled her secret to his leading actress. But along with the irony, the lady's eyes held kindness, and an assurance that, if known, the secret of her birth would remain secret.

The conversation mercifully then moved to safer topics. Not unwilling to talk, Mrs. Hathaway, on being asked, freely enumerated her line of work, or the roles she was best known for in the theatre. 'I have as many as thirty to hand, on a good day,' she said. '*Mais mon dieu*, they are so many of them *en Francais*, and so cannot perhaps be counted. I learned many while with Mlle. Clairon, a great actress and a greater teacher. But also I have Congreve and Sheridan, among others. And my favorite, Shakespeare's Beatrice, and Juliet, *bien sur*, and am accounted to be quite good in the breeches roles.' Here she dimpled at Molly devilishly, and Molly chuckled in spite of herself.

'You'll be either brave or brazen,' she said, forgetting her accent for the moment. 'To show your legs to so many?' She rolled her eyes skyward. 'I should be in a quake.'

'But in showing them to so many while on a stage is not at all intimate,' Mrs. Hathaway assured her. 'I am so amply covered with fabric, and the stage is so well separated from the audience, *non*? And if some consider it to be an invitation rather than a piece of artistic license,' she shrugged expressively, 'then that is why I have Mr. Pearce, and Jacob Freeman, and of course, Brutus, to defend my honor.'

Molly had no answer to this, as she had no idea who any of the gentlemen just named were, whether relatives, or employees, or even perhaps what might fastidiously be referred to as 'patrons'. But she was puzzled, and intrigued. Over long years of needlework and clients, she had become very good at telling the *ton* from the *nouveau riches* - those who had recently got their fortunes through trade, or bought their titles through clever marriage alliances, or advanced their stations through superior military service and a bit of smuggling on the side; or sometimes even through education. The classes of the English were more fluid than ever they had been when she was a girl, yet she could still hear the echoes of a broad north country 'r', or the slurring of the 'a's' in a Londoner's speech, try as the speaker might to eliminate such peculiarities. And those who had dragged themselves up the social scale by the skin of their knuckles often lacked the easiness of manner that attended the well born. Where the Quality might be haughty and entitled, the *nouveau riches* were merely insufferable, pompous boors.

In Mrs. Hathaway, she found an enigma. Discreet enquiries brought forth no illumination regarding her birth or heritage; she seemed to have suddenly appeared at The Swan, just as suddenly to have become a sharer in the company - nearly impossible for a woman, even in this modern age of Actor-Managers ushered in by Garrick - and equally suddenly to have become one of the leading lights of the company. Granted, all of this had come about in a period of upheaval for The Swan. It had been torn down due to space constraints, and the old fashioned, inconvenient, many times rehabilitated construction with its alarming tendency to tilt toward the street had given way to a clean-limned structure of pleasing proportions after the style of the great Wren.

Rather than keeping the company - which at the time of demolition numbered thirty, including stitchers, ticket-takers, scene operators, and the like - during reconstruction, Mr. Pearce had taken that particular moment to purge the cast and staff so that only a handful of the very best workers and actors remained to kick their heels and find what employment they could during two years' down-time. Some stayed in London and worked in other unlicensed houses that offered Opera, Pantomimes, and the like; others spread out through the Provinces to tour or to work in the many houses now thriving in outer parts of the realm.

The new structure seated upwards of 1500 souls. It was still small compared, say, to Drury Lane or Covent Garden. But it sufficed. And when The Swan reopened like a Phoenix from the ashes - spacious, gleaming, modern - auburn-haired Mme. Seraphine had been there with it, ready to charm the world with her French-inflected Rosalind, her witty Beatrice, her divine Juliet... and, of course, her legs, which were said to rival Mrs. Jordan's. But if one stopped admiring the legs and listened to the lady's voice, and watched her as she seemed simply to melt into a role - ah! This was art. Audiences laughed with her, and wept with her, and saw their own lot in life reflected in every nuance of her words, the mirror held to nature, just as Mr. Shakespeare had suggested.

There was no sign of a Mr. Hathaway, who must surely have been an English, or at the very least, a Welsh gentleman. Perhaps, the rumors went, 'Hathaway' was a name she had taken on herself in the same way that simple Dorothea Bland had become 'Mrs. Jordan' upon crossing the Irish Sea to seek her fortune on the stages of London - and in the beds of its aristocrats. Mrs. Jordan was now respectably - or as respectably as a courtesan could be said to be - allied with the Duke of Clarence. They were producing small FitzClarences at a rapid rate, and Mrs. Jordan still graced the stage in those periods when the royal Duke found himself in financial embarrassments from which only the drawing power of her theatrical ability could rescue him.

Another rumor suggested that Mr. Hathaway had been the master of a sturdy trading vessel that went as far as the Indies, and points north and south, before sinking without a trace. Yet another insisted that no, it was Mme's son who had gone to sea, and the husband killed in the crossfire of the French Revolution. These two events taken together would more than account for the deep unhappiness that haunted the lady's eyes in the rare moments when she might be caught silent and unaware of scrutiny. She guarded herself - oh, well! But those moments existed.

An obvious supposition was that the celebrated actress was the mistress of Charles Pearce, who named himself the invisible Mr. Hathaway's cousin. But as she and Mr. Pearce maintained quite separate living arrangements, and as Mr. Pearce was in the habit of maintaining one or two dollybirds from among the company's dance corps, and as nobody of Mme. Simard's acquaintance had ever seen the actress in company with any man in what might be considered anything other than the most proper manner, Madame was inclined to discount that particular story.

The actress' daughter was real enough, at any rate - she with the romantic name of Angel, fifteen years of age when she arrived with her mother on British soil after a dangerously adventurous journey across France and, one surmised, a narrow escape from Le Havre.

Mrs. Hathaway could not be in the first flush of youth, the self-styled Mme. Simard opined. Considering herself to be an expert at guessing these closely held secrets of the female heart, she judged the actress to be just on the windy side of forty years of age. Little telltale signs - the odd thread of silver that hid in the middle of thick auburn hair, the crinkles at the edges of eyes that told of much laughter, the crease between the brows that might denote a certain level of care, or perhaps incipient short sightedness - told the tale. And... could it be said that perhaps the jaw, that terrible teller of truth, was beginning to show just the merest hint of softness?

No matter. The overall appearance was charming, the modiste was forced to admit. Mrs. Hathaway smiled. She laughed. Her public face was schooled to turn a frank and friendly gaze on all the world. She appeared prepared, in fact, to be pleased by all she saw. She made no effort to correct rumors or explain her past. If anything, she seemed to waste no thought on it at all. Madame Simard thus reckoned that Mrs. Hathaway must have been the by-blow of some nobleman or another, and had been kept and then bought off by a wealthy man whose children she had borne. She was neither the first nor the last to have done so, if it were true. And as she bore her lot and her life with grace and discretion, who was Molly Boggs... er, Madame Simard... to pick holes?

Some weeks later, when the actress returned to the shop to collect her finished garment, she came accompanied by her daughter.

Angel was a tall, slender girl. Like her mother, she exuded an air of well-bred poise, but in Angel's case it came with a dose of shyness. The girl seemed just as happy to hang in the background quietly while the older ladies conducted business, chatted, and bandied light gossip. But her eyes - large, green, expressive eyes against a mass of raven black hair - saw everything. Madame could not help but notice the way the girl studied the dresses that hung alluringly on hangers in the front windows of the shop. How she read the forms, the textures, the colors, the shapes. How she pursed her lips as if coming to deep conclusions. How her fingers gently, so gently, reached out to touch a velvet or a fur, or to straighten a piece of lace.

Never having met the girl before, Madame felt already that she knew her, because she saw her younger self - oh, not so fortunate a self, but girls are the same in soul - that loved fabric, and fashion.

In retrospect, Madame realized that it had been very clever of Mrs. Hathaway to leave the girl in the shop '*s'il vous permettez, Madame*', while she went to execute several errands that would take 'not above a quarter of an hour'. Madame's permission was easily achieved, it still being early for her regular clientele to be up and about. And at that, the girl's serious demeanor evaporated, transformed into fulsome joy.

'Go on - touch it,' Molly offered, seeing Angel yearn to bury her hand - and then her face - in a pelisse edged in the most beautiful beaver fur, glossy and soft. 'What do you think?'

'I think it fit for a real lady,' sighed the girl. 'But the color of the mantlet...' she tilted her head and frowned.

'What about it, then?' demanded Madame, shocked out of her French accent.

'I think the color should be, perhaps, not so dark. For if it were lighter just by a shade, more an emerald than the color of a forest, do you see, it would be truly stunning and set both the fur and the wearer off just so.'

Madame was nearly speechless. 'Do you sew, then?'

'I made this,' said the girl with simple pride, indicating the muslin walking dress she wore. 'I had to cut it down from one of *maman's* dresses, not so much the height, you see, but the shape, which,' she blushed becomingly, 'was far too revealing, and more... *ample*... than my own.'

Madame laughed out loud, the kind of deep, delighted belly laugh that had not been awarded her very often in her recent life, and was rewarded by a dimpled giggle from the girl.

'I would like to be just like you,' Angel continued. 'I would like to dress beautiful ladies and make their clothes.'

'Some of them ladies, they an't so beautiful,' remarked Madame drily.

'But they are more beautiful when they wear your dresses, are they not? For your dresses are perfect. I would feel very beautiful in one. *Maman* most certainly will.'

The promised quarter of an hour quickly melted into a full thirty minutes. By the time Mrs. Hathaway returned, Madame and Angel were on the closest of terms, with bolts of fabric unrolled all over the shop to be fondled and caressed and felt between finger and thumb, and smelled, while the dressmaker and the girl chatted easily about the best use for this muslin, or the best style for that sober bombazine.

The following month, Angel came to apprentice with Madame and her two other assistants. 'For although I make a good living, I shall have very little for my daughter to go on with, and no dowry, Madame,' said her mother. 'And as you can see, it is textiles, not theatre, that is her born milieu.' The agreement was that Angel should return to her mother's house every night rather than further crowding Mme. Simard's limited living quarters, and be delivered safely to the shop early every morning by Jacob Freeman and Brutus - whom Molly now knew to be respected household member and faithful dog - to build the fire, arrange the windows, set out the day's work, and do all the other myriad things that apprentices do so that their masters and mistresses can concentrate on the creative work at hand.

That had been four years ago - only four years! And Madame could not imagine her life or her business without the support of Angel Hathaway, who had grown into the promise of her bones and become a graceful young lady. Although any number of young men now appeared ready to throw themselves at her lovely feet, Molly was relieved to see that Angel did not yet appear to have any preference among them, or any desire to walk out with one. In fact, Angel's only irritating tendency was that of picking up stray creatures found on the streets or in the park. There had been an endless parade of kittens, squirrels, the occasional bird, and even a parrot that now resided with the Hathaway family, to contend with. What it was that possessed the girl was a mystery, but it was useless to argue. Some of the kittens, at least, had grown into useful mousers throughout the neighborhood. And that great hairy cur Brutus was a good guardian. But as all the stray animals put together were not as distracting as one young man might have been, Molly hoped that perhaps in Angel she had at last found her partner and successor, a daughter of her heart, who would not be lost to the attractive drudgery of marriage, household, and children too soon.

Meanwhile, Seraphine and Molly Boggs had become fast friends as well. For although the difference in their respective births and background must be evident to most, they shared several vastly important attributes. First, they were women forced by circumstance to have a profession in order to earn their bread. Second, they had had children that must be looked after and set up in the world without benefit of a present father. And third, they were each in their own way forward-looking women, used to a certain freedom of thought, who had made bitter choices in order to recreate themselves and thrive in a world that punished a woman alone. If neither knew the whole story of the other's life - well. No matter there. They had seen into each other's souls, and liked the truth they saw there.

*****

If Ned Badgeley had been told of the havoc wreaked among certain female parties by the *Morning Post & Daily Advertiser's* announcement of his marriage, he would have been astonished. As far as he was concerned, marriage to Henrietta Attenborough would not change his lifestyle or chosen pursuits one iota, as it had come about as a matter of dire necessity. At issue was Ned Badgeley's deepening debt, and an urgent need to get his hands on rather a lot of money very quickly. A sizable fortune left him by his mother's father had been his for the several years since that gentleman's demise, in theory. In practice, its disbursement rested on the completion of one of two onerous but ironclad conditions: One, that he successfully achieve the advanced age of thirty years; or Two, that he marry a girl of his own station who would be acknowledged by his parents and guardians as a right and suitable alliance in the eyes of the world for the man who was to become the 5th Viscount Torrington.

Badgeley was hobbled. Four more years of waiting was an eternity his debtors were unlikely to honor. A trip to the moneylenders while at Oxford had resulted in the interference of his uncle Neville - the most tightfisted of his mother's brothers - who had, in the interest of sparing Badgeley's father embarrassment, and on being petitioned daily for a month by an increasingly distraught sister, disentangled him from that particular trouble. It had been an extremely unpleasant experience, which Ned had no wish to repeat. And all attempts to get the 4th Viscount to intercede in the Trust on his behalf availed nothing. His father was a simple and self-absorbed gentlemen, fond of his hunters and his hounds, and with an abiding interest in a very distant past in which the fabled King Arthur of the Britons figured strongly. His preferred lifestyle was placid and untroubled. He had his wife - a woman of formidable strength of mind - to oversee the running of the house. He also had a very intelligent and hardworking steward - who, if rumor was correct, was also his half-brother from the wrong side of the blanket - who oversaw the land, stock, and agricultural wellbeing of the demesne as if it were his own. Being so blessed with such ardent protectors, Torrington had no need to worry about anything that wasn't exactly to his taste. As the first sign of unpleasantness always sent him into deep anxiety, he got in the habit of using the barest hint of Trouble as an excuse to remove his person from its vicinity by inventing a desperate journey to some little known village in the far north of their country where he was sure - oh yes, *quite* sure - that remarkable evidence of Ancient Habitation had been uncovered in what was now a field of turnips, and must be investigated before the field was plowed into wheat. Thus, when cornered by his son about breaking the trust, the elder Torrington had predictably blinked hard several times, fluttered his hands vaguely in the air as if making some sort of protective incantation, and said, 'My dear boy, I shouldn't dare! It would mean dealing with Neville, and you *know* what he is!'

Ned Badgeley knew exactly.

And so, since the 4th Viscount was barely fifty-five years of age and showed no inclination to turn up his toes in a proper manner to leave Torrington and its considerable wealth to its deeply indebted heir - not that Badgeley *wanted* his father's death, mind; he was fond of the old man - marriage was the only answer.

On the surface of it, this posed no problem. At twenty-six years of age, Ned had been on the town for enough years to have cut his eye-teeth. He was tall, well-shaped, and had pleasing manners. He was favored by the ladies, as evidenced both by the sighs of many a hopeful mama and by the dressmaker's bills incurred in keeping certain opera dancers clothed in a style that put him in the best possible light. He was a fair whip, a bold rider to hounds, had an eye for horseflesh that made him a popular companion on trips to Doncaster, Newmarket, or Tat's, displayed to advantage at Mendoza's, and had the sort of charm that could woo even the sourest dowager.

But he was addicted to gambling. At the races, he chose winners for his friends and lost all his own money chasing 'a sure thing for the Stakes' according to the first groom's second cousin's best friend. The fields of sugar cane he invested in in the Indies were burned to the roots in a local rebellion. The ships whose nutmegs - or pineapples, or tulip bulbs, or silver - he staked his wealth on sank, or were boarded by Colonial privateers. And at the gaming tables of the latest and most elite hells, his luck was execrable.

So he was in hock up to his ears, showed no interest in changing his ways, did not look like inheriting a title in any but the most distant of futures, and was in real danger of having to sell his phaeton and the sweet-stepping pair of matched bays that drew it, *and* his hunters, *not* to mention having to let go the house he leased in Town, and rent rooms at a Gentleman's Hotel instead. There were even rumors that he might have to spend a certain amount of time rusticating in the family pile, or going to Italy for a year or two, until his affairs had stabilized of their own accord.

These prospects might have been laughed off by another man, but they reduced Ned to despair. What he craved was comfort and the ability to continue his lovely life for as long as he could before retiring to a long-awaited title. It seemed utterly unfair that this should be denied him, and absurd to expect him to be leg-shackled to some clinging chit bent on producing many irritating children and cramping his independent style, even if a bride and a wedding date would go a long way to quieting the voices of the many insistent creditors who would be promised full payment of debts the moment the ceremony was sealed and appropriate funds unloosed from their bonds. Funds which ought to support Ned for a good long while.

If only he could find an easy-going wife. One with her own fortune. One who wouldn't meddle in a man's affairs.

He had for a time flirted mildly with Amelia Damson, and thought perhaps she would be the right ticket. She was very pretty, with a pleasing plump figure and the loveliest cloud of golden hair. When he imagined her naked, and dreamed of the pleasures that might be forthcoming from her cushiony body, he grew quite lightheaded and very nearly popped the question at a most inopportune moment in the corner of a garden with Amelia's Mama momentarily out of sight. He had been overcome by emotion - or was it merely lust? - and, since the lady did not seem amenable to having her luscious curves and revealing dress of lightweight silk crushed against his chest while he covered her dimpled face with hundreds of kisses, and since some sort of expression of unquenched desire seemed in order, he caught her sweet white hand in his and was about to protest undying love and yes, even marriage, when Mama and the gardener rounded the corner and the loving pair were forced to jump guiltily apart and profess interest in a low growing shrub with some sort of thorn protecting an insipid-looking pink flower. Ned stooped very low, both to smell its perfume and to give his throbbing member a chance to subside.

Upon closer investigation Ned discovered that Miss Amelia's charms and property were quite entailed, and that she would not bring much more to the marriage bed than an ancient family name and her undeniable but probably fleeting charms. She was, in fact, looking for financial salvation as urgently as Ned was. The Fates and Miss Amelia's Mama had certainly rescued Ned that day.

He reminded himself sharply that there were plenty of females upon whom his physical ardor could be cooled without having to make as desperate a move as an offer of marriage. Girls like Bridie Murphy, for instance, that most delectable opera dancer of The Swan, whose affections could be bought with pretty words and a silk shawl, or a garnet pin. And as for the other issue... he suddenly recalled his childhood friend Hetty.

Lady Henrietta Attenborough had been on the Marriage Mart for an indecent number of years before gracefully disappearing and had, one supposed, given up on achieving the sort of offer her parents had hoped for her. Part of the problem was that Attenborough's wife was rumored to have had grandfather who made his fortune in Rubbish; and although her own upbringing had been unexceptionable, that taint was indelible to the upraised nostrils of Polite Society. Had the daughter been a dazzler, or shown any humility in her bearing, she might have joined herself with the younger son of some Great Family. But Miss Henrietta was instead known for her sense of self worth, and she had summarily rejected all of her most eligible suitors for the simple reason that they were only after her fortune and cared nothing for her at all. 'Well what else would you expect, you stupid, irritating girl!' exclaimed her exasperated mama. 'However else did any woman ever make a respectable match?' And so she retired from the Marriage Mart untethered, and prepared herself for some sort of useful spinsterhood.

The Torrington and Attenborough estates abutted one another, so Edward Badgeley and Lady Henrietta had grown up together. Henrietta, a couple of years Ned's senior, had, he remembered in the depths of his despair, always been a good goer when they were children, ripe for any adventure, a crackerjack rider, and with a deal of sense that kept the pair out of the more serious forms of adolescent trouble. He visited her to take her measure, found her very much as comfortable to be with as he recalled, and unfolded both his plight and his ability to rescue her from hers in return. She laughed out loud, clapped her hands, and accepted his offer without hesitation. 'For you must know, Ned,' she said in high good humor, 'you are the first man that ever proposed to me so that he could achieve his own fortune rather than mine. And with two sisters and a brother on my heels, I had rather not be in my parents' house too much longer. So we shall deal famously. And, my dear friend, you need not worry about me. I shall be quite content to go on with my life as I have, and take you as you come.'

With both families approving, a bargain was struck.

A part of the arrangement was Lord Attenborough's shrewd tying up of his daughter's fortune on any son that should issue from the union, rather than allowing the future Lord Torrington any use of it. Another part involved a conversation between Lady Attenborough and her daughter in private, in which Miss Henrietta assured her worried mama that she knew very well how to control Ned, and had no doubt that he would come to heel before very long.

Which, had Ned heard this conversation, would have sent him to Italy on the first packet, exactly as his father might have done.

This morning he was disgruntled, in part because the notice in the *Morning Post & Daily Advertiser* made the reality of his impending doom… er… nuptials… all too real. He wished for the umpteenth time that his confounded parsimonious grandfather had been a little less punctilious in the laying out of the trust that would solve Ned's pressing issues, and felt for the umpteenth time very hard done by. And it was raining, which meant there would be no point at all in taking his phaeton to the Park, because none of the young lovelies that he would have desired to take up with him would be there.

He was saved from gloom while in the middle of a rather good breakfast of ham, eggs, a hefty slab from a side of beef, a loaf of fresh bread, and a flagon of small beer, by the announcement of the arrival of his friend Sir Robert Kilronan and cousin The Hon. Tristan Neville, whose elegantly attired figures entered the breakfast room hard on the heels of the announcement, with no invitation at all.

'Here, what do you mean by disturbing a man at his breakfast,' grumbled Ned crossly. 'What on earth do I pay Simms for if not to keep rude fellows like you from my door?'

'You don't pay him at all as far as I can see, coz,' drawled Neville, helping himself to a mug of ale and throwing himself into a chair by the fireplace. 'When was the last time any of your staff received any payment from you? It's a wonder they stay on.' He took a long draught from the mug. 'Quite respectable, this,' he said approvingly. 'You've an excellent brewer in your kitchen, Ned, whatever else.'

'I'll tell you what it is, Tris,' said Sir Robert, inspecting and then sampling a stout slice of beef. 'It's purely family loyalty. Lay you a monkey those old geysers have known Ned since he was in leading strings and would rather… I say, Ned. Where did your cook find this beef?' He took a plate from the sideboard, sat down at the table, pulled the platter toward him and helped himself liberally.

Ned observed both men with disfavor. 'For all you know the food and drink you're helping yourself to is all I have to eat for a sennight.'

Sir Robert looked up from his plate with concern. 'Is it truly, Ned? For if it is, I can…'

'No, you damn well can't!' exploded Neville. 'Do not you believe a word this fellow tells you, Robin. His family could buy yours twice over, if they cared to, and come to think of it, perhaps mine, into the bargain. What is it this time, Ned? The horses? The tables? Or the muslin trade?'

Ned flushed and muttered mutinously that it was none of their business, but admitted that, no surprise to anyone, he was deeply into dun territory.

'Is that why you've agreed to be shackled to the Bluestocking? Thought she was on the shelf,' said Neville uncharitably.

'She is not a bluestocking, Tris, that's fiddle. Well. Not very *much* of a bluestocking, at any rate. And she's not above two years older than myself.'

'*Let still the man take a younger than himself,*' intoned Sir Robert sagely. '*So grows she to him. So*… damn. I can't remember the rest. Is she rich?'

'Rich enough,' said Torrington. 'We shall suit very well.'

'And you'll get your fortune,' approved Neville. 'Well played, coz.'

'Then,' ventured Sir Robert, 'does this mean that the incomparable Miss Murphy of the divine face and elegant bosom will be available for a new suitor? For I can tell you, I have been most interested in sampling that heavenly creature's good attentions. What do you say, Ned? Can a fellow Irishman, a friendly and well-meaning fellow countryman, gain access to the secrets of those thighs, the moisture of that…'

'No!' said Badgeley vehemently. 'It means no such thing, I can tell you! So you'll keep that notion out of your scheming mind and a civil tongue in your head where the lady is concerned!'

Sir Robert leaned back in his chair and smiled ironically at the younger man. 'Lady!' he said. 'Now that is not the word that comes immediately to mind, when speaking of Bridie Murphy. How will this fadge, I wonder,' he mused. 'Is the sublime Henrietta such a paragon that she will smile on such an alliance before you have so much as consummated the nuptial ties?'

'Well *of course* she will not think it at all odd,' said Ned firmly, although now that he considered it he wasn't at all sure of himself on this point. 'She as much as said I should continue my way of life just as it always has been. But,' he snapped his fingers, 'since you put me in mind of it, I must today go to a dressmaker's shop, and buy a small present for Bridie. To mollify her, you know. Something smart but not too dear.' He grinned. 'She has the very devil of a temper. If she's seen the *Morning Post & Daily Advertiser* she may be in a bit of a rage.'

'More than likely, I should think,' agreed Neville placidly. 'But if you believe she can be bought off with a chemise...'

'Of course she can, coz. She's a female, ain't she? Pretty words and pretty clothes. All it takes, swear to you!'

Neville looked doubtful, Sir Robert frankly skeptical, and if any of the women in Badgeley's life - from his mama to his intended bride to his mistress - had heard this comment, you could have laid any sum on the improbability of his seeing another dawn. He remained blissfully ignorant, however, and with two friends to advise and comment on the day's best waistcoat and the tying of his cravat, armed with the knowledge divulged by the estimable Simms that Mme. Simard's was indeed considered to be up to all the tricks in the line the young master was considering, Badgeley left his rooms two hours later feeling that his life was truly blessed after all, and that all routes were once more open to him.

*****

In the Pool of London's Legal Quays, the newly arrived East Indiaman *Adventure* rubbed gently against its mooring while ship's carpenter Chance River leaned on the deck rail and stared moodily at the loud, crowded, smoky - and truth be told, ripe - panorama of commerce, humanity, and offal that was the Port of London.

'Still aboard, Mr. River?,' asked another young man, strolling up to take his own place on the rail.

'Always summin left to do, Mr. Hathaway. You?'

'Assistant to the ship's surgeon?' he snorted. 'I won't see shore 'til hours after the last invalid debarks. Mr. Lovett, on the other hand…'

'Three parts drunk with a whore on his knee by now, I dessay,' nodded River. 'Happen he won't come back, neither, and you'll inherit the job, like.'

'I sincerely hope not, Mr. River. I've a deal yet to learn.'

'Nothing you can't larn as you go, sir. You wouldn't be the first as cut his teeth on the job. Nor yet in one a them fat books you allus got yer nose in. If you don't mind me sayin'. How hard is it to set a man's bones an' all? I reckon it be a deal like joining two pieces of wood as don't quite fit.'

Hathaway laughed. 'There's something to that, actually.' He pulled a flask out of a pocket, took a swig, then offered it to River. 'Brandy, then? Keep the heart warm?'

'I don't mind,' River took a pull and smacked his lips appreciatively. 'Some a that Frenchie stuff, ain't it? How'd you come by that there?'

'Medicinal,' vowed Hathaway.

'I should try that un,' River grinned.

'The trick is hiding it from Lovett.' He took another pull on the flask, shook it gently next to his ear to check the level, then handed it to River. 'You must be looking forward to some shore time, are you?'

River shrugged noncommittally. Took a long pull and rolled his lips together, savoring. 'How long since you was home, Mr. Hathaway?' he asked, after a long silence.

'Home? Good question, *mon vieux*. France, t'would be, until I was sent away to sea to learn medicine, these eight or nine years since.'

'You a Frenchie! Nah, you an't.'

'My father was an Englishman. We spoke both languages at home.'

'Then how'd you get aboard *Adventure*?'

'My second ship, the frigate *Liberté*, was boarded and scuttled by a Dutch privateer on my second voyage down west of the Azores. My master, the medical officer, was killed in the action with the other officers, but I was made prisoner with the rest of the crew. Name of *Sea Lark*, the ship that took us. Do you know her?'

River grunted an assent. 'Vanderoodt's ship.'

'The same.'

'Right bastard, I heard.'

'You heard right.'

'But you an't a prisoner on *Sea Lark*, and Vanderoodt wouldn'ta let 'un stroll away, like.'

'I escaped.'

'Nah, you din't.'

'*Mais c'est la verité*. There's not much to me, especially by the time I'd been on that ship a year. I could slip in and out of a tight spot easily enough. And I can swim.'

River looked at him sideways, skeptical.

'S'truth,' Hathaway repeated, hand on heart. 'One day, I was set to swabbing with two others when we were anchored outside Vieux Carré. Under the lash, we were, in the heat, every one of us sick and starving, while most of the crew was ashore. I'd had enough. When the overseer was distracted, I just slipped over the side.'

River whistled. 'They never saw you in the water?'

'There was a right hue and cry. But it's a crowded port. Plenty of cover.'

'You ought to've bin kilt.'

Hathaway stared into the past, the muscle in his jaw twitching. 'Rather die escaping than die another day aboard that ship,' he said quietly. 'That I can promise you.' He took a deep pull on the flask.

'How'd you make out, after?'

'There's always work for someone who can bind an arm or dose a fever, on the docks. Especially one with an ear for language. And... There was a Native woman, a healer...' he stopped for a moment and smiled reminiscently. 'She it was pulled me from the water, half dead. Strangest fish she ever caught, she said, but she nursed me. I learnt some valuable medicines from her, that I have used to advantage since.'

'And then...'

'And then... I thought to make my way back to Marseilles, but the Revolution broke out. There were fewer ships, and it was hard to get news. I finally heard roundabout that my family... everything I'd known, in fact... was gone. Then, much later, I received a letter that had been two years finding me. My mother and sister were alive, and got to London. So, I took ship on a trader, to Halifax. When *Adventure* came in and needed a surgeon's mate, I signed on. And since then...' he shrugged. 'The water is my home, near enough. You?'

River nodded reflectively. 'Me, I was born not far from these here docks. I don't remember as they stank so bad, but I expect they allus did.'

'I expect so.'

'I an't seen these docks in, lemme see. Close on a dozen years, I make it.'

'You ran away from home?'

'Worse'n that. I ran away from my master. I were 'prenticed, see, to a cabinet maker, and he were a good master and I were a good student of the craft, but I dunno. 'Twas allus about ships, and the water. That's how me dad come to his end, I'm told. That's how I 'spect I'll meet mine.'

'Did you know your father, then?'

'Nah. But I were told - me ma, she told me - he caught a fever and died in the Virginias. And when I run away, I shipped aboard the fastest ship I could find headed there.' He laughed. 'O' course, no ship was going to Virginia in them days, hardly, 'less they was goin' to war, but I din't know that, did I? I were a right green 'un. Ended up in the Indies, then all the way to the Antipodes. But I got to Virginia after four or five years, I reckon.'

'And did you look for your father?'

'Heard tell of him, is all. I guess it was like they said, right enough, and he died a that fever.'

'I'm sorry.'

'Nah. It were a blessing, see, knowin' that. To know he din't just scarper on me ma and me like so many others done. Anyways, I bin on ships ever since, and never one of 'em headed for England. Never thought I'd see 'er again. Then I took a notion, and hearing *Adventure*'s ship's carpenter had up and died when we was refitting in the Indies, I signed on. Cap'n thought me young for the job, and I din't have the blessing of the Crown or nuthin', since I hadn't never worked in the yards. But I had the good word from other crews, and after some hot action at sea I'd done more repair and refits than most. I persuaded him that bein' as I was young and lively and knew ships as well as any, I'd more'n likely live out the trip to Halifax and across the ocean and keep the ship afloat, too.'

They laughed, and drank.

'Will you look up your mother, then?'

River stared silently at the shore. 'Dunno as I will,' he said finally. 'Like as not she's gone where can't nobody reach her. And...' his voice trailed off and he stared into space for another long while. 'We din't have nothing, me ma and me. Only just what she got making dresses for folk. I look back and I see how hard she worked for the both of us. When I went off to be 'prenticed me ma, she told me to learn all I could and make something better of meself, and to forget all about her. I reckon I cried every night for most of a year when weren't nobody looking. But that's all gone, now. And,' he added meaningfully, 'I an't never told that to no man.'

'I never heard it.'

'You?'

'God grant *Maman* and Angel - that's my sister - live yet. As for *papa...*' he shook his head. 'I never heard he got to London. But *Maman*... I heard she's a sharer in a theatre called The Swan. Or was a year ago.'

'No lie?'

'S'truth.'

'I figured you for...'

'A gentleman? *Pas moi, mon vieux. Maman* is an actress. Very popular in Paris. My step-father - a scholar, he was, just enough of a living to rub along on. He was used to be what the English call a bear-leader.'

'A what-all, now?'

'A gentleman that - for a price - will act as guide and tutor to wealthy sprigs taking the Grand Tour.'

'Well if that don't beat all,' Chance marveled.

'Half flash and half foolish,' agreed Hathaway. 'Spent most of his time posting bail and dragging them out of bawdy houses and gaming hells as far as I can make out, but he must have been successful, for he was paid a great deal in tips from grateful parents.'

'Only time I was ever drug from a whore or a gin mill was by the constabulary, and if I spent a night in gaol, well. Too bad for me.'

'Too right. Anyway, *pere* Hathaway saw *Maman* onstage and that was that, the story goes. He persuaded her to bring me away from Paris, marry him, and move to a little village where he had a house. He taught us all our letters, she went back to work during the Season, my sister was born, and they saved enough to get me a good berth on a good French ship. *Mon pere*... must have made it possible for *Maman* and my sister to leave France. But more than that...' he shrugged.

'Got hisself killed, you reckon?'

'Probably.'

'Awful lot of people go missing, in that kinda action. Sometimes on purpose.'

'*C'est que je pense, moi.*'

'And the man who got you on your ma?'

'She never spoke of him. Could have been anyone.'

River grunted, and tugged lightly at the gold earring he wore in his left ear. 'Me ma, she done some sewing for the theatres roundabout. I remember hangin' round some stage or another pesterin' the carpenters when I was just a little 'un. Mebbe The Swan was one of 'em. Mebbe they know each other.'

'We could go looking together.'

'Nah... Mebbe... I don't rightly know. Me ma moved on even afore I left. Never said where. Mebbe she din't want me, no more. Mebbe she found a man. Dunno what to think, now I'm here. Don't seem like so good an idea as it did back in Halifax, this coming back. It ain't home no more.'

Hathaway sighed and shook his head. 'And yet...' his eyes gleamed a little wistfully.

'You ought to get along, sir, when you've the chance. Knowing where your Ma is, an' all. You ever see London?'

'No. You could show me around. I'd appreciate it.'

'Mebbe.'

'At least come to The Swan with me. There should be a good meal in it, if nothing else.'

'That's right kind, sir.'

'Stephen.'

'Chance.'

They shook hands.

'Why now, Chance?' mused Hathaway. 'Why on earth are we coming back now?'

River sighed gustily. 'Just a notion, I reckon. Not the best one a body ever had, neither. London's big and ugly, for certain. I bin used to something different. I guess I remembered something different.'

'I believe memory is like that,' agreed Hathaway. 'When I went back to our village, just a year after I left, I was shocked at how small everything looked. Our old house, the gardens, even the town. Like it had shrunk all the time I was growing.'

'That's right,' agreed River. 'That's the way of it.'

Hathaway saluted the shore. 'To coming home,' he said, and drank.

'To coming home,' echoed River, drinking in his turn.

'Even if I've never seen it before.'

'May we live through 'er.' He ceremoniously scattered the dregs of the flask on the water below them.

*****

In Southampton, an older gentleman dressed richly in with a coat of deep maroon superfine, a figured silk waistcoat of exquisite workmanship, silk stockings, and shoes that were shined and tasseled to perfection, was bowed into a private parlor of The Dolphin by an obsequious landlord who showed no sign of thinking the gentleman's wardrobe was at least twenty years outdated, but rather promised the immediate appearance of refreshments appropriate to Milord's discerning palate. The parlor was well lit and pleasantly proportioned, with a fire crackling in the grate and a window that overlooked the harbor with its skyline of masts, rigging, and wheeling gulls that sailed and mewed across leaden skies while boats of every size and configuration bobbed and creaked on troubled water. Milord allowed a servant to remove his many-caped greatcoat and take both hat and gloves from him. A silver tipped cane stayed in his possession, though he did not appear to rely on it overmuch for support.

'Denham!' exclaimed a florid figure already in possession of the room. He strode swiftly to the older man, bowed, wrung his hand, and ushered him to a high backed bench that sat perpendicular to the fire. 'The best I could do this present, sir. How was the crossing? I feared for your safety.'

'T'was taxing, I confess. But, time and tide, you know,' the gentleman waved a white hand languidly. 'We have endured far worse, dear Bev, have we not.'

Beverly Ramage eyed his old employer uneasily. Neither age nor an arduous and rather mysteriously urgent journey could account for the deep lines carved into a face whose patrician cast had settled into sallow harshness, or the slight tremor in the pale hands. Everything about him hinted at a lifetime of dissipation. 'I confess, sir,' Ramage said tentatively, 'I was surprised to receive your letter. We... I... did not expect to see you on English soil again. After so long away, that is to say, sir. Very glad tidings, of course. Very glad.' Carefully. These things must be phrased carefully.

'I surprise even myself, dear Bev. But, family affairs, family affairs. My dear late wife, you know, had estates in Buckingham that, sadly, must needs be attended to. And who else but my bereaved self to carry out a last commission on her behalf?'

'Quite. Oh, quite. I am sorry for your loss, sir.'

'I thank you. T'was inevitable, however; she was ever delicate, my Annis. The Mediterranean climate that was death to her dear deceased husband was a saving grace to her, I believe. We had quite five years together before she grew ill and departed this world. Five - lovely - years.'

'Of course,' said Beverly uncomfortably. He resisted an impulse to loosen a suddenly constricting cravat. He had forgotten, after all this time, what a sinister creature Denham could be. 'Children?' he asked.

'To call our own, alas, no. One daughter, only, from said previous attachment. She will, of course, inherit that portion of the estate that includes the dower house, unless she might be persuaded to sell. She did not desire to travel with me. I cannot conceive why, but I assume t'was childish jealousy against my union with her mama. Young girls are so emotionally unstable, do you not find, always eager to take against one on the slightest provocation. Her mama deemed in best... to send her to relatives in the country, and there she stays.' His mouth twitched in irritation. He rested his cane against the wall and spread his hands to the fire. 'The girl is to be married very well. A Count of Venice. All *her* many children will speak nothing but Italian and French. Little chance they'll be interested in a property in foggy, rainy, England.'

'But you, sir?'

'Oh, I. Quite a different issue, my dear. Of late I have had the oddest notion - you may well laugh at me - that I should like to spend the days remaining to me in the home of my birth. Most diverting, is it not? Almost, I shudder to say it, *sentimental.*'

'It has been a very long time, Denham,' Ramage remarked.

'I make it some twenty-five years. Do you think it long enough? Do you yet have doubts?'

'No. The girl was never found you know. Those most affected are dead or moved away these fifteen years and more. None to remember it, or not so it could matter.'

'But you remember.'

'I do, sir.'

'Tch. And you still disapprove. After all these many years.'

''T'was cruelly done, Denham. It went hard with the family. If you'd been here to see... the mother, you know, died of grief...'

'She need not have done so if the stupid chit's papa had seen reason and come up to scratch, Bev. All he had to do was agree to a marriage.'

'But to abandon the girl...'

'Bev, Bev, Bev. What would you have me do? Bring her home? Return her to the bosom of her family? No!' he shuddered. 'Far better she be left to take her chances than crawl home as damaged goods, no prospects at all. Do but conceive, old fellow, the scene. It quite beggars the imagination. Lost to all Polite company, no chance of being received in Society again. An embarrassment, sent quietly somewhere deep in the country to live as an elderly relative's companion and so dwindle away. No. Far better I leave her, do you not see? I gave her freedom. A rare gift, had she but the wit to use it. And of course, I gave her a trade, Bev. A pretty whore is always popular.'

'She was but fifteen years of age, sir,' said Bev quietly.

'And what is that to me? I'll tell you: *Nothing*. Can it be that you are developing scruples at this late date, my - most - trusted - steward? I recall no such tendency in your manner twenty-five years ago.'

Bev flushed uncomfortably and stared at the floor without answering.

'Come, *mon vieux*. Do not let us quibble over the past. Her papa had his chance, and lost it. It was, in fact, his own fault. I sought only to bring the issue to an end I dearly craved with the daughter I desired; even, I hazard to say, loved. I'd no notion the stupid fellow would cut her off. What could I do but cast her away? Not my fault in the least.'

Bev eyed his employer uneasily and did not respond.

'Now speak to me of the present, Bev! Where must I go? Who must I see? I do long to be back in Town. Have you eaten? Shall we leave immediately, or do we risk the sheets and stay the night? What have you procured as my dwelling, for the nonce? For 'twill be only the nonce, I assure you. I shall soon be quite a wealthy man again, Bev, with estates that must needs be managed. Who knows? Perhaps I shall even venture to marry one more time. Ah, here is our refreshment.'

*****

'*Non, non, non!*', insisted Seraphine to the choreographer of the new piece due to be performed for the first time that evening. 'You cannot have the swing there, *regardez-vous*, for there is no way to light it properly from the side without scorching the scenery and even, perhaps, catching fire to some poor dancer as she comes onstage. *Voyez-vous?*' She demonstrated where the actions were to take place, dancing lightly in and out of the shadowed wings and around the leafy swing that dominated the center of the stage, then came to a halt. '*Jeremyyy!*' she sang into the wings over the din of voices shouting as several strong men cranked huge backdrops into place, stripped to their shirtsleeves even at this hour from the exertion, while others wielded saws, hammers and nails to fashion the struts that would hold a stock pastoral scene featuring a village square in a slightly different configuration from last week's performance so that it would look fresh. '*Jeremyyy!*'

For a small woman, the choreographer marveled, Mme. Seraphine had a prodigious carrying voice. And a peremptory one.

A bandy-legged man of middle years popped his head out from behind the curtain, disappeared again briefly to bawl, 'No, ye great booby, that's up! *Uup!*', and popped back out. 'Yes, mam?'

'Please explain to Mr. Demers why it is that the light cannot properly illuminate a swing mounted at the side of the stage *here*.' She stood on the offending spot. 'I must speak to Mr. Pearce and make the proper choreographic adjustments. *Alors, mes demoiselles!*' she clapped her hands briskly as she bustled across the stage. 'All eyes on Mr. Demers, please! Doll Bridger, if you do not cease your idle chatter *Tout suite*, I'll have you turned out in the street, *par le bon Dieu!*' As she exited the stage she heard the voices of Jeremy and Mr. Demers rise into heated debate. 'Ye cannot hang it there ye great eejit,' shouted Jeremy, ''twill run the poor girl into the edge of the damned proscenium and knock the damned light over, and burn the damned house down!'

And Mr. Demers shouted back, 'I will not have my piece ruined because my girls are forced to break their pattern to dance *around* the swing and half of them in danger of being struck by it when…'

With a sound of strangled rage, Seraphine threw her hands up, stalked downstairs, and barged into the tiny theatre office. '*Ce soir*, Charles!' she shouted at the startled manager. 'This... *monstrosity* opens *tonight*! And that idiot of a choreographer - *where* oh where did you *find* that one - 'and so she went on in front of the bewildered man, gradually beginning to swear violently in French as she paced.

'Sera!' he expostulated after this had gone on for some minutes. 'Sit down, for God's sake, and speak English!'

Seraphine sat down abruptly in the chair he gestured at, closed her eyes, and rubbed her temples wearily.

'Now,' he said, straightening his wig. 'What is the matter?'

'I cannot persuade Mr. Demers that his choreography does not fit the needs of our stage. Bridie Murphy has been indulging in every form of ridiculous behavior from strong hysterics to wild imp... imp... - *qu'est-ce que le mot*? Impre-cations? *Bien* - against *les horreurs des hommes* because her lover - *quel surpris* - has abandoned her. The scenery is not *nearly* ready. You sit here in your ivory closet and ignore the chaos that is taking place all round you while I do the work, and.... And....' She fell silent, and chewed her lip.

'And what, Sera?' prompted Pearce.

'And I have grave doubts, Charles. About...' she searched for the right words, then finished in a rush. 'About you and me at our ages having the *testicules* to continue Mr. Shakespeare's balcony scene with Romeo and Juliet when we both have *children* old enough to do the roles. *Regardons nous*, Charles!' Her gesture included both of them, but in fact she chiefly referred to Pearce himself, whose current increase in girth and a tendency to baldness made him a far better choice for The Ghostly Friar than the fickle stripling Romeo.

'Ahhhh,' Pearce smile broadly, finally hearing something that made perfect sense to him. 'My dear Seraphine. Despite what the French might say and do in their own - doubtless well enough - theatrical tradition, you know it is quite true here, in the home - might I even suggest the very *bosom* - of our dear Mr. Shakespeare, that a woman *must* be old enough to play The Nurse before she can properly play Juliet. And you will play her charmingly, my dear, as you always have. You do not look a day above twenty, 'pon my honor you do not! This is just your opening night nerves, do you think? Seen 'em before, you know!'

'Charles, this is *not* about my… oh, never *mind*,' she said crossly, and wondered why it was that men absolutely could not ever to be brought to understand that women had more to think of than their figures, their fashions, and whether they looked their age or not when men, in her opinion, ought to spend more critical time on such things. Using a mirror to critical advantage might cause Charles Pearce to admit that even Capulet was a far better part for him than Romeo, no matter what wig or corset he used to diminish both years and girth.

'Tell you what,' Charles continued brightly, 'I have a capital idea. There is the matter of that very particular and delicate… erm… *package* that I mentioned, that under current circumstances I cannot possibly collect at Mme. Simard's. If you were to run off to fetch it now, rather than waiting until…'

'Charles, I am not your errand boy. Send young Harry to Mme. Simard, or let Angel know about it this evening and have her bring it.'

'No, no! Oh, no. It must be done immediately and discreetly, my dear. That is why you must do it for me. I explained it all to you earlier. Do pop over, won't you? It will do you a world of good to take a breath of air. And it will help me out of a potentially sticky situation.'

Seraphine eyed him suspiciously. 'Which sticky situation do you refer to, precisely, Charles?' she asked with awful calm. 'The one involving your debts to Mme. Simard and several other dressmakers about town? The one that involves soothing the anger of the very ambitious Doll Bridger when she finds she is not to be replacing Bridie Murphy? Or another that I do not yet know? *Par example*, last week's receipts suddenly vanishing, *pouf*,' she made a magical gesture with her hand.

'As for the receipts, why, I can explain it all very neatly, after tonight's performance don't you worry. As for the rest... If you could but go and do this errand for me, none will be the wiser, and I,' he added expansively, 'will undertake to straighten out the various artistic *contretemps* occurring on the stage. Then Doll will be... I mean...' he stumbled to a stop, and blushed.

'So it is Doll, indeed!' Seraphine pointed an accusing finger. 'You are in fact giving presents to Doll Bridger now? What, pray, happened to Mrs. Betterton? No,' she closed her eyes in resignation. 'Do not tell me. *Mon Dieu*, Charles, Doll Bridger? She is younger even than your daughter, that one. If your poor wife were alive to see you making such a fool of yourself over that *putain...*'

'Now, Sera. Sera. A man has his needs...'

'*Vil, vielle chèvre malodorante*! Please spare me hearing of your *needs*. I will do your errand, for *vraiment*, the walk will do me good and I do desire to see Angel. But if you do not have all ready for this afternoon's rehearsal by the time I return, Charles, and if you do not have all of last night's receipts in your hand for me, I swear, *moi meme*, I will wring your fat neck with my two hands, with the greatest of pleasure.'

'All will be ready, my dear,' said Pearce hastily, throwing up his hands as if to ward off Seraphine's threats. 'To the last farthing! I swear by all I hold dear!'

*****

For their parts, Messrs. Badgeley, Tristan Neville, and Sir Robert arrived in the Park just after the magic hour of noon, ready to be seen *en promenade* with a colorful mass of young gentlemen and ladies of fashion, mamas eager to show off marriageable daughters desperate to be attached respectably by Season's end, roués hanging out for well-fixed widows, and mushrooms and bounders of every stripe doing their utmost to bring themselves into the orbit of those in Polite Society by whatever means necessary. The morning's rain had moderated to a brightening spring afternoon, and a pleasing number turned out, 'it being such a soft day, after all'.

The three friends strolled the alleés chatting about the upcoming summer - who would go to Brighton, who be forced by an elderly patron to Bath, who rusticated to the country to recover from gambling reverses, what delights Town might hold in the weeks before the general exodus occurred. These speculations were of necessity disjointed, being interrupted by frequent stops to chat with lively groups of heavily chaperoned young ladies. Everyone knew by now that Badgeley was to be wed. He took no end of teasing from several forward girls, who made a great show of casting him off and throwing their attractive lures in the direction of Sir Robert and Mr. Neville instead. This caused Badgeley to redouble his attempts to charm the birds back to his hand, just as it was intended to; and in sum, he and Sir Robert competitively bathed themselves in the attentions and flirtations of the damsels in question with so much delight that a formerly dreary day was suddenly full of promise after all.

Neville found himself oddly indifferent to all attempts to attract favor. Always somewhat aloof in company due to a natural shyness, his current unease made it evident that he very much wished himself elsewhere. He glanced down every path looking for… well, he couldn't say what, but he frowned in disappointment when he did not find it. Some of the more intuitive ladies surmised that he must be missing an inamorata whose path the had hoped to cross, and made an effort to bring him out of his solemnity with fluttering lashes, or the smallest glimpse of a plump bosom or a nicely turned ankle, or by commenting upon the excitement to be had at Lady Such and Such's soiree. Tristan smiled sweetly, returned noncommittal answers, and realized that he was crashingly bored.

'I perceive, sir,' opined one bold mama in an alarming hat that must have denuded the better part of an ostrich, 'that you are one who is quite above the frippery sort of flirtation of these loose-seeming gels. Such shocking forwardness would never have been abided in my day. My dear daughter Eleanor - you have met, have you not? - Eleanor, dear, make your courtesy to Mr. Neville, that's right! - is much of the same mind as you. Are you not, Eleanor!'

Poor Eleanor, dressed most unsuitably in a pink ensemble that made her resemble an iced cake, and unattractively blue with cold, blushed an even more unbecoming shade of red, mumbled something incomprehensible, and tried to become invisible. Neville felt sorry for the chit. He bowed, smiled, wondered aloud how her mama allowed her out in such weather without so much as muff to warm her, and moved on, leaving Mama with her mouth opening and shutting indignantly. 'Inelegant rudesby!' she exclaimed to his back. 'I never was so set down in my life! I cannot suppose, my dear, that it is his fortune makes him so starchy. Five thousand a year, one hears, hardly handsome, and such a cold fish, too!'

Privately, poor mousey Eleanor had found Mr. Neville charming, and his fortune perfectly adequate. She had no illusions about her prospects, her chief ambition after one humiliating London season being to achieve a marriage that would remove her from her mama's bullying and give her a home of her own to manage - a country pastor with a respectable living, or a comfortable gentleman farmer who was not married to drink. Still, she would have been more than human not to steal a final glance at Mr. Neville as he retreated, and feel the tug of the heart that always dwells on what might have been, 'if only'. At least he had honored her with an acknowledgement of her existence. More than either of his friends had done.

'You are the oddest fellow in the world, Neville,' chastised Sir Robert when once he had caught up and found his friends momentarily disencumbered from the chattering of hopeful females. 'How you can find yourself unmoved among this garden of beauty is utterly beyond me. Myself, I have found at least half a dozen lovely flowers in need of being plucked.'

'Then you may have 'em,' remarked Neville moodily. 'I do not care for this particular garden.'

'Not like - Tris! One begins to think you unnatural,' chided Badgeley.

'Not at all. I merely dislike silliness. Have you never looked at the most delectable, most mouth-watering of these ladies, and thought that in another few years the loveliest of them will have lost their looks from childbearing and will come to closely resemble those fearsome mamas who are forever throwing them at one like minnows to a pelican? The prospect makes me shudder.'

'But Neville,' complained Sir Robert reasonably, 'that is why one keeps *mistresses*, old fellow.'

Neville frowned, and swished at a clump of grass with his cane, as if it had somehow offended him. 'Sorry, Robin. I have not found this to be a satisfactory answer.'

'Then you are one of those romantic fellows, are you? Forever writing poetry about the perfections of a metaphorical woman that has never existed? And who, by the way, never *will* exist. Or perhaps, your tastes run in another direction entirely.' He stopped and faced Neville. 'Are you that sort, Tris? Are you... *that* sort of man?'

'Why should this matter to you, sir?' He looked quizzically at his friend and was surprised to see a fleeting glance of longing cross his eyes, so immediately stifled that Tristan might almost think he had imagined it, but...

'Because,' drawled Sir Robert casually, turning a fascinated gaze to the buds of an overhanging pear tree through his quizzing glass, 'I should be forced to cut off our friendship, if you were to answer aye. And I should sorely miss your company at the races.'

Badgeley, who had been listening with an increasing sense of worry, jumped in before Tristan could respond. 'Don't you worry about Neville!' he swore stoutly. 'I happen to know of an extremely dashing Cyprian he has had in his keeping for...'

'Shut, it, coz,' warned Neville, coloring.

'I am only defending you, Tris', said Ned reasonably. 'And you said yourself, in my company, that she has simply the most delicious…'

'I was in my cups, Badgeley. I spoke out of turn.'

'Then it isn't true?'

'On the contrary, every word is true,' he smiled reminiscently, and the pleasure in that smile caused both other gentlemen a brief stab of envy. 'But as I am about to end my liaison with that particular lady I would rather not...'

'End it! *Why?*' wailed Badgeley.

'Gouging you, is she, then,' said Sir Robert knowingly, immediately restored to his sense of place in the world. 'Playing you off against another, I shouldn't wonder, too. Clever, these high-flyers. Nothing to do but give them a nice round figure for their nice round figures, and cut them loose. Don't worry about 'the lady', dear boy. She'll look after herself.'

'*I'll* look after her, coz, if you'll but tell me who she is and where to find her,' grinned Badgeley.

'You can't afford her, Ned,' said Tristan.

'But I'm to be married. Then I'll be full of juice.'

The sheer naivety of this ridiculous statement gave the other two men pause to look from the speaker, then to each other, before dissolving into helpless laughter.

'What! What have I said?'

'My dear gudgeon, if you believe your newly minted wife will allow you to collect mistresses as if they were prime hunters, you know very much less of the female sex than ever I thought,' said Neville.

Badgelely blushed. 'Now you sound like our damned uncle,' he complained sulkily. 'Always preaching common sense and frugality at one.'

'Does he really? Sounds a dead bore,' drawled Sir Robert. 'Elderly gentleman is he? Troubled with gout? '*A plague o' these pickled herrings?*' *In my day, young men would never dare?* That sort of thing?'

'*No*,' said Neville with a laugh. 'He's a prime 'un. And rather more likely to keep his distance than preach. Never see the man unless something's gone hideously wrong.'

'Exactly what I mean,' groused Ned. 'Then he appears out of the ether like the ghost of Hamlet's father, suggesting that an inability to live within one's means and to pay one's debts is… *unwise*. And a damned nasty way of making sure you never come before him again.'

'If you weren't so stupid with money, coz…'

'For Gawd'sake, can we move along to Jackson's?' drawled Sir Robert. 'I'm getting bloody damp standing about in all this greenery, and it's about to rain again.'

'First to St. Jermyn Street,' said Badgeley firmly. 'I must find something for Bridie.'

*****

In quite another part of the city, the gentleman Sir Robert suspected of being a dead bore was locked in seemingly mortal conflict in a large, bare room that echoed with the clash of rapiers, the grunts and exhortations of two men whose breathing came in short gasps, each searching for the weakness in the other's guard, each spinning and diving and parrying with deft wrist work and such agility that they could have been panthers doing battle in a forest. Both men were stripped to breeches and close-fitting fencing jackets that clung to muscular figures soaked in sweat, clubbed hair plastered against their brows. They were well matched in size, but where one was older, grizzled, and burly, the other was just past middle age, all litheness and grace. Yet it was he now on the defensive, and with a sudden dive and twist of a sword, the older fighter sent his opponent's rapier spinning and with a flourish, touched the younger man's throat with the point of his sword.

'Eh?' the fencing-master crowed, breathing like a bellows. '*Eh?*

'I submit!' gasped Nathaniel Neville. The buttoned sword point dropped and both men clasped one another on the shoulder and with what breath was left them, laughed uproariously.

'Admit it, Domenico, I almost had you,' gasped the younger.

'Never! I but toyed with you to give you a proper workout,' gasped the old Italian. And then they laughed some more.

'Come,' said the fencing master when he had regained his breathing. 'You may use my dressing room and then I shall invite you to share in some of the excellent brandy I have obtained.'

'And the package that came with it?'

'Safe. Thriving. And will be passed on tomorrow, as planned.'

'Canada?'

'Ay. If the papers you provided hold up to scrutiny.'

'They will hold.'

'*Bene.* Come, let us drink. And then you must leave me, for next I entertain the clumsiest pair of cubs I have ever met.'

'Come now, old friend. Were we not all of us clumsy when we began?'

'Never,' Domenico said, with a sad shake of his head. 'All *these* young men care about is the fists, and the pistols. No. There is no art to the sword, anymore. You and I, we are of an age that will see the end of the rapier, queen of weapons. My master, the great Angelo, would weep to see it.'

'I hope never to see that day,' said Neville. It is indeed an elegant weapon.' As they spoke, the men cleaned their foils with care and honor, and stored them, leaving a servant to tidy the room while they toweled off, dressed, and climbed with the ease of long friendship to the older man's lodging upstairs. Domenico poured the promised liquid from a heavy decanter into crystal glasses. Neville sipped, granted it excellent, and had the audacity to wonder aloud if it had ever seen an excise stamp in coming to England's shores.

'That is not for me to suppose,' twinkled the older man, and lifted his glass to Neville. 'I have the greatest confidence in my supplier, you see. But now tell me, one understands that your nephew Badgeley is to be married. Does this meet with your consent?'

'Oh, yes,' said Neville complacently. 'He is marrying to get hold of his fortune. I believe at present he thinks his life will continue as it always has, one bad venture after another. He's a devilish loose fish, you know.'

'One has heard,' grunted the other, sipping.

'But I know the girl. She may have a salutary effect on the whelp, little though he knows it now. I shan't enlighten him.'

The maestro laughed. 'Well. You must wish him happy from me, sir, and tell him that he and young Mr. Neville, *and* that Irish baronet they spend so much time with, are well overdue for a lesson.'

'By which, I take it, you mean a humiliation?'

'Oh, never that sir, never that. Merely, as it were, a call to greater art.'

They chuckled again, finished their brandy, and Neville rose, shrugging himself back into his coat. 'I shall take my leave, my friend, with thanks,' he said. 'Both for this', he gestured to the drink and the weapons downstairs, 'and for the other thing.'

'It is my pleasure. You will not stay for another?'

'Alas, no. I am commanded to my sister's side for the rest of the day and evening. There are, I am told, errands to perform in Jermyn Street before the afternoon is out, followed much against my will by a performance at The Swan tonight.'

'The Swan! Then you will see the sublime Madame Seraphine's Juliet.'

'I neither know nor care, not being an afficionado of the theatre. One must, however, agree when one's esteemed sister is up in the boughs about something or other and demands attendance, or one will never achieve peace.'

*****

Seraphine dashed through the front door of Mme Simard's shop just as the rain began to fall in earnest again, and found Madame herself engaged with a client - one of those who is determined not to be pleased, mistaking simple ill temper for a perfectionist's eye. Nearly every bolt of fabric in Madame's shop was partially unrolled on the counter. Muslin vied with velvet, silk shimmered against linen, calico did battle with brocade, in a chaos of texture and pattern. Elsie and Maria scurried back and forth from workshop to showroom, rolling up the abandoned and unrolling fresh temptations in an endless parade that Seraphine thought looked rather like a fire bucket brigade fighting a lost cause. Madame glanced up on hearing the doorbell tinkle and hazarded a harried nod and smile that carried an element of relief.

'Bonjour, Madame,' trilled Mme. Seraphine cheerily, sizing up the situation with a glance. 'Comment allez-vous aujourd-hui?'

'Tres bien, merci, madame, tres bien. Un moment, s'il vous plaît.' Madame shot her friend a smile of real gratitude. She could always count on Seraphine to say something that allowed Madame to exercise her small store of French, thus raising a difficult client's estimation of her knowledge and ability.

And so it was, for the difficult client looked from earnest Madame to the attractive, poised, and - one must admit, beautifully dressed - Mme. Seraphine and back again, and suddenly found Madame's suggestions regarding the burgundy-and-cream striped silk to be exactly what she had had in mind all along.

Seraphine hid a smile and feigned deep interest - which quickly turned to real interest - in a made-up round dress of the most beautiful muslin, printed in pomona green stripes alternating with cream panels printed with sprigs of yellow rosebuds and leafy tendrils.

'Is it not lovely?' asked her daughter, appearing behind her. 'Bonjour, maman.'

'*Bonjour, mon ange.* Indeed. Indian cotton, *n'est-ce pas*? I thought it illegal to import.' She touched the soft fabric lovingly and inhaled its clean scent.

'We may now find it again, *maman*, is it not famous? Feel the hand of it. And the smell, isn't it divine? And only look at the cleverness of the printing. One might almost smell the rosebuds.'

'*Tres belle.* But the bodice is cut so free, beneath the bust. Must we truly look so, now? Is it not like being undressed? There is barely room for a chemise, much less a petticoat.'

Angel laughed. '*Pas de tout, maman*! It is meant to look rustic, and democratic. A new simplicity, you see, that - in theory - makes the distance between the lady of birth and the simple country maid dwindle into nothing. The new republican order at work. Clothing as a political statement, do you see? *Liberté, Egalité, Fraternité.*'

'*Ce sera le jour*,' laughed Seraphine, 'when fashion and politics walk *tous ensemble* to make a statement about the changing of the world as we know it.'

'But no, *maman*, 'tis nothing but the truth! Now add this,' she took a creamy lace fichu from another stand and artfully wrapped it about Seraphine's shoulders, 'or a spencer jacket of silk in this darker rifle green,' she removed this from the same stand and held it against Seraphine's chest, 'it is really quite modest, you see. And quite stunning.' She laughed again, and exactly at that moment the door opened once more with its insistent tinkling of the bell, and Mr. Tristan Neville entered just in time to see the lovely Miss Angel Hathaway laughing merrily, green eyes shining, black hair gleaming, pale skin glowing, holding a silken green garment up to the famous Mme. Seraphine of The Swan. He stopped as if turned to stone, and stared, forgetting to finish whatever remark he had been throwing over his shoulder to his companions, who broke the spell by ungraciously shoving him from behind, suggesting that he 'move along, Neville, you slug, do! We're getting thoroughly soaked out here!'

Angel's laugh had in that split second evaporated into an 'O' of surprise, and in that split second, her eyes met Tristan's across the beautiful muslin dress, a message was sent, and received, and returned.

And then the shop was filled to the brim with young men and many-caped gabardine greatcoats steaming from the rain and beginning to smell of wet dog. The men all recognized the esteemed Mme. Seraphine, of course, and smiled gallantly and gave her extravagant bows far exceeding her station. She responded with a courtesy and the mischievous smile for which she was famous. 'Gentlemen,' she nodded, then gently removed the green jacket from her daughter's fingertips, setting it and the fichu back on their stand.

'Your servants, madam,' Sir Robert spoke for all of them.

But young Neville's eyes never strayed from Angel's face.

'I'll… I'll fetch my cousin's parcel, *maman*,' said Angel somewhat unsteadily. 'I am sure you came to collect it.' She disappeared through the curtain into the workshop.

The indecisive lady left with a neatly wrapped parcel in her own arms, and sniffed haughtily at the gallant way Sir Robert opened the door for her with a flourish of his doffed hat and a punctilious bow.

Before he could straighten up, another male figure swept through the door, removing his own hat.

'Thank-you… Sir Robert Kilronan, I presume?' said the man with polite irony, sending Sir Robert into utter confusion.

'Uncle!' ejaculated Badgeley.

'Precisely, Badgeley. Astute, as always.'

Seraphine tried vainly to stifle her humor, failed, and let out a choke of laughter that distracted the gentleman briefly. He turned his gaze to her and saw an auburn-haired beauty of early middle age hiding her mirth behind a muslin gown that would have suited her very well, had it been on her person. He found this thought so disturbing that he frowned, and turned away. Seraphine's laughter turned to puzzlement. She could swear she had seen this gentleman before, but how? A fleeting image tugged at the edge of her consciousness, but no answer came.

'What on earth are you doing here, Nat?' asked Tristan, dragging his attention from the curtain through which Angel Hathaway had but lately disappeared. 'Doesn't seem your sort of place at all.'

'T'isn't', replied the older man. 'I've been bored to death dancing attendance on my esteemed sister Lady Letitia, who is across the way embroiled in having a new scent developed for her personal use, and saw the three of you entering this establishment. Which, if I am not mistaken, specializes in the dressing of ladies?' He cocked an eyebrow and surveyed the three young men. 'Perhaps you are procuring a piece of finery for your intended, Badgeley. How thoughtful of you. You do your mama proud.'

Mr. Badgeley blushed scarlet. 'Um…' was all he managed to say.

Mrs. Hathaway had tactfully withdrawn to the farthest corner of the shop and was now in quiet conversation with Mme Simard as the dressmaker tidied the counter after overseeing the removal of the last bolts of fabric into the workroom. She thought she knew for whom such an item of clothing might be destined, and it gave her no comfort. Badgeley had caused quite enough trouble among her young dancers at this particular point in time. His appearance at the dressing room door, apologetic gift in hand, might be enough to send Bridie Murphy into a despair from which she would not soon recover. And she needed Bridie Murphy fit to work. She did not this present have an adequate replacement, being determined not to allow that replacement to be Doll Bridger.

Angel came back through the curtain, and handed her mother a package. The briefest glance hazarded in the direction of the golden-haired gentleman made her blush scarlet and glance away again; he in turn looked at her sidelong as if all he wanted to do was gaze his fill but felt he had been rude enough for one day.

Seraphine, whose business it was always to be sensitive to human emotion, saw the blush, and followed it to its cause. She frowned.

'There is a bill inside the package,' Angel said, eyes firmly on her mother's. 'If my cousin would just… put something toward it. It would be helpful. He is being a great idiot, is he not?'

'*Oui, il est*,' sighed Seraphine. 'There is no fool like an old fool. Angel…' she started.

'*Oui, maman?*'

'…*Rien, n'import*. Will you to The Swan this evening?'

Angel nodded. 'Jacob will fetch me,' she said. 'I thought perhaps I could persuade Madame to see your Juliet. She has not, I believe, had that pleasure. I do worry about her, *maman*. She seems - *je ne sais quois* - so tired, lately. And she coughs.'

Seraphine looked thoughtfully to where Madame was now engaged with the young men. 'Yes. It worries me, as well. How I wish she had someone…' She shook her head. 'Bring her by all means, if you can persuade her. I shall meet you all after the performance, and we can have supper together.' She turned to leave, but not before sending a troubled glance toward young Mr. Neville. He and Kilronan were regulars in Badgeley's company, of course, and frequently to be seen haunting The Swan's dressing rooms. She had never thought she might have to worry about Angel crossing their paths. Angel had been as well protected as possible from the attentions of young gentlemen with rank, address, lust, and ruthless self-interest in their hearts. Madame Simard's had seemed at a blessed remove from the more blatant dangers faced by silly young theatrical ladies.

But Angel was a young woman now, and far from silly. She could not anymore be protected from the ills - or the temptations - a larger world had to offer.

Seraphine allowed herself one more surreptitious touch of the beautiful green-striped muslin dress, then moved to let herself out of the shop. Seeing this, Sir Robert moved with alacrity to hold the door for her, but was beaten to this office by Nathaniel

Neville, who swept it open with a slight bow and expressed the hope that she should not be troubled by the rain.

'*Merci, M'sieu*,' she nodded, and somewhat more tartly than was her wont, added, '*Je vous assure*, I can endure both wind and weather,' and with that statement, she suddenly knew where she had seen Mr. Neville before.

She exited, parcel protected under her cloak, with her customarily good-natured public face closed and troubled. There were times, she reflected, stealing a glance at Badgeley, Kilronan, and the younger Neville through the window as she passed, when she hated - yes, actively hated - young men of the titled class. The damage they caused impressionable young females below their station was detestable and unjust.

She must speak to Angel. Experience dictated that no good could come of the attentions of a handsome and wealthy young man like Tristan Neville. No good at all.

She would not have been pleased to hear the elder Neville remark to the younger men that he would doubtless see them at The Swan later on, as Lady Letitia had blackmailed him as brazenly as any henna'd tart, and threatened dire consequences if he did not turn up to lend her box an air of consequence. He added that he fully expected to be bored unto morbidity.

Badgeley, who had up to now been sullen and jumpy in close proximity to an uncle whom he feared, actually laughed out loud. 'Oh, I think not, sir. I believe my mother intends to throw the dowager Lady Underwood in your face.'

'Good God!' said his uncle, startled. 'Who - or what - is the dowager Lady Underwood? Some female of dubious years and small fortune with whom she wishes to saddle me forever? Has it come to this?'

'No, no!' Badgeley assured him. 'She is of the first stare, actually, a cracking rider to hounds, in possession of a very good stable and, I believe, a sizable fortune. And is one of mama's *closest* friends.'

'Then how have I avoided this paragon?'

'You know mama. Her *closest friends* circulate through her life more or less like water through a sluice. I daresay Lady Underwood is of quite recent vintage, and has not yet had the opportunity to enrage mama for some terrible infraction of taste or opinion. In the meantime she seems determined that your mutual interest in horseflesh will make you admirably suited.'

'I ought to have stayed in the country,' said Neville sourly, slapping his gloves through his hand impatiently.

'Well,' said Tristan prosaically, 'you'd better get used to it, Uncle. For in my experience there is nothing females hate more than to see a man of your advanced years unmarried. All that money, all that birth, wasted? The assembled matrons of our family won't rest until they have you decently shackled to some poor respectable dab. God help you, is what I say.'

The elder Neville rolled his eyes skyward. 'What have I gotten myself into? My dislike of all of my sisters' interminable web-spinning is in equal measure to my disdain for the theatre. Silly bunch of gudgeons prancing about pretending to be someone else.'

'I believe you will like The Swan, sir,' offered Sir Robert. 'They offer fine entertainment, a very intimate setting, and quite a respectable supper. And of course, besides the opera dancers, which are very scenic, there is the divine Mme. Seraphine.'

'She being…?'

'Oh, sir! *Every*body must know Mme. Seraphine. But surely… you did recognize her?'

'Recognize who? What on earth are you talking about?'

'Mme. Seraphine, of course. That was she who was just here!'

'The auburn-haired wench? She is an *actress*?'

'Not merely an actress, sir. She is Beatrice, and Juliet, and Rosalind, and - O! The list is long. For myself, sir, I prefer her Rosalind, for she has an exceptionally lovely figure and excellent legs. But if you are there this evening you shall see for yourself and doubtless fall at the lady's feet, as have we all.'

'I thought Badgeley had already fallen at her feet.'

'Oh, no, sir,' grinned Sir Robert. 'That is another chit altogether, an opera dancer of rare beauty. And… he hasn't fallen at her *feet*, precisely. More Shakespearean than that, I believe, he has *died in her lap.*'

Badgeley blushed furiously but didn't trust himself to speak in his own defense. He wondered how it was that other people managed to get along so well with his uncle Nathaniel. It made him very grumpy indeed to think that he, alone of all around him, lacked that particular facility.

For himself, Nathaniel was aware of a rising sense of helpless rage against the iniquities of females, and a raw sense of loss that was completely incomprehensible. He also knew that, just as he had recognized her and her lovely daughter, the auburn-haired wench had recognized him. And that memory, when she placed it, could prove inconvenient.

He grumbled a curt farewell to the younger men and strode from the shop into the rain to continue his duty to his sister.

'What on God's green earth?' wondered Sir Robert aloud, observing Neville's abrupt change of temper.

'You see now what I mean, Robin?' said Badgeley. 'He was ever an odd fish.'

'No such thing!' defended Tristan. 'He's a topping fellow, Robin, honestly. But I'll tell you what, Ned. I think my aunt is playing a game that will leave her sadly burnt, if she thinks to lead him to a pasture he don't want to graze in.'

'Do I hear a wager?' asked Sir Robert hopefully, as they exited the shop.

'Not from me,' said Badgeley. 'My pockets are to let.'

'And I don't want to fleece a friend,' said Tristan kindly.

'I'll call you out for that,' complained Sir Robert. 'I demand a round at Jackson's with you, my cub.'

'Not I, Robin,' said Tristan. 'Not today. I'll leave you here, I think, and we'll meet later, at The Swan.'

Badgeley and Kilronen watched their friend stride away, with eyebrows raised.

'Did I say something amiss, Ned? I'm damned if I can think what.'

'Nothing at all, Robin.'

'Then why is he in such a taking? He could hardly wait to be shed of us.'

'No accounting for it at all, old fellow. But he's a Neville, after all. Damned queer in the attic they are, if you ask me. Jackson's?'

'*Lead on, MacDuff*,' uttered Sir Robert portentously.

They strode off in the other direction, and thus were spared the sight of Tristan Neville coming to a sudden halt at the next nearly deserted corner and unleashing a roar of anguish as he struck an innocent tree such a mighty blow that his cane cracked in half, causing several hapless pedestrians to scatter in alarm.

Tristan Neville had now twice seen the woman of his dreams, the woman he could love forever, the woman he wanted to marry. And she was a dressmaker's assistant.

*****

Seraphine found James Hemings - the imposing individual in charge of admitting or barring 'The Swan's Swains' from entering the dressing areas by virtue of their dress, their attitude, or their level of drunkenness - perched on the prompter's stool close behind the stage right proscenium, munching the last crumbs of his supper. She informed him that under no circumstances was Mr. Edward Badgeley to be allowed downstairs this evening, 'for I believe that Bridie is so utterly undone by the notice of his marriage that she is very likely to indulge in *un crime passionale*. Or worse, to go up on her lines. And that, *mon cher* Mr. Hemings, would be a *disaster.*'

'To be sure, t'would,' agreed Hemings calmly, wiping greasy fingers on his trousers. 'What with that new Polish choreography fella prancing about issuing orders like as if he was Queen of the May, and Miss Murphy's taking on hysterical-like whenever a body looks at her sideways, it's been a thought noisier than usual hereabouts. You'll be glad to have missed un,' he jerked his thumb toward the stage.

'*Mon Dieu…* Mr. Pearce?'

'Oh aye. Noisiest of the lot, him. Threatening this one, firing that one, tearing up the Polack's plans, thundering down the whole carpenter crew with that powerful deep voice of his…' Hemings shook from head to toe with suppressed laughter and wiped his eyes. 'T'was a rare taking on, Mam, truly t'was. I an't seen him like that for dunnamany months. Oh, and that prompter fella. Mr. Jakes? He come up so upset he had to repair to The Silent Woman to steady his nerves like, and an't been seen since.'

'*Enfin, un jour plus amusant,*' Seraphine marveled. 'I think I shall absent myself more often and allow Mr. Pearce his performance.' She turned to go, then as an afterthought, turned back.

'Mr. Hemings… you did say that Mr. Jakes is still at the Silent Woman?'

'Oh, ay. I doubt but we'll not see him back here tonight.'

'*C'est ce que je craignais.*' She sighed, got as far as the stairs, and turned back again.

'*Alors,* who then will prompt?'

'Jacob Freeman, mam. He reads and can keep up. And he can nip out to collect Miss Angel and be back in plenty of time.'

'*C'est bien.*' She started for the stairs again, thought of something else, and came back. '*D'ailleurs,* Mr. Hemings,' she added. 'There are two other young men that are frequently with Mr. Badgeley - Sir Robert Kilronan and Mr. Tristan Neville.'

'Yes, mam.'

'They shall not enter, either. And if they give you any trouble at all, call me.'

'Oh, they'm no trouble, mam,' grinned Hemings. 'I been dying to pop one a they's corks these half dozen weeks.' He flexed his fingers suggestively.

'*Oui, je le comprends,*' said Seraphine appreciatively. 'But please refrain, Mr. Hemings, unless pressed to the wall. The Swan cannot afford a lawsuit for battery, you know. Not against the *ton.*'

'Right you are, mam.'

Seraphine found Charles Pearce in the office, spectacles perched on nose, script in hand, pacing to and fro as he muttered and gesticulated. 'Ah! Sera!' he exclaimed jovially when she entered. 'I've been overlooking the balcony scene again, and I believe I have found something quite new to try for tonight. Would you like to run through it with me and see how it plays? Did you bring my package?'

'*Oui, bien sur*, and Mme. Simard would like some money.'

Pearce stood and reached for the packet. Seraphine held it away from him and rested her other hand lightly on his chest. 'And I also would like some money, Charles. Specifically last night's takings.'

'Sera, do be reasonable,' expostulated Pearce. 'You know that, by law...'

'...You took it and gambled it away, didn't you.'

'Not a bit! I had expenses... unseen costs... come along, Sera, do, you know that I...'

'You did lose it, didn't you.' She swore long and fluently, then hit him hard with the package. 'This must end, Charles. The money is equally ours, to be shared after paying our workers.'

'Well *of course* it is. But I, as my cousin's guardian...'

'*Canard*! You are nothing of the sort!'

'And you, as a woman, have no legal say in the matter!'

She stared at him in fury, eyes blazing. 'You are a swine, Charles Pearce. And I am leaving.'

She turned on her heel and yanked the door open.

'No! Wait! Seraphine!' implored Pearce. 'You cannot leave just before a performance, the house is full!'

'*Regarde-moi, Porceau*,' she spat.

'But the money... we can't afford...'

'*We*? If it is not my money then the loss is yours alone. I care not.'

'But I can't... there isn't enough... Sera, I thought we were partners,' he wheedled.

'Then where is my share?' she demanded.

Pearce retreated too his desk. 'I... it... you're right, my dear. I did lose it. I owed... certain sums... but,' he looked at her pleadingly, 'I'll get it back. I swear. If only you'll stay.'

'I'll stay if you give me control of the money.'

'Give you... Are you mad... No! Wait! Don't leave! Yes, my dear, of course, of course I'll give you control, if it will help. Just... I have these new ideas, you see... I thought we could try them on the new set. I'd like to know if there is blocking to change.'

'Are you sure you don't need to rest your voice?' Seraphine asked mockingly. 'Hemings tells me you were quite *rampant* today.'

Pearce mopped his brow and sighed in gusty relief. 'Ah, t'was a rare performance,' he admitted humbly. 'I was Lear, *Blow winds and crack your cheeks!* I was Capulet, *Beg! Steal! Die in the street!* - Should I be adding Capulet to my line of work, do you think? Garrick couldn't have done it better - I was young Hal, *God for Harry England and St. George!* Haven't had so much fun in years.' He beamed, rubbing his hands in delight. Then added, 'But Sera... don't expect it of me too often, will you? Such passion does take a great deal out of one. Much more your sort of thing, I would have thought.' He looked at her over his spectacles. 'Do not leave me, Seraphine. Truly, it will not happen again.'

'It will not, *Je te promet.* For from this moment I will manage the money. But I think it does a great deal of good to have the company see you *furieux.* When you rage, the company say, *Voila! C'est un homme puissant!* When I rage, I am merely a Harpy.'

'It is a sorry fact of nature,' agreed Pearce, ascending the last step to the stage. 'Ah. Here we are, then. Only look at the new balcony. Is it not perfection? Now, *a propos* of the position, I was thinking...'

They spent the next hour doing what actors do best - honing and perfecting troublesome pieces of the roles they would present that night, restaging blocking that had come to seem stale or that no longer worked on a newly configured set fancifully representing a homesick Italian artist's version of a Veronese piazza placed in a lush landscape. They added new inflections here, a slightly different reading there, a reaction that was begging to be used in another place, all in service to the play. All to make sure that what they would portray was fresh and new and surprising and moving to the thousand souls that would be in attendance that night, many of whom would be mouthing familiar and beloved words of longing from the audience, in concert with the actors.

Mr. Pearce and Mme. Seraphine may have been too old by twenty years to play Mr. Shakespeare's star-crossed lovers. But in the year of Our Lord 1793, Romeo and Juliet were characters that must be earned by long and arduous study, after playing dozens upon dozens of messengers, mountebanks, nurses, priests, and other secondary characters. Once learned, roles like these became treasured personal property, hoarded by the actors that played them. Reputations - indeed, entire careers - were built on the specific manners and methods each performer brought to the stage in offering great characters to the world at large.

Mr. Pearce and Mme. Seraphine were rightly famed as the doomed sweethearts, which, following the lead of the great Mr. Garrick and celebrated Mlle. Clairon, eschewed the presentational or bombastic, acknowledged neither friend in the front row nor patron in the gallery, but kept absolute focus in character and story; each line delivered as if fresh and never spoken before. And so new theatre tradition is born and its lineage handed from generation to generation, down the years in an ever-evolving continuum.

As the pair rehearsed, deaf and blind to all except the profound beauty of text and the deep emotional yearning for relationship that somehow cannot be adequately expressed in ordinary words, all other activity slowly quieted. Dancers and actors, then house cleaners, seamstresses, and carpenters, put down their tools and quietly straggled singly and in pairs to the stage as if drawn irresistibly by the magnetism of the couple now

working. At last the entire company stood watching silent and
rapt, and when the scene ended and the spell broke, burst into
spontaneous cheers, whistles, and foot-stompings. Mr. Pearce and
Mme. Seraphine looked up startled, as if rudely awakened from a
dream, and gazed about them in bewilderment, until,
consciousness dawning, they beamed with pleasure and gave their
audience an elegant impromtu bow that swept them in a great arc
of the stage.

'Thank-you!' said Mr. Pearce. 'Thank-you very much! I think
then… Mrs. Hathaway? That we have a success on our hands?'

'I believe we have, Mr. Pearce', smiled Seraphine, 'with critics
of this stature to comment on our work,' she indicated the
informal assemblage.

The watchers whistled and cheered some more. The actors
bowed again.

'Good!' boomed Pearce jovially. 'Now then, fun's over,
everybody back to work, and let's make success a reality!'

In moments the bustle created by fifty bodies working as fast
as they could to get a production up and running returned the
theatre to a chaotic welter of activity. To an outsider it would have
seemed pure insanity, but to anyone in the business of theatre the
cacaphony of shouts, thumps, hammering, sweeping, and
fragments of curses and collisions had an internal sense of
purpose all directed toward making an impossible mess of fabric,
wires, and broken pieces of scenery soar suddenly to the rafters so
that the exotic Veronese garden grew a backdrop whose
perspective drew the viewer's eye deeply into a blue and rolling
distance that looked suspiciously like the Chiltern Hills. Lanterns
were lit and mirrored to reflect on the set and make the most of
the actors' features. Musicians began to arrive, take their places,
and warm up, instruments honking and squeaking like so many
flocks of tuneless birds. Crises in the crowded dressing rooms
were addressed with a stitch here, a piece of extra lace there, an
adroit string or pin somewhere else. In the lobby and dining
room, the cleaners gave the brass an extra polish, the front-of-

house people made sure the night's program contained no misspellings, and the kitchen staff clattered and shouted and banged pots as they prepared the food and drink to be offered at the intervals and after the show to hungry and, it was hoped, cheerful theatre goers.

Eventually, quiet reigned again, with only the chatter of actors and actresses dressing, making up, reciting lines, and laughing, the pithy backstage conversations of the technical crew as counterpoint. This was the period Seraphine loved the most; that hour before a raucous audience shoved its way into the house to take their seats with noise and expectation, when the theatre felt as if it had inhaled and now held its breath until the first curtain opened, the first song struck up, and the first scene played. From then until final curtain, all would be a blur - backstage blending into onstage, present life enfolded into the lives of stories told, present emotions subsumed by theatrical passions. A blurred reality, shared by an audience that breathed the same air, heard the same words, saw their own lives in some ineffable way mirrored by those portrayed for them on the stage itself.

But for now, for this moment, Seraphine breathed in the quiet, the smells, the dust, the expectant atmosphere backstage, and understood once again that she was fortunate indeed to have a life that held such variety and beauty, and the opportunity to inspire people to laughter and tears and greater self-examination. It was a gift, this profession. A gift that had entailed heart-breaking work and soul-destroying decisions, *oui, c'est vrai*. But a gift none the less. She hoped she could hold it for another decade. If she were very fortunate, maybe more.

At the stage door, raised voices jolted her from her reverie and with a sigh of foreboding she left the stage. As suspected, she found Hemings firmly wedged in the opening of the stage door facing down Mr. Tristan Neville and Sir Robert Kilronan, who at that precise moment were holding Mr. Edward Badgeley by the arms and attempting to keep the overwrought gentleman from 'popping his damned cork, the damned self-important, fusty *puppy!*' while for his part, James Hemings was looking all too ready to jump into the fray himself, meaty fists at the ready, while Jacob Freeman stood firm behind him, a restraining hand on Hemings' collar.

'*Qu'est-ce que c'est?*' demanded Mrs. Hathaway in a rallying tone, which had the immediate effect of causing the would-be combatants and their doughty seconds to separate in some confusion and straighten themselves into a semblance of propriety.

'Good evening, Madame Seraphine,' said Badgeley, fighting to regain both his breath and an iota of haughtiness. 'I do not mean to create a scene, but this *fellow*...' he indicated Hemings -

'...Was just a-doing me job, see, *like* as you told me, Mam, *and* this young fella...'

'...Was trying to enter, on a very particular errand for Miss Murphy, *whom*, as you very well know...'

'*Arretez, s'il-vous plait!*' ordered Mrs. Hathaway at her most stentorian. 'Mr. Hemings, thank-you. You have done exactly as I asked. Mr. Badgeley, you are not welcome in The Swan's dressing room on this or any other night, *monsieur*, until I see fit to admit you again.'

'But... *why?*' wailed that gentleman, nonplussed.

'*Mr.* Badgeley,' said Mrs. Hathaway sternly, 'It has come to my understanding that you are presently to be married. May I offer my felicitations. In the meantime, you have been spending a great deal of time, and saying a great many foolish things...'

'I never promised anyth...'

'...to a young and very silly girl who believed you to be in love with her.'

'But I never! My intent was...'

'*Faite attention*, Mr. Badgeley. I know *precisely* what your intent was, and I remind you, *moi meme*, that I do *not* run a bawdy house, *M'sieur*. Miss Murphy is not yet of age and is under my protection - *ne parlez pas, m'sieu, pas un mot!* - *Enfin*, Mr. Badgeley, I repeat. You may not, until further notice, enter the dressing rooms of this theatre. You and your friends are, of course, welcome at any performances and in the supper room. But your relations with Miss Murphy are at an end. Do I make myself perfectly clear?'

'Madame, I hope you know to whom you are speaking in this impertinent way!' swore Badgeley, drawing himself up to his full height of birth, asperity, and wounded pride. His friends, to their credit, looked uncomfortable.

'Ned,' muttered Sir Robert warningly, and tried to put a hand on his friend's arm, but Badgeley shook it off.

With fiery eyes, Madame drew herself up to her full height as well, which, while a good six inches less than Badgeley's, was far more impressive. '*Mr.* Badgeley, I know *exactly* who you are, and I feel quite certain your *maman*, an honored patroness of The Swan, would be mortified to know you to be acting in this unbecoming manner. And if you think that you can threaten me - *moi meme, m'sieu, chez moi!* - then I shall be forced to allow Mr. Hemings to evict you in any way he sees fit - which will afford him the greatest pleasure! - *and* I will not hesitate to prosecute you for malicious trespassing!'

'Ned, old boy,' insisted Tristan quietly as Badgeley fumed, 'best to keep on the windy side o' the law, eh?' with a brief awed glance at the formidable little figure of Madame Seraphine.

'She's quite right, you know,' insisted Sir Robert. 'Private property, dear boy, and you no rights in the matter.'

'We are done here,' spat Badgeley and strode away, flinging the package that had been in his pocket into the alley, where it landed in a murky puddle.

Tristan watched this action with some embarrassment before turning back to Mrs. Hathaway with a formal bow. 'We apologize for the behavior of our friend, madame,' he said, with as much courtesy as he could muster. 'We shall endeavor to keep him from any further indiscretion.'

Sir Robert bowed as well. 'And may I add, madame, that we very much look forward to your performance tonight.

'*Merci*, my lord, young sir,' said Madame, with a gracious nod. 'And now, *si vous me permettez...*'

'Of course!' said Neville. He stooped and picked up the package. 'Perhaps you could find a use for this in the costume department, ma'am. It seems a waste to let it rot in the gutter.'

Mrs. Hathaway accepted the dripping article gingerly, and the gentlemen withdrew.

'Well,' remarked Hemings with satisfaction. 'Them's a pair of pretty-spoke gents, any road. *Not* but what I wasn't looking forward to putting young fella-me-lad onto the cobbles,' he added with some resignation, closing the stage door with a thud.

'You and me's too old for that sort of thing anymore,' Jacob Freeman advised. 'I doubt not you'd be the sorrier, once 'twas over.'

'Aye,' agreed Hemings. 'But you can't say the idea hadn't crossed yer own noggin onc't or twice.'

'Not I,' smiled Freeman. 'I'm a peaceable man. I'm off to collect Angel, Seraphine. And you, James, do you stay out of trouble while I'm gone.'

Seraphine held the dripping parcel out to Hemings carefully. 'Mr. Hemings, if I know anything of the matter, this contains a rather expensive and very nicely made linen chemise, with lace. I'll not upset Bridie Murphy further by giving it her, but I believe it might fit your young wife, might it not? The wrapper is wet, but I feel sure the contents are undamaged.'

Hemings flushed with pleasure. 'Thank-you, mam. How very kind you are indeed.'

'*Pas du tout*, Mr. Hemings,' said Seraphine. 'Call it the spoils of war.'

'I will then, mam,' he grinned.

In the alley, the two pretty-spoke gents had their own post-mortem.

'Now *that* is a formidable woman,' remarked Sir Robert as the two went along to the street to find Badgeley. 'Had me all in a quake, I swear!'

'She was magnificent,' agreed Neville. 'Did you see the light on her hair? Positively, I thought she might burst into flame. And those *eyes*!'

'Oh, dear lord,' groaned Sir Robert, and punched his friend hard on the arm. "Tis far worse than I ever imagined, Tris. You *are* a bloody romantic. It wouldn't hurt Ned to be tipped a leveler by the doorkeeper. Might teach him some manners.'

'I'll lay a pony he could do the job in three moves.'

'Two.'

'A bet?'

'Done.' They shook.

'Ah, there's yer man, surly as a bull. I think we all need a drink, don't you agree, Tris?'

*****

As dusk gathered in the corners of early evening, rain-washed streets glistened, suffused with a golden light that shone through ribbons of the inevitable fog that emanated from Thames and the soggy ground. *Chez* Madame Simard, Elsie and Maria cleaned the workshop, filled the scuttle, and made up the fire while Angel rolled bolts of linen, muslin, and cambric that had been on display all day. Gently, fondly, she examined every exposed inch for signs of damage from dirty fingers or for staining specks of dust or soot. Carefully, she measured, cut, and folded a length of ivory muslin sprigged all over with lavender and rosebuds destined to be a sweet dress for spring and summer, which she wrapped in brown paper and tied with string to be delivered on her way home to the purchaser. As she worked, her mind returned - despite all efforts to think of something, *anything*, more edifying - to the blue gaze of Mr. Tristan Neville, whose name she had managed to collect from the conversation she had pretended not to heed. Then she made a rude noise so loud that it startled Elsie into dropping a box of pins in the workshop but failed to banish those blue eyes, that burnished gold hair, from her mind.

The bell tinkled, and the door pushed open. Angel looked up to see a burly man not many years older than herself standing uncertainly on the threshold looking about him in openmouthed wonder, as if undecided whether to stay or bolt. His skin was cinnamon, his height middling, and he was very lined from being, she thought, constantly in the weather. His dress was that of a seaman, worn, but clean and neat. A pleasant scent of sawdust and salt water hung about him.

'May I help you?' she asked with a smile

The young man started, closed his mouth with a snap, and removed a hat from springy black hair that he wore in a single pigtail.

'N-no, miss,' he stammered. 'I think this be the wrong…' he stopped. 'No. That an't right. I mean, Miss. I mean, I was just… erm. Is Mrs… uhh… Madam …' he blushed, 'erm… *Simard* about, Miss?'

'Of course,' smiled Angel. 'Close the door to keep the fog out, won't you? I'll fetch her for you.' She started to turn away, then turned back and, with head tilted and a laugh showing in her eyes, added, 'Now don't bolt, will you? She has never bitten anyone to my knowledge yet, sir!' Then she went through the workshop to Madame's office, to tell her that a very nice looking if rather nervous young man was at the front door and had asked for her most particularly.

'For me?' Madame frowned. 'Why on earth? Late for a tradesman, I'd think.'

'Not a tradesman, I think, Madame. He is dressed as a seaman. Do come and see him, will you? If you delay I am very afraid he will run away and never come back. And,' she added, twinkling at Elsie and Maria, 'I am agog with curiosity. Will you come, Madame? Presently?'

'Oh, very well,' grumbled Molly. She removed her spectacles, patted her hair, hitched the lace fichu that had slipped crookedly from her thin shoulders straight again, and closed the accounts book with her quill carefully marking the spot.

'*Ouai?*' she demanded impatiently in her best French accent as she bustled through the curtain to the front of the shop. 'What do you require of me, *s'il-vous plait?*'

The young man stood backlit by a shaft of light from the big front window. Raindrops sparkled diamond-like on dark curls, and his eyes were of that melting brown, with a slight almond shape to them that Molly Boggs could never resist, upon a time. It looked, in fact, like... Molly's heart banged erratically against her ribs. She caught her breath and involuntarily clasped a hand to her bosom, her mouth making a small 'O' of shock, as if she were seeing a ghost, as if she might actually die in that moment, right then, as if an angel had come for her, to take her away...

'Do you not know me, Ma?' the young man's eyes so fearful, so imploring. ''Tis I, Jack that was.'

'Oh my lord!' breathed Molly Boggs. 'Oh my lordy-lord. Jack!' She flung herself at him with a sob, and Angel and the other two girls, who hovered open-mouthed at a discreet distance, peeping around the edges of the curtain, were treated to a sight they never thought to see, that of Madame Simard, that tyrant of the dressmaker's trade, that virago of impatient energy, that terror of apprentices, clutching a handsome young stranger to herself with all her might, and sobbing hysterically as she said over and over, 'Jack. O my Jack. O my boy. O my sweet love. O I never thought I would. O I thought you was. O my Jack, my love, my boy', and he held on to her in turn, and tears started to his eyes as he said to her, 'There now. There now. 'Tis I indeed, I thought you was gone away, Ma, awful hard it was findin' you, oh 'tis you indeed.'

*****

Like Mlle Clairon before her, Madame Seraphine eschewed the use of the heavy white lead paint and rouge that were known to raddle complexions beyond repair while causing hair loss, swollen eyes, and numerous other debilitating issues. Instead, Seraphine used a light flour paste to render her complexion pale without cementing it into an immovable mask. She likewise refused the tradition of removing her natural eyebrows and replacing them with mouse skins, instead plucking them to the correct shape and darkening them with kohl. Marianne - former slave, herbalist, healer, dresser, and now wife to Jacob Freeman - had shown her how to create rouge and lipstick from the bright juice of berries and even certain insects whose crushed bodies secreted the proper color. For older roles she might powder her hair thickly. For Juliet, she left her auburn mane *au naturel* and entrusted the artful dressing of it and herself to Marianne. And in this way the transformation from middle aged woman to youthful Juliet was made complete.

They were deep into the final moments of easing Seraphine into Juliet's dress when Jacob Freeman tapped on her door and cautiously looked around it with a broad grin creasing his battered face, rain still dripping from his head and his cloak. 'Excuse me, Madame,' he said, somewhat out of breath. 'I have just left Angel in the box office where she is feeding Brutus, and am sent by Mr. Pearce to tell you there is a visitor in the office that warrants your immediate attention.'

'A visitor? So near curtain? *Tiens*! He *knows* I cannot be troubled before a performance, Mr. Freeman. Why on earth...' but Freeman just shrugged, shut the door, and went to claim his post in the prompter's corner, chuckling. When Hemings asked what was the fuss about, he smiled as he took off his cloak, shook the rain off, and hung it on a peg, marveling, 'T'is a night for miracles, Mr. Hemings, surely. You'll see what I mean presently.'

Meanwhile, a grumbling Seraphine strode to the office and yanked the door open....

To find Stephen Hathaway - slender, weathered, worn-looking, older, but undeniably her own ruddy-haired son Stephen - lounging on the old sofa very much at his ease, sharing a brandy with Charles Pearce.

'*Stephen*!' Seraphine shrieked after a split second of disbelief. He jumped to his feet with a shout of laughter just in time to be nearly knocked over by the crushing embrace of an ecstatic mother who promptly burst into tears, ruining her carefully applied makeup. So deep and glad were her emotions at his safe return from the high seas, the unexpectedness of his arrival, that she forgot to take Pearce to task for imbibing in strong drink before a performance.

Within moments the office door burst open again to frame Miss Angel Hathaway, black hair framing her face in damp curls, face flushed rosy and eyes sparkling from what appeared to be a hard sprint. She paused, panting, in the doorway, and took in the scene before her. Her expression, just now suffused with joy, turned to consternation as she gazed at the wiry stranger in the arms of her mother. Suddenly shy, she `asked tentatively, '…Stephen?' and looked anxiously at him. 'Is it really you, Stephen?' And then, drawing affirmation from the glow in her mother's eyes, she shouted, 'It *is* you! *Stephen*! Honestly, brother, can you have forgot your *sister*?' and stamped her foot in exasperation as if to bring him to his senses.

Young Mr. Hathaway stared in confusion, blinked, looked harder at the vision in the doorway, and uttered, '*Le bon Dieu! Se peut-il que ce soit ma petite Ange?* All grown up? *Angel*!' He spread his arms wide, grinning, and she flew into them and flung hers around him and they laughed and clung to each other and then held each other at arm's length and took turns exclaiming at how well or badly the other had aged, demanding laughing confirmation from their mother about the great changes made by a few years of life abroad and the surprises still possible in this old world. And, heart singing, Seraphine tore herself away to repair her ruined make-up.

*****

Edward Badgeley's highly anticipated evening of diversion had turned to ashes. Wallowing in equal measures of rage, insult to his dignity, and the awful realization that he had in truth behaved appallingly in his stage door *contretemps* made him badly want to blame someone else. He wanted to wring Bridie Murphy's soft white neck. He wanted to fling himself at her feet and beg forgiveness. He wanted to cast her off in righteous fury. He wanted to fuck her ruthlessly and possess her completely. He could do none of these things. He hated his friends for having so cruelly pointed out that he had already ruined her. But he hadn't! He hadn't! She had wanted... he had wanted... Images of her naked body rose before him like a knife twisting in his guts. He could hardly breathe. If he could just see her... to... to...

With a strong friend on either side to keep him from bolting and creating worse trouble than he already had, Ned appeared with an ill grace at his mother's box in the first gallery after a bracing stop at the tavern two doors down, thinking to sulk and fume in a private corner. Instead, he discovered it filled with not only his mother and his odious uncle Nat, but the same dowager Lady Underwood about whom he had warned said uncle, and, to his complete shock, his bride-to-be Henrietta and her good friend Amelia Rackham, the plumply attractive girl he'd come so close to proposing marriage to before recovering his senses. He spoke the bare minimum of polite nothings to this happy assemblage and threw himself broodingly into an offered chair next to his intended, wishing the entire gathering at the bottom of Thames. Sir Robert and Tristan, after safely depositing their friend, administered the bows and light hearted repartee that made them so attractive and immediately betook themselves to the theatre bar.

The ladies were in high spirits. Miss Rackham, evidently recovered from the blight of losing Ned Badgeley to her friend Hetty, thought it famous of dear Lady Torrington to have invited them to come to the theatre, such a rare treat, was it not, for one heard everywhere of the excellence of The Swan's company. This of course rendered Ned even angrier than he had been. He listened to the ladies distractedly, responded monosyllabically, and made an excuse to absent himself as soon as he was able with the intent to follow his friends to the bar and fortify himself against the company of an unwelcome collection of ladies on a night that, having started badly, was setting up to be unendurable. His doting but worried mama was left to wonder whatever ailed the boy, and to make excuses for him. His uncle Nathaniel merely frowned reflectively before turning his attentions once more to Lady Underwood's discourse on the superiority of the country to the city, and her abhorrence of nightlife in general and the theatre in particular. 'For I do believe, do not you, that it instills the most horrifying lack of manners in our young people, who must have examples of excellence and taste before them - and discipline, of course, which the theatre cannot be held to offer...' and more along these lines until Neville began to wonder if the lady had mastered that trick known to musicians, of circular breathing that allowed them to play seemingly without pause to inhale.

'You must apologize,' remarked Sir Robert when Badgeley found them. 'You were inexcusably rude, Ned. Can't think what screw got shaken loose in your head. I wouldn't blame the woman if she never let you backstage again.'

'I've got to see Bri... Miss Murphy,' said Ned wildly. 'I've got to see her and make her understand...'

'Understand what, old son?' said Sir Robert. 'That you want to continue enjoying her considerable charms for nothing more than a chemise, while you marry someone of your own sort and give *her* the title of Lady Torrington? Not the thing at all. Never knew she was underage, makes it very much harder. No good going round ruining young girls' lives and making them into whores.'

'But she was *willing*. She *knew*...'

'Knew what, precisely?' asked Tristan bluntly. 'I'll wager you told her you loved her, didn't you?'

'I never... I only...'

'Told her that you would always take care of her?'

'Well, but I...'

'Ned, you stupid harecop,' said Tristan cuttingly. 'What won't we say to get into a succulent woman's cunny? Part of the game.

But if you were sweet-talking her, giving her presents too, you can wager that a girl like that - just over from Ireland, opera dancer for now but needs a husband, no other line of work open to her but kitchen wench or washer woman or the street unless she gets one - she was dreaming dreams very much finer than reality.'

'She *can't* have been. I never…'

'Never?'

'Well…'

'Way of females, old boy,' added Sir Robert sagely. 'Fueled with the image of those Irish wenches - what the hell were their names?'

'The Gunnings,' supplied Tristan.

'Yes. Came over on the boat and married dukes, or earls, or some such blather. Stuff of fairy stories. Now they all believe they can do that. But they can't.'

'It could be different. I could keep her the way she would like. I could set her up…'

'You ain't that rich, Ned. And when you get a child on her, then what? You ain't a Royal. Can't keep two households. Can't give your bastards your name, neither,' said Sir Robert firmly. 'Daresay the chit don't even want you anymore, after this.'

'Stick to your own kind,' agreed Neville. 'Or the dolly birds who know the game.'

'Like your Cyprian?' sniped Ned.

'Yes,' responded Tristan, unperturbed. 'I'll wager she's already set something by for a comfortable retirement. Your Miss Murphy is made of baser metal, coz. We see her sort on every street. Poxy and gin-soaked. Begging for the odd customer.'

'I'd never let Bridie…'

'Yes you would, old son,' drawled Sir Robert callously. 'First sign of trouble and you'd be off like a shot. Know you too well.'

'You know nothing at all,' grumbled Ned. 'All very well to pinch on at one about morals and poverty like those endless reformer sorts. And me without a feather to fly with unless I marry! Paying a house full of servants - leeches, every one - half a guinea a week - each! - Now *that* poverty.'

'That's funny, coming from you, Ned,' retorted Neville. 'If you'd leave gaming, you'd be plumper in the pocket than Robin and myself together. If you end up in the sponging house it's your own damn fault.'

Sir Robert yawned. 'I am excessively weary of this conversation, 'pon my soul I am. I shall have to abandon you both, positively I shall.'

'In that case, we'd all best have another drink,' said Tristan instantly, 'and prepare ourselves for the delights of the Torrington box. Lord, what a night.'

In said Torrington box, Neville the elder had descended to a hitherto unsuspected circle of hell. The dowager Lady Underwood proved herself to be as narrow-minded as she was prideful of the supremacy of her own breeding and that of the Thoroughbred horses she so closely resembled, down to the whinnying laugh. Having discoursed at length on the superiority of her horses, her admirable children, and in fact of everything and everyone in her household over everything and everyone in the great houses surrounding her own, she turned to the dress (so immodest!), bearing (such airs from an obvious mushroom!), social standing (*not* at all what one would expect!) and worth (questionable at best!) of the glittering stream of wealth and entitlement that strolled back and forth among the boxes trading pleasantries and gossip. She then deplored the riff-raff in the upper galleries as loud, uncouth, badly dressed, and noisome, and that didn't even *begin* to describe those in the lower orchestra. Neville clenched his jaw to keep himself from observing she was describing herself to a nicety. His sister had described her as a bluestocking. Half an hour in her company was enough to show Nathaniel that if she had read anything at all, it could only have been a book on the breeding of hounds.

An eternity later, Lady Underwood paused long enough to complain of a great thirst brought on 'by the uncommonly dry atmosphere of the theatre'. Neville sprang to his feet, offered to provide refreshment for all of the assembled ladies, and escaped.

'A fine lot you are, abandoning me to an entire bevy of excessively dull females,' he remarked to his nephews and their crony as he downed a strengthening glass of brandy.

'It's your own fault, Uncle,' retorted Ned. I warned you about Lady Underwood.'

'Yes. And I should have listened. But whatever it is that has you in the sulks, Badgeley, you'd best recover. The three of you are going to accompany me back to the box, laden with ladylike refreshments and entertaining conversation.'

'Not if you expect me to sit next to Lady Underwood,' stated Ned flatly.

'I do not. I expect you rather to be very apologetic and extremely attentive to your affianced wife.'

Ned blushed.

'Is Lady Underwood really that dull?' asked Sir Robert with interest.

'Yes. Inexcusably rude, as well,' said Neville. 'She talks only of horses ad her own importance.'

'But wealthy?'

'Extremely wealthy.'

'I'll sit next to her, Neville,' he said handsomely.

Tristan laughed out loud. 'You can't, Robin! She'll eat you alive.'

'Sure, I'll have her eating out of me hand before the first interval, see if I don't,' said Sir Robert cheerfully, in his best stage-Irish brogue. 'She sounds just like the great majority of me own dear raunties in the auld country.'

Sir Robert was as good as his word, and set about flirting outrageously with Lady Underwood, using the odd vehicle of breeding race horses as his medium. This strayed into detailed observations that, had the others been listening, would have caused them to blush in deep embarrassment and cover their innocent ears. Not so the Dowager Lady Underwood - she gave as good as she got, laughed immoderately, and raised Sir Robert's hopes ever higher.

Tristan undertook to amuse Miss Rackham, which, since it involved nothing more than listening, nodding, and smiling as she chattered, was not an onerous fate. Giving every impression of deep attention, he scanned the audience. Seeking her. Knowing he shouldn't. Hoping she wouldn't be present. Knowing in his liver that she was. Not knowing what he would do in either case.

Ned prepared to appease what he assumed would be the wounded feelings of Miss Attenborough, and was both slightly miffed and somewhat intrigued to discover that she hadn't missed him at all, but was mildly pleased to see him and to ask a question that had been troubling her a great deal, which was to try to discover whether the pastime of prize fighting was art, science, or mere brutality. This immediately sent Ned into a lengthy discourse on a subject dear to his heart, ignorant of how cleverly Miss Attenborough had begun to make herself so indispensable to him. In a very short time he would barely know how to get on without her.

Neville made desultory conversation with his sister. As greatly as he disliked the theatre, he was never so relieved as when at last the curtain rose and he no longer had to endure the incessant flow of inanities that emanated from the majority of the entities in the box.

On the other side of the proscenium, Seraphine stood behind the curtain by the prompter's corner and looked with satisfaction on galleries and floor packed with eager theatre-goers, bathed in light. Satisfaction turned to pleasure as the music began, the curtain rose on the beautiful set, and the dancers swirled onstage. The crowd sighed like an ocean and applauded thunder. Magically, the music was sublime, not a note out of place. The lighting was superb. The scenery, operated by complex and often temperamental machinery, moved as if borne by angels. And the players were in one of those unpredictably exalted states that actors pray for nightly where nothing could go wrong. Each act found new heights to ascend to, new meaning in old words, new emotion in songs that had been sung a hundred times or more, and the crowd hummed and laughed and wept and breathed with the performers, '*spell stopp'd*'.

When it came time for Bridie Murphy to sing, Seraphine held her breath. It had been touch and go all the way to Places as to whether Bridie would go onstage at all; in the end only the threat of replacing her with Doll Bridger forced her to flounce to her feet with a mighty pout to make her way to the wings. Seraphine trusted that once on stage the tiresome girl would respond to the attention of the audience and forget about her troubles for at least that much time, as what actor does not. And Bridie didn't disappoint. From the moment she entered, she held her public in thrall with her golden voice, her cascading hair, her melting eyes. Seraphine exhaled in relief and noted that the combination of a broken heart and the threat of losing her position to another had a most salutary effect on the caliber of the chit's performance.

To Ned Badgeley, every second of Bridie's performance was torture. On his right hand sat Henrietta Attenborough, the fiancé he had just begun to think was a prime 'un. On the stage, in a glory of golden hair rippling about white shoulders and a sweetly turned ankle peeping out from under foaming petticoats, was the object of his adoration. Now that he had been warned away from her, she appeared to him more desirable than ever she had before. His attention was so rapt that when, in a particularly moving moment, Henrietta put her hand on his arm, he very nearly threw her off with a rude set-down, caught himself in the nick of time, and turned on her a smile so sickly as to be worrying. Fortunately, Henrietta was herself much caught up in watching Bridie, so missed the moment.

In the pit, among the great sweating mass of humanity that most of us belong to, Stephen Hathaway sat with his beautiful grown-up sister Angel on one side, his friend Chance River on the other, and Chance's mother Molly Boggs beyond that. Stephen had no particular preference for Bridie over any of the other opera dancers, rather thinking that a graceful dark-skinned girl in the back of the line looked more delectable. Chance, on the other hand, took one look at Bridie Murphy and knew that there would never be another woman for him this side of the grave. His lips parted, his breath caught in his throat, his eyes could not feed enough on every inch of her. Oh, she was perfection, this girl lit by the magic of the stage. Every move she made, every inclination of her head on her beautiful neck… and when she was finished, he all but leapt to his feet to whistle and clap and stamp the floor in ecstasy. Stephen laughed at him.

'I thought you said you'd spent your earliest years hanging about in theatres,' he rallied his friend.

'Well, but it weren't like this, were it, Ma? We never saw it all lit up-like, and the outfits and the singin' and all.' He blushed mightily. 'Will that un be coming on again, you think? That's a rare un, that un, eh, Ma?'

His mother, still stupefied beyond speech at the cosmic lightning bolt that had returned a son to her, just smiled as if caught in a beautiful, ephemeral dream, and squeezed his hand.

After a lengthy interval that allowed for much eating, drinking, visiting with friends, and ogling both those in the boxes above and the seats below, it was time for *Romeo and Juliet*; or those parts of the play that Mr. Pearce deemed worthy of performance. He had not taken Garrick's trick of turning the play's ending into a happy one, but instead had deleted great gobs of language, and scenes that he thought did nothing to move the plot, so that the whole was more to his notion of what Mr. Shakespeare *should* have been doing with his play, if he had had a grain of sense. This included, of course, the addition of several songs and two full scale dance sequences, which escaped the strictures of the Licensing Act that prevented theatres like The Swan from producing serious drama.

The result may have rendered Mr. Shakespeare;'s *Romeo and Juliet* somewhat unrecognizable to its author, had he seen it, but for The Swan's audience, the result was a happy one. Seraphine, buoyed on the magic of the evening, supported by the hand of

Fortune that had brought her own son safely home to her, felt as if this one night above all others, the character of Juliet inhabited her so completely that she could do nothing more than follow her lead, speak as she spoke, respond as she responded, weep as she wept. Fueled by all the joys and terrors and griefs and hopes that mothers feel for their children, she found herself drowned in the acute sensibility of a young girl overwhelmed by the overpowering, life-altering passions of a great, impossible love, '*be fickle, Fortune! For then I hope thou wilt not keep him long, but send him back.*'

The audience grew quiet, and quieter still. In his sister's box, Nathaniel Neville found that his attention, heretofore focused anywhere but on the stage, was fixed intently on the actress known as Mme. Seraphine. It was in fact as he had been told - she was not a player reciting a part, but was the character itself. With her simple honesty and straightforward delivery, she drew the audience into the world of the words so that they all might share once more the joy and agony of first love. And damn her, on the stage she managed to look no older than thirteen. Neville found himself staring at the action - or more properly, at the lady who was central to the action - with an intensity that would have been frightening to behold, had anyone been looking anywhere but at the scene unfolding before them. Because the single most prominent emotion he felt was rage at this creature who forced him to feel, forced his heart to break again. He wanted more than anything to throttle the sorceress that caused him such pain.

Beside him, Tristan Neville, glass to eye, scanned the orchestra seats once more. And suddenly, there was the young woman - *his* young woman - smiling and rapt, her face reflected in the light of the stage, eyes sparkling, mouthing the lines that filled the hall with such resonance. His hand tightened on the glass involuntarily and his stomach lurched. The young lady sat in company with her employer, the old fraud who called herself Mme. Simard, and two young men, one of whom she seemed to be on terms of some intimacy with. Neville the younger felt himself flush, and forgetting that he had determined never to give the lady another thought, entertained a sudden desire to murder the hated stranger, who in normal circumstances would have seemed a perfectly pleasant stranger.

On the other side of the theatre yet another figure, dressed elegantly in a manner that had been fashionable twenty years prior, entered his box just in time for the final, dreadful scene in the Capulet tomb. While the audience gasped and moaned and wept, the older gentleman made a long study of the occupants of all the other galleries within the sightline of his glass, wondering if after all this time away he might find somebody whom he could recognize. Only then did his eye travel to the stage and the auburn-haired woman who held the audience so rapt. His stomach gave a sick twist.

It couldn't be. No. Impossible. He had only known one wench with hair of that shade, and she… but no. She had not survived, and this was merely a trick of the light, an actor's trick. Of course it was. It was being in London again - the familiar sights, the sounds, the memories. It had his mind playing up against him. Besides, even if she had survived - which was impossible - the chit could never have had the wit or the means to have found her way back to England. And there had been revolution in France since then, with everything known turned *'into something new and strange'*. So no. Not possible.

'Are you quite well, my lord? You look very odd,' said Ramage, seated beside him.

'No, no. Merely weary. It is the shock, you know. One finds oneself inhabiting two worlds when returning home after so many years. One, the world of one's memory. The other, the world that is. So many differences, dear Bev. And so many things the same.'

Ramage grunted, and turned his attention to the stage.

'Who is the actress playing Juliet?' Denham asked casually.

'The bill proclaims her one Madame Seraphine. A sharer in the company, one is made to understand. But as I am not in the habit of attending theatrical performances, I have little more to offer. Frippery nonsense, if you ask me.'

Denham made a noncommittal noise. 'And where is this Madame… er… *Seraphine* from, one wonders?'

'Just another Frenchy emigré, I suppose,' remarked Ramage dismissively. 'Taking bread from the mouths of good British citizens. Only look at that mass of people below, sweating and weeping; wasting what little substance they have earned on sheer delusion. It's my belief Walpole did not go nearly far enough in restricting such fantasies.'

'I'd no notion, dearest Bev, that you were of such a puritanical nature,' murmured Denham, his eyes still fixed on the stage. 'I am honored that you should have agreed to accompany me to such a den of iniquity.'

Romeo And Juliet wound to its inevitable conclusion, with a song written by Pearce himself performed by the company to mourn the dead lovers as the curtain rang down. The applause, the stamping of feet, the whistling and shouting, shook the chandeliers, and curtain calls were numerous. But at last the interval before the after-piece occurred. The box holders resumed their visiting, comparisons of this person's head dress, that one's gown, the other one's latest clandestine match-up, and the political tattle of the day. Both Nevilles surfed the crush of gaily chattering theatre goers to obtain another round of refreshments. Finding his uncle in a brown study, Tristan peeled away in search of better entertainment. He carefully maneuvered himself between several women notable for their immense girth and even more immense head dresses featuring very tall wigs and enough feathers to have denuded a swan, without spilling a drop of his own drink. Having safely negotiated this particular hazard, he turned around, and collided heavily with the object of his internal disquiet.

'Oh!' exclaimed that lady, reeling back.

'Here!' exclaimed her escort. 'Have a care, sir, can you not?'

Tristan's free hand shot out and caught the lady by the elbow as she staggered. He apologized profusely, blushing like a youth, and maintained a steadying grip until she gently pulled away. 'I am so very sorry, mistress, it was, you see, the very large ladies with the plumes, and I was momentarily blinded...' He gestured helplessly at the ladies in question with a smile that invited the pair to laugh with him. The lady's lips twitched, and when her fine eyes touched his with a quick, direct glance they flashed with humor. Then, just as quickly, she blushed rosily, looked away, and would not meet his gaze again, which drove him to despair. The other gentleman - tanned from long exposure to the elements, fit, and slender - just looked wary. 'I trust I have done no damage?' Tristan added for his benefit. 'May I make all better by procuring for you a glass of champagne and a biscuit? But forgive my manners. I am Tristan Neville.' He held out his hand to the gentleman.

The stranger thawed somewhat, and startled Tristan by looking at him squarely as an equal, rather than deferring to a gentleman of rank as he ought to. 'Stephen Hathaway,' the man said, returning Tristan's handshake firmly. 'May I present my sister, Miss Angel Hathaway.'

Tristan's bemusement evaporated. 'Your sist... Ah! But are you then related to the divine Mme. Seraphine herself?'

'We have the honor of being her offspring, sir,' acknowledged Miss Hathaway, and hazarded a peep at Mr. Neville from under thick lashes as she curtsied. Her eyes were very, very green. Tristan wanted to fall into their depths and never come up for air. 'I...' he started, then cleared his throat. 'I do believe we have met before, Miss Hathaway, have we not? Do you not assist Madame Simard in her... in her shop?'

'Angel is soon to be Madame's partner, sir,' Stephen Hathaway answered for his sister with pride. Neville glanced up and read a warning in the man's face. He met Hathaway's eyes evenly.

'But - but that is wonderful,' he responded. 'I salute you, Miss Hathaway.'

Angel smiled. 'Thank-you, sir, but your felicitations are premature. My brother exaggerates the matter.'

'Not by so very much, I'll wager.' He glanced up just in time to find Sir Robert bearing down on him in one direction, and the fearsome dowager Lady Damson, belatedly arrived at the gala affair and now with daughter Amelia in tow, in the other. 'I believe I owe you a champagne and a biscuit, do I not?' he smiled winningly and made his escape.

'A very pretty bespoke gentleman,' remarked Stephen to his sister. 'You mind him, Angel. He has taken a fierce shine to you, or I am very much mistaken.'

'No such thing,' reproved Angel. 'I am not at all the sort of girl a man of the *ton* wastes his time on.'

'On the contrary, you are *just* that sort of girl. And what, pray, do you know of such things?'

'As I work in a dressmaker's shop, which counts many of the *ton* as its clients, among them Mr. Neville - who, by the by, is the son of an earl - I know a great deal more than you might think, brother.'

'If he is the son of an Earl, and a client of your employer, he is absolutely dangerous for you,' repeated Stephen with asperity. 'If he tries anything…'

'He will not. And if *you* think for one moment that you can take control of my life just because you are returned from sailing the seven seas for years beyond comprehension, you've another thing coming, Stephen. I am fully of age, I have been raised in the theatre, which can hardly be called a sheltered existence, and I'll not be bullied by you or anyone else!'

Stephen's jaw tensed, and his face colored in the beginnings of anger.

'But I have said my piece now, and we may begin to know one another again,' she laughed up at him, deftly deflecting a public argument while happily hugging his arm. 'Oh, I am *so* glad to see you again, Stephen. You have grown very handsome, you know. All the ladies envy me tonight.'

Stephen laughed back a little uneasily, and squeezed her hand. 'And I am glad to be reunited with my family,' he said. 'Though it

is all very strange and unfamiliar to me, *tu connais*. All these…
these *Anglaises.*'

'They are not so different than *les Francaises*, after all,' she said.
'But we must seem oddly parochial to you, after sailing the known
world and having adventures.'

'*En verité*, I can do with fewer adventures for awhile,' he said
firmly. 'Some of them were pretty near to be the end of me.'

'*Mon Dieu.* I am all agog, and expect to hear every word,'
vowed his sister.

'And I shall be pleased to make the hair on the back of your
neck stand up,' he twinkled back at her. 'Wait here a minute; I'm
going to get a proper drink.'

His departure gave Mr. Neville just the opening he needed to
approach the beautiful Angel, standing for the moment unguarded
by her jealous brother. Having carefully dodged both the ladies
bent on ensnaring him and the insistent presence of his cronies,
he took immediate advantage of this brief and fortuitous moment
to swoop in, bestow a glass of champagne and a comfit on Miss
Hathaway, and ask far more casually than his fluttering stomach
dictated if she was wont to walk in the park on a fine day.

'In general I do not, sir,' the lady said, more quellingly than he
would have liked. 'For as you have seen, I must work for my bread
and have little time for idling away the day.'

'I am sorry to hear it, Miss Hathaway. To idle away a fine
spring day in the company of friends is, I believe, one of life's
simplest pleasures.'

'Do not be sorry,' said Angel, meeting his gaze squarely. 'My
work is useful, and I take pride in it. But perhaps you may find this
distasteful.'

'Not at all,' he swore. 'It is certainly revolutionary, however.'

She laughed, and her laughter sounded to him like music. 'It is
mere necessity, I assure you. But even were it not,' she added
reflectively, 'I believe a woman must have some certain right to
earn her own way in the world and not depend on her existence as

a mere wife. Ah,' she frowned ironically. 'Now I have incensed you.'

'Merely provoked me to further thought,' responded Neville gallantly, though he was, in fact, rather taken aback. 'You are a most unusual woman, Miss Hathaway.'

'No such thing, sir,' she remarked drily. 'You may find a dozen of my like, anywhere you look in London.'

'You cast me down, Miss Hathaway. But I must disagree with you. For I have, I assure you, looked at many hundreds of women in London, and I have not yet met one remotely like yourself.'

Angel's gaze met his in surprise, then, finding nothing in his expression but warmth, hers turned to wonder. 'I beg your pardon, sir,' she relented. 'It is not my habit to... that is, I am more accustomed to...' she made a defensive motion with her hand.

'I pray you will not push me away, Miss Hathaway. I intend you no harm. Come. Surely you cannot work all seven days of the week?'

She blushed, and looked away. 'I... perhaps I was exaggerating just a little, sir,' she admitted. 'Monday is, in fact, my half day. I *might* sometimes be found in the park with friends on that afternoon. To give my dog exercise. And... I do love to watch the horses.' She blushed again, blinked several times, and took a deep, sustaining breath.

'But how wonderful,' said Tristan promptly, his expression immediately brightening. 'I often exercise my horses in the Park. Are you, then, a student of horseflesh?'

'Only an admirer, sir. When I was a child in France, I had a demon of a pony. I did dearly love to ride about the countryside, and often dreamed...' Her expression turned wistful for a moment, but just as quickly she laughed. 'I am sorry! What a deal of nonsense I am speaking!'

'Nothing of the sort,' smiled Tristan, with an uncommon desire to swoop Miss Hathaway away from what he thought must be a tawdry life and into something finer. 'Do you miss your home, Miss Hathaway?' he asked instead of doing anything so rash.

'*Oui, tout,*' she admitted. '*Encore* my demon pony. But,' she shrugged, banishing the memory, 'I have much to be grateful for, do I not? For now I live in London, which has many beautiful parks, after all.'

'It does. And perhaps we shall meet in one of them on a fine Monday.' Still smiling,, he took her hand. She tried to resist; her hands were red and chilblained, and the half mitts she wore to warm them could not hide that humiliating fact. But he persisted, and kissed it lightly. And in spite of herself, Angel smiled back, and allowed herself to feel a shiver of possibility.

'*A bientot*, Miss Hathaway,' he said, bowing.

'*Au revoire, m'sieur*', she bobbed a curtsey. And watched as he wove through the crush, smiling at this person, sharing a light word with that one, enjoying a flirtatious comment with yet another. The man was that handsome, his form just that trim, and his address that elegant. Light glinted off the dark gold of his hair. And the eyes... She shook herself. *Stupid girl. Do not be a stupid girl.* The slightest hint of a mild flirtation with a man like Tristan Neville would damage her reputation and enrage her *maman*. There must be no meetings in the park on Monday or any other day. She sighed in disappointment and downed the rest of her champagne. Sometimes life was entirely unfair.

The bell rang, the announcement was made to return to their seats for the after-piece, Stephen appeared to reclaim his sister's arm, and Tristan Neville made his way back to his aunt's box.

'Where the devil have you been?' demanded Sir Robert, when Lady Torrington's party had reconvened. 'Left me alone with that dreadful hag Lady Damson and her vacuous daughter, nowhere to hide until the interval ended.'

'I thought you well occupied with the fascinating dowager Lady Underwood,' said Neville archly. 'Who you seem to have taken by storm.'

'My irresistable charms,' Sir Robert admitted modestly. 'My broad knowledge of… er… horse breeding. Where on God's green earth has Badgeley got to? Anybody seen him?'

The general consensus was that nobody had, and that he had probably met with some crony and rolled off to the latest gaming hell, having forgotten all about the play and his fianceé. Which would be, his mother agreed with a great deal of annoyance, very typical of her Edward, who showed every sign of being exactly the sort of man his father was, didn't her brother Neville agree? To which Nathaniel responded that he had no notion of any such thing, and in fact, didn't much care who the whelp resembled as long as he came to his senses and began to resemble a grown man. This earned him a sharp rap across the knuckles from Lady Torrington's well-aimed fan.

It might be thought that at this point Miss Attenborough would be reconsidering her impending union with a man as unstable as Badgeley. Henrietta was, however, a lady of strong resolve, a trait learned well from her mother, the daughter of a rubbish picker who had, by dint of unceasing labor and a clever eye to the main chance, become the owner of several junkyards whose pickings yielded an enormous income. His granddaughter was thus well versed in the virtues of patience and hard work. Besides, she was fond of her childhood friend Ned, and knew his foibles. The news that he was nowhere to be found merely caused her to smile reassuringly at his irritated mother, safe in the conviction that Badgeley's life would see improving changes once they were married, and that, when the time came, she would fill the position of Milady Torrington with all the grace and aplomb the position required.

Lady Underwood returned on the arm of an elderly gentleman who handed her back into the box with patent relief. She reclaimed her spot next to Sir Robert, with whom she declared she must continue a comfortable cose. Lady Damson chattered as aimlessly as a yard full of chickens, Miss Rackham tried by all her arts to engage Tristan Neville in conversation, and

Tristan's overwrought mind kept repeating, *I have fallen in love with a shopkeeper's assistant.* It was an impossibility, inconceivable. He could not fall in love after seeing a woman three times. *The love of my life is the daughter of an actress.* He would not go into the park on Monday; he would go into the country for a week instead. This could go no farther.

As the divine Miss Murphy and the dancers made their final appearance, a message was delivered addressed to Mr. Neville. Nathaniel accepted it, read the garbled contents, cursed violently under his breath, and quietly excused himself to his sister. 'Matters of politics,' he murmured, with an admirable attitude of regret he was far from feeling.

Instead of finding a chair and setting off across town to the Embankment, however, he strode around the building, through the little alleyway that led to the stage door, and presented himself there to Mr. Hemings, who, after a moment of surprise during which Nathaniel introduced himself as the recipient of the note, indicated silently that he should follow him downstairs.

Jacob Freeman stood at the door to Pearce's office. At a nod from Hemings, he opened the door to admit Neville, who found his nephew laid out on a sofa whose contents had been rapidly swept to the floor, a large and bloodstained handkerchief clutched to his nose, and his clothing torn and stained.

'Badgeley,' demanded Neville unfeelingly, 'What the hell are you playing at?'

Badgeley turned a swollen and purpling eye to his uncle. 'I didn't want you!' he exploded through the handkerchief in tones rendered both muffled and ridiculous by the young man's general appearance. 'I wanted Tristan!'

'Yes, well, as the note was addressed only to Mr. Neville, it came to me.'

'I had to see her,' Badgeley complained petulantly. 'Does no one understand?'

'You don't got to see no one in this here company, young man,' said Hemings vehemently. 'Them was your orders, and them was my orders.'

'It's outrageous, Uncle! this *fellow* -' Ned indicated Hemings -

'Did his job, did he?' Neville filled in conversationally. 'And popped your cork while he was about it?' He turned his back on his graceless nephew and looked appreciatively at James. 'Hemings, is it? You display to advantage, sir, I saw you once at Tunbridge Wells. I always wondered why you retired from the ring. At the top of your game, were you not.'

'Thank-you, sir. That's as it was, sir,' beamed Hemings with a respectful nod. 'But I married a young wife, sir, and it an't no life for a family man, sir, and I got this here offer.' he shrugged. 'Mr. Pearce and Mrs. Hathaway, sir, they run a respectable business here, sir, and treat 'un proper. Innit so, Mr. Freeman?'

'Aye, e'en so,' agreed that gentleman.

'They are fortunate to have you.' He sized Mr. Freeman up, eyes lingering on the battered face. 'I feel somehow we have met. Now how…' he asked, puzzled.

'I misdoubt we have passed on the street', said Jacob pleasantly. 'Nothing more, sir.'

Neville eyed the flattened nose, the scars, the ravaged hands the size of hams. 'My mistake,' he said smoothly, and turned back to Hemings. 'I apologize for any disturbance my nephew has caused you. The cost of any damages should come directly to me, and I shall see them paid. Come on, you great gudgeon, on your feet. I'm taking you home.' He handed his seething and now humiliated nephew a fresh handkerchief.

'You can't take me anywhere!' Ned said thickly, trying and failing to stand. 'Not until I see Bridie!'

'I won't have you a'bothering Miss Bridie no more. Sir', said Hemings flatly.

'We have an understanding,' said Badgeley hotly. 'It is a stupid mistake!'

'Ah!' frowned Neville, comprehension dawning. 'Made certain promises, did you, and the lady read the *Gazette* this morning.'

'That's the way of it, sir,' said Hemings. 'It an't usual to say so, sir, begging your pardon, but The Mistress, she has very strong views on this kind of goin's on, if you take my meaning.'

'The man's lying, Nat! I must see...'

'A doctor, perhaps. And do *try* not to bleed all down my new coat, won't you.' With Freeman's help he pulled the disheveled young man to his feet, manhandled him out the door and up the stairs. They met no one on the way; from the backstage area a roar of applause and shouts from a happy audience flowed over the stage while the entire cast danced on to accept their thanks and take final bows. Neville gave each of the wardens a generous coin, and ferried his charge out the stage door. Hemings closed it firmly behind them, muting the interior sounds of success and joy, and blotting out the magic of the lit stage and its actors in costumes as bright as birds. In the sullen night air of the rain-slicked alley Ned struggled to stand on his own. After several failed attempts he stood swaying, one supporting hand on the sooty stone beside him.

'I would not so lower myself as to tell you what I think of you in front of men like Hemings and Freeman, Badgeley,' said Neville savagely. 'Have you completely taken leave of your senses? No, do not speak. To use your entitlement as a weapon, to allow your cock dictate whatever bird-brained action that takes your unthinking, self-indulgent fancy - I took you to be green, but to behave like a regular johnny flat... Do *not* speak, sir. You have trespassed upon private property, despite being warned against it. You have abandoned your duty to your mother as the host of a party that includes the woman who is to become your wife. And you have lowered yourself to brawling in the backstreets of a *theatre*. Good *God*, man. Even you could not sink so low, one would have thought! If I find you behaving with such stupidity as to try to force yourself where you are clearly unwelcome once more, Badgeley, I swear I'll have you horsewhipped.' He dragged the staggering young man to the street, flagged down a chair, and bundled Badgeley into it. 'I fully expect all proper apologies to be made in this matter. An I do not hear of them, you will hear from me, rest assured.' He gave the carriers Badgeley's address and a coin and watched as the conveyance made its way into the flow of evening traffic.

'Torch, sir?' a ragged child appeared from the front of the theatre hopefully, lantern at the ready.

'No', said Neville curtly, 'I'm going back in'. But he flipped the boy a ha'penny first.

A world away from this unpleasant scene, The Swan's curtain rang down for the final time and the house gradually emptied; some of its denizens to their homes, some to their clubs or locals, and some to partake of the post-show meal offered for a fee in the supper room. In due course, these were joined by some of the actors and The Swan's two sharers, who were roundly applauded again as they arrived. Seraphine barely had time to come through the door when she was accosted by the company's patroness Augusta, Lady Hensleigh, acknowledged bluestocking and one of the recognised leaders of London's cultural life. 'Mme. Seraphine!' she exclaimed, bearing down on the actress like a ship in full sail. '*Such* a triumph, my dear. Your Juliet - oh! Profound! Heartbreaking! One would almost think you were nothing but a *child*, you impossible creature. *Darling* Seraphine,' she continued in a more wheedling tone, 'it appears that I must play hostess to one of those *tiresome* political dinners that George so adores. There is a vote afoot in the Commons that he very much hopes to turn to his advantage before this session ends, and I find I desperately need a woman of address and intelligence to make the numbers even. I know this sounds *dreadfully* like damning you with faint praise, but *do* my dear say you'll come, for besides that it will give me a great deal of pleasure to see you, it will also make an otherwise potentially deadly evening quite tolerable.'

'*Merci du compliment, madame*, but you know I am not in the habit of political conversation,' smiled Seraphine.

'But that's quite the point, you see. It's meant to be an evening of *pleasure*. Sheridan will be there, and the Birnams, not that he is a pleasure by any means, for he proses on endlessly as if he alone had the key to the Tree of Knowledge, and as for his wife, a sillier woman I have yet to meet, but she is very much bullied by her husband, poor thing, and hardly dares peep without his consent, so one must forgive her. And then there will be Miss Berry of course, and, oh, some several others who are very likely to talk forever about the state of Paris, and that book the alarming Mr. Paine has recently published from there. Please do say yes. It will be *such* a help to me.'

'In that case, I must count myself honored, *Madame*,' Seraphine laughed.

At that moment Nathaniel Neville, having interrupted Badgeley's cronies in the middle of their supper to inform them of his nephew's latest indiscretion, turned toward the exit and was faced with the ladies. With an ill-tempered frown, he bowed punctiliously. 'Lady Hensleigh, how pleasant to see you. Mme. Hathaway, your artifice almost creates the illusion of real feeling.' And he passed on.

'Artifice... almost creates...' stammered Seraphine. '*Quel diable*! Does the gentleman mean to insult me?'

Lady Hensleigh patted her friend's arm comfortingly. 'I believe, my dear, that it was meant as a compliment.' She looked in the direction of his departing form speculatively. 'Mr. Neville is one whose eloquence in his element, in the Commons, could charm a nightingale. I believe he does not properly understand your *milieu*.'

'*Je le jure*, his *compliment* would curdle milk. I suffer indigestion *quand je lui regard*.'

'Pray do not judge him too harshly, my dear. He suffered greatly as a young man, you know. His pretty young wife and child died of a fever while he was away fighting in the Colonies that were. I believe he has never quite been the same.' She frowned, remembering. 'He sold out of the army and became a very different sort of man altogether. And he has never married again.'

'Surely there are enough desperate young women and well-bred widows about that would be glad to share his income.'

'Perhaps that is the problem,' pointed out Lady Hensleigh prosaically. 'Would you want to marry somebody desperate for a roof over her head, or somebody interested only in your wealth or station? After all, even in the most liberal *marriage de convenance*, one must occasionally discourse with one's espoused life partner over the breakfast ham.'

'In that case, it must suit him better to remain single,' said Seraphine bluntly. 'And as usual, you are the height of practicality, *Madame*.'

Seraphine's progress when they parted was hampered by many short conversations with well-wishers whom she had no wish to alienate in any way, even though she was growing hungrier by the moment. One pushed a glass of champagne into her hand, which she sipped to be polite. She tried to attract Mr. Pearce's attention, as he seemed as usual to have procured a platter of food with no trouble at all and therefore might be expected to bring her something. That erstwhile gentleman was deep in discussion, however, with a large lady wearing an alarming headdress of many plumes and a sequined bodice cut so low that Seraphine thought her breasts must at any moment spill from what little confinement the fabric allowed. Which, on reflection, was probably exactly what Mr. Pearce most hoped for. Shaking her head in exasperation, Seraphine turned away from her cousin and was extremely pleased to see Stephen, Angel, Molly Boggs, and the young man who must be Molly's long lost son entering the room together. Angel and Stephen were confident, and moved through the crowd as if born to power. Molly and her son hesitated just inside the door, and the son looked ready to bolt. Seraphine waved. Molly, hugely relieved, waded toward her, and introduced Jack - now Chance - River to her with palpable joy. She clung to her son with starry eyes and could not stop patting his arm as if to remind herself that he was real. Chance, for his part, gazed around him with something akin to amazement. Stephen chaffed him.

'I believe Mr. River is looking for that Bridie Murphy of yours,' he grinned to his mother. 'She has a great and immediate admirer in Mr. River.'

Chance blushed furiously and tried to deny any such thing, which only sent Stephen and Angel into gales of laughter. It was as if the young people had known each other for years, Seraphine thought, which gave her great satisfaction.

At that moment, Denham appeared in the doorway beyond Stephen's shoulder, framed by light, looking insolently through his glass at the room and its occupants.

Twenty-five years fell away as if they had never existed. That mannerism, that walk, that dissatisfied curve of the mouth, all were carven on her memory as if on a granite stone that could never be erased. Seraphine felt her heart squeeze, and her breath come in short gasps. If this had been a stage romance, she would have clutched her heart dramatically, rolled her eyes in horror, and uttered *YOU!* in faltering accents. But this was Seraphine's life and no romance. Her glass slipped from fingers suddenly grown numb and smashed on the floor, splashing champagne all over the hem of her dress. And without so much as a moan, Seraphine crumpled.

Stephen caught her before she reached the floor. 'Air,' he said tersely. 'We need to get her some fresh air. Help me, River. Mme. Simard, Angel, cover us, will you? We don't want a fuss.'

'Through that curtain,' said Angel. 'Is she...'

'She has merely fainted. This way, River.' And with great aplomb, he and Chance spirited Seraphine's sagging form through the curtain Angel indicated that hid a long hallway to the backstage area, while Angel and Molly covered their retreat and fetched the house manager to take care of the spill and the glass.

All was done so quickly that no one else was aware it had happened; only some few people looked round and noticed that

Mrs. Hathaway did not seem to be present anymore. 'Probably exhausted, poor dear,' said Pearce jovially to the big breasted woman. 'Fearful strain, that Juliet. Romeo too, for that matter. But I am built for these sorts of parts, you know. No delicacy about my constitution at all, eh?' He took the moment to hazard a surreptitious brush against the lady's bosom and was rewarded with a promising giggle and a rap with the lady's fan as she coquettishly chided him for being a *naughty* man and simultaneously leaned somewhat closer to him so that his view of her cleavage was headily unobstructed.

Seraphine awoke on a sofa set just inside the stage door, which was ajar to let the evening air flow in. 'I cannot think what came over me,' she remarked weakly. 'I believe it must have been want of food. I have been very hungry ever since the curtain came down, you know, and I could not seem to find anyone to bring me a plate.'

Stephen frowned at her. *Je ne pense pas, Maman,* he said. 'You saw something, or someone, did you not?'

'Nonsense, Stephen. 'Twas no such thing.'

'You were perfectly well, *Maman*. Then you looked up, and it was as if you had seen a ghost.'

'*Mon cher, non. Ce n'est pas possible.* Now,' she sat up carefully. 'I am quite well again, you see. Only I shan't hazard that stuffy room again. Could somebody *please* bring me a plate of food and something to drink? And please, no word of this to anybody, *hein*? T'would be far too embarrassing.'

Stephen frowned again and shared a puzzled look with River. River shrugged; his attention had been elsewhere at the time. He volunteered to go fetch a plate of food. Perhaps that Bridie Murphy would be in the supper room by now.

'Now, *Maman*,' said Stephen firmly. 'No more lies. What - or who - did you see to cause you such distress?'

'You always were a deal too observant, Stephen,' remarked his mother. 'Even when you were small, one could never…'

'And a good thing, too, or you'd have been on the floor with the broken glass,' he responded.

She took her son's hand. 'Indeed, my love, indeed, I am so very grateful that you are here. Oh, Stephen, you cannot conceive my joy. It has been a long and tiring day for all of us, has it not? But you are here now.' She could not help herself then, but wept a little, clutching her son's hand. And while he still lacked the answer he sought, Stephen was sensitive enough to know that no further information would be forthcoming tonight.

When Chance returned with not only a plate of food but also Angel and Molly, Stephen took his leave and walked back to the dining room. There, he accepted a glass of claret and retired to a corner from which to study the diners, looking for anything that might not fit. All he could see that seemed at all out of place was an old court card of a roué, dressed a generation out of date, who spoke with Pearce. For no reason he could name, the sight of the gentleman made the hair rise on the nape of his neck. The man's mouth smiled, but the hooded eyes that looked cynically upon the room seemed somehow dead. As Stephen studied him dispassionately, Denham's eyes were drawn inexorably toward him and the serpent-like gaze bored into him. Stephen met that gaze boldly and without fear. Not for nothing had he been at sea all these years. This ruined man was but one of a type found in every port in every land of the known world. So it was Denham's eyes that widened, Denham's face that paled as if he saw a ghost, Denham whose gaze slid away first, Denham who turned and left the room.

Stephen stayed at his post, watchful. Accustoming his eyes to the dress and manners of *les Anglaises*, accustoming his ears to a babble of accents in this, his second language, that said much about class, about region, about birth.

When none but the theatre company and cleaning staff remained, Seraphine and Angel joined him, and they sat down together for the first time in a decade, sometimes talking, sometimes in silence, just taking each other in; the changes, the twists of fate, the lives lived, the time gone by. There was so much to tell. Of how Stephen had come to be on an English vessel at all, much less a vessel that included Chance River. Of Seraphine and Angel's journey to England from Le Havre in the rain and dark. Of the failure all had had in locating George Hathaway, whom they feared dead. Piece by piece, they filled in the missing time, finding each other at once familiar and strange. After the giddiness of being reunited, starting to patch together a present that might include a common way forward. At length, having talked as much as they could talk, they wound their way homeward, with Jacob Freeman, and Marianne, and Angel's lurcher Brutus. Seraphine showed Stephen to the sofa in the morning room, promised better accommodation on the morrow, and wearily went to bed.

There she gave way to a bout of fearful trembling that nobody could ever be allowed to see. She drew the covers around her and looked at her room, her walls, her safe house, visualized all the people she loved that were around her. She was not that child anymore. Sara Finister had died. Seraphine Hathaway was alive. She was strong and had power and property and people who would look out for her at need. She was safe from the past.

But if the opportunity for revenge she had longed for were now offered, she would take it with both hands and exult in it. '*I would eat his heart in the marketplace*,' she said fiercely to the darkness. And she would, God help her. She would. There were those in the world whose evil was such that they deserved to be destroyed, with not another thought given.

She could not, would not, live in fear. The past could not be allowed to flood a present she had spent these many years crafting. She would not be caught flat-footed again. After tonight, she would be in control once more.

And on that note, Seraphine finally slept. Outside her window - which against the prevailing wisdom of the time she always kept open to the fresh night air - a blackbird warbled a song as liquid as moonlight while the streets grew quiet and night gave way to foggy pre-dawn.

*****

It was Marianne who awakened her much later, by putting a tray of breakfast on a small table by the window, which she closed against a raw breeze.

'Marianne!' said Seraphine sleepily. 'There was no need for this care, you must have other things to do besides wait upon me.'

'You had a shock last night, Sera. It seemed right to let you rest. I've made you a *tisane* that will fortify your circulation, if you would like to have it in bed?'

'No, indeed! I'll get up. I'd no idea it was so late. Will you join me?'

'I brought an extra cup,' grinned Marianne, pulling a second chair to the small table.

Seraphine climbed out of her warm bed and into a wrapper and a pair of slippers, then, as Marianne discreetly turned her back and poured tea, used the chamber pot, poured some water from a decanter on the nightstand into a basin, rinsed and dried her hands, then joined Marianne at the table. Picking up the mug that held the *tisane*, she smelled it gingerly, then with appreciation, and took a deep draught.

'Heavenly,' she sighed.

Marianne smiled. She had an apothocary's mind, had Marianne. She had learned the properties of plants, insects, and animals from her enslaved grandmother. She knew remedies to reduce a fever, cure a toothache, ease chest inflammation, even help to mend a bone. It was whispered that a desperate woman might go to her for a mixture that would rid a belly of an unwanted pregnancy. Or even, in the most dire of situations, create a poison from certain fungi that would create an illness that appeared as a slight indisposition, disappeared again, and returned much later to cause its subject's death in a manner untraceable to

the source`. Marianne, who valued her life and did not intend to
be hanged as an African witch, never admitted to this knowledge.
In another world, in another age, she would have made a fine
apothecary; but that world did not exist yet.

Born into slavery on Saint Domingue, Marianne had served a
mistress who, after years on the coffee plantations of father,
husband, and finally son, had brought her young servant with her
to Paris just as Saint Domingue's slave rebellions were heating up.
In Paris, her first action was to free Marianne and raise her to a
position of respect in the household. The mistress ailed from a
wasting disease that no doctor could cure. Marianne's skill made it
more bearable; and at the last, perhaps provided a quiet exit from
the pain of this world. No one would ever know.

The mistress left a small legacy 'to her dear sister' - a
relationship never acknowledged in life - that permitted Marianne
some freedom of choice in finding an occupation that appealed to
her sensibilities. She gravitated to the ready Parisian community of
the theatre, where her skill in concocting *macquillage* from plants,
and for creating medicinal packets for persistent and even
uncommon ailments, was valued highly. No one there asked for
credentials, or flinched from the color of her skin. They were
grateful for help, and respected her talents.

One day she met the young Mlle. Seraphine, a rising light on
the stage; another woman alone in a male world. They quickly
became friends, and Marianne slid easily into a position as
Seraphine's dresser and companion; a bond that continued after
the actress met and married the earnest *Anglais* George Hathaway.

It was several years afterward that Jacob Freeman entered the
story, discovered late on a rainy night collapsed at the back door
of the cottage Hathaway shared with wife, young children, and
Marianne. Jacob was nearly naked, half dead, and horribly scarred
of face and body, his skin raw with tracings of a brutal whipping,
and ropy with ridges from previous ones. Jacob had heard,
whisper to whisper to whisper, that this certain English gentleman
had been useful to people like himself. He pleaded for help, and

was taken in. Marianne came down from Paris, where Seraphine was currently playing, to tend his grievous wounds, there being no question of calling a doctor who might immediately alert the authorities to the presence of a fugitive in the Hathaway house. In the long days of the man's recovery, Hathaway saw advertisements offering a substantial reward for the apprehension of one Japhet Wiley, who had murdered his master, a Virginia gentleman visiting Paris to deal in tobacco and slaves, and disappeared. Hathaway watched Jacob closely for signs of instability or violence, drew his own conclusions, and asked no questions. And when the man who called himself Jacob Freeman was finally brought back from illness and injury, Hathaway showed him the advertisement. Jacob wept.

'I had no choice, sir. That man took everything from me, everything. Home. Wife. Family. Humanity, sir. Everything. The last time... I thought he would kill me. I thought I wanted to die. And then I realized that I did not.'

Hathaway sighed and rubbed his brow wearily. 'You can stay here for awhile, Freeman. But you must be useful. What can you offer?'

'I am a very good cook, sir.'

Hathaway looked at the enormous man and blinked. 'You... cook?'

'Indeed, sir.'

'Then I find we are in need of a... cook.'

Jacob was more than a cook, of course. The Hathaway home was a ramshackle affair, neither of the heads of the household being precisely grounded in the practical needs of daily life. Seraphine or her husband were frequently absent, she for the theatre, he on other sorts of work. Jacob saw a need, and filled it. When there were vegetables or grains to harvest, or chickens or a goat to slaughter, he knew best how to kill them (a process that young Stephen very much enjoyed) as well as how to cut, dress, preserve, and cook each part of them (which Freeman insisted young Stephen learn). When strength was needed, there was no man more powerful. Much later, when Hathaway deemed it necessary to send Seraphine and Angel out of the country for their own safety, Jacob abandoned his idea of staying in France to take on the role of escort and protector.

Marianne would not leave her friend Seraphine. And so they all came together to Le Havre, thence to Southampton, and on to London. As strangers in a new land, there was no question but that the emigrés would thrive far better as a household than they could separately. When Seraphine found a small house, they all moved in. And within a short period, the household of mutual need and shared experience became a household of kindred souls.

Jacob and Marianne were married in London; a marriage that now no one could tear either of them from. Together, they discovered the city's African community. On hearing Olaudah Equiano speak on the evils of slavery and his own rise to freedom and autonomy, Jacob began attending meetings of The Sons of Africa. As the years since that terrifying night that had found him on George Hathaway's doorstep passed, he breathed more easily. He dared to dream.

'Marianne,' Seraphine said carefully as they sipped their *tisane*, 'I am trying to remember the name of a mushroom that has a mortal capacity.'

'Oh?' asked Marianne lightly. 'And are you planning a murder?'

'No, no,' laughed Seraphine a bit unsteadily. 'I am rather... thinking about a play Mr. Pearce would have me write, and it must entail a poisoning.'

'There are a dozen that will suit. The amanita mushroom for instance, very beautiful, very deadly. The Old Ones used it to receive visions, but it is mortal in larger quantities. Then there is the innocuous little...'

'I am thinking rather of something more insidious. Untraceable.'

Marianne put her mug down and looked steadily at her friend. 'I think you are not talking about a play, *m'ami.*'

Seraphine blushed, and looked out the window. Silence grew.

'We will not speak of this again, I think,' said Marianne, after long minutes had passed. 'But if you require my help… you shall have it.'

Later, in the kitchen, she told Jacob of the incident.

'It seems so small when I speak of it here, but there is something troubles her,' she said. 'Something that happened last night. Perhaps from her past. Perhaps she is in mortal danger.'

Jacob thought for a moment and shrugged. 'There is much we never know about one another,' he said. 'What we face. What follows us. Perhaps, like me, she had to steal herself one time.'

'She was never a slave,' scoffed Marianne.

'Enslavement has many faces,' he responded.

Madame Seraphine

II.
"I do love nothing in the world so well as you -
is not that strange?"

- William Shakespeare, *Much Ado About Nothing*, 4.1

Madame Seraphine

A passable bed chamber was created for Stephen by emptying a narrow attic under the eaves of the Hathaway house of buckets, boxes, bits of furniture awaiting repair, and household supplies of varied description, which involved moving most of it either to the small shed next to the privy at the foot of the garden or to an already crowded closet beneath the stairway via a set of extremely steep and inconvenient stairs. The cleared room was barely tall enough in the center for Stephen to stand upright, but once thoroughly scrubbed it looked welcoming enough, with small windows at either end that allowed for light and ventilation, and views in one direction over many shapes and configurations of chimney pots and roofs, and in the other, a large and noisy construction project. Stephen and Jacob scavenged a serviceable bed frame and straw mattress from the jumbled workshop of a used furniture dealer several streets along, in trade for several broken upright chairs. Pillow, spare sheets, and a blanket were rustled from the house store, a rag rug with hardly any holes in it was placed by the bed, and several strategic pegs were added to serve as clothes hangers. A snug spot for Stephen's sea chest under the window carried his medical books, a brass candlestick of antique design, and some few mementos from his time in the Indies, rendered the room quite homelike by morning's end. Stephen pronounced himself *parfaitement à l'aise*, adding that it was much more private than any shipboard quarters he'd known, not to mention smelling a great deal better.

That settled, he set about investigating his new city with his friend Chance River. A long acquaintance with foreign ports made the pair more discerning and certainly more worldly than most of their contemporaries, but in London even they found a breadth of culture and diversity of dress and language that they agreed had much to commend itself.

The following morning, Stephen came down the stairs to find his sister in the kitchen before him, already putting on her cloak while Brutus stood by the door wagging his brushy tail.

'*Ah, c'est parfait!*' exclaimed Angel, wreathed in delight. 'Stephen! I must be at the shop early today, we have such a deal of work to do. Might you escort me, so that Jacob may go to Smithfield?'

'*Avec un plaisir le meilleur grand*,' bowed her brother. 'But what then must I do with *le chien gros*?'

'Oh, he will stay with me,' Angel assured him. 'He has been my great protector, you know, from the moment I rescued him from some horrible boys when he was but a poor little puppy. He has been very loyal and brave ever since, *n'est-ce pas*, Bruté?' She ruffled his head and Brutus grinned at her, yellow eyes glowing with adoration.

'*Tiens*. I suppose then that I must be glad of him,' remarked Stephen, in whose life dogs had not loomed large in recent years.

As they walked, Angel named sights and landmarks, Stephen described more of his adventures abroad, and Angel described her own struggles of leaving France behind and learning to live an entirely new life.

'It must have been very difficult, *ma soeur*. But I have so many questions. Where, for instance, does this Pearce come in? Are he and *maman*... Er...'

'Lovers?' Angel laughed. 'Do not blush, *mon frere*. I am not so innocent. *Pas de tout.*' She wrinkled her brow in thought. 'As I understand it it... and I may not understand the whole, *tu comprends*, there are things of which *maman* does does speak - *papa* had an arrangement with his very unwise cousin Pearce. *Papa* lent him money for The Swan, to rebuild after a fire that burned it. But in return, Pearce must promise that *Maman* should have a place there, if it were needful that we leave France.'

'But... how could *Papa* know that you would leave? I find this difficult to understand.'

'You were away, Stephan. You could not see all that happened, even before the Revolution. I think... that *Papa* became involved in dealings that were perhaps not quite *comme il faut*. I remember conversations that I was not allowed to overhear, and people coming and going from the house at strange hours, all sorts, and *Papa* being gone for days and then coming back without the people he had gone away with. He was dirty and exhausted, oh, often. It was a frightening time. But somehow... when it came time to leave... we had money. And our cousin Pearce to come to.'

'Then why did they send me away? I wanted to study medicine at Montpélier. If I had stayed, perhaps I would still have a home, and a profession. Perhaps I could have helped him. And had a part in the Revolution.'

'Yes, and perhaps you would be dead. *Stephen*,' said Angel in exasperation. '*Papa* loved you as his own son. But he had a whole family to look after, not just you. *Je pense, moi*, that sending you away on a ship has been a very good thing for you, for I look at you and you are handsome and strong, and know so much of the world. And me, maybe I would rather have stayed home, and married a prosperous man, and lived in a beautiful *chateau* with fields and orchards and animals. But I am in London, with *Maman*. I am a *modiste*, and earn my own bread. This is no bad thing, you know, to be able to make one's way in the world. *Papa* of all people knew that. I cannot be other than grateful, that he did what was necessary to bring us here.'

'No,' Stephen admitted. 'You are right, of course. Who can know the future, after all. So you left France, and you were not paupers. How is it that you were not robbed, or worse?'

Angel giggled at the memory. '*Maman* and Marianne and I took all of the money had been hidden away *comme une écureuil* and sewed it into the hems of our clothes. They were so heavy that we could barely walk. *Maman* is very clever with business, you know. When we arrived in London we found our cousin Pearce to be not a very sensible man. Too many women. Too much drink. And gambling, which he thinks we know nothing of. The Swan was nearly bankrupt. But *Maman* had both money and skill to make the theatre successful again. Only she would not agree to giving my cousin a *sous* unless she was made a half owner, in *Papa*'s name. On paper, even! And so, we prosper.'

'But,' he frowned, 'how is this possible?'

'*En verité*, I am not certain at all how she made this happen. I think it is because here in England, she may own property, if she becomes a widow — *le bon Dieu empeche* - the property that had been her husband's, can then be hers. I do not know precisely how she managed this. I know only that our *maman* is *very* persuasive when she wants something.'

'And if *Papa* returns?'

'Then,' she said with confidence, *'ce n'est pas plus un probleme. Papa* will take care of us.'

'On espere,' said her brother doubtfully.

Arriving *Chez Simard*, Angel let herself in, Stephen agreed return to escort her home at the end of the day, and thus armed, he set off. Past the market stalls and carts set up for a day's business selling everything from fresh meats, early vegetables, the morning's haul of oysters, cockles, and mussels, to refurbished clothing, 'barely a stain on it sir, worn by a gentleman of note, it was', to 'a song for your lady love sir, written for you right here', past shop windows filled with every sort of temptation an aspiring tulip or budding lady of fashion might require, past bakeshops and coffee houses whose tantalizing aromas made his stomach growl, into parks with wide vistas, grazing sheep, placid water, and blossom-filled trees and gardens, past the Palace with wide estates visible behind closed gates and guards, around the Royal Mews with horses, carriages, grooms, and soldiers riding out in working attire for exercise, and down to the familiar smells of the river with its gulls crying and dock workers shouting, rigging slapping musically against masts, water lapping against hulls, and the ripe smells of rotting seaweed and raw offal; always those smells.

The tide was on its way out. Mudlarks clambered down ancient algae-slick stone steps to newly opened shoreline and began their daily trolling with rake, shovel, and bucket to see what Thames might have brought them that day. All of this a part of the great City his father had described to him when he was small: its riches, its poverty, its mix of culture and language, its taverns, its great houses, the apparent ability of a man to make his way in the world by dint of hard work, clever dealing, and a hefty load of luck. Or conversely, to lose everything and end in a pauper's grave.

And yet, he himself stayed in France, Stephen reflected, and though he made sure his wife and children spoke flawlessly the language of his heritage, made no push to bring his young family to a London home. Instead he had become wrapped in the heady rhetoric of Republicanism, and taught the principles of the great philosophers to local children. It had been, Hathaway thought, a quixotic venture at best, to try to impress high ideals on a population whose main concern in rebellion was to bring the price of bread down.

Stephen had not much use for philosophy. It was medicine that fascinated him, and the extraordinary discoveries made daily, it seemed, by scientists of the mysteries of the human body. But there was no avenue for the son of an actress, stepson of a tutor, to study this art. Unhappily apprenticed to a butcher, he had incurred many punishments for spending more time examining the way the wings of geese were configured, or the manner in which pigs' joints and muscles were designed to allow mobility, than serving *Madame*'s desire for a Sunday joint. It became very evident that the butcher's life would not do for young Stephen, so his stepfather found him a berth on a trading vessel bound for the Indies as a surgeon's mate, in the theory that such a calling would either kill him or turn him into the physician he longed to be. And he had learned much - of medicine, of course, but more of the world. He had learned discipline, survived storm and battle, been captured and treated as a slave, escaped and made his way in an alien culture and climate, found friendship, lost love, and learned compassion. He had picked up different languages and the odd exotic disease. For all that experience, he supposed he could be grateful.

When he eventually received a battered, filthy, and almost unreadable letter from his father detailing his mother's and sister's flight to London, his intention to follow when he could, and the address of his cousin Pearce at The Swan, the news was nearly two years old. He was relieved beyond words that his mother and sister still lived, and had found security here. But for himself... an

English name and command of the language did not make him an Englishman. He was French, by every measure that mattered. Yet with no recognizable France to return to, and nothing that could be called home, he was as rudderless as the hordes of other emigrés now filling the cities of Europe from France, from the Americas, from the Indies. Except, of course, that he had a family. Virtual strangers they might be, in an unfamiliar setting and with new lives. Family nonetheless.

He stopped in coffee house for a bowl of coffee and a meat pie, and eavesdropped as he ate and drank. Here, near the markets, he heard business being transacted and gossip disseminated in thee or four different languages and innumerable regional accents that might as well have been another language. Here, there was discussion over a cargo of wool and the price of its safe carriage to mills in Antwerp. There, an argument raged about yet another bill coming up in Parliament that would end the slave trade, which a group of merchants loudly descried as an end their to livelihoods, and a group led by an educated-sounding ship's surgeon equally hotly condemned as an immoral trade in human life. In yet another quarter, a table of men that included at least one Frenchman discussed the radical notions set forth in Paine's new treatise *The Rights Of Man*, but could not agree on whether it had more merit than the moderate views of Mr. Burke. And everywhere, of course, there was gossip - who was in power, who was about to be out, who had created a scandal by flaunting an *affaire* with an aristocratic lady under the nose of her husband, who was suddenly called abroad after a clandestine meeting with swords; all of the currency that turned the wheels of society everywhere.

When he left the coffee house restored in mind and body, he realized that he'd been so intent on his thoughts while walking that he'd ended up on a very crowded street utterly unfamiliar to him. After several failed attempts, he found one who was familiar with the neighborhood he sought; and with two more pauses to recalibrate, finally found his way back to the narrow street in which lay his mother's home.

It was a modern structure, one of many new terraced buildings that would when finished look out on a pleasant little square that was currently muddy and bushy, torn apart by an army of gardeners that were turning it into a civilized version of something natural and wild-looking, with paths that crossed it from all sides and what might turn out to be a tiny water feature in the center. One large old remaining tree in what had only recently been a small meadow would give welcome shade in the height of summer, and the whole green square would dampen the sound of traffic on the main thoroughfares. But for now, the neighborhood was deafening with construction.

Mrs. Hathaway and her household had been among the first to move in. Though narrow, the house gave the appearance of spaciousness with high ceilings and a great deal of light. From the first floor parlor it looked upon the park-to-be from a pleasant bow window, and the kitchen at the rear of the ground floor opened to a tiny garden that held the privy, a small shed, a tidy kitchen garden of herbs and, in season, vegetables, as well as Jacob's pride, a hopeful young apple sapling espaliered against a warmth-giving wall.

When he let himself in through a kitchen redolent with smells of baking, Jacob grinned and said he was on the point of producing coffee and fresh biscuits. His offer of help having been turned down, Stephen found Seraphine upstairs at her desk, sifting through bills in windowed light, parrot on her shoulder. With a brilliant smile she put her quill down and held her hand out. 'Stephen! You are just in time to rescue me!' she greeted him.

'Will it bite?' Stephen looked doubtfully at the bird as he took her hand.

'Only if you poke at it, isn't that right, handsome boy?'

'Handsome boy,' agreed the parrot.

Seraphine laughed, delivered the bird to the top of its cage by the window, and invited her son to join her on the sofa. Marianne and Jacob arrived with coffee and biscuits, and all helped themselves with the ease of long friendship to talk over the news of the day. To Stephen's joy, the conversation was all in French, whose cadences and music fell on his ear like rain on parched earth.

When Marianne and Jacob left, his mother turned to him brightly. 'You really are in the way of rescuing me,' she said with a twinkle. 'Now that you've had a chance to acquaint yourself to your new surroundings, and we've all gotten to be comfortable with each other again, I'd like to enlist your help in a matter of business. It concerns The Swan, and money.'

*****

During his first week on shore, curled nightly on the old sofa in the tiny flat over his mother's shop with his heavy cloak as a blanket, Chance River missed the roll and salt smell of water as it slapped against a ship's walls, the creak of wooden timbers, the calling of the hours, the bells. He did not miss being confined with men whose unwashed bodies stank, who farted and snored and mumbled through the sleeping hours between watches. So he would have been perfectly comfortable where he was had his sleep not been interrupted by the troubling sound of his mother in the next room, coughing, coughing, coughing, drawing ragged breaths in between. On his first night he arose to ask if there was something the matter, and if he could help. She insisted that it was just a little infection she had caught and that she would be right and tight presently. But Chance was no fool. As he lay awake thinking and listening, he drew the obvious conclusion that his mother was suffering from consumption. This sent a shiver of misery through him that was surprising in its intensity. He had not thought himself capable of feeling so powerfully for the woman who had cast him away, as he thought, so easily. Time in her presence brought home to him the anguish she'd suffered on letting her only child go to what she thought must be a better life.

Any notion he had entertained while bitterly in his cups of his mother happily married or in the keeping of some other man, with a whole litter of snotty-nosed children at her beck and call, had evaporated on his first glance at her shop, her solitary living conditions, how careworn and frail she appeared to him from this distance of years. When he had chaffed her, telling her how he had imagined her living circumstances while he was away at sea, she was startled, and then laughed.

'Another man, Jack! More children! How should I desire that, when I waited so long for your father? When I hoped so much for you? No, Jack. What need I for another man - under me feet, as like as not, and drinking up all me profits. No need, nor no time!'

When she questioned him on his intentions and he spoke of looking for another vessel that needed a skilled carpenter, she barely managed to withhold her tears.

'Ah, you'll not leave me again, Jack? Say you'll not? Ah, 't'would kill me to lose you again, my dearest love, so it would. Or if you must go, let it not be soon. I'll find you a bed of your own, dearest, and we'll shut off the end of the room for you, see. We'll be so snug, you and I.'

He couldn't help but laugh. 'I'd eat you out of house and home, ma,' he said. 'You'll be wishing me in the Antipodes before a month is out.'

'No, no truly!' she'd exclaimed. 'What, turn out me own Jack, ever again? No, I would not. There's plenty for both, I've some set by. You'll see.'

'No need, Ma.' He took her rough hands and kissed them. 'No need. I've saved some blunt, there being nohow to spend it at sea, and I've the skills to set this place up shipshape. I'll be useful, see. It won't be me drinking away all your takings.'

'You'd never,' she swore seriously. And then, a malicious grin lighting her elfin face, added, 'I'd beat you out the door with me stoutest broom an you did, so I would!'

So, he had a berth, and a mother. But if he stayed, what the hell would he do? All he knew was the sea, and ships. Even when he thought about being on shore, the words that came were a seaman's words: *out of me depth*. Or: *all at sea*. Prowling London - a city he barely remembered - with his mate Hathaway did more to enhance his sense of unease than to dispel it. London was large, and indigestible. The farther he walked from Thames, the more lost he felt.

So, on this fine spring morning he rose with a plan beginning to form. He dressed, tidied his gear away into a corner, and was out the door almost before the first chants of the ragman and the flower girl were heard, passing Elsie and Maria as they busied themselves about with opening shutters, sweeping both shop and street front, fetching coal for the scuttle, and kindling a fire in the big old fashioned fireplace that heated kitchen, shop, and flat. They greeted Chance pertly and seemed more than ready to flirt, but Chance escaped with a stammer and a blush into the early morning air.

He made his way to the waterfront, senses awake to the smells and sounds and sights of the city he'd been born in. The inflections of different neighborhoods, the slang of different regions, the accents from afar - French, Dutch, southern European, Colonial, African. A city that harbored all comers, for good or ill, depending on each person's ability to scratch together the kind of work that might make a life. At a bakeshop he bought a small loaf of fragrant bread. At an ale shop he quaffed a pint to swill it down. He found his way to the great pile that was Somerset House, and to Thames beyond, freshened by all the rain and not so fever-ripe as it would be later in the season.

All his life it had been river and sea. Sea and river. On different continents, in different seasons, harbor and river mouth, journeys on and by water. A life determined by water, and all that lived on it. Could he live away from it? Could he sleep comfy, far from the slap and roll of water on wood? The smells of salt and timber, canvas and tar? The sound of gull and tern and albatross?

Filled comfortably with good bread and passable ale, he knew that he could certainly eat better here on land. And there were only so many storms, so many battles both sought and narrowly escaped, that a body could survive before the sea claimed him forever.

Chance - whose name had come because of his prosaic ability to measure them, take them, and use them to his advantage - began by daylight to think he might like to settle somewhere, truth be known. Thought he might like to walk out with a plump and pretty girl (here he warmed, thinking of the rosy charms of Bridie Murphy). Thought he might even like to have his own shop, and raise children that wouldn't have to fight for every crumb but could figure and write and earn their way and hold their heads high.

As Chance did, he realized. As he had fulfilled his mother's dearest wishes, albeit it not in the way she'd imagined. He was a man with skills, after all, learned year by year in shops and shipyards and aboard the big ships themselves on dunnamany voyages. He knew how to put a vessel together, and how to make her yare. He'd long admired the fleet clippers beginning to make their appearance on the tea runs to China and India, even crossing the wild weather of The Horn to reach the other side of the world. There were ships like that being built in The Pool, he knew, and, as the number of ships entering the Port of London increased, a huge industry in repairs.

As he thought and walked, Chance drifted into the dockyards, and the building yards. He struck up the odd conversation, he was given the odd tour by a prideful master carpenter, he asked the right questions, he raised interest from some of the men he spoke to, and that elicited further conversation and the sharing of a certain number of experiences.

By noontime Chance River had a good job, with good wages, that would allow him to stay right in London and still be next to the water that was his lifeblood.

And in the evenings, rather than haunting taverns, he found himself loitering in The Swan Theatre's backstage area in the hope of catching glimpses of the divine Bridie Murphy, until James

Hemings grew tired of falling over his burly form and set him to work pulling the curtain and moving scenery. The opportunity to be a part of the magic of the stage pleased Chance no end. And he had a ringside seat for every one of Bridie's performances.

Still, there remained a niggling shadow in the back of River's mind, and so one early morning found him in Bishopsgate Ward, entering a prosperous-looking yard stacked with timbers and boards, swept clean of sawdust that lay in a neat pile, smelling sweetly of sawn lumber. A woman somewhat older than himself opened the facing door as soon as he knocked and frowned. 'We're not hiring, just now,' she said shortly, and made to close the door. Chance put his hand against it.

'Is the master about?' he asked.

'I told you...'

'I got business with the master.' He took a small pouch from his pocket with his free hand and gave it a shake.

The woman's gazer turned sharp. 'The master an't well', she said, eyes straying to the purse.

'Do you be his daughter, then?'

'In a manner of speaking. His son's wife. We be running the business, now.'

'Old Mr. Alden was always an honest man. Be you the like?' He gazed searchingly into her eyes. She didn't blink.

'I am that,' she said with a short nod.

'Then,' he extracted two gold guineas from his purse and held them out to her, 'you give him this for me, and tell him Jack River, son to one Molly Boggs, owes him. And Jack River, he always pays his debts.'

*****

Edward Badgeley woke up long after the rare springtime sun had transformed the sodden mess of many weeks into a wonderland of blossom. Fruit trees bloomed in clouds of pink and white in parks, squares, and tiny gardens, fragrant bluebells in wooded lanes, constellations of violets in every patch of earth and new grass, and old, gnarled trees unfurled tiny new leaves of tenderest green to prove the sweet power and heady smell of new beginnings. The world warmed, birds sang, and suddenly it was that kind of spring that poets sing about.

Its beauties were lost on Ned. His mind recycled horrifying images from his actions of the previous week. His response - to drink himself blind for the ensuing days and nights, refuse all but the lowest company, and nurse a deeply self-indulgent sense of injustice - had erased neither the images, nor the actions. A powerful facer from the redoubtable Hemings, followed by a body blow that not only leveled but completely humiliated him, might, within the confines of Jackson's Salon, have resulted in bruises worn as badges of honor. To have been made a complete fool in such short order in a rain-soaked alley at the stage door of The Swan theatre in plain view of performers and technicians, was mere street brawling. Worse still, it had brought down the wrath of his terrifying uncle, before whom his weak protestations of undying love for an Irish opera dancer now looked both risible and squalid. And he had a really heroic hangover.

Pulling the covers over his aching head with a moan, swearing yet again that females were to a woman faithless and troublesome baggage, Ned resolved to henceforward adopt an attitude of cynical abstinence that he supposed must be held by Nathaniel Neville himself. This new and romantic thought of himself as a weary man about town, sneering at the shallownesses of the world, allowed him to reach the conclusion that the entire *affaire* had been the fault of Bridie Murphy and her scheming harridan of an employer, Madame Seraphine. Clearly, they had conspired against him from the start. Well. They would know better in future than to meddle in the affairs of Edward Badgeley. He would see to *that*.

Thus cheered, he thought he might just be able to face breakfast.

Then he remembered that his appealing new role of world-weary acetic wouldn't fadge, since he was engaged to be married to Henrietta Attenborough, whom he had essentially abandoned in his mother's box at The Swan without so much as a word, and ignored completely ever since.

He was not so lost to all sensibility that he didn't realize the inexcusable nature of this solecism. Nor was he ignorant of the horrible financial straits he would be in if his intended cried off and thereby deprived him of the inheritance he so badly needed.

A handsome apology and a drive in the park were immediately required. And he would take her flowers. That would be safe. Ladies always love flowers. Don't they? He would have Bellamy see to it.

Armed with new determination, he arose and allowed Bellamy to begin the long and arduous process of dressing him so that he could be face forward to the Polite World. These ministrations began with the absolute need of a bath. He smelled appalling after his week's bender; even Bellamy, who was paid to look after his needs unquestioningly, could barely hide his distaste. When his master had been made tolerable once more, Bellamy wielded his skill in the artful use of the haresfoot to disguise the enormous bruise blooming across the better part of the left side of Badgeley's face and one eye. That this was achieved with only minor moaning from Ned and the lightest of tutting sounds from the sainted Bellamy proved to the young man that he was, in fact, behaving very bravely. As soon as he was in shirt and breeches he dashed off a note to Miss Attenborough that bore what he thought was an eloquent *mea culpa* and the suggestion that she be ready to accompany him to take the fine air sitting beside him in his phaeton in two hours' time. It never occured to him that Miss Attenborough might have other plans for the day. What else had she to do but wait on him, after all? And he was offering a rare treat. It wasn't every day that he invited a Female to ride with him in the equipage that was his pride and joy.

This and a hearty breakfast made Ned feel halfway to sainthood, so that by the time he had gone out from his house, mounted the step of his phaeton, and collected the reins of a lovely pair of matched grays from his head groom Jason, he felt very much the London man of fashion and birth once more.

*****

Tristan Neville departed Town with relief, mounted on his favorite hack. Leaving it to his man Hubbard to follow along as best he could having packed such things as might be considered necessary to a young gallant intent on spending a week in the country, he pointed himself in the direction of the family seat, struck off across country as soon as possible, and within a few easy hours of riding found his spirits raised by the sights, smells, and agricultural industry of spring, untroubled by anything more than a few passing showers and a fairly minor detour necessitated by one essential bridge being out due to the season's earlier floods. His mood lifted even further when he arrived at Ashcroft Manor and found that his mama, brother, sister-in-law, and all their children were at present away to visit cousins in the next county, and were not expected to return for a sennight. Tristan therefore enjoyed several extremely pleasant solitary days rambling about the green countryside paying visits to old friends, fishing in his brother's well stocked streams, and partaking freely of his brother's excellent cellars in the evenings in front of a cheerful fire in the the small parlor he'd always favored, after having eaten an excellent meal created in his brother's kitchen. Christopher might have inherited the estate and the title that went with it. It was still Tristan's childhood home. As such, Tristan felt neither a hint of envy regarding his elder brother's entitlement, nor a moment of restraint in partaking of his generosity.

When news got out that he was in the area, invitations arrived, and he even enjoyed a light flirtation with the younger sister of a childhood friend that extended as far as a picnic that was rained out halfway through and an evening that included supper and a lively hand of whist for penny points. The sister, Arabella Montjoy by name, had sparkling eyes, a mischievous smile, was a dashing rider, and was fetchingly apt to defer prettily to all of his opinions. When Tristan wondered why their paths had not crossed in London, she explained that a fever had caused her to miss what should have been her first Season, but she showed no particular tendency to repine the loss. Tristan began to feel settled again, his world tilting back into a comfortable orbit of known events and predictable rhythms that erased his mental turbulence. He began thinking that a woman like Miss Arabella Montjoy might suit him very well. He resolutely stuffed down images of a darker, more complicated woman by replacing Angel Hathaway's elfin face with Arabella Montjoy's fair one whenever the dressmaker inserted herself into his thoughts. He persuaded himself that Angel was coarser, not nearly as accomplished, and infinitely more unbecomingly forthright than Miss Arabella Montjoy. And after all, Angel Hathaway was a poor dab of a thing. Arabella was a true English Rose. Really, he couldn't think what he'd been about.

He returned to London in a state of smug complacency, and the following morning arose betimes to accompany Sir Robert Kilronen to Tattersall's to inspect a consignment of hacks, hunters, and carriage horses from the estate of a Young Gentleman Of Quality (according to the carefully worded announcement) who was being forced to sell to settle his debts. In a circle as small as that inhabited by Neville and Kilronen, it would have been strange if the gentleman in question had been unknown to them, and on arrival at the sale, immediately recognizing the cattle and equipages on offer, they realized that this was, in fact, the case.

'Devilish loose screw,' commented Kilronen, shaking his head. 'Can't tell you the number of times he had to be carried out of some hell or another without a feather to fly with. Fell into dreadful company. I had to cut him loose, you know. I believe most did, toward the end.'

'Where's he gone to now?' asked young Neville, as they strolled up and down, studying the make, shape, and usefulness of horses, tack, and carriages.

'Italy, one hears. Staying with a distant relative near Florence or some such place.' He shook his head. 'Bad blood there, dear boy,' Kilronan said.

'As long as the bad blood don't extend to his horses,' remarked Neville prosaically. 'I shouldn't like to waste the day looking at filled tendons and broken wind. I say, I do like the make of that curricle. Look at those springs.'

'Can you afford it?'

'No,' admitted Tristan regretfully. 'It's not just the buying, it's the keeping.'

'Ay, there's the rub,' agreed his friend.

They pushed their way with difficulty to the edge of a sawdust ring, packed six deep and shoulder to shoulder with every part of humanity from titled members of the first degree to burly hostlers from area posting inns to colliers, cabbies, vanners, and ragmen, and even the odd doctor or hunting parson up for the day to find a sound covert hack at a cut rate price. It appeared that a great deal of amusement was to be had in the bidding. The horses paraded, offers were shouted, jeers and catcalls uttered, and cheers to two competitors who drove the price of a neat pair of bay cobs to an unseemly level just because the two bidders hated one another. The hammer fell, the horses moved out, a new lot brought in. By the end of the session Tristan found himself the owner of a tidy brown mare with a star and one white sock that he didn't need but felt might make a very nice lady's hack (Arabella Montjoy's likeness was forcibly superimposed on quite a different mental image), then a young Irish-bred chestnut that he bought just because he liked the look of it and the price was right. Kilronan was pleased to discover a solid bay gelding with the kind of bottom he liked for a hunter in certain heavy-going countries. In the end, satisfied with their purchases and the entertainment value of the morning, they agreed to retire to their habitations and reconvene later on to give their new horses a test ride in the Park.

This was not, perhaps, the wisest decision either gentleman had ever made. Having been but lately brought up from the country, neither the chestnut nor the bay were accustomed to the crowds, smells, or noise of the city, so their progress was less one of elegant procession than it was an adventure of spooking, snorting, prancing, and - in the case of Neville's young chestnut - the odd plunge. Sam Bolton, Neville's childhood friend-*cum*-headgroom, rode soberly beside them on the much more experienced brown mare, and opined with a weary shake of his head that he'd warned the young sirs of this activity on green 'uns, and that an early morning before the streets got busy might have been the better choice for a first go-about. But as the young gentlemen in question were both skilled horsemen, they eventually arrived safe and laughing to the relatively quiet confines of the Park.

'You see, Sam,' rallied Neville cheerfully. 'All right and tight, and no bones broken!'

"T'wasn't *your* bones as worried me,' opined Sam. "T'was alla them people in the way of youse, which I thought for certain you was in the order of running over.'

But of course his words went unheeded.

A brisk trot and energetic canter took care of much of the horses' excess energy, and put Neville and Kilronen in a self-congratulatory mood over money well spent. The way back along the track at a more relaxed walk allowed them ample opportunity to socialize with friends and acquaintances who were using the best the day had to offer. The spring air was rich with the scent of a hundred kinds of shrub and flower that grew in banks beside *alleés* and bridle paths, beyond which stood ancient oaks and ash trees with new leaves framed sheep grazing the park's green meadows with their new lambs. The men inevitably encountered Badgeley, looking *point-device* in his phaeton drawn by its greys, Miss Henrietta Attenborough - who had quietly canceled all of her other plans for the morning - seated beside him, gaily attired in a walking dress of deepest rose with a matching cap that had an ostrich plume jauntily curling from its brim. Behind them sat Miss Attenborough's maid, trying to look properly stern, but clearly having the time of her life.

Ned drew his equipage to the side of the path under the branches of a newly green-clad chestnut tree. Tristan and Sir Robert set about chaffing their friend on his execrable taste in horse flesh and received like treatment in kind, then they outdid one another in flattering Miss Attenborough, suggesting that she was far too fine a diamond to be wasting herself on such a lost cause as Badgeley, whose bruises were still visible under Bellamy's carefully applied *maquillage*. Henrietta was in general honest, practical, and unaffected by self-delusion, but she blushed prettily under the onslaught, and looked quite remarkably lovely. She responded handsomely that although they were terrible liars they were such pretty liars that she was sure her head would be completely turned by their words and instructed Ned to take her away from such sweet turn-ups immediately, lest she be overborne. They departed on the best of terms, and Ned began to think himself quite a fortunate devil to be seen in the park with as elegant a lady as his intended, forgetting for the moment that he was nursing a broken heart and a deep sense of the injustice of the world in general and certain dollybirds in particular.

It was a good thing his attention was elsewhere, or he would have seen Bridie Murphy herself, in an oddly configured group of strollers that included *Mesdames* Simard and Seraphine, Stephen and Angel Hathaway, Chance River, and the hound Brutus. Molly Boggs would not ordinarily have been out strolling on such a day, rather preferring to use precious time in taking care of her little flat and tidying her shop accounts. But Chance had persuaded her that a walk was just the thing to clear her lungs-like, and that she would benefit from breathing the sweet air of blossom and green leaves. 'I been to the tropics where there's flowers as big as your head, Ma', he said. 'And I've smelled oranges and lemon trees as would make you swear you was in Heaven. But to my way of thinking, there an't anything so sweet smelling as a homely patch of bluebells on a London path.' And by the time Stephen had appeared at the shop to collect Angel for her half day, his cause had been won.

For her part, Bridie Murphy preferred the company of the other girls in the chorus, a noisy and flirtatious group whose taste in friends was louder, ruder, and entirely more jolly than this lot, and whose idea of entertainment leaned more toward a cockfight, a hanging, or a dumb show than a placid walk. Seraphine had all but dragged her to the park, insisting Bridie avoid her usual haunts while she was mending her heart. In reality, she desired to keep a close eye on the chit in case she should decide to do something idiotic that would prevent her from performing. Like drowning her sorrows in blue ruin, for instance, or deciding to accost Mr. Badgeley at his home, neither of which was beyond the impulsive dancer's scope.

Meeting with other young people did improve Bridie's ill humor. She was a bit in awe of Angel, with her cheerful demeanor and quiet authority. She was also in awe of Angel's skill with a needle, which had transformed many a tatty old costume into something fine and magical with just the addition of some ribbon, a neatly placed piece of lace petticoat, or a reshaped bodice. The interesting presence of both Stephen Hathaway and his friend Chance River raised the level of entertainment exponentially. Two such attractive young men - one darkly beautiful with ringleted hair the color of a blackbird, the other ruddy complected with hair of glossy chestnut - were balm to a broken heart. Although Chance River was becoming a common sight backstage at the Swan, she had largely ignored him. Properly introduced, he became so tongue-tied that she almost thought him simple, until a look into his deep brown eyes made her realize with a jolt of pleasure that he was deeply smitten. Unable to restrain herself, Bridie found herself flirting outrageously with both men, chatting more easily with Angel than she would have expected, and sharing in a good deal of easy banter and ready laughter that lifted her spirits and made her feel that the world had much to offer after all.

Until they came to the end of the path that intersected with the Serpentine. Until she saw Ned Badgeley in his exquisite phaeton chatting with his friends on their fine horses, and - the worst insult of all - Miss Henrietta Attenborough, the nasty trollop who had stolen her Edward from her, sitting beside him looking every inch the ravishing lady, with a hand gloved in palest lavender kid resting easily on Ned's shoulder. Bridie's wounded breast swelled with rage and then, as the phaeton began to move off and Ned not even glancing in her direction, with crashing despair.

It was Chance River who caught her before she fainted, steered her to a bench and sat her on it. Chance River, who smelled so sweetly of sawdust and the sea, and whose arm was comforting and strong. But she wanted Ned Badgeley. She loved Ned Badgeley. She wailed, showing signs of going into deep hysteria while Chance chafed her hands and Seraphine raised her own skyward in exasperation, muttering about this stupid, silly, naive imbecile of a child, which Bridie Murphy didn't understand a word of since it was all in French. Then, just as a fit of vapors seemed inevitable, Molly Boggs produced a vial of smelling salts from her deep pockets & held them under Bridie's nostrils, which had the immediate effect of bringing Bridie back to her senses violently as she choked and pushed the salts away with revulsion.

'There,' said Molly with satisfaction. 'Now pull yourself together, girl, and stop making a scene.'

Bridie leapt to her feet theatrically. 'I was not making... I was overcome... to see that... that... oh, *no one* understands!' She made to flounce off, but Molly stood in her path, eyes blazing, and slapped her smartly. Bridie gasped, stopped, and put a hand to her stinging cheek.

'You ungrateful little baggage!' said Molly roundly. 'Look at you. Got your fingers burnt, din't you, messing about with what you *knew* was bound to end badly? At least you an't with child and no way to support it. Count your blessings, girl, and don't you go blabbin' your silly little piehole off like as if Madame Seraphine and me - two mothers, raised our kids by ourselves, we did, mind - *don't understand*.'

And then Molly fell to coughing and had to sit down and recover herself and all attention - especially that of her son - swiveled from the self-deluded Bridie to the tough little dressmaker.

Molly waved away all the attention. 'It an't no use pretendin' I got the breath I used ta,' she gasped. 'The silly chit made me that angry, so she did.'

'I am sorry, Madame Simard,' said Bridie, in a small voice. Then lifted her chin. 'And I am *not* a baggage.'

Molly clamped her mouth tight, nodded briefly, rose, and said, 'Right. I need a pint and a bite after all this brouhaha, and that's a fact. C'mon.' And they all meekly followed her lead as she stomped off on a diagonal across the park.

Chance found himself next to Bridie again. 'I hope you won't take against me ma,' he said. 'She'm a right un, but she'm notional.' He shook his head and grinned ruefully.

'Oh, I don't,' said Bridie quickly. 'She reminds me of me own ma, in Dunlo.' She laughed shakily, and they walked in silence for awhile. 'And,' she continued with a long, shuddering breath, 'she's right. As me own ma was right, and warned me how t'would be. I been stupid, and that's a fact. All this time I been play acting up on that stage, and people giving me flowers and clapping for me and setting me up, it got to me head, see. Got me thinking I was something I an't.'

'You're worth twice than what that gentry-cove is,' Chance said vehemently. 'And you deserve everything… everything that's good. You need… you just need… to have… to be… Practical.' he stumbled into blushing silence.

Bridie grinned at him and patted his arm playfully. 'Like your ma?' she teased.

Chance mumbled something incomprehensible.

'I do got to be practical,' she admitted. 'Only, I would like to learn how to dress like that lady. Like a beautiful flower.'

Meanwhile, Stephen fell in beside Angel. 'I feel there's a story behind that little contretemps. I gather the gentleman in the phaeton...'

'That was Mr. Edward Badgeley, and his affianced wife beside him,' said Angel with a laugh. 'Stupid girl, Bridie let Mr. Badgeley persuade her that he loved her. Which of course, is anything but the truth. *Eh bien, elle n'est pas rien que son putain.*'

Stephen was silent for so long that Angel felt compelled to elaborate. 'If you are thinking that The Swan is nothing better than a bawdy house, Stephen, you are very wrong. *Maman* is very straitlaced, *elle-meme. And* strict with her opera dancers. The temptations are great, however, in such a business.'

'And *Maman* does not...'

'Take lovers? No, Stephen she *does not*,' she said firmly. 'She has tried only to get news of *Papa*. You have lived your own hell, Stephen. So have we lived ours. *Maman* and I, we have achieved a small happiness. A small success. We mourn *Papa* oh, every day. It is hard, this not knowing. But we choose life, *tu comprends*. With both hands we choose life, because we must.'

Stephen shook his head. 'It is a deal to absorb, *ma soeur.*'

Their talk was so deep that Stephen and Angel had stopped paying attention either to their surroundings or to Brutus, and Angel's grip on his lead was lax. When a taunting rodent bounced away from the lurcher all but inviting him to give chase, Brutus finally lost all sense of propriety and with a mighty roar, leapt forward violently, and tore his lead out of Angel's hand. Squirrel and dog, dog gaining ground with every leap, shot down the path and crossed the Serpentine with Angel in hot pursuit, shouting '*A moi! A moi Bruté! Chien mal, venez!*' in vain. The squirrel found its way blocked by oncoming traffic doubled back, was nearly run over by a bay horse that was trotting beside a brown and a chestnut, the dog nearly barreled into the horses which shied violently, Angel ran out onto the track still yelling Brutus' name, Stephen caught her by the arm, the chestnut horse bucked and neatly unseated its rider, the rider cursed loudly and fluently at the dog and the woman chasing it and as fast as a tumbler bounced to his feet still holding the reins, dragging his horse around with arm and crop raised high to kill the dog. Angel screamed '*Non! A moi, Bruté!*' and shaking Stephen's restraining arm off, launched herself at the dog, grabbed him by the collar, and hauled him off the track as the rider, still swearing, held his plunging horse and shouted, 'You stupid little doxy! I should have you and your dog...' and then with a gasp realized exactly who he was addressing, just as Angel recognized him and drew herself to her full height, eyes round with fear and defiance.

'Miss Hathaway! You...' he stammered, blood draining from his face.

'Mr. Neville, I...' panted Angel stiffly, her face white.

'Your damned unruly dog should never...'

'Your poor frightened horse should not...'

'That cur...'

'...I was wrong, *m'sieur*, to lose control of my *lurcher*...'

'Damned right you were! That *thing*...'

'I make every apology for my *lurcher*'s behavior and my own negligence...'

'You're lucky I wasn't injured! Or my horse! That... insufferable *beast* has no business in the Park...'

'*Your unmanageable horse*,' interrupted Angel heatedly, 'has no business in the Park!'

'*My horse*! Do you have any idea...'

'*Si vous m'écoutez!* I will be most happy to make it good however I may!'

'You had to business to be anywhere *near* this avenue...'

'I thank-you, *my lord*, for reminding me of my place in the world!' Angel stopped him in freezing accents. 'I believed the Park to be a place open to the Public! If there is nothing else... *my lord*... I will leave you, now.' She sank into a deep curtsy that managed to convey a world of contempt.

'No! Miss Hathaway...' managed Neville. 'Please! It was... I never meant to call into question... but the dog was... I was unseated, madam, and it made me angry,' he said finally. And when this elicited nothing more than a scornful stare from Miss Hathaway, coupled with a low growl from Brutus, added, 'That dog is clearly dangerous, and should be dealt with.'

'That horse is clearly unschooled and nearly as unmannerly as his master. *Sir.*'

'As his... *Miss* Hathaway, your behavior, coupled with that of your damned *cur*, has pushed my temper beyond endurance!'

'We shall remove ourselves from your sight with the greatest of pleasure. My lord. *Should* you require restitution, you know my direction. *Allons-nous, Bruté,*' she ordered with a sharp snap of her fingers. '*Venez.*' Brutus obediently turned with her and they stalked away.

'I say, Tris,' said Sir Robert, approaching his friend. 'Isn't that the chit that...'

'Stow it, Robin,' said Neville shortly. He gathered himself and his horse, remounted, and jogged off toward the gate in seething silence.

Since the event had not ended in the authorities being called, the rest of Angel's group treated it with gales of relieved laughter, although Angel, her rage spent, felt only an odd sense of loss. The story gained dimension and hilarity when repeated to Charles Pearce at The Lamb And Flag later on, although that gentleman moderated his laughter with a remonstration to his young cousin that it wouldn't do to make a joke of a man like Tristan Neville, so please not to repeat the story lest it come back to haunt them all.

'I do not see why it should,' said Angel tartly.

'Stature, my dear,' said Pearce. 'He is a gentleman, after all.'

Angel curled a lip. '*Stephen* is a gentleman,' she said. '*Mr. River* is a gentleman. Mr. Neville is merely a nobleman.'

From a moment of shocked silence, another shout of laughter, but above the noise rose Seraphine's theatrical voice, '*Ça suffit!* All of you!' and brought it to an end. 'Angel,' she continued when she had gained the attention of all the young people, '*je te comprends, ma fille.* But you were in fact at fault. And you must not speak so of those people who support the Swan and in fact our livelihood in this most public place.'

Molly Boggs deftly turned the subject with several very clever caricatures of current extremes of fashion and the ridiculous figures attempting to wear them, Bridie met her impression by impression, and laughter returned, but Angel maintained an obstinate silence. And while the others were occupied with eating, drinking, and chatting with acquaintances well met, Pearce drew Seraphine a little aside.

'I had an odd experience meself today, Sera,' he said, and told her about how he had been called to the front of the theatre to meet an older gentleman. 'Name of Denham,' Pearce said. 'Claimed he was an old friend, and wanted to know how to find you.'

Seraphine grew pale, but maintained her poise. 'I remember the man. We had... dealings... oh, many years since. He is not an acquaintance fit for me or mine, *mon cousin.*'

'Thought there was something devilish havey-cavey about the fellow,' Pearce nodded knowingly. 'At first I thought p'raps he had news of George. But I realized it couldn't be that; for if he had, surely he would have told me.'

'Did you mention George by name?'

'No. He kept fishing for information about you. How long you'd been here. What your history was. Made my skin crawl, I don't mind telling you. A damned loose fish. I turned him away. Did I do right? You are not in any trouble, Sera, are you?'

'No, my dear,' she comforted him. 'You did right. And there is a story, which I will tell you in time. But... let us not increase his knowledge of us, *hein?* In this you are correct. He is a very bad man.'

And then a burst of laughter claimed their attention, another round appeared, and the moment passed.

*****

On the evening of Lady Hensleigh's gathering Seraphine dressed carefully in a silk gown of rich old gold that had been cleverly tweaked on more than one occasion by Angel to keep it up-to-date. In its current iteration it showed more decolletage than Seraphine was comfortable with, which caused her daughter to roll her eyes. '*Maman*,' she reproved through the pins in her mouth as she twitched a piece of fabric into place, 'after all these years of seeing almost every part of you exposed to the public onstage, it astonishes me that you are such a prude when you are off it.'

'Would you rather I went about like the opera dancers, all gauze and bosom, flaunting myself to the ogling beaux?'

'No,' said Angel. 'I shouldn't like that at all.'

'I thought not. So the decolletage…'

'…Will stay as is the style. Modesty is one thing, *Maman*. Dowdiness quite another.'

And of course, Angel was right, thought Seraphine, turning to view herself in the small mirror on her dressing table. The gown - tasteful, elegant, with barely a hint that it had survived several seasons of wear - set Seraphine's rich russet hair, worn *sans poudre*, to perfection. A simple necklace of amber and pearl with a matching bracelet finished the ensemble, and a voluminous cloak would protect all from the weather, which was wet again.

A hired chair set her down at Hensleigh House just as two carriages arrived from different directions to disgorge famous playwright and prominent Whig Mr. Richard Sheridan and Miss Mary Berry of Audley Street, famous bluestocking and longtime ward of the esteemed Mr. Horace Walpole. The three darted up the steps to the house together exclaiming and laughing over the rain, to shed wet cloaks into the hands of waiting footmen. Lady Augusta greeted them fondly, then turned her attention to the

next pairs to arrive: one a very officious gentleman named
Birnam, whose timid wife he corrected, talked over, or answered
for every time a question or comment was directed toward her;
the other a dyspeptic gentleman named Sir Michael Everard
whose wife, Lady Matilda, countered his leanness by being large,
colorful, and fruity of tone. 'Ohh. The *actress,*' she uttered
dramatically as Lady Augusta made introductions. 'I dearly fancied
myself to be an actress when I was very young. I was *such* a
favorite in our schoolroom pantomimes, you know; *all* the other
mamas were in raptures over my 'Lady of the Lake'. Such a
romantic calling, do you not think?' she asked Seraphine, then
before Seraphine could answer that it was bloody hard work more
often resembling drudgery than romance, continued, 'But of
course, you know, my dear papa would not have it that I should go
on the stage. Not good *ton* at all, he said, and of course he was
quite right.'

Seraphine smiled wanly, murmured something suitably
noncommittal, and moved on, guided by the strong hand of her
hostess.

'I believe you have met Mr. Nathaniel Neville?' Lady Augusta
nodded to him.

'Only in passing, ma'am. How do you do, Mr. Neville,' she
said neutrally.

'*Enchanté, Madame,*' Neville responded, sounding anything but.
He bowed punctiliously.

'You have seen her affecting Juliet, of course,' declared Lady
Augusta brightly. 'You must try to see her Rosalind. A *tour de force,*
Neville, simply a *tour de force.* And,' she added archly, with a tap of
her fan on his arm, I am told the gentlemen are *quite* over the
moon regarding the shapeliness of her legs in the breeches parts.'

'Oh, I was accorded to have had the most *beautiful* leg, when I
was a girl,' Lady Matilda gurgled behind them. '*Not,* of course that
any but my dear Everard has ever seen them, but he will tell you,
won't you, dear Everard?'

'I will do nothing of the sort,' exposulated her spouse, eyes protuberant with alarm.

'I do not find the sight of women parading in men's attire appealing', Neville said grimly. And then, realizing that something more encouraging might be required, added, 'But I found your Juliet almost... erm... believable.'

Seraphine's shocked gasp and Lady Augusta's sharp intake of breath were fortunately covered by Lady Everard.

'*A rose by any other name would smell as sweet*,' she trilled dramatically, fan clasped to her bosom, eyes cast heavenward. 'Oh, I was famous for my Juliet, in the county.'

'At least two of your relations, Mr. Neville - Mr. Tristan Neville, and Mr. Edward Badgeley, is that correct? Are great supporters of the theatre,' interjected Seraphine, recovering herself by sheer force of will.

'Would it were not just the theatre they supported. I believe one must apologize for the behavior of one's nephew Badgeley.'

'As to that, it ended well. My felicitations to your nephew on his nuptials.'

'I cannot see how the affairs of Mr. Badgeley can be of interest to anyone outside of his family and friends,' said Neville crushingly. 'Ah. Hensleigh, a word,' he added, seizing on the sight of Lady Augusta's husband with evident relief. 'You will pardon me, *madame*.' He bowed slightly again and left.

Seraphine looked after him in open dislike. 'Are you sure this wasn't a dreadful mistake, Augusta?' she asked her hostess. 'I cannot think why my presence in this group can cause anything but consternation.'

'Not a bit,' responded that lady stoutly. 'You are just what the company requires for a bit of color and a dose of reality. You shall have Mr. Sheridan and Miss Berry to lean on at need. Will she not, Richard?' she added, plucking that gentleman's arm.

'With the utmost pleasure!' beamed Sheridan instantly. Then asked in mock consternation, 'To what dreadful nonsense have I just agreed, Lady Augusta?'

'I was just saying that I am quite certain you will find Madame Hathaway's views on the current situation in France to be extremely edifying,' pronounced Lady Augusta, and she sailed onward to the next group.

By the time dinner was announced, Seraphine had navigated her way safely through all of the guests and settled into a fascinating discussion with Miss Berry that began with Burke's *Reflections On The Revolution In France*, and wound its way to Mary Wollstonecraft's recent and already infamous *Vindication Of The Rights Of Women*, which they both agreed should be the subject of a *salon* for further investigation. Taken into supper by the silent Mr. Neville, she mercifully found herself seated next to Mr. Sheridan, whose plays and work as a sharer in Drury Lane she admired very much, and who could be counted on for dry and witty observations that parodied society without showing him to be a dog biting the hand that fed him. His practiced charm made up for the presence on her other side of the stiffly disapproving Birnam, who opined heavily if inaccurately on any number topics on which he considered himself an expert. Upholding her end of a conversation with this gentleman required little effort on Seraphine's part, as he asked her for no opinions whatsoever and clearly did not expect her to have anything to add. Her entire role was to periodically utter, 'Ah yes', and 'how fascinating' and 'Well!' Every now and then he would appeal to his wife, seated across the table, to support the veracity of all he said, and that poor woman, seated between Mr. Neville and Sir Michael, would jump nervously and squeak, 'Oh yes, of course, Mr. Birnam, it is exactly as you say.' Seraphine felt very sorry for the woman.

'One hears,' said Lady Augusta brightly from the bottom of the table, 'that your son has returned from sailing the known world after the most extraordinary adventures, Mrs. Hathaway. I vow I shudder at the very thought of all he endured to find his way back to the bosom of his family.'

Predictably, conversation came to a halt and all eyes swiveled to Seraphine. 'Indeed, ma'am,' she smiled. 'Angel and I are most grateful to have him with us for some little time.'

'But how is this?' blustered the ponderous Mr. Birnam. 'Your son, here in London? Surely he was on a French ship? Has he been properly registered with the authorities?'

'His journey began in France, sir, nearly a decade since, as a surgeon's mate,' said Seraphine. 'But through misadventure, some years on, his ship, the *Liberté*, was unmasted and boarded by a Dutchman, and he was captured.'

'But how extraordinary!' uttered mousey Mrs. Birnam, wide-eyed.

'Preposterous!' blustered Mr. Birnam. 'If he was taken prisoner by the Dutch, how should he now be walking free in London?'

'He escaped, sir,' said Seraphine, eyes wide with theatrical wonder.

'Escaped!' exclaimed Lady Everard. 'How very romantic!'

'But why not go back to France?' demanded Birnam. 'Surely his father...'

'My husband is English, sir. We have had no word of him since we left France.'

'Your husband was sympathetic to the Revolution?' asked Neville abruptly.

'He was sympathetic to the cause of the common man,' Seraphine corrected him. 'I assure you, he had no hand in overturning the Monarchy.'

'Robespierre is offering amnesty to returning emigrés. What stops you from returning?' asked Sheridan.

'Do you believe such an offer to come without a cost, *m'sieu*? I have no such faith.'

'So you instead continue to avail yourself of our British hospitality?' suggested Birnam snidely.

'And to pay for it with British pounds, sir,' she said sharply.

A stray gust of air rattled the windows of the large dining room and caused the candles to gutter, despite the heavy curtains. As the shadows in the room wavered across the features of the diners, Seraphine looked again at Neville and with a shock, realized where she had seen him before. She gasped, and then laughed as the others again looked at her and waved the attention away.

'*Je vous en pris, messieurs, madames,*' she said. 'All this talk brings back memories that are very troubling. Not, perhaps, the best for the table?'

After an eternity of eating, drinking, and conversations that nearly bored Seraphine to tears, Lady Augusta lifted an eyebrow meaningfully at the ladies, and they withdrew gracefully to the Hensleigh's attractive drawing room. The staff had built a welcoming fire and set hot beverages and sweetmeats within easy reach of comfortable chairs. There the ladies made desultory conversation about children, the difficulty of finding good staff, the inconvenience of having the fashion houses of Paris interrupted while unruliness was rife in the country, the horror still felt by all present regarding the recent beheading of poor Louis XVI and his Queen, along with the shocking loss of their families. Everyone in the room - everyone in the city - was affected by the deaths of so many. The chain of European nobility, though small, was far-reaching. Each death rippled through the whole.

'I declare I am almost afraid to go out of the house,' said Mrs. Birnam anxiously. 'What shall we do if the unwashed masses come to our gates and pull us out, as they did in Paris? What if, God forbid, we are betrayed by our own servants?'

'It is very unlikely to happen here, ma'am,' Mary Berry said consolingly. 'The situation in France is very different.'

'But the chaos! And poor Marie-Antoinette, who merely suggested that the people eat cake if there was no bread to be had, though how this can have happened, I've no notion, for have they not the very best of bakeries there?'

'Yes dear,' said Miss Berry gently. 'But it is not the quality of the bakeries that is at issue, you see. It is a matter of the price, which many cannot afford to pay. And of course, a very wet season that spoiled a good deal of the wheat crop last year.'

'But… what has *that* to do with it?' asked Mrs. Birnam in confusion.

The gentlemen chose that moment to join them. Mrs. Birnam's eyes went to her husband in a patent relief tinged with fear. Birnam, not noticing, retired to the window, looking angry. Hensleigh, conversely, seemed rather pleased with himself, the dyspeptic Sir Michael almost cheerful, and Sheridan positively bubbling. Not for the first time, Seraphine reflected that she would rather have been in the dining room with the men than retiring so meekly with the women. It would have been interesting to see exactly what had transpired to cause so many changes of expression.

She glanced up to find Neville's gaze resting on her frowningly. She raised her eyebrows at him inquiringly, he turned away, and she responded, 'Indeed!' in awed accents to something Lady Matilda had just said, which seemed to be exactly the response that lady expected.

'I think we must have some music to lighten our hearts before we part,' announced Lady Augusta gayly. Lady Matilda, would you like to play for us on the harpsichord? I vow it has been an age since…'

'No, no!' exclaimed Sheridan gleefully. 'Let us have a story, instead. Something to cap the night with adventure. What do you say, Lady Augusta? Lady Matilda? Shall we have a story? Mrs. Hathaway, do please regale us with the hair-raising tale of your escape from France.'

Seraphine, startled, tried to demur, but was overridden by all the ladies.

'Oh yes!' exclaimed Miss Berry. 'Do tell us, Mrs. Hathaway, we are all agog!'

'I've been trying to tease that story from her the whole of our acquaintance,' applauded Lady Augusta. 'Come now, Mrs. Hathaway, the moment has arrived. You must sing for your supper.'

'But did you have to escape in a horrid wagon of turnips, or something of the sort?' asked Birnam's wife timidly. 'I fear I should never...'

'No, no,' laughed Seraphine. 'Nothing *quite* so uncomfortable as that. But it was a wagon of produce, and we did dress in the clothes my son and my husband reserved for tramping about the countryside. I may tell you that they itched horribly, and smelled dreadful.'

'You dressed as *men*? 'Pon my soul, I'd no notion your life was so exciting,' remarked Lady Matilda with an eager shudder, 'I should have been frightened to death. Tell on!'

Seraphine sighed, and looked inward, drawing the memory forward. '*Apres la Bastille*,' she began, 'we were hopeful that there would be a *rapprochement*. That there would be a new Constitution. A new way of living. It was very exciting, at first, you see, the world seemed new again and full of possibility, as if the human race could be reborn into perfection and harmony. But of course, we were naive. All became increasingly chaotic. There were soldiers demanding money for protection. There were bands of thieves and cut-throats, taking all they wanted and killing those who resisted. There were people informing on their friends, their neighbors, to get their land. George - my husband - set about making it possible to leave France together. He contacted his cousin - Charles Pearce, of The Swan, as you all know, I'm certain. He provided me with letters and I took the money that we had both been putting away, just in case we might need to act quickly. These we sewed into the linings of our clothing. But in the end... there was a letter to George, from Paris. He would not tell me from whom, or even what it said, except that he must stay back for some few weeks. He insisted that we - my daughter Angel and myself - should leave as soon as we could pack some few belongings. I did not at all wish to leave my home, *vous comprenez*. I did not wish to leave my husband. My son was at sea, we knew not where.'

'But… surely you had *staff* to accompany you?' Asked Lady Everard.

'No staff, but household members, who would not stay behind.'

'Freed slaves, both,' nodded Lady Augusta sagely.

'And you trusted them?' gasped Mrs. Birnam in alarm.

'With my life, *Madame*. Quite literally.

'Jacob Freeman designed that we should travel in a wagon full of produce. It was an idea, oh, of genius. We should never have got through otherwise, we should have been robbed and murdered for whatever we had about us, and my daughter and Mrs. Freeman and I, were we discovered not to be men…' she hesitated, and allowed that simple statement to make its mark on the ladies, 'but we were fortunate. And Mr. Freeman was an imposing deterrent. *Eh bien*, we set off across the countryside, in our wagon, with joy, with song, with patriotism, but mostly with vegetables and even bread, for as we went, we fed people. And when we ran out of food, we unharnessed the horse and turned it loose. We walked the last miles by night and hid by day. It was frightening and cold and damp, but we got to the harbor safely.

'There we found everything in disorder. There were warehouses on fire. The docks were crowded with people trying to get onto a ship, any ship. There were horses rearing and shots fired. There was a young lord with his lady shouting at his man to give money to the soldiers that surrounded them. I saw the man refuse, and turn away while the soldiers dragged the young lord away, and his wife, who was screaming…'

Seraphine stopped, reliving the scene, mouth half open, eyes far away.

'Mr. Freeman… dragged us to a boat, thrusting through the crowd. I was nearly pushed off the dock. He pulled me back. We stumbled into a boat and the boatman rowed us out to the ship we were to board. Mr. Freeman argued with the captain, who tried to deny our arrangements, and cheat us of the fare.'

'Damned Frenchies,' muttered Birnam.

'It was a British ship, *M'sieu*. The tide was on the point of turning; if we missed it, the ship would leave without us and I doubt we would have lived through the night. But we did not miss it. Mr. Freeman prevailed, I know not how. As I stood on the deck thinking our troubles were at last over, I looked back to the docks and was horrified to see a man running for his life, and behind him, a group of soldiers shouting and firing into the crowd. There were so many screams. The man, he was fast, like a cat, but the crowd was thick and the soldiers pushed on. He did not stop to get into a boat, but kept running to the very edge of the wharf, stripping off his coat as he ran, and then... he dived into the water. All this I saw from the deck, lit by the fires, and heard the commotion. My daughter was weeping, terrified, but I could not look away. Our ship began to haul anchor and just then I saw the man's head come up out of the water and he was swimming, swimming for the ship. Mrs. Freeman and I shouted and pointed and pleaded with the sailors to stop, stop and help this man. We were moving slowly and he swam closer but the ship picked up speed with the tide. Mr. Freeman ran to the side of the ship and threw a rope far, far out into the water. The man was able to grab hold - the ship was moving faster now - but Mr. Freeman and two sailors pulled, pulled on the rope and as shots rang out from the shore, they pulled him up onto the deck, where he collapsed.

'It was then the captain ordered me to take my daughter and retire below decks. And that is where we stayed. The weather was calm, and although I am quite sure the captain and the crew lived in constant fear of being overtaken by a French ship, we came safe to London. And the rest, you know.'

There was a lengthy silence, during which nothing could be heard but the wind moaning around the windows and the fire crackling.

'But what… happened to the poor gentleman on the wharf, and his lady?' finally asked Mrs. Birnam timorously. 'Was there nothing…'

'I do not know, *Madame*,' replied Seraphine gently. 'I do not think it was a happy ending.'

'Even more difficult to get out now,' reflected Hensleigh. 'Look at Thomas Paine. You'd have thought him to be a *cause célebre* in the revolution. Instead, he moulders away in the Bastille.'

'The *on dit* is that he will be released sometime this year, if he doesn't die of a fever beforehand,' remarked Neville, who had not ceased staring into the fire since Seraphine began to speak.

'Good God, Neville, surely you haven't spent time in the Bastille yourself!' said Birnam.

'Certainly not,' said Neville. 'But I have been frequently to Paris, on trade matters. One hears the reports.'

'If you ask me, those who couldn't see the writing on the wall deserved what they got,' sated Birnam heavily. 'Overthrow a perfectly good government for some Jacobin ideal? Nonsense. An invitation to Rule by Rabble, which is as much to say the utter demise of civilized society.'

'But dear Mrs. Hathaway,' demanded Lady Augusta, deftly turning the conversation, 'what of the man who swam to the ship? You said not another word about him.'

'I never saw him again, *madame*,' shrugged Seraphine with a sad smile. 'He ran, he dove, he swam and struggled, he was rescued and hauled aboard. And that was the end of it.'

'A mystery!' breathed Miss Berry ecstatically.

Seraphine laughed. 'In the hands of one of our more accomplished novelists, perhaps. Something on the order between the domestic and social critiques of Fanny Burney and the terrors of the unknown as styled by Mrs. Radcliffe.'

Birnam snorted. 'I should never allow my wife to read such nonsense,' he said predictably. 'Damned unsuitable occupation for a woman, to write novels.'

'Even if that is the only way to earn their bread?' asked Seraphine sweetly.

'But I thought you were much taken by the writings of Miss Hannah More, Mr. Birnam' protested his beleaguered spouse in surprise. 'You have always encouraged me to read her works.'

Her spouse's complexion darkened in anger. 'Miss Hannah More instructs in the art of domestic intelligence,' he said stiffly. 'As such, she must of course be admired, as far as that goes. As for her crusading on the topic of good deeds, well. One cannot but be repulsed. Were she to have found a husband, I feel sure that such leanings must have been…'

'*Not until man is made of some other metal than earth*,' murmured Seraphine.

'I beg your pardon, ma'am?'

'Excuse me, sir. I could not resist an allusion granted by Mr. Shakespeare to his redoubtable heroine, Beatrice, who abhorred the idea of marriage.'

'In a *play*, madam. Yet another piece of folly I cannot conceive of having any merit. Do you not agree, Neville?'

'I admit, sir, that the theatre is not a forum I find edifying. And I deplore the morals of its players.'

'Oho!' pounced Sheridan. 'What have you to say to that, Mrs. Hathaway?'

'That the morals displayed by actors reflect those of the society in which they exist,' said Seraphine smoothly.

'Of course you would say that, ma'am,' said Neville. 'But I know of no well brought up lady in our society who would stoop to displaying certain parts of her anatomy so freely in public. It smacks of whoredom.'

'I see,' said Seraphine. 'But undoubtedly you speak from your own experience, sir.' She smiled and was gratified to see Neville flush with suppressed anger. 'And of course I had forgot,' she added, taking it in turn to gaze at each of the male members of the party, 'that if one is not born… er… 'hosed and shod', *c'est ça?*… one must be rather nicer in one's appearance before the world than, say, milady so-and-so who allows any number of *cisisbeos* to assist in her dressing, even to the placement of her patches or the putting on of her stockings, in what to my my mind is a shockingly intimate manner. Or milady such-and-such who has had any number of lovers both high and lower born and whose children may not resemble one another at all. Oh, pardon me - except for the... ah... heir and the... *qu-est-ce que le mot...* spare, of course. They must needs be honest.'

'Mrs. Hathaway. Seraphine...' reproved Lady Augusta agitatedly.

Seraphine ignored her. 'And what of milord thus-and-such, who is allowed to ravish a naive young girl with complete propriety, up to and including ruining her reputation and leaving her, perhaps, no other recourse but to work upon the stage or with a pen. Either of which must be preferable to taking in laundry, or mending. Or turning to the streets. At least with pen and performance, one may live by one's wit. But what do I know of the world, *messieurs*, after all? I am but a poor actress upon a stage, born to speak, as Beatrice again would say, *all mirth and no matter.*'

There was a small silence; an intake of breath in which the women fussed with their fans and the men took long pulls on their drinks.

'You may not like it, ma'am,' conceded Neville, alone in meeting her gaze. 'But it is the way of the world.'

'I am very weary of that world, sir,' said Seraphine. 'And now,' she took a deep breath and stood, 'I must leave you all. Lady Augusta, Sir William, my deepest thanks for a most edifying evening. *Je donne à tous une bonne nuit.*'

She curtsyed deep, let herself out of the room, and informed a surprised and sleepy young under-footman in the corridor that she required her cloak and a chair, immediately. Lady Augusta, she was certain, was even now mending an evening that had gone tilting out of her control, and would be busy for some few minutes yet.

Which indeed was true. By the time that lady came bustling from the room to find her friend and mollify her, the lady had already departed.

'In a chair, you say?' she demanded of her austere butler. 'Without even a single escort at this time of night?'

'I did think to send Octavius along with her, very discreetly, of course, ma'am. He is a good man with a cudgel. She shall come to no harm.'

The distance between Hensleigh House and Seraphine's quiet street measured by foot was not far. But measured by the strictures and straits of Society, Seraphine's direction might as well have been to another country. As the chair took her from the broad thoroughfares of St. James into the smaller, crowded streets that housed people like herself - drapers and shipbuilders, lawyers, doctors, and merchants - Seraphine felt herself relax. On this growing edge of London - noisy, squalid, in constant ferment, full of accents from all parts of the world - a new class of Englishmen and women rose. They occupied the crescents and terrace houses that sprang up everywhere on buildable ground, extending the city's boundaries and its reach, adding to the creative stew that made London endlessly interesting and variable. They all paid ground rents that enriched the very people who occupied palaces and great houses like Hensleigh and Clarendon and Somerset. Would a revolution like the one in France change this? Or would a new order of entitlement merely rise to replace the old?

She paid the drawers of the chair, gave the discreet Octavius a coin and her thanks, let herself in through the kitchen, and lit a lamp from a twist of paper kindled at the banked grate. Its light made fantastic shapes on the walls and spread dim fingers into the night-cloaked shadows of the hall as Seraphine paced wearily to the front of the house and up two flights of stairs to her room.

She must needs apologize to Lady Augusta for her behavior, she thought as she undressed, shook out her clothes and hair, and put on a bedgown. Her abrupt departure had been inexcusable.

She could not think why she had been invited to such a gathering. She had been rendered nearly speechless with rage by the intolerable opinions of the Birnam, who was nothing more than a common bully. And as for that damned Neville… well. Perhaps he had spoken the way he did to punish her for her story. For it had been he that swam to the ship that left Le Havre that night.

Seraphine yawned cavernously, crawled into bed, and burrowed under the covers. She was asleep almost instantly.

*****

The next morning, Seraphine sat at the table in the window of the small, light-filled morning room, sipping her favored hot chocolate and nibbling at one of Jacob's excellent biscuits. The view from her window always gave her peace: this morning a drifting post-rain mist shot through with bars of golden sun that touched the edges of wet roof and sparkling tree and slowly unveiled the day, like a curtain pulling away to reveal a beautifully lit set. With nothing facing her but The Swan's endless accounts, she was attired simply in a striped dimity dress with a figured fichu across her shoulders and her hair *en deshabillé*, a green ribbon threaded through it to keep it from falling across her eyes. Having eaten the last crumbs of a biscuit and sipped the last dregs of chocolate, she contemplated the rather cluttered glass-fronted desk in the corner with resignation, but was saved from tackling the mess by Marianne's appearance in the doorway, announcing that a Mr. Neville had presented his card and wished to see her.

'Mr. Neville?' asked Seraphine, puzzled. '*Which* Mr. Neville?'

'Mr. Nathaniel Neville, he says. Here is his card. He is an older gentleman.'

'Older! Would you call him… '

'Older than the younger Mr. Neville,' opined Marianne, a dangerous twinkle of the eye ruining her prim demeanor.

'Please tell the gentleman I cannot possibly receive him just now, Marianne. It is far too early, and I am far too busy.'

Marianne's lips twitched. 'I did so, but he was quite insistent, and said that another time was not at all *convenable* for him this present.'

'Convenient! For *him*! *Tiens*. How predictable these men are. I'll go down and tell him so myself.'

'It will be quite useless, I think. He is very determined. But I will try to slow his progress so you can prepare.' She left, chuckling.

Seraphine tapped the edge of the card against the top of the table, marveling at how quickly last night's chickens were coming to roost. She rose, shook out her skirts, and stood next to the chair she'd been sitting in, the better to use the morning light to her advantage. 'Mr. Neville,' announced Marianne in her best imitation of a haughty butler with barely a glimmer of a lifted eyebrow. She stood aside to let him enter. Neville hesitated on the threshold, took in the whole of the small room at a glance, and smiled appreciatively at the picture presented by his hostess, sunlight gleaming on a mass of chestnut hair and hinting at a creamy shoulder and bosom beneath the translucent fabric of the fischu. It might have undone a lesser man.

'Charming, Mrs. Hathaway,' he approved. 'You look fully ten years younger, set just so against the light.'

'*Mr*. Neville,' Seraphine said with asperity. 'I feel quite sure that you did not call upon me at this early hour to insult me before I have finished my breakfast.'

'Was I insulting? I rather thought I was paying you a handsome compliment.'

'Then your delivery is somewhat lacking, sir. How may I assist you?'

'Because it is a very soft morning which will, I fear, turn once more to rain by noon, and because there are very few people of any consequence stirring at the present moment, you may assist me by accompanying me for a drive in the Park.'

'And you are willing to risk being seen in the park seated in your carriage beside one whom you consider to be little more than a whore because no one of consequence will view such a spectacle at this hour?'

'Oh, that stung, did it? Rest assured, I am very republican in my tastes. Many women far less well mannered than yourself have been seen driving with me in the Park, even at the height of the Promenade.'

'In that case, I decline the offer, sir. That is not the sort of company I choose to be associated with.'

'Then allow me to be more direct. Mrs. Hathaway, last night you told a story that could have been disastrous to me. This being the case, I believe you owe me the courtesy of a private meeting, which might best be undertaken in my carriage, in the park, at a time when few are about, and we are able to speak freely without being overheard. Do you not agree?'

'You may safely say whatever is on your mind right here,' she responded. 'You need fear no one in this house.'

'Charming as that prospect may be, I cannot risk it,' he said.

Seraphine unbent a little. 'Very well,' she agreed. 'But I shall be half an hour dressing.'

'Being a gentleman of leisure, and accustomed to the complications of female attire, I am prepared to wait.'

'There is chocolate in the urn, and I recommend one of Jacob Freeman's biscuits, if you're feeling peckish, sir.'

'Mr. Freeman is a cook?'

'A very good one. There are also books to peruse, should you desire.'

'Every comfort looked to, in fact. But will you not invite me to your boudoir to help with… er… I believe you mentioned the selection of stockings?'

'I most certainly will *not*. I find the very suggestion repugnant,' she said firmly, sailing by him.

'*Touché*, he said, hand to heart. 'I am undone.' But he was already alone in the room.

Seraphine returned in rather less than half an hour, neatly dressed in the severely cut walking dress she'd had from Madame

Simard those several seasons ago which, with Angel's help, still kept its shape and hugged her figure beautifully. As she re-entered the room, gloves in hand, Neville held up a copy of Thomas Paine's *Common Sense.* 'Have you actually read this?' he demanded.

'Of course I have read it,' she said crisply. 'Why ever else would I have it in my possession? I find that Mr. Paine - for all his many peculiarities, among which is the almost intolerable stench he exudes - has a great deal of worth to say. And I have, before you ask, also read Burke's *Relexions sur la revolution en France.*'

'Good God. I thought perhaps it belonged to your son. Instead I find that among *your* numerous other peculiarities, you are a bluestocking.'

She hid her eyes dramatically with a graceful hand. 'My secret is out,' she uttered. 'I can never hold my head up in Polite company again. And how did you know I have a son?'

'You mentioned him last night. And it was my pleasure to meet Mr. Stephen Hathaway in person while you were dressing,' he said, rising and ushering her out the door. 'I felicitate you. I found him a very likely young fellow with a deal of useful experience, for his years. If it is medicine he longs for, I see no reason for him not to make a success of it.'

'You are being ironical, sir. You know full well he cannot do so without a patron.'

'He strikes me as a resourceful sort. He puts me vaguely in mind of someone,' Neville added with a frown. 'I cannot at the moment think who. No doubt it will come to me.'

Finding no one in the front hall waiting for them, he helped himself to his gloves and hat, which had been left on a table, then opened the front door and bowed Seraphine through it. When it was closed once more, Seraphine took a large key from her reticule and locked it.

'What, Mrs. Hathaway. No butler?'

'Now you *are* being ironical, sir. How should I afford a butler? We all do our part, in this household. How, pray, am I to get into this conveyance safely?' She cast a dubious eye on the lightly built curricle and the glossy bay pair that drew it as it rounded the corner with Neville's head groom handling the lines.

The groom jumped down from his seat and went to the horses' heads. 'Put your foot there', Neville pointed to a small step, 'and your hand here', he offered his. With only a couple of small unladylike bounces, Seraphine was able to get into the carriage with dignity reasonably intact and displaying only the smallest glimpse of ivory petticoats and shapely ankle. Neville sprang in beside her and took the reins, the head groom jumped onto the perch behind them, and Neville carefully maneuvered the pair around the square, weaving in and out of tradesmen's carts, piles of stone and bricks, and foot traffic that made the street busy even at this hour.

'You must tell me more of your intriguingly democratic household,' invited Neville as he expertly threaded the bays through the traffic of the main road.

'It is a matter of necessity,' said Seraphine. 'My occupation being an uncertain one, all that I earn must be parsed carefully between the costs of living and saving toward an eventual retirement from the stage, if I am to remain at all comfortably situated.'

'And are you? Comfortably situated?'

'*C'est comme vous voyez, m'sieu.*'

'You are a woman of many parts, ma'am.'

They continued on the main road at a steady jog maintaining a surprisingly comfortable silence, and arrived shortly at the Park and its pleasant track. The meadows and paths were filled with pockets of mist and golden light that dappled the roadway invitingly. Neville allowed the horses to lengthen into a smart ground-eating trot. Seraphine allowed herself to breathe in the moment - the soft air, the greenery appearing out of the mist as they bowled past, the scent of blossoming shrubs, the musical chink of harness brasses, the rhythmic power of the two bay horses with their arched necks and broad hindquarters. She sighed contentedly.

'It quite spoils a woman, to travel in such a vehicle, behind such a pair,' she admitted, when he shot her a questioning glance.

'Spoiled? In a curricle? *Madame*, I assure you, this is a sporting vehicle, not remarkable for its comfort. For that you must surely have a chaise, or a barouche.'

'As the great bulk of my experience has been either a gig or a wagon, I assure you, a curricle is heaven,' she retorted. 'And I know enough to be aware that a gentleman's racing curricle is far more spartan than this, and quite unsuitable for a lady.'

'And how should you come by that sort of knowledge, one wonders?'

'I am, as you said yourself, a woman of many parts, *m'sieu*.'

'When did you recognize me?' he asked abruptly, bringing the pair down to a relaxed walk.

'Not until partway through dinner. Before then I knew I had seen you, but I could not bring a picture to mind. You, I believe, recognised me far earlier, *ce n'est pas vrai?* At that first encounter Chez Simard.'

'It is my business to remember faces', he answered curtly. 'Why did you tell that story?'

'It is my business to tell stories.'

'You could easily have left certain details out.'

'I wanted to see your reaction.'

'Now you have.'

'Your reaction is to take me for a drive in your curricle? I must try that line of flirtation more often. Unless you mean to murder me and leave my broken body behind a shrub in the deeps of the Park.'

'The thought occurs,' he retorted.

'I hope you will not act on it, however. I had no way of knowing I was putting you in danger. In fact, I have only your word that I have.'

'Let us just say that I have certain interests in France which, if known, would put any number of people at risk of death, not the least of which is myself. I cannot allow that to happen, Mrs. Hathaway. And having said that, I have already said too much.'

She studied his profile for a moment in silence. 'You need have no fear of me, Mr. Neville,' she said. 'I do not believe that I betrayed you by so much as a glance.'

'Agreed,' he admitted reluctantly.

'And, I was in a high state of emotional turmoil and there was little light that night. I have no idea who that poor man was, for indeed, I never saw him again. I am only glad he was rescued from what I am certain must have been a horrifying end.' She shuddered theatrically and widened her eyes.

'You are very good, madame.'

'*Bien sur.* There is a difference, however, between being a teller of stories and a carrier of tales.'

'Even when certain knowledge gives you power?'

'I have no need of that sort of power.'

'Not until it is required of you.'

'Then may it never be required.'

'It was Jacob Freeman who pulled me from the water?'

'*Oui, c'est ca.*'

'I owe you both my life, in effect.'

'*Non. Pas du tout.*'

'Was there ever really a Mr. Hathaway?'

'Of course there was,' she said, nettled. 'What reason have I to invent that? I had thought, in fact, that... perhaps, in your line of work... you might have run across him.'

'My line of work?'

'*Je ne suis pas un imbecile, M'sieu.* I need not elaborate, I am sure.'

Neville shook his head shortly. 'Tell me about your husband.'

'He is the third or fourth son of a family on the Welsh marches, or so he told me. An academic, of necessity. He came to Europe as a... bear leader? *C'est l'expression?* - of young gentlemen making the Grand Tour, I believe.'

'And as you were an actress...'

'...he saw me on stage one evening, *oui.*'

'And succumbed to your considerable charms and made you his wife?'

'The circumstances of our marriage can be of no interest to you, sir.'

'You cannot know that, *Madame*. You have already surmised my... interests... abroad.'

'Then... we were useful to one another, and we prospered.'

'A *marriage de covenance.*'

'*Si vous voudrez.* He was a deal older than myself, a widower with no living children. This his cousin Charles Pearce has affirmed, though I had no reason to doubt it.'

'And you were caught up in the Revolution?'

'George was idealistic and utopian in his thinking. I was the more practical. When the Revolution that he dreamt of occurred, it was not what he had imagined.'

'So he sent you and your daughter away.'

'*Oui.*'

'But not your son?'

'*Non.* Stephen had already been at sea for several years. We...' The sudden tears surprised her. She struggled against them. 'We thought... it would be... Was... *Excuez-moi, m'sieu,* to talk about that time...' she looked to the side, breathing deep, forcing her thoughts back to order. Neville tapped the horses back into a trot, eyes ahead, thoughts unreadable. When they reached the end of the track, he turned the equipage in a grove before traveling back they way they'd come.

'Perhaps your husband will reappear,' he said neutrally.

'*Je pense que non, m'sieu.* By now there must have been some word.'

'I will do what I may to find your husband, Mrs. Hathaway,' he said suddenly.

Seraphine raised her eyes to him in startled gratitude. '*Le bon Dieu vous guardez, m'sieu,*' she said.

Then, almost casually, Neville added, 'And perhaps you can do something for me.'

'*Bien sur.*'

'Have you, in your travels, met a man by the name of Denham?'

The effect on Seraphine was electric. Gone were the goodwill, the relaxation. She flinched, and color drained from her face. 'Our paths may have crossed, in France,' she said, tightly controlling the tendency of her voice to tremble. 'Why?'

'He came to an earldom, long ago,' said Neville. 'The third Earl Denham, his father, was a gamester and a womanizer, and when he died, he left little more than debts for his eldest son to inherit.'

'It is an old story, sir.'

'Ah, but it gets better. Following in his esteemed father's footsteps, the younger son gambled away the remnants of what had once been a considerable fortune in a surprisingly short time, despite all efforts of the elder brother - now Fourth Earl Denham - to curb his habits. Not long after inheriting the title and estates, that young Earl died in a hunting accident...'

'*Mon Dieu...*'

'...precisely... leaving his younger brother to inherit the whole. The story goes that his indebtedness was so great that his only recourse was to marry an heiress. His reputation, however, was such that very few mamas who cared for their daughters were willing to trade a title for a daughter's wellbeing.'

'*Naturellement.*'

'He ran off with the daughter of a local landowner - Sir Robert Finister - whose wife's people had properties in The Indies. The girl in question was, I think, still in the schoolroom. Denham meant to force the father's hand by ruining her, but Finister cut up rough and refused. And in the ensuing fracas, Denham disappeared, and the girl, too.'

Seraphine studied the interlacing tree branches that passed above them and sighed. '*If this were play'd upon a stage now, I could condemn it as an improbable fiction.*'

'Over the years, one saw Denham from time to time,' Neville continued. 'In Germany, in Italy, in France - always with a new wife. Or always having just become a widower again. But no sign of the girl. The family spared no expense, looking for her. But she had disappeared. It was an immense scandal.'

'Perhaps the family did not look in the right places, *m'sieu*,' she said, after a time.

'Perhaps not.'

'It is… a dreadful story. I wish it were less common.'

'Less common!'

'The rape of young girls for the sake of title or money? The ruination of those with no prospects for momentary pleasure? In my business it is not uncommon. What is your interest in this story, *m'sieu*? It can hardly have affected you.'

'On the contrary, Mrs. Hathaway, I have an abiding interest in the workings of injustice. The cost to the girl's family was disastrous. I knew the elder brother at Oxford. From him I knew the details, and that the mother never recovered. After her death the family moved to Jamaica, to make a clean start. Edward is still there, but the younger brother, Julian, came home to run the family estates in Herefordshire. And there the story should end, except that Denham has suddenly resurfaced in London, and as it happens, was seen at The Swan last week. So, being naturally curious, and there being many unanswered questions surrounding the gentleman, I wondered.' He looked at her piercingly. 'You have not answered my question, Mrs. Hathaway.'

Seraphine was saved the necessity of responding by the sight of Mr. Tristan Neville trotting up the track toward them, mounted on the same chestnut horse that had caused such consternation a few days since. He raised a hand, Neville steered his pair to a halt on the side of the track, and his nephew came up beside them.

'Good morning, Uncle! Good morning, Madame!' he greeted them, managing to display only a flicker of astonishment at seeing this particular pair together.

'Good morning, Tris. Where did you get your hands on this young 'un?'

'At Tat's. One of Cleveley's dispersal.'

'I shouldn't have thought there was anything worth the taking.'

Tristan laughed. 'Well, there were a good many puffy hocks and filled tendons, but this fellow was too young to have been spoiled yet.'

'Looks as if he'll make a fine hunter.'

'I expect he will, sir. He... can be a bit, um... *erratic*... being green...' he glanced at Seraphine briefly and colored. 'So I thought it best to bring him out before the main crowd arrives and give him a chance to acclimate himself to the new sights and sounds. Um... Loose dogs. And the like. And become a bit more mannerly.'

Neville looked from Tristan to Seraphine, eyebrows raised slightly. 'Loose dogs... and the like?' he asked mildly.

'Yes,' Tristan said uncomfortably. 'I daresay Mrs. Hathaway can explain that statement to you. I must be on my way. Perhaps I shall see you at Jackson's?'

'Not I. I leave town later today. But I expect to return to London within the fortnight.'

Tristan saluted his uncle, bowed to Seraphine, and went his way.

'Loose dogs... and the like?' repeated Neville as he touched the bays lightly with the whip and told them to walk on.

'Oh,' Seraphine laughed lightly. 'It was quite ridiculous, and I missed nearly all of it, arriving just at the end. But as I gather, the great hairy lurcher that is my daughter Angel's chief protector couldn't resist the sight of a squirrel, ripped its lead from her hand, and as it happened, ran directly in front of Mr. Neville and his friend Sir Robert Kilronan. The chestnut horse spooked badly and unseated Mr. Neville. This was, of course, a blow to his pride. So after swearing that the dog should be put down for its behavior, he gave my daughter a harsh set-down.'

'And she, being alike in spirit to her mother...'

'Flew into a rage. She has a very strong sense of justice, sir. Prior to that moment I had thought Mr. Neville a most gentlemanlike young man, not inclined to lean so heavily on his entitle...' she stopped short, and drew breath. 'I am sorry, sir. I have no right to...'

'No. You have not,' Neville said, coolly. 'The world may be changing, Madame, but England is not, I thank God, France. So while I deplore the tendencies of my nephews to create spectacles in public places with those not of their world, the thing I deplore most is their neglect of the obligations of their breeding. I think you understand me, ma'am.'

'*Je vous comprehends parfaitement, m'sieu,*' said Seraphine, stiff with humiliation. 'We are nearly at my street, sir,' she said tightly. 'You may drop me here, and I shall walk the rest of the way.'

'Don't be ridiculous. I shall certainly...' then he cursed angrily, and pulled the horses up short, because Seraphine had already stood up in the precariously balanced curricle and yanked open the door. As soon as the vehicle was stopped, before the groom could jump down from his perch to go to the agitated horses' heads, she had clambered out ungracefully, and cursed like a sailor when the skirt of her favorite - indeed, only - walking dress caught on the edge of the step & tore badly.

'I had begun to think you a different sort of man, *m'sieu,*' she looked up at Neville, eyes blazing. 'I shall know better from now on. Rest assured that your *business,* whatever it is, remains safe with me, despite my failings of birth. *Bonne journeé. Monsieur.*' She swept Neville a grand and mocking curtsey, spun on her heel, and strode away to lose herself quickly in the narrow streets and growing crowd leading from the park.

For his part, Neville's rage was so great that his hands on the reins clenched harshly and caused the bays to jig and skitter. 'Mind that pile of bricks, sir, do!' expostulated his groom anxiously. 'Let their heads go!'

'Do *not* presume to tell me how to drive my horses, John!' swore his employer, and sent the horses forward. Never had he wanted to punish anyone as badly as that ill-mannered, red-haired shrew.

Seraphine entered her house through the kitchen, where Marianne, who had just sat down with a mug of cider, took one look at her and poured another mug from a saucepan poised on the ledge of the fireplace.

'Oh, your poor dress!' she exclaimed, refraining from commenting on its wearer's thunderous expression. 'Come and sit, Sera, take some cider with me while I mend.'

Seraphine sat stiffly, accepted the drink, and watched Marianne deftly mend a tear in a linen petticoat, which was oddly soothing. Finally, with a sigh, she said, '*Marianne, je ne comprends du tout ce monde, pas du tout.* We are all born in the same way and die in the same way, and eat and drink and fuck and piss in the same way… and yet people like myself are penalized for our birth, and people like you are penalized for your skin, and both of us are penalized because we are women, and who makes these determinations but men of title and influence? And why is it so hard to progress against that power? When all any of us want to do is live in peace, with a roof and enough to eat.' She downed the cider in one gulp and made to hurl the mug into the fireplace.

'You'll be very sorry if you break that,' said Marianne, catching Seraphine's hand with her own. She held on until Seraphine's breathing stabilized and her grasp loosened, then gently removed the mug from her and set it aside. 'In France, they are trying to make a different world.'

'In France, it is still a world powered by men.'

'*Bien sur.* It is always about power, and always men who wield it.'

'There must be a way. Some little way. For us.' Seraphine rose and shook out her skirts. 'I am so distressed about my beautiful dress, Marianne. I cannot afford to replace it. Can it be repaired, do you think?'

Marianne reached out to examine the jagged tear. 'I think it is a job for Angel,' she said. 'But first I will clean it, and that will make her part easier. Leave it for me when you go to The Swan. Do you need help with your dressing?'

Seraphine shook her head. 'No. Thank-you. You have other business, and I don't want to come to depend too much on your good will.' She walked out to the hall to go upstairs. Marianne looked after her, concerned for the rare forlornness that had overtaken her friend. 'I'll be there an hour before curtain,' she called after her.

*****

At The Swan's stage door, Seraphine was greeted by James Hemings, who informed her that Lady Augusta had just arrived by the main entrance, and wanted to see her.

'*Mon Dieu*,' sighed Seraphine. 'My penance continues. Is she in the dining room?'

'I thought it best, ma'am. I had them in the kitchen give her a glass of lemonade and a plate of iced cakes.'

'*Bien joué*, Mr. Hemings. *Merci*.' Stopping by her dressing room only long enough to remove her pelisse and bonnet and tidy her hair, Seraphine quickly went up the stairs, across the stage, and through the house to the dining room off the lobby, which gleamed with brass and polished wood from the light of windows now open to soft air and the sounds of tradesmen and afternoon traffic that floated up from the street.

'Lady Augusta,' said Seraphine contritely, curtsying prettily. 'How can I possibly apologize enough for my behavior last night. It was inexcusable.'

'Oh, Seraphine, no,' uttered Lady Augusta. 'Truly, truly, the blame must all be mine. What, Hensleigh asked me, what on earth must I have been thinking to have cast you in the midst of that horrid group of people! I only thought to have introduced a bit of levity into what seemed doomed to be an evening of frightfully dull political chat. And instead I threw you to the lions, dear girl.'

'Nonetheless, I did not mean to forget myself so far as to allow men like Birnam and Neville get under my skin.'

'No,' Lady Augusta frowned. 'It was not your finest hour, I will say. But Birnam is the most awful sort of bully, as you know. It was Neville who shocked me. His behavior toward you...' she shook her head. 'Frankly, I was appalled, and told him so.'

'Ah,' said Seraphine. 'That must explain, then, why he arrived at my house just as I was finishing breakfast with the intent of taking me for a drive in the park.'

'Good God!' said Lady Augusta, looking horrified. 'At the *breakfast* hour? He never did! Did you go?'

'He did, and I did.'

'And did he apologize?'

'No. We quarreled again. Before that though,' she tipped her head sideways and contemplated, 'I believe the worst epithet he threw at me was to accuse me of being a bluestocking, after remarking that I looked ten years younger with the light behind me.'

'Good God, Sera! What *can* he have been thinking?'

'Other than that, I believe I was quite in charity with him. Until he found it necessary to forcibly remind me of my position.'

'No! Did he give you a set-down?'

'Indeed, ma'am.'

'The insufferable brute,' said Lady Augusta, frowning. 'However,' she continued briskly, 'We need not dwell on Neville. I am exceedingly happy that *we* understand one another, and that all is well between us. I must dash. Tell your Mr. Freeman that his cakes left me swooning. I shall steal him from you, Seraphine, mark my words!' and with that cheerful parting shot, she departed.

Seraphine sat at the table a little longer, absently eating a small cake and wondering what web from the past might be threatening to entrap her. She tugged mentally at every strand of her life. None seemed to cross another in a way to pose a threat. But Neville was a deal too perceptive and too much an enigma to be trusted. And the troubling appearance of Denham could not bode well. She sighed, and rose too her feet just as Jacob appeared from the lobby.

'Seraphine, you're wanted onstage, if you please. Mr. Pearce and Mr. Demers are about to come to fisticuffs. Over a dance, it appears.'

'Of course they are,' sighed Seraphine. 'You don't seem too troubled by it, Jacob.'

'Not I,' he grinned, his battered face creased with enjoyment. 'It's as good a play as I ever saw!'

Seraphine laughed. Then as she walked by him said, 'By the way, Jacob, Lady Augusta sings the praises of your cakes, and says she wants you to leave us and be her cook.'

'That is kind in Lady Augusta,' said Jacob equably. 'But Marianne and I are quite content as we are, for now.'

'She would certainly pay you better than I can.'

'Between employment and servitude is a great and mighty river, ma'am. To others this may not seem so. To we who have been enslaved it is a large distinction. And Marianne and I have larger plans than domestic service.'

She looked for a moment into Jacob's eyes, deep with experiences she could not begin to name and that no words could measure. Finally, she nodded briefly. 'Thank-you,' she said simply, and passed by him to go to the stage.

'Gentlemen!' she clapped her hands sharply as she entered the house. 'Gentlemen, *s'il vous plaît! Ecoutez-moi, maintenant!*'

An hour later, fisticuffs averted, Hemings greeted her return backstage with the knowledge that a parcel had been left for her in her dressing room.

'A parcel? What sort of parcel?' Seraphine asked, perplexed.

'I'm sure I don't know, ma'am.'

'I don't recall having ordered anything,' she said. 'Perhaps it was meant for Mr. Pearce. Or Miss Angel. Who brought it, did you find out?'

Hemings shook his head. 'It's been that busy, ma'am. The boy didn't leave no name, just said t'was for you and for me to make sure as you got it. P'raps,' he said, eyes twinkling, ''tis something from an admirer, ma'am. I was saying to the missus this very morning as how it's a shame all these opera dancing chits get all the attention, when it's our Madame Seraphine as deserves it.'

'Mr. Hemings, one more word, and I will believe you are flirting with me,' she laughed, and Hemings blushed to the roots of what little hair he had. 'I will go myself and see. Perhaps it will be something *mervelieux, n'est-ce pas?*'

And in fact, it was something marvellous. For when she opened the package, what appeared before her was the very gown she had admired *Chez Simard.* The beautiful muslin she had so loved, printed in pale green stripes alternating with panels that carried sprigs of yellow rosebuds and leafy tendrils on their cream background. The little spencer jacket of deep green silk. Seraphine lifted the dress tenderly and held it to herself, inhaling the clean scent. She could not imagine who could have known about her desire for this very dress, or who, knowing it, would have given her so extravagant and costly a present. Molly couldn't afford to give away such a garment. Angel couldn't afford to buy it. Stephen showed absolutely no consciousness of any style of dress whatsoever, no matter the wearer. She searched through the packaging, but found no note and no explanation. Surely, it was a mistake. She should take it back. But... she fondled the material caressingly. It was such a lovely dress. All she could do was ask Angel, who must know the identity of the purchaser.

And in the meantime, Rosalind beckoned. She put the dress and its protective wrapping aside, and began the process of turning herself from Mrs. Hathaway, sharer in The Swan, to Madame Seraphine, its fiery haired leading light.

As You Like It went off without a hitch that evening, with another full house. Although Mr. Neville, that avowed tyrant to players, was not there to observe the performance, the better number of the gentlemen in the audience were properly appreciative of Mme. Seraphine's shapely legs, even clad as they were in concealing layers of leather and wool. She gave life, joy, and vulnerability to the plight of Rosalind, the girl dressed as a boy to hide her true identity and win her lover. Bridie danced like an angel, golden hair catching the light and shining as bright as the stars, or so ardent Chance River thought, watching from his perch backstage next to Hemings. Bridie still paid him little attention. She still nourished a broken heart. But faced nightly with his cheerful demeanor, steady presence, and popularity among the other girls, even she grudgingly allowed that Chance River was a proper man.

The only potential crisis of the night arose at the end of the evening when Charles Pearce, having been told by the box office that Mrs. Hathaway had the night's takings in her control, sought her out as she finished her supper and demanded an accounting.

'For I have needs, if you must know, and you haven't any right to remove the takings before I've looked at them, Sera, you know you haven't.'

'It's not the looking at them that worries me about you, Charles,' said Seraphine serenely. 'It's the helping yourself to the lion's share before anyone else has been paid.'

'You have no right! The Swan is mine! And the money is mine to do with as I please! I have...'

'What you owe your mistresses and bookmakers is nothing to me, *Mr.* Pearce. In case you have forgotten, fully half of The Swan belongs to me...'

'To your *husband*, Madam! And as he is not here, you haven't the legal right to withhold...'

'I am not withholding anything. You will get your portion of the pay on Thursday week, with the rest of us.'

'Thursday week! You cannot possibly think... There are important expenditures... *No*, by God, this is *unacceptable*. Hand over the blunt this moment, Seraphine, or I swear I will...'

'I don't have it.'

'You... *what did you say?*'

'I don't have it.'

'*You've lost the night's...*'

'*Pas du tout, mon cher.* Nor, unlike you, have I gambled the lot away. By now, I fancy, Stephen and Jacob have delivered the money to Mr. Henson, who will see it deposited to The Swan's account in just a few hours. Do sit down, Charles, before you have an apoplexy.'

'*You... You...*' Pearce sat heavily and mopped a face that had become alarmingly red. 'You *viper.* You *serpent at the breast.* I gave you a home. I took you in. And this is the thanks I receive? By heaven, Mrs. Hathaway, I will have you turned out for this.'

'You may, of course. But when I go, I will take my investments with me. In cash.'

'You *cannot.*'

'I can, and I will.'

'But the theatre cannot...'

'Survive without me. Yes. I know.'

A crafty gleam grew in Pearce's rather bulging eyes. 'As to that, Sera, you know by law that you cannot own property yourself. And, as seems likely, my cousin George is in fact deceased, then all that share that was...'

'Mine...'

'...in his name, becomes mine.' He sat back in satisfaction. 'I have hesitated to bring up so painful a subject before now, but you must see, my dear, that you have nothing to say in the matter.'

'Yes, Charles, I do, actually,' said Seraphine with a calmness that Pearce, expecting tears and recriminations, found inexplicable. 'I meant to tell you this before, but as the time never...' She looked up at the door, her face brightening into a smile. 'Stephen! I've just been telling our cousin Pearce that your father's share in The Swan has been passed on to you as his advocate three days since.' She looked back at Charles. 'Do not you worry, Cousin,' she said to him soothingly. 'Stephen has a very good head for business and will protect our investments as I know you would were they all your own. Shall we have a celebratory drink?'

'Gladly,' grinned Stephen wolfishly. '*Mon cher cousin* Charles, I am so very happy to be able to help my mother and yourself with the great responsibilities of this wonderful theatre. *Je suit a la hauteur.*' He raised his glass. '*Aux partenariat!*'

Seraphine looked from Pearce's expression of stunned disbelief to Stephen's devilish grin and laughed out loud. In this moment, it almost seemed that the whole tilting world had righted itself and begun to spin again as it was meant to. 'To partnerships!' she agreed, and raised her glass.

*****

Fully five days after The Incident Of The Dog - an event that he hated to admit still caused him no end of lost sleep - Tristan Neville was stung to the quick to hear an anecdote bruited about downstairs in his own house, that quoted the lady who was the source of his anger and confusion as daring to call him - him! *Mr. Tristan Neville! Son and brother of an Earl!* - 'only' a nobleman. Not a Gentleman. Oh, yes, he heard that. His head groom Sam's sister's husband had been in the selfsame tavern at the very moment the statement was uttered, no matter how quickly the conversation had been squelched by the chit's mama, and that hurly-burly fellow had wasted no time in ensuring that the comment became generally known to Tristan's entire staff. This, of course, enraged him even further. Though very aware that his status in the world sprang purely from an accident of birth, he never questioned that he was due a large degree of respect because of it. It had never occurred to him that this might make him a snob.

His first notion was to fire the lot of them, turn them out on the streets, and good riddance. On reflection, he realized that although immediately gratifying, it would only make his case worse. He fired Sam's sister's husband instead, as a general warning, then redoubled his efforts to show the rest of his staff how important they were, and how much their loyalty meant to him. And with that, his staff came to the wise decision that really, Mr. Tristan Neville was a good and generous employer, and life became calm again.

Except for the issue of Miss Hathaway. Having all but persuaded himself that she was common and a bit coarse in comparison to Miss Arabella Montjoy, his drastic re-introduction found her... unapologetically dignified. Even when holding that great, hairy cur. Even when nearly being run over by three horses. And she not only scorned his status, but had delivered him - *him!* - a set-down worthy of a Duchess. It was disconcerting. It was refreshing. He wanted to teach her a lesson. He wanted to dive into her green gaze. He wanted to make her suffer. He wanted to strip her bare and fuck her. He avoided the theatre. He took no pleasure in sparring at Jackson's. He quarreled with his friends. He picked holes in the behavior of his groom. He sent a perfectly good dinner back to his kitchen, then slammed out of his house and spent hours walking. He went to Brooks' and found it insipid. He went to a rout held by the mama of a young lady who was accorded one of the Season's greatest Beauties, and couldn't find a single reason to stay beyond what was strictly polite. He drank a great deal too much. He rode his young chestnut hunter in the park and through the streets at all hours until it was accustomed to every horror London might offer an equid. He hoped he would see Miss Hathaway. Even more, he hoped she would see him. Why? To repine, of course. To see what she had... what? Missed? But there was no trace of her anywhere. And he would not - no, he *would* not - lower himself to going within two streets of *Chez Simard.*

The only avenue left him for the assuaging of his frustrations was a visit to a certain lady with whom he had a standing engagement that, to be honest, had been cooling in recent weeks. When later they lay spent and tangled in her sheets, Tristan's overriding sensation was not satisfaction. It was despair. His mistress, with the understanding of long experience, recognized the signs and took the moment to tell him with quite a respectable attempt at a tear in her limpid eye that alas, she feared they must now part forever. Which solved one problem, but not the other.

At the end of a week, he found himself in front of *Chez Simard*, as if his feet had known this had always been his goal, even if his head did not. Through the great bow window, past the displays of stylish jackets, pelisses, and a hanger that bore a divine drape of deep primrose watered silk designed to lure ladies of fashion inside, he could see figures moving about their business. Then - his heart jolted - there was Miss Angel Hathaway herself, laughing with a young matron who was wrapping herself about with a gauzy length of sarsnet. He studied her through the window, devouring her features, her grace, her easy manners. Angel Hathaway, damn her green eyes, was a poised, gracious, and beautiful young woman, secure in a world he had no knowledge of at all. And she did not pine for Tristan Neville.

He caught himself from an impulse to rest his head against the cool glass of the window. *Pull yourself together, Neville! She's just a chit in a dress shop!* He gave himself a mental shake and strode purposefully to the end of the street, and into the nearest tavern.

*****

There really had been a Madame Simard, once. Molly Boggs had never met her, but she knew they shared the same physical dimensions, because she had once bought a dress of the best French design and workmanship, clearly by a very fine atelier, from a pile of cast-offs. And the name stitched into the lining read '*Mme Simard*'. Molly had been very taken with the dress - beautiful amber silk with a gold lace overlay and the loveliest low neckline, designed to make the most of a small woman's charms. When she bought it off the cart of a friend - a month's wages, it was, and cheap at that - she wondered what had caused Mme. Simard to sell it, for it was in near perfect condition with barely a stain or a tear upon it. Had she been an emigré fallen on hard times? Had she fallen ill? Had she even, perhaps, died? When Molly wore the dress she tried to imagine the lady for whom it had been made; who she was, how she carried herself, what she thought about.

Unconsciously, Molly Boggs began more and more to become the Madame Simard of the dress. When finally it had to be remade to maintain its fashionable mien, she picked every stitch out and studied with what care and attention to design it had been created. By the time she moved her shop, the dress was long gone, but Molly Boggs and Madame Simard were One, and the little *modiste* had learned how to create stitches easily as fine as those in the transformational garment.

Today, the interior of the shop was in full bustle. Lady Attenborough and Miss Henrietta Attenborough arrived quite early in he day, to decide which of the luscious materials just arrived in the shop in anticipation of the frenzy of cutting, sewing, and designing that would occupy the next weeks, would suit for the upcoming wedding. On the counters were silks and crepes of the dreamiest ivory and cream, satins of every hue from palest primrose to deepest rose to richest lilac. There was lace of ivory, silver, and gold. There were spools of ribbon in every color, pattern, and width. As the ladies pored over Madame's patterns, Angel and Madame herself gently steered them away from the most egregious fashion excesses of the moment, and tactfully pointed out those bearing simpler and more elegant lines. Madame persuaded Lady Attenborough that the overpowering plum satin she wished to swathe her ample form in was perhaps a shade that might prove alarming, and that this pretty lilac was *tres elegant*. Miss Hathaway pointed Miss Henrietta away from the unflattering pastels much favored by her mama, demonstrating to a nicety how the deeper, rosier colors of spring became her rather brown complexion and tawny hair to best advantage. She further suggested that this once a slightly more daring décolletage might be not only seemly, but *ravissant* stitched and shaped just so to set off a smaller bosom, which the bride's mama acknowledged regretfully was neither as full as one might wish nor as plump as her own had been at the same age. But then, her own looks, Lady Attenborough fondly recollected, had been rather finely drawn in their golden-haired and cornflower blue-eyed perfection. Her daughter, she opined, sadly took after her dear grandmama, who had been as dark as a gypsy. Since Miss Henrietta had heard this story for most of her life, she treated it as the merest background chatter requiring only an occasional nod of acknowledgement, while Madame and Miss Hathaway simply smiled encouragingly and said 'what does madame think of the gold lace at the decolletage', or 'this cut through the bosom must be bound to please Mr. Badgeley, and show his intended wife to be enviably beautiful'.

When the ladies Attenborough finally retired from the shop to refresh themselves elsewhere, Madame, Angel, Maria, and Elsie set about the arduous job of making some semblance of order out of the colorful chaos that had been created. They labelled everything that was to be the bride's gown, a traveling dress, and a new day dress, as well as Lady Attenborough's gown. They set these pieces aside carefully, then gently folded and stored the fabrics and lace that would be used in other projects. Molly and her 'prentices took everything left over into the workshop, and Angel stayed in front to tidy the exhibits.

When the doorbell jingled she looked up with a smile ready on her lips. But when she recognised Mr. Tristan Neville, the smile faded, the mouth grew tight, and the lady colored slightly, finding a sudden desire to shake out a chemise that appeared to need straightening on its form.

'Miss Hathaway,' started Tristan uncomfortably, 'I came… that is to say I feel that… that is… may I have a word with you, please? Preferably in private?'

'I am very sorry, sir, but as you see I am quite busy at present. It is time for us to close the shop. If m'sieu is looking for something to please a lady…'

'No. No! I am not looking for anything at all. I am looking to see you. But what I have to say…'

'Anything you have to say may be said here, sir,' Angel said with some trepidation. 'We are quite private for the moment.' She moved behind the counter and rested her hands on it. For balance, perhaps. For protection, certainly.

Tristan looked helplessly at her, her face, her form, the defenseless hands that rested on the counter, chapped from the long winter's chill and already showing the signs of a life of hard work. At that moment what he wanted most of all was to take those hands and kiss them. And tell their owner that she might never have to work that hard again in her life. But this was too radical a thought for him to fully comprehend at the moment, and he realized that he knew so little of Miss Hathaway that any unguarded comment could in fact offend her deeply. Perhaps she didn't want to be taken away from her work. Perhaps she didn't want his protection. In his experience, this was a concept almost too alien to countenance.

'You wanted to say something, Mr. Neville? If it is about Brutus... I can assure you...'

'Brutus? Who the hell is Brutus?' he demanded, nettled. Then, 'Oh. The dog. No, Miss Hathaway. I am not here about your damned cur.'

'Lurcher.'

'Um. I am here to apologise for my behavior in the park, which I realize was inexcusable. Even if I was badly provoked. I have a very short temper, you see. I must learn to mend it.'

'Yes,' agreed Angel.

'And... I am exercising my young chestnut much earlier in the morning now,' he went on, embarrassed at his desperation, desperate to make her understand... 'He is already growing more accustomed. To the sights and sounds. Of the city.'

'Mr. Neville, the schooling of your horse can be of no interest to me.' She turned away.

'He is country bred, you see,' Tristan rushed on imploring. Angel hesitated. 'He was... a bit overwhelmed.'

Angel turned back. 'I understand you sir,' she relented. 'I have made sure to remind Brutus of his manners on a lead. His job is to protect me. Not to chase squirrels.'

Tristan ventured a smile, his relief palpable. 'Then, Miss Hathaway, are we friends?'

'Yes, if you like, Mr. Neville,' Angel said stiffly.

'Then… to make it up to you… may I escort you home?'

'No, thank-you, sir. My brother will be here to walk with me.'

'I could wait… in case…'

'There is no need, sir,' said Angel firmly.

'Angel, *qu'est-ce que c'est?*' Came a voice from the rear of the shop.

'*Un moment, madame,*' she called back. '*Ce n'est de rien.*'

Not satisfied, Molly Boggs poked her head around the curtain that led to the workshop. '*Allo?*' she demanded. 'Angel, is this gentleman troubling you?'

'No, madame,' said Angel. 'He was just looking at a piece of lace for his sweetheart. Are you not, *m'sieu.*' Her eyes looked steadily and uncompromisingly into his.

'Yes. Thank-you. You have been most helpful. I am… I remain… your servant, ma'am.' With no other action remaining to him but to leave, Tristan bowed, settled his hat onto his dark gold head, and departed.

Madame sighed in annoyance. 'Such a pretty gentleman he is,' she said. 'And I think, not here to look at lace for any sweetheart, dearie.'

'No,' admitted Angel. 'He was not. He came… actually… to apologise for his behavior in the park.'

'Did he, now,' said Molly approvingly. 'And very handsome of him, too, I say.'

'Yes,' agreed Angel a little shakily, picking up some scraps on the counter and tidying them away. 'I thought… Oh, *Madame*, I was very frightened. I thought he might try to take Brutus away from me. Because I was at fault. I should not have let him pull the lead out of my hand. *Excusez-moi, Madame.* I am just so relieved.'

'Yes, yes,' said madame shrewdly, patting her arm. 'Those Nevilles, you know,' she shook her head.

'What do you mean by that, *Madame?*'

'Well. Not for me to carry stories, but 'tis a known fact they can be temperamental. And they take themselves very serious-like. I only wish...' she shook her head again, and folded the goods in the window, leaving it empty of temptation to late night thieves looking for easy pickings.

'You only wish? *Madame*, you are being very enigmatical,' complained Angel.

'You an't like most of us, are you, Angel? I never yet saw you walk out with a young man, nor fancyin' one beyond a laugh and a joke all friendly-like, and that's good enough in itself. But if you was ever to marry, Angel...'

'I don't think there's any danger of that, *Madame*...'

'That's just what I'm talkin' about, girl. You won't never be happy with just a pint and a tickle and a solid roof over your head.'

'*Madame!*' exclaimed Angel, shocked. 'Are you calling me a snob, *moi-meme, qui vous adore*?'

'Now you come down outta the trees, missy. All I'm sayin' is, you read things, and you think on things, and you'd be deal of help to any professional man. But that sort don't marry girls in shops. And I know what you're goin' to say,' she warned, finger wagging. 'You're goin' to say this here world is changin'. But it an't changin' fast enough for the likes of you nor me. Now where's that brother of yours? You ought to be on your way home by now. It's coming on to dusk.'

Angel laughed. 'He probably got sidetracked by a cockfight or some such horror,' she said. 'If he isn't here by the time we've done cleaning up, I'll just start walking. There is plenty of daylight left. And I have Brutus.'

After an hour, the girls brought in a scuttle and started a welcoming fire in the back of the shop, then set about assembling bread and stew for their long-awaited supper.

'Stay here with us, won't you, and share a bite,' Molly invited. 'It don't go easy with me, you settin' off all on your own.'

'Nonsense,' said Angel firmly. 'I'll be fine. Brutus can bite, and I can run.'

When she collected the brindled dog from his spot behind the house, she looked at the sky with some trepidation. The daylight she had so blithely counted on was damped by cloud, and a fine mist began to send its fingers up the narrow streets from the river. Angel's heart quailed a little. She thought briefly of turning back to the shop, but after a moment's hesitation gave herself a firm internal shake. She took a shorter hold on her loyal dog's lead, forced herself to stride forward with confidence, and though she did pull her hood up as a partial protection against prying glances, she kept her head up and eyes fixed forward. But her heart thumped.

The roads were crowded. She was bumped several times, saved only from falling by the pressure of Brutus' solid body against her. And on two occasions it was only his threatening growl that kept her from being accosted by men that looked too interested. She began to count the blocks and to hurry a little more.

As she reached a corner of the main thoroughfare, a shadow detached itself from a wall and stood in front of her. Angel stifled a shriek. Brutus growled menacingly, moved in front of her, and pressed himself against her legs protectively.

'Miss Hathaway! Please, do not be alarmed, it is I, Tristan Neville.'

'*Ah le bon Dieu*!' breathed Angel. 'You gave me such a fright! You would have been well served if Brutus had attacked you!'

'As to that... if you could just call him off...'

'*A moi, Brutus. Ca suffit. Tu es un chien formidable.*' She ruffled his coat and scratched his ears. With just one more sidelong growl at Neville, and having done his job, he relaxed and panted happily at his mistress' side.

'That is a fine watchdog,' remarked Tristan. 'I shall never abuse him again, I swear.'

'Mr. Neville,' demanded Angel incredulously, 'have you been standing here all this time?'

'I have, actually,' he admitted. 'And I have had the most interesting time of it, too. I have discussed a cure for curbed hocks with a coster who gave me a very promising recipe for a poultice that he swears works a charm. I have discovered where I may find the very best flowers of the season for far less than the usual sellers will take me for in Covent Garden or on the steps of St. Paul's, and have paid well for this knowledge. I have observed many gay parties of weary but cheerful people in their workaday clothes going to the local for a pint after their day is done…'

'Mr. Neville, do not romanticize. I hardly think they were cheerful about lives that I know to be full of thankless drudgery…'

'Then the cheer must have been for the proximity of the tavern. But I must insist, Miss Hathaway, they were definitely cheerful. I have,' he continued, 'also turned down an invitation to join one especially rough-looking group who I feel sure would have been happy to roll me in an alley and rob me.'

'All admirable, sir. But you know of this world, surely. You and your friends are no stranger to either these streets or their various cockpits and taverns.'

'And whorehouses. I know you are not forgetting the whorehouses.'

'I was not,' she said primly. 'But a lady does not speak of these things.'

'As it should be,' he relented. 'But you know, I visit these neighborhoods always in the company of my own sort. We are always armed. We do not encourage familiarity. I am rarely alone as I have been this evening, to stand, and listen, and watch. It has been most edifying. And now I have the pleasure of walking you home, with the aid of your fierce dog. Your brother has forgotten you, has he not?'

'Yes,' Angel admitted. 'But I assure you, I do not require…'

'…my help. Oh, but you do, Miss Hathaway. Whether you like it or not, I would be less than a… er… *gentleman*… if I were to allow you to travel about these streets at dusk with only a dog for company. So try to make the best of mine, will you?' He offered her his arm. The dog growled. She shushed it, and took the arm.

'Your hand is so cold, Miss Hathaway. Have you nothing to cover your fingers?'

'I do well enough with my mittens, sir.'

He said nothing, but tucked her hand more securely into the crook of his elbow.

She admitted to herself that she was relieved. They walked, stiff and formal at first, and in relative silence. But Neville's ability to maintain a one-sided stream of amusing observation finally had the effect of making Angel relax and even chuckle, and finally respond. So that their brisk progress dwindled to a stroll. They talked of everything and nothing. They shared anecdotes of their lives and families. They laughed over mutual experiences with certain prominent London characters who would have blushed if they'd heard what was said about them. They found that they had much the same taste in reading, argued hotly about the execrable taste the other had in music, and shook their heads at the ridiculous extravagances of extreme fashion. If Angel made a literary or theatrical allusion, Tristan parried it neatly. If Tristan opined too generally on a topic of social or political importance, Angel put him on the spot with an incisive comment or question.

And far too quickly, they were on her street and at her gate. Suddenly shy and formal again, Angel thanked Tristan punctiliously for accompanying her this long way, and bid him a good night. She had ushered Brutus through the gate and was about to follow when he stopped her, blurting suddenly, 'Miss Hathaway. May I call on you?'

She hesitated, with a startled catch of breath. 'I… I think not, Mr. Neville,' she said, regaining her composure. 'For me… for you…' she steadied herself, and began again. 'Our worlds are so very different, you see. Mine will always be a curiosity to you. And I would be so very unwelcome in yours.'

'You are no doubt prudent, Miss Hathaway. But I think…'

'Mr. Neville,' Angel cut him off. 'I do not know how to say this… delicately… but say it I must. You have been in the habit of running tame about The Swan with your friends. You are aware of my mother's profession, and… and all the… *conjecture*… that accompanies it. And… because of the behavior of… certain members of The Swan's company… you may have developed an idea about those of us who are of a certain… station… that may have led you to some inaccurate conclusions.'

'Miss Hathaway…'

'No, you must let me finish, sir…'

'Miss Hathaway', he said more firmly, 'I do not think you a loose girl. When I first laid eyes on you I thought you were…'

'Something finer than I played?' supplied Angel, with an ironic smile.

Neville had the decency to look uncomfortable. 'Miss Hathaway, you do not mince words. Yes, then. Something finer. Something quite out of the ordinary, in fact. When I saw you in Madame Simard's shop… yes. I admit to being shocked. And disappointed.'

'And in that you were correct. Mr. Neville. Do you not see? It cannot be.'

'Miss Hathaway…' he hesitated, unsure what he should say next, and almost without thinking, implored, 'can we leave these larger questions aside? Just for now? It seems… I find… odd as it may be, wrong as it most probably is, Miss Hathaway… I do desire nothing more than the simple pleasure of your company.'

Angel's heart - O, so human and so young - gave a little skip at that. She studied Tristan's face and found nothing there but candor, and anxiety, and even a certain hopefulness.

'You do not even know me, sir.'

'I should like the opportunity to know you better,' he said.

She knew she should refuse. She knew it. But just this once… 'I will not sneak about in secrecy, Mr. Neville. And I most certainly will *not* be your mistress.'

'I would not dream… I would not *presume*…' he cleared his throat. 'I do not expect that, Miss Hathaway. But if, perhaps, we were occasionally to meet… and talk… or walk… on your… your…'

'My half day, Mr. Neville. You may call it what it is. There can be no pretense about what I am.'

He sighed. 'I would like to understand your world better, Miss Hathaway. I would like to try to make mine more comfortable for you.'

'Perhaps, sir. But now you must go.'

'*Au revoir*, Miss Hathaway.' He took her chapped hand and kissed it lightly. And they parted ways.

'*Merde,*' she muttered after he had disappeared into the mist, with a force that would have shocked her swain, had he heard it. 'Brutus, what have I done? Do you think I am being stupid?'

Brutus wagged his tail and grinned.

'No. Of course you don't, you silly dog.' She sighed and followed him through the gate.

*****

As she reached the side door she was alarmed to see a small, cloaked, human-shaped bundle curled beside it, weeping its heart out. Brutus trotted forward, wagging his tail and trying to lick the form's hidden face.

'Who's there?' asked Angel sharply.

The figure gasped, and rose stiffly. 'It is only I, Angel, Bridie Murphy. I did not… I did not know where else to come, Miss,' and she flung herself into Angel's surprised arms and burst into fresh tears.

'*Venez, venez,*' soothed Angel. 'Come into the kitchen, let's, and get you warm. *Venez ici.*' She struggled to unlock the door while holding on to Bridie and pushing the unhelpful dog out of the way, finally managing to wrestle all three parties into the warmth of the kitchen, lit only by the reflection of the banked fire on the walls. 'Sit, Bridie,' ordered Angel, settling her on a bench by the long table that was the kitchen's most prominent feature. She kicked the fire to life, kindled a lamp, set it in the middle of the table, collected a steaming kettle from the hob, and poured two mugs of cider, pushing one toward Bridie.

'There,' she said, finally, sitting next to the girl. 'Tell me what's amiss, then. Why are you not at The Swan? Is it that Badgeley? Has he bothered you again?'

'No! No, Angel, not that. No, it's...' she struggled against her tears, 'It's me mam, Angel. Me mam is gone.' She took a crumpled letter out of her pocket and flattened it out on the table. 'O, Angel, I got the letter just today, from me sister Mary 'twas, I had Mr. Hemings read it me. Mary... she said Mam was took with a fever and they thought... they thought she would come right after a few days but then of a sudden... O Angel, me Mam is dead,' sobs wracked her body. 'And now I'll never see her again, never. I shouldn't never have come here, I should have stayed home, stayed with Mary and Mam...' she pulled a handkerchief as crumpled as the letter had been and blew her nose violently. 'But they wouldn't have it, see. When me da passed... he was a teacher, he was, he taught all of us in the towns around our letters, only that I was never so good in the way of it, see, the letters, I couldn't make 'em be still, but I could remember most anything I heard, could sing and dance with him on the road, like, for some extra coin, only the traveling was hard, Miss, so hard... so when he died of an ague and left Mam with the six of us, 'twas,' she blew her nose again. 'and me brother Seamus no more than a babe in arms...' she stifled a sob, 'me Mam and Mary, they said to me, Bridie, you got to go on now, you're the beauty, you can sing and dance, you got to cross the water and be like that Mrs. Jordan, that Dorothea Bland as was, or them Gunning sisters what married Dukes or some such. And so I come to London, and I been sending money home to them regular, I have, and I thought I'd go back, see, in a carriage with fine horses and fine clothes on me, but O Angel, none of it matters anymore, none of it, because me Mammy is gone and I can never help her and I been nothing but a fool.' She wept again, helplessly. 'O, Angel,' she managed finally through her tears, 'Mr. Pearce and Madame, they told me I shouldn't go onstage tonight. But I couldn't be in that little room all by meself, with nothing but stupid girls about me, no more I could. So walked and walked and walked 'til it got dark, and then I come here, and I hope you don't mind, miss. I didn't know whatever to do. I don't know how to go along without me mam.'

'Of course not,' said Angel, thinking fast. 'You must stay here with us. There's a truckle bed in my chamber, if you don't mind sharing a room with me. But I am so sorry, Bridie,' she hugged the unhappy girl.

There was half a loaf of bread left from breakfast, and some cheese, and a bit of stew still warm in the pot over the fire. Angel laid all of these out on the table and refilled their cups. Jacob came in well before they had finished eating, greatly relieved to find Angel at home, 'for,' he said, 'Stephen was detained from coming to meet you by a brush with the law.'

'With the law!' exclaimed Angel. 'Oh no, what on earth can have happened!'

'That's for Stephen to tell, which he will, presently. But your mama sent me out to find you, and as I found the shop shut up and you gone home alone, I was right worried for you, Angel. You should have waited. You knew I would come, at need.'

'I'm sorry for your trouble, Jacob,' Angel said contritely. She repeated her story, stumbling only slightly when she came to the part that involved Tristan Neville, at whose name Jacob's gaze intensified and Bridie looked up in interest. But she skated over it quickly and brought her story to its end with the discovery of Bridie on the stoop.

Jacob stated his condolences to Bridie with a kindly voice. He told her how it was that he had lost his own parents, when he had been sold away from them and taken to a new home far away. How he had resisted and had been beaten, and tried to run away, and been beaten even worse. 'It was a terrible time, to be without them,' he said.

'But…' asked Bridie, wide-eyed, 'did you never find them again?'

'No, Bridie, I never,' said Jacob.

Bridie looked from Jacob to Angel, wonder in her eyes. 'Then we're all the same, an't we,' she said. 'All lost souls.'

'Except we in this room are blessed with friends,' Jacob pointed out. 'A roof over our heads. Enough to eat, most days, and good work to do. The way I see it, that's all our mamas and our papas would have dreamed for us. So do you look at it that way, we honor them every day, by being. And that is how we must remember them, by what we are become.'

*****

Sometime later, Stephen came in with Marianne and Seraphine and found Angel and Bridie still at the table, talking. The two women immediately took Bridie in hand and bustled her upstairs to find dry clothes and make up the truckle bed while Stephen sat by his sister to explain his abandonment of her.

'The *law*, Stephen!' Angel exclaimed in disbelief before he could begin. 'Jacob says you were taken up by the *law*!'

'*Vraiment, ce n'était pas de ma faute!*' protested her brother defensively. 'Do but listen, Angel, *s'il te plaît*. I went to a coffee shop and met there a group of emigrés - Girondists, who fled Robespierre. They were so interesting, these men, full of information from inside France, of how the Revolution has evolved into something far more radical than ever it was, so that…'

'Stephen!' interrupted Angel. 'How were you taken up by the authorities?'

'Another patron overheard us speaking in French - we had become, perhaps, louder than we ought - and thought we were plotting a revolution in England.' He barked a laugh. '*Quel idiot.* He called the authorities and we were detained. The others had papers to prove themselves, *mais moi-meme*, what do I know of papers, who arrived on a Britisher from Canada less than a month since? What do I know of this ridiculous Aliens Act, me? I was brought before a justice of the peace who found me in violation and threatened me with prison. I was never so angry, Angel. I was hours arguing with this man, who was bound that I am a Jacobin spy with a false identity. *Enfin,* I mentioned *Maman* and it seems this justice of the peace is her great admirer. *Alors,* even this relationship he doubted, and nothing would do but I must escort the gentleman to the theatre to make *Maman*'s acquaintance and prove it.'

Angel, listening to this story open-mouthed, began to giggle. 'Oh, Stephen,' she said unsteadily. 'I am so sorry you had such a day. But the thought of you being paraded to the theatre by a... a... justice of the peace.... Were you bound?'

'*Oui! Par les mains*! Stop laughing! It was humiliating in the extreme!'

'I am sorry, *mon frere*, but... oh, it is too absurd!' and she went off into gales of laughter.

'*Oui, c'est ca*,' Stephen admitted with a grin, 'It was absurd. And then to see this silly, self-important fellow *fawning* over *Maman*, while she came over all *Francaise* and fluttery...' he demonstrated with waving hands and fluttering eyelashes.

'I can picture it...' managed Angel...

'...So that finally he must admit that I am indeed the... er... *fortunate son of such an illustrious mother...*'

'Oh, no, he did not say that!'

'*Main sur mon coeur, il se dit*. And then promised her - she is utterly outrageous, you know, she was gazing at him with her eyes *comme ca* -' he pantomimed fatuous adoration - 'that he would have the proper document ready for me tomorrow morning, and I have but to collect it to end... erm... *all my troubles while on these sceptered shores*. Graciously, as if he were the King.' Stephen bowed with a kingly flourish, sending Angel into whoops.

'Oh well done!' she crowed, clapping her hands. 'Our clever *Maman*.'

'Yes. I should be disapproving, I feel, but she is...' his brow wrinkled with effort, 'how do these English say it... a... a Complete Hand, *c'est vrai?*'

'*Oui*. A complete hand.'

He nodded, then added seriously, 'But to hear these *Girondists*, Angel, who love their country and are now refugees with nothing to their names... all they have been through, and to be in England with no jobs or prospects... there are so many like them in the streets, Angel, not just French, but other nations, too, who come here in hope or in desperation. Needing so much. Your England cannot be so blessed when there are those who lack even basic necessities. There is a great deal to be done to aid them, *ma soeur*. I have it in mind that I may help, somehow.'

And the next day, he unpacked his kit in his attic room, and set about finding space for his medicaments and instruments in the kitchen pantry. Marianne, with her own wide experience in herbs, fungi, bark, and unguents, took a deep interest in his actions, and before long they were deep in discussion about the merits of this salve or that tonic, each adding to the other's store of knowledge. When Stephen deplored the lack of a certain ingredient, Marianne offered to show him where it might be found, or pointed out a certain small and innocuous plant now growing in her medicinal garden that, when gathered at the right moment and processed in the right way, might provide similar results. They both understood well the responsibility inherent in handling these plants, and in not allowing the tincture of one to contaminate the jar of another. Some plants were healing, if the leaves were crushed or steeped or infused, but deadly poison if raw or if the roots were powdered; some had healing properties no matter what parts were used; others only when in a very particular state of maturity. And both recognized that, while the established medical professions discredited these old remedies or viewed them with suspicion, use of them had to be judicious, and, for Stephen's purposes, as an adjunct to the recognised practices for which he desired to become licensed.

His knowledge was put to use sooner than expected, when The Swan's foreman Jeremy fell from the stage rigging and broke an arm an hour before curtain. Stephen oversaw the careful moving of the man to the green room table, then set and splinted the bone. While he was occupied with these arduous and - to the victim painful - tasks, he sent Marianne to procure a list of medicines from the house, and she returned forthwith to help ease the poor man's pain and apply healing tinctures and unguents before binding of the whole in clean, undyed and unsized muslin from the costume shop. Stephen also forced his patient to drink a powerfully foul tincture that he said would guard against infection despite Jeremy's resistance and howls that he and the blackie were trying to kill him, so they were. Only the unflinching intervention of both Pearce and Mrs. Hathaway quelled the man, and the tincture duly swallowed.

The scene struck fear into the hearts of the other stage hands, for they depended on and trusted Jeremy, and were liable to believe what the now blessedly unconscious man had shouted out about Mr. Hathaway and Mrs. Freeman. It took dire threats from Pearce about deliberate injury to life and limb to get a mutinous crew back to work. The show eventually went off without a hitch, though the mood backstage remained volatile.

'In truth, Hathaway,' apologized Pearce afterward, 'they're an ignorant lot, and superstitious. If it isn't the sawbones with his laudenum and his leeches, they don't think anything good can come of it.'

'If it makes them feel better, I can certainly find leeches, though I would as soon just bleed the man and be done.'

'Perhaps. And perhaps 't'would be better if Mrs. Freeman were not helping dispense the medicaments. The fact that she...'

'Is African?' Stephen finished, face flushing with anger.

Pearce looked uncomfortable. 'I was going to say, because she is a woman. But as you have mentioned it...'

'I'll not allow superstition or prejudice to determine my choice of assistant, Cousin Pearce,' warned Stephen. 'But,' he breathed and steadied himself, 'you needn't worry. I've experienced this sort of trouble shipboard. One of our surgeon's mates was an African whose touch, it appeared, was repugnant to a swabbie who had broken a leg. It took three strong men to hold him down, just so as to set a bone that had come right through the skin, and...'

'Yes, yes, I'm quite sure,' said Pearce hurriedly, turning rather green. 'I'm sure you're correct, young Stephen. When Jeremy comes back to work, they'll doubtless be clamoring for none but you. And Mrs. Freeman.'

And so it proved when Jeremy, healing quickly enough to hold court and deliver orders to all his underlings from an ancient armchair brought onstage for him from the green room, his arm well wrapped and in a sling, changed his accusations of murder to songs of praise for Mr. Hathaway and 'that clever Mrs. Freeman'. So Stephen and Marianne found themselves in demand for every ailment and injury that might be suffered by a human being working in a theatre. Not one of these people could pay, but Pearce saw to it that Stephen was well fed, 'for', as he put it, 'a long drink of water like yourself might well eat his mother out of house and home, else, so you might as well do some of that eating here.' Small gifts appeared, too: a posy of flowers 'to brighten the senses, like'. A fresh-caught fish from an appreciative husband. Some mending that a grateful wife might undertake. In the meantime Stephen began to spend more time in the coffee houses and taverns frequented by emigrés, where he might speak the language of his home, and where he and Marianne were able to work their way into a community that badly needed the services they could offer. Stephen Hathaway began to think that London might not be such a bad place, after all.

*****

Bridie's entry into an already crowded household was not uneventful. Having grown up in a large family in much poorer surroundings, she was not afraid of work, and became indispensable at once in helping with the shopping and the mending and the cleaning. This was of course what Bridie most hoped for, since the Hathaway household improved her circumstances exponentially.

More difficult was her love of drama. Wallowing in the injustice done her by Edward Badgeley, she embraced the role of poor, cast-off waif, which, coupled with a strong if misplaced sense of guilt regarding the death of her mother, made her prone to very public dramatic languishing. Backstage, her melting sighs might gain a rapt audience of sympathetic opera dancers. In the Hathaway household, she was ordered by Seraphine to pull herself together, and by Stephen to stop flouting her charms about the house like a Covent Garden Nun, 'unless, of course, you intend to live your life as a whore, in which case, do it elsewhere.' When she attempted to treat Jacob and Marianne - both of them better spoken, better educated, better traveled, and more worldly than she would ever be - as a lower form of servant, they looked at her with such a mingling of mild surprise and pity that instead of feeling important, she felt small and stupid. And when, in a fit of pique, she announced to Angel that she had a mind to 'shift off to lodgings where a lass might have a bit of fun', Angel merely remarked that she would be glad to have her chamber to herself again.

Then, when life looked its most dire, someone would praise her for a task well done, or ask her opinion on the general treatment of the dancers that proliferated on the City's stages, and listen to her answers. And she would decide to stay, and become the lady she aspired to being.

For his part, Chance River thrived in his new job as an assistant to the master builder of one of the fleet new clippers being built in the London Pool. He was a perfectionist, was River, and demanded perfection of those working under him. In his world, attention to detail saved lives, not just ships. The fact that he knew ocean-going vessels inside and out made him a valuable employee. The fact that he had been at sea for so many of his years, and had seen so many places and had so many experiences, made him a font both of ideas and of stories - hilarious, gruesome, and cautionary by turns - that made him a popular figure among the other men. And the fact that he was one of them - born and raised by the water and loving its every mood, loving the boats that worked it, knowing the bells that announced the times of day and the conditions of the weather - made it easy to accept him.

If there was the odd jealous man or two who thought to ambush Chance on his dark walk home and cut him down to size, well. Of the few bruised and battered men that reported to work the day after such an attempt, none was Chance. Likability, he knew well, was easy; respect had to be earned. Having learned this with his fists aboard many ships in many ports, he understood to the fraction how much the lessons of respect must cost, and how heavy their burden must be.

The master was aging, and a man of Chance's ability and ambition might well aspire to his position and its benefits in time, if he learned well and played his hand right. This thought allowed Chance to dream of a small terrace house of his own, maybe one of the new ones in the vicinity of Bedford Square, where he might remove his ma from the endless drudgery of her life and give her some of the ease she so richly deserved for the time she had left. And if he had a wife... someone like Bridie Murphy, for instance... and if they all kept working to help to earn their way into that new lodging... well, they might just be able to pull it off. He still had the better part of the prize money earned from several of his voyages. He was not without the means to dream.

He went to The Swan most nights. Sometimes Molly came with him, and they would sit together in the audience. Other times she slyly suggested that he wouldn't be wanting her in the way, which made him blush. Chance made no secret of his admiration for Bridie Murphy. Sometimes he brought her a flower 'that was the gold of her hair,' or 'the blue of her eyes'. Bridie, used to far richer gifts than primroses and cornflowers, was at first merely polite on receiving these offerings from his callused hands. But the admiring looks Chance received from the other girls, several of whom did their best to turn his attention from Bridie, led to a stab of jealousy, and the glimmer of a new attraction. Surreptitiously, she began to look for Chance's solid form sitting by the curtain in the prompt corner with Hemings. On the nights that he was not in attendance, she felt oddly piqued.

Her former lover Badgeley, who without ever knowing it had started the evolution of an entirely new state in this very small but deeply human corner of the world, gave up going to The Swan altogether, declaring it very poor entertainment. He was often preoccupied with matters of his upcoming nuptials, the heady receipt of his fortune, and even a passing interest in his bride.

He continued to enjoy his usual schedule of visits to Tat's, or Jackson's, or Brooks', or the Promenade, or even the lower forms of entertainment provided by cockpits and bare knuckle boxing. The latest gaming hells that throve on separating young blades from their money and required secret passwords or the sponsorship of a crony could never fail to be of interest. And there were social occasions that marked the Season - routs, suppers, trips to Ranelagh; not to mention the odd dollybird that still aroused and then slaked his lust.

But even these delights seemed not to hold his attention in the way they had done formerly. Neville and Kilronan wondered how a simple female could bring about these changes in their rackety friend; Miss Henrietta Attenborough could have told them. She merely looked to Badgeley for guidance in all matters of fashion and the world. She asked him for answers and advice.

She made him indispensable. Badgeley would never know how brilliantly tactical Henrietta's actions were, but the simple device of being treated as an intelligent and capable man steered him unconsciously in the direction of behaving more like one.

Of course her actions were calculated. Of course most of the advice she got from him was complete rubbish. But Henrietta did not want to die a spinster, nor would she settle for a mere Mister. She had been raised in the expectation of an aristocratic marriage. She now required it just as surely as Badgeley required the fortune that would keep him from ruin. Having erred grossly in holding her self-worth too high during her years on the Marriage Mart, with neither dazzling beauty nor a bottomless fortune to offer as an attractive challenge to the highest of eligible bachelors, she had lost no time in acting decisively when her childhood friend Ned laid out the scale of his grievances to his childhood friend. No other lady must have the opportunity to solve Badgeley's pressing money problems simply by saying 'Yes'. Having attached him with lightning speed, she set about the longer game of subtly shaping the young man to her ideas by allowing him to think that they were his own. Henrietta Attenborough was wasted as a woman; she would have made a brilliant military commander.

'I'll tell you what it is, Tris,' said Sir Robert mournfully one day, as they made their way back to Town from an exceedingly gruesome hanging that had proven to be one of the chief social events of the week because of the famous highwayman that met his demise that day. 'Badgeley's becoming a dead bore. Reminds me more and more of his father. Get up there!' he judiciously flicked his whip at the nearside horse of the eye-catching skewbald pair he'd acquired to draw a phaeton rented for the Season. 'I'll lay you a pony that Attenborough chit is at the bottom of it. Frighteningly capable, that woman.'

Tristan laughed. 'You're one to talk, you and your widow. Now there's a winter campaign, if you want my opinion.'

''Tis a work in progress, a work in progress,' opined Sir Robert piously. 'Nothing determined, nothing spoken. But you know, Tris,

I could do worse than a woman like that. She keeps a damn fine stable. Her house is orderly and her staff excellent. And she has plenty of blunt, which is something I need, old son.'

'How you can even contemplate a union with that woman and her irritating, starchy ways…'

'A man may contemplate far worse than that, when he has a gun to his head.'

'Do you, Robin?' asked Neville, startled. 'Have a gun to your head?'

'My pockets are all to let, old son, truth be known. My estates in Meath will take a packet to restore. I've three sisters of marriageable age, and no Mama to present them. I am duty bound to continue the line with an heir. And before you say I can do better than Lady Underwood, let me just tell you that I won't hear a word against her. I'm serious, Neville.'

'Point taken, my dear. I'm sorry if I misspoke. But you cannot tell me you love her. That's doing it too brown.'

'I don't. My heart, such as it is, has been given to no avail.' He glanced briefly, longingly, at Tristan, then quickly back to the road to steer his team around a coach that lurched into their path, loaded with very drunk and merry young men who hung off of every surface in a state of high jollity. Nothing like a hanging to make people grab at life with both hands.

'I know you guess, Tris, how it is with me,' Sir Robert continued, with another sideways glance. 'I will say only that Hannah and I understand one another… very… well.'

'Ahhh,' said Tristan carefully. 'One has heard whispers…'

'Let them stay but whispers. She gave her late husband the heir he needed, and more than enough extras. She has indicated that she is not yet too old to offer me the same, after which we may do as we please and be friends. And for that simple favor she will rescue my family from penury and me from hanging for my sins.'

'Then what's in it for her, if you don't mind my asking?'

'I would lend her and her children a home, the security of controlling what is rightly hers, and countenance. She is a considerable heiress, Tris, and of course in her current state the target of every kind of fortune hunter, any one of whom will certainly bleed her dry given the chance.

'Of which you are one, I might point out.'

'Naturally. The difference being that I do not wish to bleed her dry. I wish only to live my life as I may, which is her wish as well. We offer one another a mutual understanding which cannot but make up for all the rest.'

'Will you stay in England, then?'

'Ah, now that's the beauty of it, me boyo. My estates have some of the best hunting country - and the finest horses - in our fair isle. To spend time in Ireland will be a pleasure to us both, as we share a passion for hunting, racing, and horse breeding. And then, perhaps, my sisters might join us here for the Season to be brought out and respectably married in their turn. Apart from that, we may come and go as we please.'

'A mutually beneficial business contract. Impressive, Robin.'

'Thank-you.'

'If it comes to pass that she agrees to marry you.'

'I have painted what I feel is an irresistable portrait for the lady, and you know, Tris,' he simpered and fluttered his long lashes seductively, 'I can be very persuasive.'

Tristan laughed. 'Robin, you are incorrigible,' he vowed.

'Yes, but if it does come to pass that Lady Underwood will agree to be my wife, I will count myself the most fortunate man who ever married out of desperation.'

'What, including Badgeley?' exclaimed Tristan, feigning horror.

'Well, perhaps I shouldn't go *that* far,' Sir Robert admitted, and they laughed so uproariously that Sir Robert's parti-colored pair attempted to bolt and nearly unbalanced Sir Robert's groom, who grabbed a handily placed leather safety strap and swore.

Not long after, Sir Robert's equipage and its elegant skewbalds swept around Grosvenor Square with a flourish and set Mr. Neville down in front of his lodgings. Instead of immediately going in, Tristan gazed about at an early evening that continued unusually fine. Gentlewomen and gentlemen strolled in the square, nurses sat on benches gossiping while they watched small children dashing about on stubby legs with hoops, balls, and toy boats in hand. Even the ragman and the delivery boys looked hopeful. Tristan set off at a brisk walk toward Jermyn Street with a suddenly invented errand to attend to at a small shop near the Arcade, and was rewarded as he came out, small parcel in hand, to see Miss Hathaway, attended by the faithful Brutus and the watchful Jacob, coming out from the alley that housed *Chez Simard*.

Angel had changed the workaday pinafore that covered her simple rose-colored muslin dress for a spencer jacket of deeper hue to keep off the chill, and a gay chip hat decorated with spring flowers and ribbons of rose, lilac, and cream. The whole set off her dark hair and ivory complexion to a nicety, and every inch of her was, to Tristan's eyes, modest and beautiful. A close observer might sniff that the garment was not in its first youth, but had been repurposed from an older one which had been carefully cleaned, then redesigned to disguise evidence of old stains or places where the color had slightly faded. But the wearer showed it off as if it were made of the finest of new materials. And then there were the eyes, those green eyes that sparkled as he drew near and nearly overset Tristan's dignity.

'Miss Hathaway,' he greeted her, sweeping his hat off with a bow. 'What a surprise to meet you here. How do you do, Mr. Freeman. Hello, Brutus, no, don't jump, you horror, I don't want to be all over dog hair and slobber, I thank-you.' He sidestepped the enthusiastic dog neatly as Angel commanded him back to her side and smiled up at Tristan.

'What clever timing on your part, sir,' she laughed. 'I might almost believe it to be deliberate.'

'Well then, Miss Hathaway, you've bubbled me, for you were in fact the intent of my journey.' He fell in beside her. 'Mr. Freeman', he suggested meaningfully, 'perhaps you will allow me to escort Miss Hathaway home.'

'Mr. Freeman will certainly *not* allow anything so improper,' rumbled Jacob firmly. 'But if the lady approves, you may accompany us.'

'The lady approves,' dimpled Angel, and although Tristan would have much preferred to have this beautiful girl to himself, he acquiesced with grace.

'You have strict guardians, Miss Hathaway,' he observed.

'Would you have it otherwise, sir?' she asked quizzically.

'Selfishly, yes. Both dog and man are dreadfully *de trop*. But... no, Miss Hathaway. I would not have it otherwise.'

'Then I am content,' said Angel.

'As am I,' added Jacob.

They strolled awhile in companionable silence, with a question whose surface lightheartedness had answered one that was deeper, and infinitely more important.

At length, silence gave way to conversation. Angel regaled the others with stories of the foibles of the clients that had come through *Chez Simard* in recent days, and the ridiculous heights certain customers' tastes went to as they sought to outshine others in their group, or the lengths that certain young bloods were willing to go to procure just the thing to attach a certain young lady of easy virtue, or to mollify a jealous young wife. She was careful to leave out names, but he recognised some acquaintances instantly from her humorous and pointedly accurate assessments. Since he had been the target of at least one of her barbs in the recent past, he began to wonder if there had been others, a thought that made him both awkward and resentful, agreeing with Mr. Shakespeare's Benedick that *she speaks daggers, and every word stabs.*

'But how have you spent your days, sir?' Angel asked him with an encouraging smile that jolted him from this unproductive reverie.

'I, as a man of no useful occupation, have spent my days fully indulging in pastimes of absolutely no worth whatsoever,' he said with a lightness that was a little forced. 'I fenced with the great Domenico and was thoroughly humiliated. I was forced to dance attendance at Almack's and was bored nearly to death. I gambled on an illegal prize fight in someone's dark stable and lost a great deal of money. I went to Brooks' and won it all back at Casino...'

'No, you didn't! Really?'

'S'truth,' he swore solemnly.

Angel studied him, torn between laughter and concern. 'But are you one of those frippery fellows who will be content to waste his days and his talents on nothing that matters? I would not have thought it.'

'And are you,' retorted Tristan, stung, 'one of those dull puritanical misses that must disparage those who are not forever doing good deeds and supporting worthy causes?'

Jacob choked down a laugh.

Angel blushed. 'Perhaps I am being unfair, sir,' she said coolly. 'It is not, after all, my business how you spend your days.'

Tristan sighed. 'Let us not quarrel, Miss Hathaway. You are quite right: I do not intend to be merely a frippery fellow, but even now am casting about for a useful occupation. But I hope you will not judge me harshly, Miss Hathaway, if I continue in my passion for fast horses, a certain amount of gaming and swordplay, and general gaiety.'

'How could I hold that against you, Mr. Neville, when I nurture a passion for beautiful things and have, I confess, never championed a worthy cause in my life that I am aware of?'

'Except for your kindness to animals.'

She laughed. 'Few would call that worthy. *Idiotic* is the kindest word I've heard. But what sort of *worthy* occupation attracts you?'

'I was thinking, perhaps, the law. Just today I saw the notorious Jem Banderall swing for his many sins. It was the social event of the season, I never saw such a crush of people so vastly entertained by the sight of such a rascally fellow dancing and soiling himself at the end... Miss Hathaway, are you all right?'

Angel had stopped moving and stood in the center of the path, color drained from her face. 'Oh,' she uttered. 'Oh. I am so sorry, Mr. Neville, but I cannot... that poor man. It was France, you see... Every day, there were... hangings. Innocent people... friends...' she shuddered and closed her eyes as if to ward off the visions, the purpled, contorted faces, the stench of emptied bowels, the bodies hanging like so much meat, the way her father had tried to pull her away, hide her face, but she could never unsee the horror...

Neville exchanged a quick look with Jacob, who nodded toward a bench. He sat her there gently and took her chapped hands between his strong ones. 'I am so sorry, so sorry. My dear... Miss Hathaway... I was insensitive. I had forgotten all that you have been through. It may help to know that Banderall was a ruthless criminal, who caused a great many people pain and suffering. I would not be averse to helping rid the world of his sort.' He dared not - could not - add that all he wanted this present was to hold Angel Hathaway in his arms and take her somewhere where she should never have to experience such fear again. Instead, when she regained her color and balance and was able to stand, he tucked her hand in the crook of his elbow and guided her forward, talking of occupations he had found attractive as a young boy - chimney sweep, pirate, ostler - until she finally remembered how to laugh. When they reached the garden gate, Jacob tactfully walked through it and left the young people alone. 'But mind you follow directly,' he admonished Angel.

With Jacob gone, Tristan brought a small packet out of his pocket and handed it to Angel.

'What...?' she asked, confused.

'A small token only, Miss Hathaway.'

'But you must not, sir. I cannot accept...'

'Believe me, Miss Hathaway, it is nothing that can offend, I feel. I am known to be the most unromantic and hideously practical man alive.'

'This from your vast experience of womankind?'

'Yes. And we need say no more than that. Good night, Miss Hathaway,' he bowed and kissed her fingers lightly. 'Until we meet again.'

'You'd best watch yourself, Angel,' said Jacob from the shadows where he had retreated. 'Young Neville may be a right one, but I'll wager, not for you.'

'I know. Oh, Jacob, I know.'

But every part of her vibrated with passion and longing, swept along on the powerful riptide of the human imperative to couple, to mate, to procreate, to love.

When they entered the kitchen, brightly lit with fire and lamp, and redolent of a hearty meat pie for supper, she unwrapped the packet. In it lay a beautifully made pair of ivory kid gloves, each figured with roses and vines. With a swelling heart, she tried them on and flexed her fingers. How welcome these would be in the cool mornings and evenings for her aching fingers. She smiled, and held her softly gloved hands to her face, breathing in the scent of clean leather and linen thread, bathed in this one perfect and transient moment by the love of a beautiful, practical man.

*****

After the lights were down and the music ended, the adrenaline and hard work of playing *As You Like It* in front of a full and boisterous house drained from Seraphine, replaced by a wave of weariness. In the relative quiet of her dressing room, she removed her costume pieces - both women's weeds and male garb - and put them away to be brushed and cleaned later. Her famed Rosalind, who wins her love while protesting that *love is merely a madness* (to the sighs of the ladies) and *my love hath an unknown bottom… like the Bay of Portugal* (eliciting whoops from the men) was always a favorite. Her famous legs, covered to the knees by a richly embroidered tunic and amply protected from there to her boots with heavy, many-buttoned leather garters that added a full inch to their proportion without displaying an inch of flesh or stocking, still had the power to elicit whistles from the men and more than a little wishful envy among adventurous women. She found these roles - Rosalind, Viola, Imogen - freeing; young women who spoke their minds and controlled their destinies with clever wordplay and a bit of a wink. With words in their mouths that no respectable female could venture safely in daily life. Of course, the roles had been played by boys in Shakespeare's time, leading, no doubt, to a great deal of confusion to audiences faced with boys playing girls playing boys. The return of theatre-loving Charles II to the throne of England a hundred or more years since had birthed a new category of player, that of 'actress', for which Seraphine and others like her stood in gratitude. It was a good profession, if a demanding one. Seraphine hoped that frugality, stringent savings, and the gainful employment of her children might keep her from destitution when the time came to retire.

But this was fatigue talking. She shook herself, rubbed her face clean of makeup, and massaged it with the floral cream that Marianne had sworn would keep her complexion youthful. Then she clothed herself in the beautiful mystery dress that had become her favorite, pinned her hair up, and set off to the supper room.

As she worked her way through the crush trading good wishes and bandying light but unexceptionable retorts to those whose ardor wanted cooling, a hand touched her arm, and a familiar voice said smoothly, 'I have your supper here, *Madame*, and your table ready. Your pardon, *mesdames, messieurs*, but I must claim the lady.'

'Mr. Neville,' she said coolly. 'I never thought to see you again, sir.' And then swiftly amended herself. 'Not that I am not delighted, of course.'

'It is the prospect of food, and not my appearance, that elicits such delight, I feel sure,' he said drily, steering her to a chair and setting the plate he carried in front of her.

'Hunger is, I admit, my motivating emotion, at the moment.' She eyed the food anxiously. 'I wonder, sir, if you will give me a withering setdown if I attack this meal with unladylike abandon.'

'I will endeavor to hold my tongue,' he said nobly, and watched, eyes lit with amusement, while Seraphine set to with gusto.

'What brings you to The Swan, sir?' she asked between bites. 'When I know you to hold in contempt the...' her brow creased in thought '...pretenses of ... what did you call it... *play-acting*?'

'I was told that Madame Seraphine's legs were something not to be missed, ma'am.'

She stared at him suspiciously, a forkful of peas suspended halfway to her mouth. 'And did they live up to your expectations, sir?'

'Do eat your peas before they fall from your fork,' he said. 'The suspense is killing me.'

'You are the most provoking man!' she complained, and ate the peas.

'Yes,' he agreed. 'I've often been told so. You look charmingly in that particular dress, ma'am.'

'Oh,' she laughed. 'It is the most mysterious thing possible. It arrived on day...' She stopped, and her eyes widened. 'You!' she said, food forgotten. 'It was you who sent it me.'

He bowed slightly.

'But... *why*?'

'I have been called many vile things by women in my life,' he mused elliptically. 'I have been slapped, I have had heavy domestic objects hurled at my head, and I have endured any number of episodes of both the vapours and strong hysterics. But never has a woman risked life and limb by dramatically leaping from my carriage, ma'am. And torn what I feel was a rather fine garment in the process. For that, an apology was required.'

'But I can't accept… this was surely not…'

'On this I remain firm, Mrs. Hathaway. It is not a gift, but a reparation. And I hope you will accept it, as I remember you admired it.'

'Then… thank-you, sir. I accept the…the reparation. You leave me… a little speechless, sir.'

'You astonish me, ma'am.'

'I also think you did not come to The Swan to see my legs, *m'sieu.*'

'No, Mrs. Hathaway,' he said gently. 'I did not. I told you that I would look for your husband.'

'I did not expect…'

'I honor my promises, *Madame.* I am just lately returned to Town from some business abroad. And while in Paris, I am very sorry to report, I did find the trail of George Hathaway.'

'And he is dead.'

'Yes.'

She paled, and sat silent, staring vacantly at her hands, now clenched together in her lap. 'And you know this because…'

'Because he was betrayed by another. He had been working in a printers' shop, under the name of Pearce. But someone in that shop recognized him, and laid information against him. He was taken in the night, from his bed, and imprisoned.'

'Oh, no. Oh, George… he suffered from weak lungs, sir…'

'Just so. He faced neither noose nor guillotine, but died of a fever of the lung in prison, less than a year after you arrived here.'

'Oh my God. If I'd stayed! If I'd been there to…'

'You and your daughter would have suffered a similar fate, *Madame.*'

'There is no chance, no possibility…'

'None. Mrs. Hathaway, please believe me. Your husband is gone. You already suspected it. Now you must accept it.'

She looked around her blindly. 'I must leave you, sir. I must…' she started to rise but before she could move, Neville was on his feet and at her side.

'I will escort you, ma'am. We will use the side entrance, so you will not be disturbed.'

'No! Sir…' she tried to pull away, but he held her close, putting his form between her and the rest of the room.

'This way,' He steered her through the curtain into the side hallway, and waited by the stage door while she gathered her cloak and belongings, having notified Hemings that Mrs. Hathaway had received a bad shock and must now go home. Hemings, always astute, looked sharply at Neville. 'Her husband?'

'Even so.'

'Don't you worry none, sir. I'll notify Mr. Pearce and close up here. No, no, sir. I don't need no payment. But here's our Mrs. Hathaway, sir. Goodnight, sir. Goodnight to you, ma'am.'

It was a soft night, barely drizzling, close and dark. A lamp in front of them bobbed with the stride of its young holder, who was assiduous in pointing out puddles, uneven cobbles, treacherous piles of horse and dog shit, and curbs that randomly protruded from optimistic walkways.

Neville made no effort to break into Seraphine's reverie, but remained a solid and comforting presence by her side. When they arrived at her gate, she allowed him to pay the lamp boy, who she suggested had earned a handsome tip, and bid him thanks and goodnight. With a sigh, she lit a taper from the lamp left burning on the hall table, and set about gently awakening the household. It was a solemn and subdued gathering that sat around the kitchen table after Seraphine repeated the details of Neville's news. There were no tears yet; time's passage made the news less a shock than sorry confirmation of what each had suspected anyway.

Even so, to know it, to comprehend it, meant something different to each person in the room. To Seraphine, the loss of a gentle soul who had given her the protection of his name at a time when she sorely needed it.

To Angel, a father who had doted on her, told her stories as she sat in his lap, taught her to read both French and English and to develop a neat hand for writing and figuring.

To Stephen, a threat to the bond between mother and son, but also a firm mentor who had taught him to speak and understand English as fluently as his native French, insisted that he think clearly and rationally rather than acting through blind passion, and taught him - sometimes harshly, always effectively - that when taking dead things apart to see how they worked, the primary motive must be compassion for the life that had departed. Compassion was not a condition familiar to Stephen in his early years, except from his mother. But he learned it well from George Hathaway.

To Marianne, Hathaway had been an employer and champion of her skills as a healer, which he encouraged her to pursue and perfect in the event that she might someday be allowed to practice in public as a respected member of the society that so far showed little sign of honoring her personhood.

To Jacob, the hand that pulled him to safety, giving him purpose, position, and the possibility of a future.

To Bridie, who had no role in the proceedings but couldn't resist sitting in, it was a reminder of the mother she had but so lately lost, and she wept quietly and bitterly from her place at the table, with the candle flickering in the center and playing over all of the expressions on all of the faces as they sat in the shadows and grieved.

'There is no hope at all that Mr. Neville could be wrong?' asked Angel, after a long interlude.

'None, I fear,' said Seraphine.

'Stephen?' asked Angel imploringly. 'Do you think...'

Stephen shook his head. 'We have all known in our hearts that he was gone,' he said. 'When I finally received his letter, I knew how to find you. But nobody could tell me about our father. Only that the house had been searched and ransacked just after all of you left, then set to the torch.'

Angel choked back a sob. 'Then how can we mourn him properly, not knowing? How can we honor him, with no body, no grave?'

'We honor him with our actions,' said Seraphine. 'Every day. And we mourn him together, in our hearts. And, my dears,' she added gently, 'Although his death is long past, it is still very new to us. So may I suggest that we allow ourselves some few days to mourn and to remember him, without the intrusion of the larger world.'

Bridie, who had stopped weeping, dabbed at her eyes, and said in a small voice, 'If it's all right, ma'am, may I stay with you? I never have been able to grieve me mam proper, see, with no funeral nor no wake. And I would be that grateful if I could just… be with you. And if we was to have a sort of service of our own, just something small, in the garden, maybe, then perhaps… could I sing a little? 'Twould make it seem more proper, an I could sing a bit.'

'Of course, Bridie,' said Seraphine, looking at her as if for the first time. '*C'est une ideé de toute beauté.*'

'We must notify my cousin Pearce,' said Angel. 'And Madame Simard.'

'Hemings will do so,' said Seraphine. 'But Jacob, would you mind…'

'I'll tell those who require it,' he assured her.

And so it was settled, and the family went to their separate beds, with their separate thoughts. All relieved that years of not knowing were now put to rest. None certain that their lives were the better for it.

*****

Denham needed money.

The English estates inherited from his departed wife, the Countess Levigne, were not at all what he had been led to believe. The country they inhabited was well enough, near to Chipping Camden with its thriving communities, cream-colored stone, and productive fields. There were the attractions of hunting and shooting, for those who appreciated them. But the buildings were, to a mind schooled to nothing but the most gracious, both rustic and pokey. There were irritating entails that he had not been properly apprised of that prevented its immediate sale - here he cursed that damnable wife of his for being less than well informed about his future properties - and the various rents and incomes were not nearly enough to support a man of his expansive tastes.

After two nights in a lumpy bed with a chimney that smoked, his temper frayed. After a day closeted with an extremely obdurate set of lawyers and stewards who deferentially but firmly repeated that yes, the law and the deeds were quite clear on every contended point, that no, there was nothing that could be done about it, and that no, there was no possibility of further income being derived from the properties as they now stood, an angry vein began to throb in his temple. When they added that if My Lord stood willing to invest in the improvements and modernizations that the place sorely needed, they were certain that the future of the estates could be quite promising, My Lord's response was vicious. He was not remotely willing to put money into the estate. He wanted to take money out of it. At last the rage that he had attempted to throttle grew to such heat he excused himself from the meeting, called for his man Tibbs, and strode angrily to a small study where he smashed a large, hideous, and extremely valuable vase in the fireplace. Tibbs, recognizing the signs, merely cleared the shards and set about quietly building a fire having once ascertained that the chimney was not clogged by rooks' nests, then set out a tray containing a rather elegant crystal glass and a decanter of French brandy, a small keg of which he had discovered in a dusty cellar. These he placed gently on a small table near a capacious wing chair in which he suggested his master sit to recover his temper. He placed himself solicitously near the table, as if ready to pour the brandy. His real aim was to be in striking distance of saving the tray and its precious contents in case the master thought to send it the way of the vase, which might have gotten them a tidy sum at auction, had it not been reduced to rubble. He wisely did not point this out to his lordship.

The loyal but increasingly troubled Bev Ramage was left to have refreshments served to the various officials left kicking their heels in the study, and make apologies for My Lord's sudden fits of pique. When he had done all he could to assuage their bruised sensibilities, he ventured across the hall and looked in on Denham to see which way the wind blew. Tibbs caught his eye, frowned, and shook his head imperceptibly. Ramage withdrew as quietly as he had entered. He recrossed the hall, made his excuses to the waiting gentlemen, insisted that My Lord had their ideas and thoughts well in hand - which those worthies correctly doubted very much - and ushered them out while assuring them of another meeting at a later date - which all knew would not occur.

When the large front door had been closed behind them, Ramage leaned against it for a few moments, deep in thought. It was increasingly clear to him that the mercurial man whose family his had served for two generations was now showing signs of the same dangerous imbalance his father had been prey to. In the older Denham there had been moments of sweet lucidity. The current Earl was infinitely more dangerous. Ramage was not fool enough to think he could leave the man's service without repercussions - perhaps mortal ones. He had wondered in all the years of the Earl's absence whether the rumors of his behaviors had perhaps been exaggerated. Several weeks in his presence made him certain that the monster that had been painted was no more than the truth. Denham was not only mad, but indeed capable of every cold blooded and self-serving crime whispered about in Polite circles in half a dozen countries.

But what was Ramage to do? Denham was protected by his title. Society might avoid him, but there was no removing him from its august membership. Authorities had failed to find anything but coincidence in the deaths of his wives, or in the sudden disappearance of at least one child of said wives. Coincidences there were that defied the laws of happenstance. But no proof. Ramage quailed internally to think who might be next.

With a sigh, he steeled himself and, knocking first, let himself back into the study.

'Ah. Ramage,' said his employer from a window where he now stood, glass of brandy in hand, staring out at a garden that had been let grow wild. 'You are just the man I want to see.'

Ramage hoped that his master might have regained his composure, but a glance at the level of the brandy in the decanter on the table showed it to be less than half full. In other words, the air of composure masked seething emotions underneath. Ramage cleared his throat. 'Sir?' he asked neutrally.

'I am sorely disappointed by the turn my affairs have taken since my return to these shores,' he said.

'It must be rather a shock, after so long...'

'It has been more than a shock, Ramage. It has been a leveller.'

'Will you,' started Ramage, hope rising in his breast, 'return to Italy, sir? Or France?'

'No, Bev, I will not. Neither of those benighted countries is at all *convenable* for me at this present.' He raised as languid hand and gazed thoughtfully at the great ruby that glowed on his third finger. 'No. What I require, my dear, is a business opportunity.'

'A business opportunity, sir?'

'Insurance has always appealed to me,' Denham said, examining a pulled thread in the lace at the end of a shirt sleeve.

'Insurance!' Ramage's brow creased in confusion.

'Precisely. So many things can so easily go wrong, say, in a theatre.'

'A... theatre? Sir?'

'There is no need to repeat everything I say to you, Ramage,' Denham frowned. 'In fact, I find this tendency extremely... ah... *irritating...* to my nerves. Do you understand me?'

Bev swallowed uncomfortably. 'I do, sir. I am sorry, sir. What sort of... theatre... did you have in mind, sir?'

'Take, just for instance, a small theatre such as, perhaps, The Swan.'

'But… why would The Swan need insurance from us, sir?' asked Ramage, thoroughly perplexed.

'That is for you to discover, dear Bev. In every place of business there must always be one who is, shall we say, less than content. Who might, for a fee, help us to illustrate a reason for having… protections. Against, oh, any number of events, don't you think?'

Bev's heart began to thud uncomfortably in his chest. 'But sir… to do such a thing… it is illegal sir. And, if I may say, unethical.'

Denham looked coldly at his man. 'I do no recall asking your opinion, Beverly.'

Ramage could feel cold sweat beading on his brow. He resisted the desire to mop it away. 'No. Sir. Of course,' he said jerkily. 'But if we should be… discovered… sir…'

'It is your duty to ensure that we are not.'

'Yes, my lord. When should I… how soon would you need…'

'All in good time, Bev. All in good time. Several things must needs be in place. First, I wish you to find everything in this god forsaken house that may be sold. *Everything*, Bev. The jackals and scribes have *kindly*,' his lips twisted in anger, 'left me a list of goods not specifically tied to the estate, which is to be your guide. I want it done quickly. I need money, immediately. Do not fail me in this.'

'I will not, my lord.'

'Next, I must remove me from this… this….' He looked around the room with distaste, 'I hardly know what to name it… and return to London. I shall depart at the first possible opportunity in the morning, Bev, and I require a private chaise, and rooms near White's from which I can work. You will please tell that horror in the kitchen that I require a properly dressed meal, properly aired sheets, and a fire that does not smoke this evening. After I am settled once more in the City, I must pay a visit to The Swan, I think. And introduce myself to Madame Seraphine.'

Ramage began to ask why, then choked the question back.

'Wise, dear Bev,' approved Denham. 'You do understand me completely?'

'I do, sir.'

'That is all, then, I think.'

'Sir.'

'Then go.'

Ramage did, with alacrity.

Madame Seraphine

III.

'The sins of the father are to be laid upon the children. Therefore I promise ye I fear you.'

- William Shakespeare, *The Merchant of Venice,* III.5

Madame Seraphine

The Hathaway household had been tucked into their various beds for a bare two hours when someone beat a tattoo upon the front door that, if not enough to raise the dead, certainly raised Brutus to a crescendo of vicious barking, and sent Jacob to the door with remarkable speed clad in nothing but nightshirt and cap, lamp in one hand, cudgel in the other.

'Hang on, you daft bugger! We're coming!' he boomed, put the lamp on the table near the door, cleared Brutus out of the way with a foot, and unlocked and opened the door a crack, cudgel at the ready.

'Please, I am looking for Mr. Stephen Hathaway!' said a voice urgently. 'I come from Lady Hensleigh. Her husband, my master Sir William, has had a fall and is insensible. Please, sir, we need Mr. Hathaway, a carriage here awaits!'

'*Je suis en route!*' Shouted Stephen from the tiny window in the attic.

'What of Lady Hensleigh's physician?' asked Jacob sharply.

'Gone into the country, sir, to tend to his sister. Please, sir, we must have Mr. Hathaway, sir; here is a note from Lady Hensleigh herself, sir.' Jacob opened the door wider to reveal a very frightened half-dressed footman with a lantern, and took the note.

'Stephen!' he called, having glanced at the contents.

'*Oui, je viens*', said Stephen, clattering down the stairs, shirt barely tucked in to his breeches, shrugging himself into his coat, calling for Marianne, who was already running from the kitchen armed with cloak and bag, as the rest of the household gathered around the stairs and the door wearing wraps hastily thrown around night clothes. He read the note and passed it to Seraphine. '*Maman*, I do not know Lady Hensleigh's hand. *C'est ça?*'

'*Oui*,' said Seraphine, looking at the scrawl and the Hensleigh imprint on the paper. door. 'Oh *mon dieu*, whatever can have happened?'

'Lost his footing into his carriage, ma'am, he did, the step being that slippery,' blurted the footman fearfully. 'Please, please do hurry, sir.'

'*Bien. Allons-y. Venez*, Marianne.' He showed her through the door and they jogged behind the footman to a barouche with the Hensleigh crest on its doors that waited at the end of the lane.

The groom sent the horses forward at a brisk trot through dark and empty streets to Hensleigh House, no time to marvel or even take notice of the tufted velvet seat or superb comfort of the equipage. The butler was looking for their arrival and opened the door quickly while the footman showed them in, and took their outer clothing. He hurried them them forward across the hall and up two shadowy flights of stairs to a well-lit chamber on the second floor.

'Oh, thank God you are come!' cried Lady Hensleigh. Rising from her place beside the bed where her husband lay inert. 'It is the stupidest thing, Mr. McGrath would choose this night to be away and I could not think what to do, oh Mr. Hathaway I do so hope you are able...'

'How long has he been like this?' interrupted Stephen tersely, as he went to work examining the man on the bed, brow clammy, pulse erratic.

'More than an hour.'

'What happened?'

'He was coming home from Brooks, and missed his footing getting into the carriage. He must I think have hit his head, or twisted something as he fell...'

'Did anyone see this? ...There, Marianne, feel there, I believe there are ribs broken... and here... I fear the wrist...'

'I do not know, there must surely have been, but oh... will he live, Mr. Hathaway?'

'I cannot say this present, *Madame, mais je pense que oui*, the fall was in all probability not mortal... And here, Marianne, at the base of the skull... no, do not probe too heavily but gently, gently, feel that? *Oui*... but he is a large man, and older, he clearly fell very heavily, *Madame*, and there are several injuries, but... he is breathing, *oui*? And this is well. Most well. It appears that the carriage did not roll over him.'

'Roll...' Lady Hensleigh gasped and choked on a sob. Stephen nodded at Marianne and gestured with his eyes to the distraught woman. Marianne took her gently by the arm and settled her in a chair close to the fire.

'Do you sit here, Lady Augusta, and stay warm,' she soothed. 'Mr. Hathaway will take care of your husband. And you are close if he needs you. Here, this will soothe your nerves. May I call your woman to you?' She took a kettle from the hob and poured some water in a mug, then added a few drops of something fragrant that reminded Lady Hensleigh of summer gardens in the country. She sipped cautiously, then relaxed and sipped more. She gestured weakly to the bell pull and Marianne tugged it.

With the help of Hensleigh's man and a footman, Stephen got the injured gentleman stripped naked and gently eased into a night shirt, then raised him gently on pillows to take pressure off the ribs and lungs. Halfway through the process, the gentleman swam to consciousness with a pitiful groan and tried to move, an action which caused him to cry out in pain.

'*Maintenant, m'sieu, restez tranquillement, m'sieu*, you have taken a fall and are injured, *vous comprenez*. You are at home sir, just be still while we make all as comfortable as we may,' he kept the patter of soothing words coming in a steady, monotonous continuum, using nods and gestures to show the others what he needed done. As well as gently feeling every joint and bone, he took time to put his ear to the gentleman's chest, alert to the kind of whistle or gurgle that might indicate a lung punctured by a rib, but was relieved to hear nothing out of the ordinary. Working quickly and deftly, he treated the ribs with a heavy ointment of his own making, and wrapped the whole area snugly to keep it stable while explaining his actions to the anxious attendants and Hensleigh's even more anxious wife. Marianne rose at a glance, measured out a dose of laudanum, and coaxed the injured man to swallow it. She followed this with an elixir of barley water and a tincture made from the inner lining of birch bark that smelled pleasant and, with the laudanum, would ease his pain and send him to sleep

'Sir,' Hathaway addressed him, 'I must hurt you now, to set your wrist, which is broken. I will make it as quick as I am able.' He nodded to his helpers to hold their master firmly by the shoulders and upper arms, and gently, carefully, listening with sensitive fingers, manipulated the damaged bones into alignment. Hensleigh cried out and tried to writhe away, but finally it was done, and the hand and wrist heavily anointed with more salve to help both the inflammation and the healing. Then, with a light, flat splint to keep the whole stable, he wrapped it in layers of clean white cloth.

The medication began to work. Hensleigh's breathing steadied, and he slip into a deep sleep. Marianne gave his man a bottle containing other ingredients which, mixed in boiled water and a few drops of brandy, Hathaway said, 'will help with the inevitable fever. This should be alternated every several hours with the barley water,' and yes, if Lady Hensleigh wished she could certainly cool her husband's brow with cool lavender water as well. 'But mostly', he said firmly, 'what the gentleman needs is rest. And now, *Madame*, so do you.'

Finally, wearily, he and Marianne went out into the light of a new morning and were taken home.

After several days Stephen could be very pleased with his patient's progress. Marianne's tinctures and Stephen's salves were potent and effective on their own; better for the fact that the patient was wealthy, had a staff whose sole employment was to look after his needs, and a larder well stocked with all the nutritional amenities that speed healing of any sort. It was a far cry, Stephen reflected, from the rough-and-ready methods used aboard ship in the middle of a voyage or in the aftermath of a battle. Yet, in his experience, it was precisely those rough methods and medicaments that often gave birth to new and better systems.

On day four, he found Mr. McGrath in command of the sickroom. Knowing medical practitioners to be jealous of both their methods and their patients, Stephen presented himself in the room with due humility. But he found in Mr. McGrath a man of both quick intelligence and generosity. He praised Stephen's work, was curious about his methods, and was not afraid to admit that Stephen had very likely saved Hensleigh's life. Within minutes, the two men were deep in discussion about fevers, humors, broken bones, illnesses of brain and body, and all the useful, damaging, new, and tried-and-true methods of looking after these things. McGrath was particularly interested in the contents of Stephen's salves and tinctures, and was anxious to ask him further about French methods he had learned aboard ship as well as those that came from his time in the islands.

'I will take over the care of Lord Hensleigh now, but if it please you, call upon me at your convenience,' he remarked as they parted. 'Word of your work will get around, you know. It will be most inappropriate for you to encroach on another's business with your lack of proper training, of course. I might, however, not be averse to taking you on as an assistant to our mutual benefit. What think you? Will it serve?'

Stephen's gratified delight was answer enough. And when as the young man left the house, a grateful Lady Hensleigh tucked something into his hand that chinked and was satisfyingly weighty, he felt he could have walked on air, or danced all the way back to his new home. His enthusiasm bubbled over when he came through the kitchen, told Marianne and Jacob about his adventure, and spun Marianne in a laughing jig around the kitchen. Then he spilled the coins out on the table, and gave her half. She tried to demur and push them back to him, but Stephen wouldn't allow it. 'Aboard ship, when we take a prize, all get their share. We rise together. That's the code. It's your share, Marianne. You earned it.'

Her shining smile, and Jacob's nod of dawning respect, were more thanks than ever words could say.

*****

Chance River could not go on living at his ma's flat. She needed the little space she had, and truth to tell, he needed a way to spread out. The sort of terrace house he imagined - something like that now inhabited by the Hathaway family - was beyond his current means, even with his savings. And he had to admit that his vague idea of taking his ma away from her shop to retire somewhere farther from the center of her universe wouldn't wash. His ma would die in harness, like an old dray horse. And, he fretted, listening to the coughing that wracked her, that end might not be so many years distant. He spoke of her condition to Hathaway, and received some decoctions and syrups made by the medic and that Marianne Freeman who helped him, to ease his ma's state. Molly flatly refused to try the stuff, but on one particularly bad night Chance persuaded her to swallow one of the syrups. It had helped her so wonderfully that now she was happy to use whatever Hathaway and Marianne gave her. Stephen cautioned Chance that nothing he had could cure Molly; it could but help her go on longer than she might otherwise. And, he assured his friend, when the time came and his ma could no longer work, there were other medications he could make, that would ease her final stages. It was not anything Chance cared to hear, but knowing it gave him comfort.

Given his ma, given his new situation in the yards, given his abiding interest in on one Bridie Murphy, Chance found himself daily less eager to sign up for another three year voyage. He liked his job; putting down some land roots mightn't be a bad move. He knew, as every seaman knows, that each voyage taken was a step closer to an end in an alley in some foreign port, or stitched into an old sail and sent overboard in the middle of some ocean, or killed in the process of defending against boarding by privateers. He'd earned his name by an uncanny ability to take a calculated risk and come up on the right side of the coin. He reckoned there was a number attached to those risks; that Fortune could hunch her shoulder and turn away at any time.

But not just yet, it seemed. One evening as he returned home, Chance found an elderly gentleman of wispy hair and bewildered eye standing outside Molly's shop in the rain only partly clothed, waiting, he said, for Margery to come home. Margery, it turned out, was the gentleman's wife. Trouble was, she'd been deceased these ten years or more. The gentleman so happened to be the holder of the head lease on the building that included *Chez Simard*, the mantua-maker next door, and the lodging above.

Chance saw no reason that kindness and opportunity should not be one and the same. On helping the man back up the steep stairs to his lodging, he took note of the small but comfortably furnished flat that, like Molly's, had a living area with a curtained-off bedroom beyond, but unlike Molly's had a gable on either side of the room that let in a pleasant amount of light and air, a fireplace built into the brick chimney that made up a part of the far wall, and the bedroom large enough to fit a reasonably sized bed with curtains, a clothes press, and a privy closet. The main room was simply furnished with a sturdy desk and several comfortable chairs, a cupboard that held the man's store of plates, mugs, utensils, and various belongings, a good rug on the floor, and a painting of a ship on the wall that separated this flat from Molly's. That wall had decorative paper on it. Chance thought the paper might hide a bricked-over doorway. If that were the case, a man of Chance's skills could break through the old doorway and turn two small flats into a spacious one that might do very well for his future needs, if Fortune smiled.

The old gentleman was a retired sea captain, name of Jos. Seymour. The painting on the wall was his ship, *Fortune*, which Chance recognized as a sign.

Old Captain Seymour was respectably cared for by a housekeeper who brought him his meals, kept the lodging tidy, the clothing washed, and, with the wife gone, whatever other needs a man might never grow too old to enjoy. She also, Chance suspected, routinely made off with whatever small and salable possessions might easily be hidden in a pocket. Chance had no quibble with this; Seymour was clean, fed, and well kept, and so the housekeeper, who did not seem to be a confirmed drunk, could feel entitled to a tip.

Befriending the old man was no trouble at all for a fellow mariner. Seymour plied River with stories of his days at sea, which, were they even half true, were many, exciting, and varied. And Chance gave as good as he got, so that a pint of ordinary provided by Chance to open a pleasurable jaw-wag became a regular occurrence.

Discreet enquiries during Seymour's cogent periods yielded the information that the old man had no family left living in England. A son had died at sea, his wife remarried and his children raised by another. A daughter and another son were gone to Gloucester, 'or mebbe 'twas Halifax'. Seymour had hardly known them, being always at sea. By the time he retired, they'd been gone. After his wife died, he'd given over the operation of his business dealings to an agent whose name and address Chance took care to know from his ma. Now, his health failing, he stayed close to home, except when his wits wandered and he went wandering with them.

Occasionally Chance took Seymour to the docks to see the ships, which made the old seaman merry and sparked a fresh stream of reminiscences. Once or twice he dropped the captain off at one of the taverns frequented by elderly seamen, tipping the barkeep handsomely to keep an eye on the old bugger 'and don't let him wander off alone, see, even if it's to take a piss', until he finished work for the day and could come to collect him.

More often, though, Seymour was too sleepy or distracted to walk abroad. He regularly asked a question or made a statement, then forgot it and repeated it not ten minutes after. He fretted that Margery wasn't home to see to his comforts. He raged against persons unknown who, Seymour insisted, were after his gold. Given the apparent light fingers of the housekeeper, Chance expected that any gold that once existed had disappeared long before. But he reassured the old gentleman as best he could before leaving him to his mumblings.

River was close-mouthed about his dealings with old Captain Seymour. Bridie Murphy, missing his constant presence at the theatre, began to think another woman had slipped into his orbit without her knowing of it. And suddenly she thought that this was a very ill thing indeed, because Chance River, a man with a job, prospects, and no vices to make a wife's life a misery, was a rare opportunity to let escape like water through her fingers. Bridie wasn't one to make a mistake twice over.

*****

There had been a deal of discussion in the Hathaway family regarding its new status - no longer awaiting news of a loved one, but accustoming itself to the fact that George Hathaway would never join them in London. Seraphine's first instinct was to go into deep mourning, which would have entailed her immediate and indefinite removal from the stage of The Swan. This prospect - and the inevitable loss of income that would result - so alarmed Charles Pearce that he immediately went to work to illustrate the folly of the idea.

'For after all,' he reasoned, 'the poor man is dead and gone this four years and more. To mourn him as if he had died under your roof - no, damme. It wouldn't be right, Sera.'

'*Peut-etre*. But I must still grieve, *mon vieux*. It is not the information that I hoped for.'

Charles took her slender hands in his meaty ones. 'Of course not, Sera. Of course not. Nor would it be seemly of you to go gayly about town as if nothing at all had occurred. But might I suggest - if you were to wear the trappings and the demeanor of *light* mourning - to be seen onstage, bravely carrying on despite this ill wind - it would be not only respected, but very affecting indeed. I'll tell you what. We could do *Richard III*. To see you as Anne, following her husband's body onto the stage, with the scheming Gloucester already in attendance...'

Seraphine released her hands from his. '*Cher mon cousin*,' she smiled ironically. 'You are so very considerate. Both of my feelings and of the success of The Swan.'

'Then you'll do it? Capital!' he rubbed his hands together. 'You must allow me to order the correct garments for yourself and Angel. They must of course set the proper tone,' he looked at her with his head tilted sideways and hands held out as if to frame her. In spite of herself, Seraphine laughed.

'No, Charles, you will *not* dress us, *s'il vous plait*! It will cost far too much.'

'Well. If you insist,' conceded Charles. 'But you must allow me the feathers for your caps, my dear, and a bit of ribbon. It's the very least I can do for my poor cousin. I won't have you looking shabby on his behalf.'

It did not occur to Seraphine that there would be further repercussions to her widowhood. But as the days went on, small gifts, posies of flowers, and even the odd very bad poem began to appear in her dressing room; followed by a small but determined procession of hopeful and extremely ineligible men. Each of them begged her favor - or, more correctly, her favors - and all of them had to be evicted despite protestations of rank, prestige, and undying love with polite firmness by the combined powers of James Hemings and Jacob Freeman.

One fine Sunday afternoon, she thought to escape these unwanted attentions by walking in the park with Angel, Bridie, and the inevitable Brutus. The two younger women being very apt to stop to chat with their many acquaintances, Seraphine walked on without them, but before she had gone more than a few hundred yards suddenly found herself flanked by no less than three aspiring beaux, all unknown to her, who jockeyed for position by her side and did their best to steer her down a side path away from the main crowd. Neither hints that they were unwelcome nor direct requests that they leave availed in ridding herself of their company. Strongly holding to her path, walking as briskly as she could with her hands and arms clutched tightly at her waist, she began feeling more vulnerable than was her wont, and looked about her for a familiar face.

She was never more glad to see Mr. Nathaniel Neville strolling toward her with friends. Pausing to acknowledge her, quickly reading the mute appeal in her eyes, he made graceful excuses to the ladies and gentlemen of his party, announcing that Mrs. Hathaway was just the person he had most hoped to see. Within moments, a combination of icy politeness, subtle blocking tactics with a body both lithe and strong, and a few veiled but menacing threats, he had gotten rid of Seraphine's obnoxious admirers, at which point he dropped his ardent demeanor as rapidly as he had assumed it.

'Mrs. Hathaway, what, may I ask, are you thinking by walking in the Park at this hour with no escort?'

'It has always been my habit, sir,' she retorted, rattled. 'And I am walking with Angel, Bridie, and Brutus....'

'None of whom are at this moment in sight...'

'They are not far behind, sir. We were on our way to meet my son at the corner, and how I choose to walk in the park is *not* your concern. I have never in my life had this sort of trouble before, and can't think what the reason might be now.'

'I can think of several,' he said somewhat grimly. 'Not the least of which is that your newly official widowhood makes you a prime target.'

Seraphine gasped. 'I *beg* your pardon?' she demanded in frigid accents.

'Need I be coarse, *Madame*? It is now generally known that you are free of even a hint of the protection afforded by a husband. As you are a rather *public* figure in this town, there are many men who will view your insistence on walking alone as an invitation to accept, shall we say, a sheltering arm.'

'But I do not at all wish a sheltering arm! I have no desire to give up my independence to serve as some tyrannical man's wife.'

'I do not think marriage is what most of your admirers intend. You are an actress, ma'am. Not an heiress.'

Seraphine stopped in the middle of the path and stared at him in speechless rage. '*Merci du compliment, m'sieu*. Is this what you think of me! That I am a common whore to go from hand to hand like poor Mrs. Robinson and so many like her?'

'What I think is immaterial,' he said curtly. 'It is what others think that is at issue here. I am sorry if you find the truth so inconvenient.' He started to say something else, then, closing his lips tightly, raised his face to the sky in frustration. And Seraphine, observing him closely for the first time, realized that the gentleman was nearly grey with weariness. Which gave her a pang. She gently touched his arm and encouraged him forward.

'Sir, I am sorry. I am indeed grateful that you came to my aid. *En verité, je vous le dit*, I was quite desperately worried. And I see that you are very weary, and would rather yourself anywhere else but here, *c'est vrai?*'

He looked at her in surprise. 'I… no, *Madame*. It is… something to do with my work. I have lost a rather important… international… package. And it is distressing in the extreme.'

She looked at him in sudden understanding and dropped her hand. 'Ah. I am so very sorry, sir. And the family…'

'You are far too perspicacious, ma'am. I ought not to have spoken. But yes. It will cause great pain.'

She nodded. They walked in silence. He found himself comforted by her presence. She found herself comfortable in his.

At the corner, Angel and Bridie finally caught up with them, flustered and apologetic, and together they found Stephen, just arriving. Neville took his leave promptly. Stephen looked after him with knitted brows. 'What business have you with Mr. Neville, *Maman?*' he asked her.

'None at all,' she said. 'We met quite by chance.'

'Indeed? This seems to occur rather too regularly to be pure chance.'

'Your concern is touching, *mon fils*. But as Mr. Neville has no interest in older actresses, and as I find him quite the most infuriating man I have ever met, *je vous assure*, you need waste no time in worrying. My honor, such as it is, will survive.'

*****

Later in the day, Bridie danced to the door to find Mr. Tristan Neville on the doorstep. Apparently, she had been expecting someone. Clearly, Tristan was not that someone.

'Oh, it's you,' she said, casting a jaundiced eye upon him.

'Good evening, Bridie,' said Tristan brightly. 'I didn't know you lived here.'

'It's a new arrangement,' Bridie said. 'You'll be looking for Mrs. Hathaway, I imagine. She an't here.'

'*Mrs*…. Why on earth would I be looking for *Mrs*. Hathaway?'

Bridie shrugged. 'All sorts is looking for Mrs. Hathaway, these days. You wouldn't believe the…'

'Bridie,' he interrupted, 'I am looking for Miss Angel Hathaway. Is she about?'

'I'll see,' said Bridie, and as Tristan was about to set foot over the threshold, she shut the door in his face.

'Tristan Neville! What on earth… Bridie!' expostulated Angel from her place at the kitchen table when she received this news. 'You left him *outside*? You never took him up to the parlor or offered him any refreshment?'

'Why should I?' countered Bridie belligerently. 'I an't a servant around here!'

'Bridie,' said Angel in exasperation, 'Less than a fortnight since, you told me, *moi meme*, you wanted to learn how to be a lady like Miss Attenborough. You have to start by being polite to people. It's common decency.'

'Well maybe I just changed me mind,' Bridie retorted. 'Maybe I don't care about bein' no lady after all!'

'Well good, then. You can find another place to live, and I shall be happy to have my room back!'

Bridie's eyes widened. She opened her mouth to fire back, changed her mind, and flounced out of the room. A few seconds later, Marianne and Angel heard the front door open and voices drifting from the stairs to the first floor.

'Marianne, what should I do?' asked Angel, in a panic of indecision.

'You must at least see what the gentleman wants,' she said practically. 'But if you go walking, mind you make that Bridie go with you. Our censorious world is at its worst regarding people of another color like myself, and young ladies with no prospects, like yourself. Your bearing, your comportment, all, must be unimpeachable.'

Angel blushed, and looked down. 'I do remember, Marianne.'

She went upstairs and found Tristan Neville standing by the parrot's cage, holding one finger gently. Suddenly she felt rather shy. Somehow Neville seemed too large for this room. Too expensive. Apollo suddenly landed in a dusty village, having overshot Olympus.

'The parrot bites,' he said.

'You would bite too, if someone entered your house unbidden,' she responded callously. 'Good day, Mr. Neville,' she curtseyed, trying to disguise the fact that her heart was beating much faster than it should. 'I apologize for the pedestrian view we have to offer, and for our lack of manners.'

'Good day, Miss Hathaway,' he said, with a bow. 'I confess, my own rooms do not look over so many rooftops, nor do they include a busy construction site. But the... er... *refreshing* manners of your household allowed me a few extremely fascinating moments studying your front stoop, your very shiny door knocker, and what I assume will one day become a pleasant park across the way.' He finished with such a twinkle in his eye that Angel laughed for the first time in days. And that made him twinkle more.

'I hope, sir, that it does not injure your dignity to consort with our kind,' she said. 'For this is very much the way we live, you see. Once the novelty has worn off, and the *refreshing* nature of informality has begun to irk you… you will doubtless never darken our doorway again.'

'Oh, I am hardly *consorting*,' he said solemnly. '*Consorting* is what one does when spending one's time with rogues and wh… um… other persons of ill repute. Which,' he admitted ruefully, 'is quite often what makes my esteemed mother and brother despair of me.'

'Ah, well,' said Angel sagely. 'No doubt they know you better than I, and fear for your immortal soul.'

'I think it is the family fortune and posterity that they fear for, quite frankly,' he said. 'I don't believe they've ever given a second thought to anyone's immortal soul, least of all mine.'

'Why are you here, Mr. Neville? It does not seem at all the thing, if you ask me.'

'But I did not ask you. I am here, Miss Hathaway, to see if perhaps you would care to walk with me, it being a very fine evening, and the early roses blooming.'

'But it is about to rain, sir. And I have but recently returned from the park.'

'Then let us be content with a turn about the square. Come, Miss Hathaway. I have but lately heard of your family's loss, and I am most heartily sorry for it. If you feel it too wet to go walking again, so be it. But when my own father died of a fever, I found it very soothing to walk or ride outside among living things.'

'That is most kind, sir. And for that kindness, I stand ready to accompany you.'

As if on cue in a farce, Bridie, who had doubtless been listening at the door, burst through without a hint of a polite knock. 'Here I am, Angel, ready and right,' she said saucily, remembering at the last moment to sketch a curtsy to Mr. Neville.

'Will you be joining us then, Miss Murphy?' asked Tristan, admirably disguising his disappointment.

Bridie drew herself up to her full height and took on an air of hauteur that would have done the starchiest lady's maid proud. 'I am to lend countenance to this delightful expedition,' she drawled with an arch look. And then, having come to the end of her well-rehearsed idea of a posh accent, added, 'So as you, a man of the town, don't try no funny stuff with our Miss Hathaway. *Not* but what I think there's any danger of that from *you*, sir, for you - for the most part - are a pretty behaved gentleman, *un*like some as I could mention.' With that, and a haughty sniff and toss of the head, she marched back out of the room.

Angel turned to Neville in horror, an apology on her lips, but found that gentleman convulsed with laughter. 'I am... so relieved... that your honor is in such good hands, Miss Hathaway,' he managed breathlessly. 'I cannot tell you how I might have worried.'

Angel giggled and shook her head. 'I am very sorry, Mr. Neville. Bridie's great ambition is to be a top-lofty lady like Miss Attenborough. I fear her studies are rather oddly shaped at present.'

'I wish her well in her endeavor,' said Tristan, now in control of himself, 'but it would be a terrible shame, you know. She is so very much her own person as she is. Shall we?'

He showed her out of the room with a bow, but was brought up short at the bottom of the stairs when Angel snapped her fingers and Brutus appeared from the kitchen.

'Er... said Neville, momentarily at a loss, 'Is it absolutely necessary for Brutus to come along?'

'Yes,' said Angel firmly. But as she put on her cape and donned the gloves Tristan had given her, she smiled up at him with such mischief and pleasure that his heart lurched in desire.

The three humans talked generally as they walked, Angel greeting neighbors, tradespeople, and neighborhood dogs alike, Bridie freely expounding on the passing parade of people: whose hat was unseemly in its size of feathers, which color of walking dress she should very much like to wear, had she the ready, and did Mr. Neville think it a good idea to have gold braiding and buttons. He answered truthfully that too much gaudiness would brand her as an upstart at best and a courtesan at worst, but that gold buttons, if not too large, might certainly do well with one of her coloring, and yes, that too many feathers were astonishing rather than attractive. These comments satisfied Bridie very well, and she dropped a few paces behind, the better to observe and think about the manners and dress of the people she most desired to emulate.

Neville, for his part, was bemused by the informality that existed between Angel and Bridie, and indeed with their neighbors and acquaintances, despite very clear differences in birth and opportunity. Some spoke in the broad accents of regions to the west and north. Others with syntax that was far from perfect. Some had manners. Some, like Bridie, had none. Some were educated, some boasted of children who were the first in their family to have achieved this. To Tristan, these differences branded the speakers as inferior, though the easy familiarity with which they treated one another was imbued with confidence.

Except when they looked at Tristan Neville, stiff with breeding and discomfort, a peacock in a chicken yard. Where they met Angel eye to eye with a smile, they glanced sideways at Tristan, bobbed their heads, touched their caps, did not linger.

Angel's heart sank. '*Mon dieu.* I think now this outing was a mistake. It has so easily lead to discomfort on all sides.'

'Not at all,' Tristan tried to reassure her 'It is only… I am very unfamiliar with… that is to say, that these sorts of people are more generally….'

'…seen to exist only to serve you?'

Tristan blushed. 'We provide many livings for many people. And as they are beholden to us, and have no living without us, and certainly no birth to speak of, they rank below us. Do you have no staff at all?'

'We hire a daily woman to empty chamber pots and clean, but she has a family and other employers to go to. Jacob grows the garden and cooks. Marianne is my mother's dresser, and a skilled herbalist. *Maman* and I have our jobs. We all share in the work of the household. We all share in the expenses. We all eat together in the kitchen.'

'How very Utopian of you,' muttered Tristan.

'Not at all. We often argue heatedly. But it is efficient. Have you ever even been in your kitchen, sir?' Angel teased.

'No,' admitted Tristan. 'Not since I was very young, at any rate. Cook was used to sneak me sweetmeats. I did love those moments with Cook. The kitchen was always warm, and smelled wonderful. Unless the slops were being emptied for the pigs out on the farm, that is.'

'But did no one in your family come up from nothing, as they say? No intrepid soldier or sailor of fortune? No tradesman?'

'Not that I can think of,' he said. 'Not in the last two hundred years or so. Our family's holdings have always been land. There are military officers, of course, or those in religious orders, which are traditional livings for younger sons like myself.'

'You cannot tell me that your father has never invested a part of his fortune in spices, or bulbs, or - God help me - slaves, or shipments of furs and timber,' she scoffed. 'What is that, if not trade?'

'We only invest in these things. We don't take part.'

'Ah. So if your hands are not dirty, it doesn't count as trade, is that what you're saying?'

'You are not making this easy, Miss Hathaway. I did not invent the system.'

'No. You did not. But you do prosper by it, so it would be useful if you thought about it.'

'Miss Hathaway...'

'Oh, dear. I know,' she said soothingly. 'You are not accustomed to being spoken to like this, especially by a female, and absolutely not by one whose social standing dictates that she should be flattered by your attentions.'

'I… you… Nothing of the sort!' expostulated Neville, though indeed, it was exactly what he had been thinking. 'Miss Hathaway,' he continued with asperity, 'I believe you to be the most vexing woman I have ever met. Ever!' he finished.

'I know,' agreed Angel equably. 'I am sadly trying. I shall try henceforward to confine my remarks to the weather. Do you not find it a bit wet for this time of the year?' she enquired so sweetly that Neville nearly ground his teeth in fury.

He was spared an ill-thought response by a male voice urgently booming, 'Miss Murphy!' and the approach of a strongly built, cinnamon-complected young fellow with the rolling gait of a seaman.

'Well, Mr. River,' smiled Bridie. 'Wherever have you been, these last days? Never mind. You are come just in time to spare me languishing with boredom.'

Chance halted, saw Neville, and looked surreptitiously for an escape. Angel could feel Tristan stiffen beside her.

'You are well met, Mr. River,' Angel greeted him. 'Miss Murphy was forced to come out walking with us to preserve my honor, and is finding it extremely dull. Will you join us?'

'Happen I will, thanks,' said Chance, eyeing Neville with trepidation, and bowing. 'That is, if… Good day to you, sir.'

Tristan nodded. 'Good day… Mr. River.'

'It's all right, Mr. River,' said Bridie confidentially. 'He an't going to bite, or anythin', are you, Mr. Neville, sir?'

'Er…' said that gentleman.

'What's that you've got, Mr. River?' Bridie dimpled, eyes dancing in the face of everyone else's discomfort. 'Did you bring me something?'

'Oh. Yes. Here,' Chance handed her a flower the color of cornsilk. 'For you. Because…' he glanced at Neville and Angel and blushed. 'Well. Because.'

'Why Mr. River, thank-you,' smiled Bridie. 'It is just the color of my hair. Do you put it in my bonnet for me, will you?' She handed the flower back to him after smelling it and positioned her head prettily, cocking an eyebrow at Tristan as if to say, *see? This is how it's done. Sir.*

Chance gently wound the sunny bloom into the collection of silk flowers on her chip hat and declared himself satisfied. Neville looked on bleakly, Bridie's message not lost on him. He wondered whether any woman of his acquaintance would be delighted by so simple a gift. He knew for a fact that Bridie Murphy would not have been content with a yellow flower from Ned Badgeley.

But then, Ned Badgeley had not been offering his heart. He had been striking a bargain based on lust: for sex, for money, for position, for goods. A different bargain than that struck with Miss Henrietta Attenborough, but a bargain nonetheless. The sort of bargain, he realized, that he himself was expected to offer a genteel woman like Arabella Montjoy, and receive in return her bargain of loyalty, children, fortune.

One need not, in other words, have love. This he understood as well as he understood the bargains made with mistresses or horse dealers. But where did Angel Hathaway fit in?

Mr. Neville felt unbalanced, as if the earth had suddenly tilted. His parents - indeed, his whole acquaintance, and most of their ancestors - had built a world on the solid foundation of their innate superiority. But that superiority, he was beginning to realize, was slippery, reliant on the hard work, good nature, and belief of all those who supported it. A vast number of people. Who aspired, bled, wept, loved like any other human on any other scale, while either directly or indirectly in the service of a gentry and an aristocracy that maintained their power through birth, position, land, and... yes... with extravagant clothing and carriages and the exquisite manners and bearing that formed the hallmark of Polite Society.

But what if those whom it was meant to inspire - or cow - stopped believing? What was left? When he looked at River, Angel, Bridie, and their ilk, what he saw was young people like himself carving a niche for themselves that did not directly rely upon the largess of those far above them. That, in fact, existed almost entirely without the interference or patronage of people like himself. Content with the gift of a flower… and all that a flower might mean for the future.

And what were Tristan and his peers doing at the same time?

Competing for the better marriage, the better alliances, the better station. Working, in fact, to stay exactly where they were now, with the argument that this was the way it had always been and therefore had merit in the eyes of God.

It was he, and not Chance River, that now looked furtively for a means of escape.

Angel was, of course, already a step ahead of Tristan's thought processes. 'And here we are, home again,' she said with a brightness she was far from feeling. 'I thank-you, Mr. Neville, for strolling with me this hour. You were perfectly right, it was just what I needed. Let us part friends here, sir.'

Shock ripped through Tristan like a bolt of lightning. 'But Miss Hathaway, I… that is… The pleasure… has been mine. Please… I beg of you… allow me…'

'*Au revoir*, Mr. Neville,' continued Angel briskly. '*A bientot.*' The voice was breezy. But the eyes - those green eyes - held pain, and a hard question. Tristan stood rooted, as if on the bank of a wide river whose dangerous current made crossing impossible.

Receiving no answer, Angel Hathaway turned regretfully and left him where he stood.

He wanted to believe that the silly little chit owed him the flattery he deserved. That she should try harder to win his favor, for the distinction he showed her in simply being by her side. Then he could have despised her, just as he despised all those who flattered, and fawned, and curried favor.

'God *damn* the girl!' he swore with violence, and strode in the direction of St. James.

For her own part, Angel returned to her room, struggling against tears of anger and despair. He loved her. He did. She knew it. There must be a way, there must.

And then it occurred to her that she sounded very like Bridie Murphy had when she had heard the news of Badgeley's engagement.

*****

Tristan eventually arrived home in a brown study, having failed to find amiable company in any of his usual haunts. Upon entering the house, he deeply shocked his butler Caine by asking after the health of that gentleman's family.

'Whatever would he be a doing that for?' he asked in the kitchen later. 'Ask after my fambly? Do you reckon he'd be about turning me away, and was in the way of finding who may be harmed? After all these many years?'

Cook - Mags Bromly to her family and friends - was about to reply when she looked over Caine's shoulder and spied a figure that made her eyes nearly pop out of her head. 'Mr. Tristan, sir!' she exclaimed, rapidly wiping floury hands all over what had been a reasonably clean apron and sinking into a blushing curtsy more befitting a Duke than the second son of a Viscount. Caine whirled and goggled, the footman and the upstairs maid, who had been having a comfortable cup of tea at the far end of the table, leapt to their feet stammering out their own courtesies, and all stood awkwardly gazing at one another, wondering what to do next.

'I am sorry,' Tristan said uncomfortably from his position in the doorway. 'I realized… that is to say… it occurred to me suddenly that… I have been in this house for many seasons now, and I have never once seen my own kitchen.'

'Never seen…' began Cook, then lapsed into bewildered silence upon being poked hard by Caine's elbow.

As silence once more reigned, Sam Bolton came briskly through the kitchen's outer door, stamping mud off his boots and complaining as he divested himself of a soggy coat, that 'That fine day we was just a-starting to enjoy is like to being a right nasty night, on a sudden. Why I barely…' then he looked up and saw

Neville. 'Why, Mr. Tristan, sir, what in the name of the Almighty above are you doing a-standing there?'

'He an't never seed his kitchen afore,' supplied the upstairs maid in a stage whisper.

'You ain't never… well if that ain't the most corkbrained thing I ever heard, then I'm a muffin,' said Sam roundly. 'Whyever would you want to see this here kitchen when you got a whole perfectly good house to look at, with art and doo-dads and all?'

Tristan straightened himself into a more dignified pose and began to wonder if this had been a good idea after all. Subduing a strong desire to retreat in disarray, he took a deep breath and tried again. 'Well, doesn't it seem reasonable to you? That a man might desire to see his own kitchen at some point?'

'Begging your pardon sir,' said Caine, regaining his own poise. 'It's quite irregular, sir. If there is a problem, sir, something that ought to be addressed, you've only to…'

'No, there's nothing that needs to be addressed, dammit!' said Tristan, growing nettled. 'You all do your jobs perfectly well. It simply occurred to me that I rely a great deal on all of you without showing the least interest in where you actually spend your time, or even what it is that you all do to make my life as comfortable as it is. And I thought perhaps I should.' He surveyed the assemblage in front of him, all perfectly upright, all at attention, all bewildered except his old groom, who clearly thought him unhinged. 'And now I have. So well done. Carry on.' And he turned on his heel and bolted.

On his departure, they all sagged into chairs at the table. 'Well.' Said Cook. 'Well I never.'

'He's such a handsome gentleman, I allus thought,' said the upstairs maid dreamily.

'You don't suppose he's a-going mad, do you?' asked the footman.

'Nah,' said Sam dismissively. 'I think it's them Hathaways as he's been keeping company with. Them's all Republicans, like. Got him thinking a bit different than what he's ever done.'

Caine said firmly, 'I'll tell you what. It isn't natural, is what. I don't hold with it. See his own kitchen? What on earth for? Next thing we know, he'll be wanting to cook his own eggs.'

'He'd never!' said the footman, awed.

'Don't worry about that none,' said Sam stoutly. 'Got his own affairs, hasn't he. And running the house and the stables, well that's our affairs, innit?' All agreed that it was. 'So he won't meddle. He'm just showing a interest in us, like. Making sure we 'uns is in right rig and getting along, like. And I call that true gentleman-like, I do. But p'raps, Mags, if'n it should happen again... you could offer the gentleman a nice cuppa.'

'His father the Viscount would never have deigned to do such a thing! He was one as knew his place in the world, and kept it,' said Caine in austere horror.

'Yes, and damned top lofty, too. I'd rather not be treated like one a me horses, nor yet a piece of furniture, I thank-ee.'

'Ah, bless his soul,' agreed Cook. ''Twas right flattering, when you think on't. Ella, where be those currants as I was a saving of? I think a nice batch of currant buns is just what the master needs.' She jumped up and began bustling. 'And you lot are in my way,' she said firmly. 'So get back to work, alla youse.'

*****

It would not have occurred to a man of Denham's rank to appear at the stage door of The Swan to demand audience with Madame Seraphine, so a very flustered front-of-house assistant jogged backstage to announce the presence of a 'niffy-naffy genlman' to Hemings, who took one look at the ravaged features and dead eyes of the punctiliously dressed Denham, and informed him pointedly that Madame was unavailable. His attempt to escort the supposed gentleman to the door was prevented by an elegant ebony cane that appeared suddenly between the door and the jamb, and the Earl's oily-rich voice suggesting that he bore information that he fancied Madame would like to hear. Thus outmaneuvered, Hemings accepted the man's card and left the him to cool his heels in the lobby while he marched the length of the house, trotted up the stage stairs, down to the dressing rooms, and rapped smartly on Madame's door.

'There's a gentleman to see you, ma'am, says it's business, but he's as queer as Dick's hatband if you ask me, fair made the hair stand up on the nape of me neck, he did,' he said, handing her the card.

Seraphine's eyes widened briefly on reading the name on the card. She knew this moment to be inevitable. She knew that continuing to put it off served nothing. 'Thank-you, Mr. Hemings,' she said calmly. 'Show him in, will you? But...' she hesitated and then went ahead with her thought, 'Stay in close contact, please. One never knows, with these 'business' people.'

'I'll be right where you can get me fast, like, an you need me, ma'am,' vowed Hemings.

Seraphine used the moments left her to steady her heart and school her expression to one of cool disinterest. Hemings returned with Denham, whose temper was on a slow burn at having been required to wait for long minutes with neither chair or refreshment offered. Being shown into what he considered a singularly cluttered and tawdry office did nothing to improve his ill humor. Mrs. Hathaway, seemingly unaware, rose, curtseyed, and said with gracious coolness, 'My Lord Denham. To what do I owe the honor, sir?'

'Mrs.... Er... Hathaway, I believe?' he asked, mustering suavity. 'I have been desirous of making your acquaintance, madame.'

'Have you, *m'sieu*? I must surely be gratified. *Asseyez-vous, s'il vous plait.* I fear I cannot offer you refreshment at the moment. As you see, I am embroiled in the endless work of a theatre company, and *comme vous avez vu*, the distance between this office and the dining room is lengthy.' She indicated a chair set comfortably near her desk, and made neither apology nor an attempt to clear several scripts and a tatty costume from it, rather leaving him the choice either of removing the objects himself, or standing.

'I shall stand, madame,' he said curtly, glad of the support of his cane.

'*Bien*,' said Seraphine. '*Maintenant, je vous en pris*, how may I serve you today? Mr. Hemings said you were here on a matter to concern me? What might that be, *on se demande*, my lord?'

'I will come to the point,' he drawled, hooded eyes watchful. 'I came to offer you protection, *Madame*, from the... er... *slings and arrows of outrageous fortune*, if I have my *Hamlet* correct.'

Madame looked confused. '*Comment?* Protection? *Je ne comprends pas, monseigneur*. If it is a question of patronage, I am of course very happy to add you to our list, for The Swan is very fortunate in its subscribers from - oh! - The highest echelons of the Polite world. *Mais peut-etre c'nest pas ca que vous se dire?* I am sorry, my English comprehension is not always so very complete, my lord. Perhaps you will explain?'

'Oh, 'tis well done, *madame*. Well done, indeed,' marveled Denham cynically. 'Whoever could have believed such a complete transformation? From the little slut Sara Finister to the respected Madame Seraphine.'

'*Escusez-moi?*' Madame asked blankly. '*Quest-ce que vous direz?*'

He had expected - what. Hysteria? Prevarication? A sudden capitulation? At least a blush that would play better into his hand. He realized with a jolt that he had erred grossly in basing his assumptions on a memory now twenty-five years old. The girl he had known, barely more than a child, had been full of fight and an aggravating tendency to shriek and deploy her nails, if memory served, but ultimately, a child, that he had broken and cast off with ease. The woman before him - mature, powerful, in complete control of her emotions - now fixed him with utter bewilderment and - could she dare? - An utterly unexpected *grise* of pity. It was outrageous. It could not be allowed.

'Perhaps I am mistaken, Madame,' he said, watching her carefully. 'You remind me so strongly of... another.'

'Ah,' the brow cleared. *'Je comprends,* my lord.' Seraphine
reached out and rang a little brass bell in the shape of an
Elizabethan lady, while saying, 'I am so very sorry, my lord
Denham. Memory serves us such tricks, does it not. And, my
lord,' she said gently, as if he were an old and failing grandfather,
'you do not look well, *hein*? I am sorry to disappoint you, but here
is Mr. Hemings to show you out. It has been a pleasure to meet
you, sir. I hope you will join us at The Swan as soon as you are
feeling well again. Thank-you, Mr. Hemings.'

Hemings stood expectantly by the door and Seraphine
gestured toward it invitingly. There was nothing left but to leave.
Denham gave a brief bow, and with admirable control of a rage
so deep that it made him tremble, hissed softly, 'First round to
you, Mr. Hathaway. There will be others. You shall see. Life is not
all… what is the proper term? Ah, I have it… a walk in the park.'

He turned away, and so missed the small satisfaction of seeing
Madame Seraphine's eyes widen just slightly. He followed
Hemings' lead, barely avoiding grinding his teeth as the man
solicitously recommended that he 'watch that step, my lord,' or
'the floor is uneven here, my lord', as they moved across the stage
and back up the aisle toward the lobby. And saw a chestnut-haired,
loose-limbed young man stride down the next aisle toward them,
whose figure turned the already shaken Denham almost to stone.
He stopped in his tracks, breath coming shallow, blood draining
from a white face, eliciting a penetrating glance from Stephen,
who demanded, 'Are you quite all right, sir?' Then, taking a curt
motion from Denham's hand as affirmation, he continued
carelessly on his way, cheerfully greeting every stage hand and
cleaner he met.

He wouldn't know that Denham's gesture was one designed to
ward off a ghost.

'Here we are, my lord. Shall I procure a chair for my lord?'

'No,' Denham snapped.

He had never been so grateful to stand on a street crowded
with the daily affairs of living.

Hours later, when he had returned to his rooms, berated Tibbs for being a clod, changed his clothes, ogled the upstairs maid with such lewdness that she escaped to the kitchen and fell into a fit of strong hysterics that took the efforts of the cook, the butler, and the footman to bring her out of, his lordship recovered from the day's unlooked-for setback in a comfortable chair by a cheerful fire, with a bottle of cognac at his elbow. Staring moodily into the flames, he recalibrated his thinking. It was the Finister chit, it had to be. Against all the odds. Not merely living, but thriving. And the young man… as if his own brother walked again, before… no. Never mind *before*. But… *her* son? *His* son? If he was right, if she was in fact who he thought… it was possible. Denham's face creased with a slow smile as he contemplated. This made his road rather more complicated than he had previously thought. But also, just possibly, far more satisfying. Nobody humiliated Denham in the way he had been humiliated today. Nobody. There was a price to be paid. And that trying child who had ruined his life should have died. Deserved to die.

He rang for Tibbs and sent a message to Bev Ramage, ordering him to meet at White's for supper.

*****

'Madame Seraphine?' Ramage asked in surprise as they attacked a large portion of roast beef somewhat later. 'The same girl you…' he caught himself before the words 'raped' and 'abandoned' came out of his mouth, '…took to France? Doing it rather too brown, Denham. It's accepted knowledge the chit died there.'

'But it is, you admit, possible.'

'For God's sake, man, her family searched for years. If she'd lived, surely they would have found her.'

'France is a large country, *mon vieux*.'

'Yes, and a revolutionary one. There are a thousand reasons for her to have died, and none I can think of for her to have survived. A gently born girl like that, alone in the middle of a strange country… I'm sorry, Denham, but it was ill done, very ill indeed. Did you never think to look for her yourself?'

'I, look for her? Why should I? That little slut ruined my life, Bev. If she died it was no better than she deserved. If she lives… she owes me a great debt.'

'Owes you… no, really, Denham, you go too far. You abandoned the girl.'

'It was her own fault. Had her father but agreed to the marriage, all would have been well. I have been away from my own country for twenty-five years, Bev. Ripped from a home and a fortune that should have been mine. Is not that punishment enough for any man? No, Bev. If this Madame Seraphine is, in fact, Sara Finister, then she owes me a very large sum indeed, to make all right. And you, my dear, will help me to collect it.'

Ramage put his utensils down, appetite gone. 'I won't do anything to set me on the wrong side of the law, Denham. By God, I won't. I've already put myself in enough danger on your behalf.'

'My dear sir, that is why I requested that you find another to execute the gathering of information that I require. Have you done so?'

'Indeed, sir. I intend to see him again in a very few days.'

'There, you see? I wouldn't dream of putting you in a position that would compromise you. Legally or morally.'

'But you have, sir,' insisted Ramage a little desperately. 'Simply by reminding me regularly of certain documents in your possession, which name me among a list of traitors to the Crown. Which you know yourself, sir, was never true.'

'Of course I know, dear Bev,' Denham said soothingly. 'It's the appearance of things, as you know, dear boy. Still, they are safer in my hands than they would ever be if made public.'

'They would be safer yet in my hands, and then burned, as they should have been long ago.'

'But they will be, Bev. They will be.'

'When?'

'When I have achieved my ends, dear fellow.'

Far from being comforted, Ramage began to see either a noose or a skillfully used shiv between the ribs in his future. The image made him ill. He had thought himself safe from all such ends. But that devil Denham never forgot anything. Not the smallest thing. Ramage was trapped.

Unless he could find a way to remove the man, once and for all.

Denham watched him and idly twirled the stem of a glass of dark ruby claret. 'I know what you're thinking, Bev,' he said, his voice light but the tone sinister. 'Do not, I pray you, make such an attempt. You will be doomed to failure.'

*****

At The Swan, Seraphine leaned back into her chair and closed her eyes.

Sara Finister. Twenty-five years since that name had been attached to her; twenty-five years since she had so much as heard it spoken aloud. *Sara Finister.* That poor, high spirited girl of fifteen, whose life had been as predictable and proscribed as any gently bred girl could have hoped for. Who as a child had yearned to be a romantic figure - a highwayman, a pirate on the high seas - and had indeed written several thrilling and fantastical stories about these figures which she acted out for the entertainment of her siblings. Who had looked forward eagerly to the upcoming treat of coming out in Society. Of taking London by storm, and being married to a dashing young man of title and fortune, who was perhaps a highwayman on the sideline, as noble as Robin Hood.

Richard Whately, Fifth Earl Denham, stole that future, and replaced a girl's dreams with a woman's endless dark horror of pain, blood, bruises. Until somewhere in France, she was thrown into a ditch by the road like so much detritus and left for dead.

She had been discovered by the fat landlord of a local inn and his good-hearted wife. Horrified, finding her still breathing, they attempted to discover her identity, but she, too weak to speak clearly, struggled to say, '*Sera…Phinne…*' And with that, Sara Finister died, and Seraphine was born.

They nursed her to health, those goodly people, and it had been a slow process because her body was badly depleted and covered with injuries the sight of which made her hostess gasp and cluck and mutter. The emotional damage was equally great. She did not speak for weeks. She showed no inclination to return to wherever she had come from, and all attempts to find out where home might be were met with a blank stare. When she was strong enough to repay her saviors by working, she proved a disaster in the kitchen and in the care and cleaning of clothes. She could safely wield a mop, though, and dusted and swept with a will. As her desire to live - and, alarmingly, her belly - grew, she began to sing while she worked, in a voice both clear and beautiful. The tavern keeper and his wife set her to singing in the evening for their customers, and as word got round, business grew and money flowed. Many young men came in, just to see Seraphine and hear her sing. Her hosts hoped one of these would take her fancy, and that she would go away with him. But Seraphine flinched away from all men, and could not bear to be touched.

She bore a son. She thought to hate him, but was surprised by love. The tavern keeper and his wife began to hint that two mouths were too many.

On a rainy night, a traveling theatre troupe came to the tavern for shelter, and set up their play in the courtyard behind. Their leading lady had been ill when the troupe arrived, and worsened as the moment approached for the performance that would pay their bed and board. In desperation, they asked Seraphine to fill in, and Seraphine proved so adept that the leader of the troupe asked if she might want to keep the job. Seraphine said yes. On their return from the south, headed for Paris as winter closed in, Seraphine and her baby son Stephen went with them.

No question Denham would do her mischief, if he could. Even an old dog may deliver a poisoned bite with what teeth it has left. To her advantage, he might assume that the woman he sought to frighten was merely an extension of the girl he tried to kill. For - Seraphine's mouth twisted bitterly - his entire experience and classification of women was that they were weak souls to be bent and bullied into whatever shape he desired. Knowing only of the death of Sara Finister, he could know nothing of the growth of Madame Seraphine.

She had no doubt that her very survival would be enough to enrage him, a monster who could not bear to be bested. Nor did she doubt that, had there been proof of his many indiscretions and secrets, he must have been tried, found guilty, and hanged long before now.

Which was why she could no longer harbor the secret she had kept close to her soul for twenty-five long years, and why she must have a plan, quickly.

As if in answer to this last thought, Stephen rapped lightly on her door and entered. 'I thought you'd like to know that we may have nipped the cold among the opera dancers with a tincture Marianne and I created. One can only hope. But what *I* would like to know,' he continued, barely drawing breath, 'is what is between you and that horrifying old court-card I have now seen here twice. And no,' he added, raising his hand to stop her speaking, 'do not tell me it is nothing, because I am not so credulous. It is something concerning your past. Our past. I deserve the truth, *Maman.*'

'You'd better shut the door then,' said Seraphine. *'Parlons nous en francais, n'est-ce pas? Alors, personne ne nous comprendra.'*

He nodded, closed the door, removed the clutter from the one comfortable chair, and sat. 'It does have something to do with that ancient *roué*, does it not? I just passed him in the aisle. When he saw me, he looked ill.'

'He might very well. You are the image of his older brother.'

'His...'

'There is no easy way to say this, Stephen, so I will just say it quickly and hope you will hear me out. That man is Richard Whately, the fifth Earl Denham. And, it grieves me to say, he is your father.'

'My *father*! But how...'

She took a deep breath, and told him.

When she finished, the silence stretched so long that they could hear dust settle, the clock tick, the distant voices of people in the dressing rooms, the thumps and scrapes of scenery being moved across the stage above them; even the occasional shout or call from the street. Still Stephen sat with eyes lowered, face pale, jaw tight, lips pressed together.

'And you have carried this secret all these years?' he asked, finally.

'Yes.'

'Did *Papa*... did... *pere* Hathaway know any of this?'

'I do not know. I do not think so. I never meant to come back to England, Stephen. When we did... I had heard - as one always hears - that Denham had gone to Germany, then to Italy. I thought myself safe. I never imagined he would return to this country, or worse, to walk into The Swan.'

'And he came to see you today.'

'Yes. He came to threaten me.'

'Threaten you! But what harm can you possibly do him?'

'He is a hereditary Earl. I am an actress. Were I to speak out, none that mattered would believe me. But he is a beast who must always have his way. He intended me to die. My survival is a reminder of his perfidy, and his exile. He will blame me for it, and try to find a way to destroy me and mine.'

'But you were a child! You can have had nothing to do with his folly!'

'He will not see it that way. He sees only himself. He is a very dangerous man, Stephen.'

'He is a very old man,' responded Stephen. 'And if I am correct, also very unwell.'

'Do not underestimate him. He has spent a lifetime doing harm to others for his own gain. If he finds anything - *anything* - to use as a tool of destruction, he will not hesitate. Oh, Stephen,' she rubbed her face with her hands wearily. 'I hope you will not hate me.'

'Hate you!' He took her hands. 'I think you are the bravest person I have ever met. That blackguard, though,' he added flatly, his voice harsh with suppressed anger. 'There is a special circle of hell awaits that *canaille*.'

'Yes,' agreed Seraphine. 'There is. But oh, Stephen. I so hope he ends up there without destroying more lives first.'

*****

Chance River was settled on a pile of comfortable oak timbers, finishing a meat pie purchased at a stall early that morning for his break, when a young fellow dressed as a clerk's apprentice trotted breathlessly into the yard looking harried and searching urgently, it turned out, for him. The master carpenter, having suspiciously ascertained that River was not wanted by the law, gave Chance leave to go, reminding him that his pay would be docked accordingly. Chance was not pleased at this interruption of his day, but the young man insisted that the business pertained to Captain Seymour, and would not keep - here he tapped his temple suggestively. Chance packed his gear, promising the master as quick a return as was in his power.

He arrived to a strange scene. The old mariner sat regally at the head of his oaken table in an ornate wooden armchair with a large pillow behind his back to support him. He was in full if faded dress uniform, had a very outmoded wig on his head, and a feverish but cogent gleam in his eye.

'Took your damn time, River,' the old man barked. 'This is Penrose.'

River looked curiously at the neatly dressed middle-aged man standing beside Seymour, and didn't fail to notice the housekeeper, who stood sullen in the background, arms akimbo, mouth set, sharp eyes attentive. The weary clerk stationed himself by the door in an attitude of watchfulness.

'Mr. River,' said Penrose, hand extended. 'I have served this last decade as Captain Seymour's agent in his property holdings, which consist of this building and its occupants. I know your… mother, is it? Madame Simard?'

'Ay, sir,' said Chance cautiously, accepting the handshake.

'A hardworking woman, sir. Never late with her rent or her taxes. And unflinchingly honest,' he cast a brief glance at the housekeeper, who snorted scornfully. 'She must be very happy to have you back at home, after… how many years at sea?'

'Better'n a dozen, I take it, sir.'

'And will you find another ship?'

'I think not, sir. Me ma, she an't in prime twig, sir. It's in me mind to abide, like, and do what I can for her.'

'And you have a job. In the Pool, I understand.'

'That's right, sir. Like to be head carpenter, before long, I dessay.'

Penrose smiled encouragingly. 'And after that?' he asked suggestively.

River smiled, shrugged. 'Too soon to say, sir. But onc't I'm settled, like, down the road a piece, 'twould be grand to own a piece of that ship, sir, innit.'

'Indeed,' said Penrose, looking at him thoughtfully.

'Begging your pardon, sir,' said River. 'I oughter be working. I reckon I an't here to talk about my prospects, sir, so…' he let the sentence hang.

'Sit down, River,' Penrose indicated a chair on one side of the table and took the one opposite. 'Captain Seymour, are you with us?'

'Ay,' said the old man, though his gaze, as so often happened, was a little less sharp than it had been a moment ago. He pulled himself up straight again, looked first at River, then at Penrose, and ordered fiercely, 'give him the lot.' And then, equally fiercely fixing River with a hard blue stare, 'But mind you see me out proper, and bury me decent, with my Margery.'

'I…' said River, nonplussed. 'What are you saying, sir?'

'He means to make you his heir,' said Penrose calmly.

'Me! But an't you got family in Quebec or some such?'

'All they wanted was my gold. All she wants is my gold,' he jerked his head toward the housekeeper. 'Well they can't have it. You been decent to me, boy, you're cut yare. And I like your ma. So me and Margery, we decided…' He looked confused for a moment, then lapsed into muttering.

River looked questioningly at Penrose.

'There is no gold, River,' he said. 'But there is this building. The lease has fifteen years to run. It is not an inconsiderable property.'

'There an't no other will?'

'There was. All left to his wife. And now to you. I wanted to see today whether you were an honest fellow, or a rogue. If the latter, I should have witheld the document.'

Chance rubbed his head. 'Well I'll be blowed,' he said. 'I don't hardly know what to say, Mr. Penrose. I got no great experience about property, me being a mariner and all.'

'I will be happy to help you with that when the time comes. Which, by the grace of God will not be for some time yet.'

But as it happened, it was God's grace to gather the old man to his ancestors sooner rather than later. Perhaps the over-excitement of this meeting, or the relief of having his affairs ordered to his liking, had something to do with it. But not two days later Seymour wandered out into the rain as he sometimes did, and forgot where he lived. The furor this caused required the combined efforts of Molly Boggs, Chance River, Angel Hathaway, both of Molly's apprentices, the mantua maker, and the housekeeper to find the old man, who was discovered trotting toward the harbor with shirt tails flapping, pursued by a pack of boys who jeered and threw stones.

No amount of solicitous care could prevent his contracting a chill, then a fever, and his mind began to wander badly. Stephen came to look at him, and although the various medicaments prepared by himself and Marianne soothed the old gentleman greatly, his wits did not recover. He called often for Margery and other friends and relatives probably long dead. He relived old battles and resettled old scores, shouting imprecations and waving his arms. He babbled about his gold. He lasted a week in this state, but when on his last visit Stephen noted that his ramblings had become weaker and less comprehensible and his breathing more labored, it was clear Seymour would not recover. Chance and the housekeeper settled by the old seaman to wait, neither trusting to leave Captain Seymour in the hands of the other. The old man passed in the grey of pre-dawn.

'Well,' said the housekeeper. 'That's that, then.'

Chance stood wearily and straightened this tired back with a grunt.

'Played your hand well, dint you,' the woman continued acidly. 'Playin' up to the old bugger like as what you did, and you gettin' the whole at the end.'

'Twas no more than Christian kindness,' said Chance. He walked into the front room. She followed.

'And me, what took care of him all this time, *all* he was needful of, what happens to…'

'You was paid fair, and I an't said nothing about what-all you helped yourself to, nor I won't.'

She gasped in rage, strode up to him, and raised her arm to strike him. He caught her hand and held it close, and just then, there was a powerful voice that said, *'Well?'* In outraged accents, and it was Bridie Murphy in the doorway, wild-eyed and windblown, as if she'd run all the way across the town.

Chance may have been besotted, but he was far from unbalanced, and he was very tired. He looked from one woman to the other and said wearily, 'I got no time for shrews. You, Jennie Mudgett, I'll be needing you to help out here, to see the old man laid out decent, and I'll see you get all you deserve. Just go off with you now, and fetch the crowner and a priest, and bring 'em back here.' Jennie made to refuse, but saw the glint of hard coin in Chance's hand. 'There's more a this an you come back with un,' he said, holding it away from her when she went to grab it. She stood looking at him murderously for a second, then nodded curtly, and held her hand out. He gave her the coin and she left.

'Well, Chance,' said Bridie, rather impressed by his masterful behavior.

'Well, Bridie,' said Chance, looking at her cautiously. 'What brings you here, and so early-like?'

'I an't seen you at The Swan this sennight past. I got to wondering what you was up to. Angel told me about your old seaman, so I come to see for meself. He's here?'

'Ay,' he gestured to the other room.

'He's passed on?'

'Ay.'

'Do you mind?'

'Ay. I'd got right fond of the old bugger.'

'And now what? What happens to all this?' she gestured around the room.

'It's all to be mine.'

'*Yours*?' her eyes widened in awe.

'Aye.'

'But... what will you... how is it...'

'I'm thinking I'll settle in, like,' he said, a hint of mischief playing about his eyes. 'Open her up so's me ma has more space. Mebbe find someone who'd like to go in with me.'

Bridie gasped. '*Find someone to go in with you*? Like a *wife*, you'd be saying?' She demanded, drawing herself up to her full height.

'If I can find a woman pleases me to look at, and can help out. And who ain't a shrew,' Chance acknowledged, and turned away to look speculatively at the ship painting, and the doorway that might lie behind it. He reached out to run his fingers along the wall to find a seam.

'Chance River,' said Bridie behind him in stirring accents, 'If you think you want a good woman in your life, you'd best not look any further than this room right here!'

Chance turned at that, and there stood Bridie, her dress pooled on the floor, standing only in her shift with her opalescent skin, her beautiful curves, all on display. Chance lost his breath at that, and his reason. He went to Bridie Murphy in a dream and put his hands on her arms, her shoulders, pulled her close and traced from her neck to her round breasts, to her back, to her full bottom, kissing her deeply, searchingly, with force, lowering her gently to the floor, where he spread her out and entered her with the fullness of him and worshipped every inch of her with mouth and hands, and when she cried out in fiery ecstasy it was his name on the beautiful mouth he possessed in every way, while the husked body of an old man cooled in the next room.

That evening, after Bridie, after a message to his employer at the Pool, after an official report of death, after the mortal remains of Captain Seymour had been removed to prepare for burial, Chance sat brooding at the table in silence, uncertain of his thoughts. With a sigh, he rose and took down the painting of the ship *Fortune*, and using his knife to pry it up, stripped off the wall paper behind it. There was indeed a doorway, long boarded over. With pry bar, hammer, and saw from his toolbox next door, Chance tore out tough old oaken planks to reveal a short, narrow passage behind the vast chimney with a similarly boarded up door beyond to Molly's flat. Chance raised his lantern and studied the wide brick surface of the chimney's side and found a nook exactly where he'd thought it would be. In the nook lay a small, heavy, dust-covered strongbox. And inside the strongbox was Captain Seymour's gold.

Chance laughed long and low, thanked the gods of fortune for leading him home, promised to do good with all he had, and returned the box to its alcove, safely out of sight.

Old Captain Seymour was buried with the ceremony due his rank, his uniform brushed, his official mourners well paid, and a headstone carved with an image of his last ship. Sometime later, Greenwich Hospital received a generous donation in the Captain's name from an anonymous source for the care of old and infirm sailors. No matter that the Captain himself would never have thought to waste his blunt on charity; Chance River knew what was owed to the fickle gods that ruled seamen.

On his next half day, he was seen in the shop of a jeweler, selecting a small golden ring inlaid with a chip of stone the color of Bridie Murphy's eyes.

*****

After a spell of hanging about in the public houses and taverns in the neighborhood of The Swan, Ramage met a young rigger named Tom, who needed money to impress the opera dancer Doll Bridger, who had been his sweetheart until Charles Pearce charmed her with his gifts and his flattery and his position. Now she was Pearce's mistress. And Tom, because Doll was not shy in taunting him with hints of her inside knowledge of their employers' lives, and further hints that she expected to become the next Mrs. Pearce, an she played her hand well, was jealous and angry.

So it was not long before Ramage, for what represented a very modest sum to him but which Tom perceived as a potentially bottomless source of income, got a pretty fair understanding of the inner workings of The Swan and its sharers and employees, as well as gossip regarding the internal politics of the place and the general makeup of the Hathaway family. He was interested to learn that Mrs. Hathaway had not one, but two children; an older son lately returned from the sea, as well as the daughter, 'a prime piece of horseflesh,' who assisted a local dressmaker named Madame Simard. Yeh, there was 'sposed to be a Mr. Hathaway, on a time in France. Nah, rumor was he'd got caught up in that Frenchie revolution what had brought so many Frogs to London (Tom spat as he said this). Nah, Mr. Pearce (he spat again) wasn't Mrs. Hathaway's lover, nor she dint never seem to have no suitors hanging about, strait-laced as a nun she were. And nah, she nor that prissy daughter of hers didn't never go out unattended, but always had Hemings or young Mr. Hathaway or yet that blackie they called Freeman who they was a great deal too familiar with, he as nasty a piece of work as ever you seed. And who did they think they were, the lot of them, poncing about giving themselves airs, he wanted to know.

Ramage passed the parts of this information that seemed useful to Denham, who absorbed it thoughtfully and wondered what this Tom might be willing to do in terms of mischief, should the chance arise. 'Of course, there would be a bonus for such work,' he said smoothly.

'Will you meet him, then?' asked Ramage, hoping for some relief.

'Good God no, Beverly. That is why I employ you,' responded his employer. And Ramage felt himself pulled deeper into Denham's web, no way to escape.

Denham in his day would have assumed that an easy mark like Tom might sing from either side of his mouth, and taken steps to correct that impulse. Time and dissipation are not the friends of wit, however, and Ramage, a simpler and far more fearful man than his employer, had neither cunning nor the desire to play chess with human lives. So when Tom the rigger inevitably boasted to his mates about 'a certain acquaintance that was good to us, very good indeed', to explain the sudden improvement in his finances, and went about his work with a certain knowing sneer and insolent swagger that had never before been a part of his demeanor, James Hemings took note.

Hemings duly brought his suspicions to the sharers. Pearce was ready to haul the young man before them, call him to the carpet, force an admission of from him that might encompass anything from stealing their prized songs and adaptations of plays to finding a way to dip his hand in the till, and sack the nasty little bugger.

'No, Charles,' said Seraphine, just as troubled but far more reasonable. 'If we turn him away, then we have an enemy with no better aim than to be revenged on us for his wrongs. Might it not be better to keep him in our sight, and see can we discover what mischief he is up to?'

'Watching is best, this present,' agreed Hemings.

Pearce grudgingly assented. When Hemings had gone, he looked soberly at Seraphine. 'Sera, what is all this about? This fellow is surely not being paid to do me ill. It must, therefore, be something that has pursued you from France. Something, perhaps, pertaining to George.'

'*J'ai peur que oui*,' admitted Seraphine, rubbing her brow
wearily. 'It is something - someone - from France. Not connected
with George, but from my earlier life.'

Pearce sighed. 'I know so little about you, you see. Only that I
made a promise to my cousin, which must be honored.'

'As you have, my dear. And I think I have given you no cause
for regret.'

'None, I assure you! In truth... The Swan would not be where
it is today without your financial investment or your talent. But...
I cannot countenance any danger to The Swan. if we go forward
as partners, I must understand the whole, Sera.'

'*Oui, bien sur*.' Seraphine stared for a moment into a middle
distance of memory: dark, filled with terror; any glimpse of joy
shadowed by the threat of that horror catching up to her again,
tearing her life apart, again. She realized at that moment how very
tired she was, how great a weight her past had been. Although she
shrank from the thought of exposing herself to those she loved
most, perhaps she owed them that trust. Perhaps in the telling, she
might finally knit together all the pieces of a tattered soul.

'As we are dark tomorrow, Charles, come and dine with us,'
she said. 'If you can but wait another day, I will tell you, all of you,
a story that it is time to make known.'

*****

'My name is Sara Finister,' Seraphine spoke into the dusk that
gathered in the corners of the withdrawing room, whose small fire
illuminated every beloved face that sat around her. 'I was the
daughter of Henry Finister, a wealthy squire whose home was in
Gloucestershire.'

'*Maman*,' cried Angel in spite of herself. 'You were born in
England? But how...'

'Angel,' Stephen shushed her. 'Listen.'

'The Denham estates were not far distant from my father's.
The old Earl, Gervase Whately, was a renowned gambler and a

drunkard. After the death of an elder son in a hunting accident, the younger son, Richard Whateley, inherited title and land. He was easily as great a rakehell as his father before him, and must needs look for a wealthy wife to help rebuild what little his father had left of the estate. He thought to fix his interest with my sister, who had just come out. He was well over thirty years of age; she was eighteen. She was rightly frightened of him, and my father refused the match. Being crossed enraged Denham always, but my father couldn't know that; the man was rarely at home and news of his behaviors came through the usual channels of gossip and hearsay.

'So, my father thought the matter closed. My sister became engaged to another. And then one day, when I was out picking berries with my nurse and my small brother, Julian... Whateley appeared out of nowhere and joined us. He tried to be ingratiating, tried to take me aside to talk. I resisted, of course, and Nurse and Julian tried to send him off, but it was no use. He became loud and abusive. He shoved my nurse and knocked her down, and when my little brother went to attack him, I thought Denham would kill him. I threw myself at him and started screaming for help. He grabbed me then, and dragged me away. I bit, I scratched, I kicked, I screamed... it was no use. His carriage was by the road, and there was a groom to help him. I was fifteen years old. I don't know what Denham thought he was about. He was prone to act in rage, without thought.' She paused, staring into the fire. 'I... had ample time to know that of him.'

She took a deep breath and continued. 'He took me away. I do not know where. He said my father would now be forced to marry me to him, or risk ruining me forever. He did not touch me at first. He had just that much honor. But we kept moving from place to place. I was at all times guarded and locked up. His temper grew worse and worse. He drank more. My father was unreasonable, he said. He didn't really love me. If he did, we would be married and all Denham's problems solved. Somehow he made it all seem my fault. That I was not amenable enough. Loved enough. Appealing enough.

'And then, in another drunken rage, he beat me. And raped me. And made me his whore. He took me to France, where the ill treatment became much worse.' She stopped again, eyes fixed in the past. 'I will not describe it to you. Those of you who are of the world have seen it. Felt it.' Jacob hissed through his teeth. Marianne sat like a statue. Stephen frowned into the fire. Pearce and Angel gazed at her round-eyed, a stranger suddenly landed from a distant star.

'I tried to escape - oh, many times. He always found me. And the beatings were horrific. It became clear after some months that no one looked for me. That no one would rescue me. He did not know - I barely understood myself - that I was pregnant. I tried once more to leave, but of course he caught me. He beat me senseless, and left me by the side of the road to die. And I nearly did.

'Then, in a stroke of incredible fortune or Divine intervention... I was found by a tavern keeper and his wife on their way home from market. They saved me, and were kind, and I worked hard for that kindness. Stephen's birth was my rebirth. I became a new person. Seraphine. I left with a group of players and began a new life in Paris, on the stage.' She stopped. Took in the people ringed around her. 'And the rest, you know,' she ended, into the thick silence of an entire room that had inhaled and held its breath.

Then, a long, slow exhale. All of the household blinking around them as if awakening from a dream. But not, Seraphine noticed, looking at each other. And not actually noticing where their eyes rested. None of them would be able later to describe the room. The landscape they struggled to understand lay entirely inside their minds. Except for Stephen. Stephen, who watched, and calculated.

'So after all those years...' Pearce mopped his brow. 'Finister's daughter. Good God.'

'Indeed.'

'But…' faltered Angel, 'why did you not come home? After? Surely you knew your family looked for you. Surely…'

'They did,' supplied Pearce. ''Twas a great scandal. They say it killed your mother, Sera.'

'But I did not know,' said Seraphine. 'Denham… had me completely in his power, you see. He made me understand that my worth was so little that my family had cut me free, and did not care about my fate. That is how… men like him… operate. Not only by controlling, and hurting, but by cutting their victims off from friends and family and showing them that it is because of some fault in themselves.'

'But after. Surely, after…' insisted Angel.

'For a long time, I was far too ill, and broken, to think beyond my misery. Who would have believed me? Word of any search for me would not have penetrated to the village I was found in. Then, as I returned to health, and Stephen was born…' she stopped, and stared once more into the past, finally shaking her head. 'Can you imagine a penniless young girl, dressed in borrowed clothing, baby on her hip, appearing at an Embassy and claiming to be the lost daughter of an English squire? I should have been jeered out of the building. Even returning to my former home, what would I be? Damaged goods, certainly unmarriagable, an embarrassment to the family but too well bred to go out in the world as an actress to make my own way. Stephen would have immediately been taken from me and fostered. And I would have dwindled as the companion of some elderly lady, no better than a servant - no better than I deserved - for the rest of my life.'

'But… they could not be so cruel…' Angel persisted imploringly.

'Oh, but they could,' said Pearce pragmatically, 'And call it Charity. Your mother has, by some miracle of Providence, created a successful life, with recognition, and even, I may say, a certain social fluidity that would never have been hers had she attempted to reclaim her true identity. If you cannot see that, my girl, you are a bigger fool than I have thought you.'

Angel could not give up that easily. 'But now? ...your brother... you said you had a sister... they would be glad to see you, to know you to be alive.'

'Would they, my dear?' asked Seraphine, looking deeply into her daughter's eyes. 'Imagine, if you will, any one of your clients at Madame Simard's. How well do you think they would welcome a stranger coming into their homes, announcing themselves as a long-lost sister? With two children by two different men? Who worked as an actress? Do you think they would open their arms and welcome this stranger - a clearly low born one at that - into the bosom of the family? I think, rather, that she would end in Bedlam, or Newgate.'

Angel flushed deep red. Marianne, sitting next to her, took her hand. 'I am sorry, Angel,' she said gently. 'There is nothing about this to make your current situation better.'

'And Stephen... O Stephen, this monster...' tears rolled down Angel's cheeks.

'Is my father,' finished Stephen grimly. 'I have God, our *Maman*, and George Hathaway to thank that he will never know.'

'I have no doubt that he has already guessed,' said Seraphine.

'But only guessed.'

'Cannot this Denham be brought to justice?' asked Angel plaintively.

'A Peer of the realm? After all this time? Not likely,' said Jacob.

'From what I have learned, he is suspected of having killed two wives, one in Germany, another in Italy. And who knows what else he has done, in the interim. But he has never so far been brought to justice. Nor will be, I fear,' added Stephen.

'Which brings us to the next thing we must talk about', said Seraphine. 'For Denham means us mischief, I believe.'

Angel gasped. 'But... *why*?'

'Because I survived. He - his kind - cannot bear being bested. To him, my existence is an insult. To him, I am responsible for his exile. And for that, I assure you, he will never forgive me or anyone close to me.'

'It means all of us must be extremely wary,' said Stephen. 'So Angel, you must at all times be accompanied by myself or Jacob or even Chance River, if you should be out with Bridie. And of course, I need hardly say that Brutus must always be with you. Take care, though, that someone does not try to poison him by offering him a treat.'

Angel gasped. 'Poison! But who would…'

'No one that means you well.'

Angel rested a protective hand on Brutus' collar.

'The same goes for you, *Maman*,' Stephen continued. 'Jacob or myself or Hemings or our cousin Pearce must always be with you when you are away from the theatre.'

'Oh, but Stephen,' chided Seraphine. 'Surely I…'

'*Maman*,' said Stephen seriously, 'In this world I have seen and treated innocent people targeted for the worst sorts of crimes and unspeakable deceits. Not one expected to be the recipient of these horrors. Some did not survive them. If we are constantly vigilant, perhaps together we can find a way to bring this Denham to justice.'

'Never was a man so ripe to swing,' pronounced Pearce. 'Or so unlikely to.'

'There are other ways to remove him,' said Jacob quietly.

Stephen shot him a warning glance. 'Let us not speak of that. May I just say that… revenge is a son's revenue.'

'Stephen!' uttered Seraphine, appalled. 'You cannot mean…'

'At this present, I mean only to keep you safe, *Maman*,' he said. 'You have carried too much for too long. It is time for it to stop.'

The rest of the company nodded, growled, mumbled, or spoke their assent. Seraphine looked at this, her collection of friends - no, her family, the best of families - and felt their love.

'Thank-you,' she said simply, and in those words lay a lifetime of gratitude.

*****

Tristan Neville could not go on much longer without some conclusion to his friendship with Angel Hathaway. He knew he should give the girl up. He knew he must. Daily, he resolved to find her and tell her that she had been right all along, that they must not see one another again. Daily, his courage failed him. Daily, he wished he had never seen her. Daily, he wanted to possess every inch of her. Daily, he contemplated buying a set of colors and soldiering his way across the continent, where he would probably die in action, her name on his lips. Daily, he thought of venturing to the Indies, where he would doubtless die of some exotic disease. Daily, he found himself loitering about the streets and stopping-places frequented by her, instead.

Recently, these desperate journeyings had been unsuccessful. The thought that she might be ill, or injured, worried him. The idea that perhaps another man, a man far more suitable than himself, might have taken her fancy, nearly drove him to distraction.

Turning the corner into his street much too early one morning, downcast from missing her yet again when he'd thought to encountering her on her way to work, he found himself face to face with his uncle Nathaniel. Other than exclaiming 'Uncle! What brings you here!' in a fashion so guilty that he felt like a small boy caught in the middle of a prank, he could think of nothing more to say.

'I desire a word with you, Tris,' Neville said, saving him the need.

'Certainly, sir. Join me for breakfast, an you will. I have just been...'

'Looking for Miss Hathaway. I know. Don't be a gudgeon, Nephew,' he smiled cynically as his nephew stood, mouth opening and shutting like the very baitfish. 'Did you think your fancies secret? London is not that large, my boy.' They entered Tristan's house, talked generally as they divested themselves of outer garments, and stood by the bow window of the front room while Tristan ordered a breakfast suitable for two hungry men.

'First of all,' said Neville, 'I've come to warn you that my sister is in town on the instant, and she is under full sail.'

'My mother! Good God!' exclaimed Tristan, deeply shocked. 'Why on earth?'

'Because, my dear nephew, she is laboring under the impression that you are about to make a most dreadful *mesalliance* with a lower sort of *bourgeosie*.'

'A *mesalliance*! Who told her that?'

'Lady Torrington, of course. Who had it in turn from that other singularly idiotic young man I must claim as nephew.'

'Badgeley! I've been bubbled by *Badgeley*? Of all the stupid, unconscionable… I'll wring his damned neck.'

'A sentiment he has often elicited in my breast,' agreed Neville. 'But to the point: it true?' Tristan didn't answer, so after a moment of tense silence, Neville continued. 'I have held the opinion that you are in general a man of good sense and tact in the handling of your *affaires*. When it came to my attention that you had been seen in the company of… I quote… 'a smashing dark haired chit', I naturally assumed it to be a woman of our world, or at least a woman who knows the game. Now instead I find that the woman in question is none other than Miss Angel Hathaway, a dressmaker by trade, and daughter of a woman who is cloaked by…'

'Cloaked by? Cloaked… by what?'

'That is immaterial at present. What on earth are you *thinking*, Neville?'

Tristan flushed to the roots of his hair. 'What I am thinking and who I choose to spend my time with need be of no concern to you, *Neville*,' he retorted curtly.

'Quite right. It is not. But when your mother arrives in my house, telling the world that her darling son is in the clutches of a designing female whose mama, an *actress*, is trying her best to force a marriage...'

Tristan gave a shout of exasperated laughter. 'Oh no, is she really saying that? And under your roof, too? I'm very sorry for you, Nat. Why did she not send Kit to rescue me? Surely he, as the head of the House...'

'I have been informed that Lord Neville was so deeply shocked that he retired to his study and has not come out since,' intoned Neville primly.

'Probably skinned out the back window with his fishing rod and retired to the Blue Boar. Left it to Lady Lydia to deal with our mother's freaks.'

'I should think it extremely likely. A great deal of sense, the Viscount. Not so his wife. Nonetheless, they share a deep notion of their place in the world, and it is a rigid notion, Tristan. They will join forces with your mother to scotch any threat of what they consider to be scandal-broth of the worst sort.'

'But I haven't created one,' insisted Tristan. 'And as for Mrs. Hathaway throwing her daughter at me... as far as I know, Mrs. Hathaway is not even aware...' he colored. 'Dammit, Nat, you make it sound as if I'm dallying with the girl,' he finished defensively. 'I assure you, that is not the case.'

'Then what is the case? Do enlighten me,' invited his uncle with a smoothness belied by the dangerous glint in his eye.

Tristan stared out the window and watched streaks of rain traveling down the panes twist buildings, carts, and people into odd rainbow shapes.

'Sir,' he said abruptly. 'As a younger son with no need for occupation other than to marry well and dance attendance on various members of a family whose tastes are not mine and whose minds I find to be inexpressibly mundane, I have no real purpose in life. I could buy a set of colors, but a soldier's life is not for me, I think. Nor am I cut out for a life in some rural church, ministering to a congregation made up of the same people I dislike so heartily.' He sighed. 'I do often envy those who go out to work every day, earning their way, or those who do things that enrich the lives of others. I should like to find such an occupation for myself.'

'There are fortunes to be made in The Indies, and the new America, if you like. Also the China trade, with new and faster ships.'

'I am not at all certain I want to make my fortune on the backs of slaves, Uncle.'

'You are more naive than I thought, if you assumed your family's comfortable fortune was made solely through rents and crops.'

'I am not at all that naive, I thank-you. I have merely come to prefer a rather different form of livelihood.'

'Then, since I have never noted a poetic bent in your nature, and cannot imagine you up to your elbows in blood and medications, there is left the law. Or politics.'

'The former of which, in fact, I have been wanting to speak with you about. I must do something useful, Uncle. But...'

'Your thoughts have been derailed by... er... *a smashing black-haired chit*, and all the parts of life that she opens to you, that you have never had cause to think about before.'

'I knew you'd understand, sir.'

'I do not understand one thing, however: how will you end your... association... with the lady? For, edifying as it has no doubt been, end it must. Your family will never agree to a match.'

'My family has nothing to do with my actions.'

'They will if they cut you off. Use your brain, Tristan.'

'That would be most inconvenient, I admit. But I have my own means, Uncle. My circumstances may be straitened, but they will not be disastrous.'

'Are you telling me you won't give the girl up?'

'I...' Tristan hesitated. Gulped. Hesitated again. Then said somewhat roughly, 'I am.' Thinking, *there. You've finally admitted it.*

'*Why?*'

'Because… she shows me how to be a better man. She questions my assumptions with a bright and enquiring mind. She is beautiful, of course. But that is the smallest part of it. I have never met anyone like her, Nathaniel.'

'Please don't tell me you can't live without her. I shall die of *ennui.*'

'Of course I can live without her,' his nephew scoffed. 'But the better I know her… the more I know I'd rather not. Though why it matters to you, I cannot imagine.'

'It matters to me not a whit.'

'I thought not. And… in fact…' he took a deep, steadying breath, 'you perceive me about to take steps to settle the matter.'

'And you are now contemplating a run to Gretna Green?'

Tristan snorted. 'I hope I am not such a flat. But… my great-aunt Charlotte still buries herself near Faringdon, does she not?'

'She does. As irascibly as ever.'

Tristan grinned thoughtfully. 'It might just serve,' he said.

'If the young… er… lady… agrees.'

'It will take a bit of persuasion.'

'You surprise me.'

'She's already told me not to call again, for all the reasons you list.'

'A woman of rare foresight.'

'Yes, but it will not serve.'

'Whyever not?'

'Because my mind is made up, Uncle. I will have Angel Hathaway to wife.'

Caine knocked discreetly and entered at that moment, announcing that breakfast was served in the dining room. Tristan and Nathaniel duly migrated to that room, filled mugs with small beer, loaded plates with rolls and ham, and sat at the table. Time enough for the elder Neville to realize that he had handled this conversation badly; that rather than discouraging Tristan's actions, he had unwittingly caused the young man to resolve himself. He cursed himself silently.

'Should you run away with this girl,' he said wearily once Caine had closed the doors, 'you must be acutely aware not only of the durability of your feelings, but of the unpleasantness which will follow such an escapade. For I assure you, Tristan. It will be very, very unpleasant.'

'Thank-you, Nat,' said Tristan. 'You have, as always, given me a great deal to think about.' He looked steadily at Neville, eyes clear and mind finally settled. 'I appreciate your support.'

'I attempted to talk you out of an impossible situation, and in fact have made it worse.'

'Just so, sir. But I should have arrived at the same conclusion in time, you know.'

Caine knocked and re-entered. 'Mr. Tristan, sir. Lady Neville is here to see you, sir, with Miss Arabella Montjoy.'

'*Arabella Montjoy*! Damn her!' swore Tristan. 'And why the hell is... Oh *God*', he cursed, putting down his utensils with a clatter. 'I suppose it's too late to turn them away, Caine.'

'I have shown them to the parlor, sir, with suitable refreshment,' said Caine. Will you care to join them there?'

'I'll make my escape, Nephew,' said Neville, rising with alacrity. 'I bid you good day. And good luck.'

'The door had closed and Nathaniel's footsteps sounded rapidly on the stairs.

With thoughts more tumultuous than he expected, Tristan took a few moments to straighten his neckcloth, flick any stray specks of dust off his immaculate coat, and school his face into a perfect mask of bland affability before strolling into the parlor with a well bred air of careless elegance. He greeted his mother punctiliously, and did his best to put Miss Montjoy at ease, as she, not insensitive, clearly felt the tension in the room. She relaxed as they chatted about the pleasures of Town and her lively expectations of seeing all the sights, including the treats of Ranelagh and the Pantheon. She was bright, she was pretty, she was dressed perfectly, and had impeccable manners. Nothing about her could offend, or vex, or challenge. A perfect catch for some fortunate man.

'Arabella has been all agog to see you again, Tristan,' purred his mother. 'I have assured her that you will be very happy to be her squire this next sennight, for a more amiable guide she could not find.' She smiled meaningfully. Tristan's smile remained fixed.

'Alas, ma'am, Miss Montjoy, I shall be away from Town on business beginning tomorrow, and will not be available for such a delightful duty. I am certain, however, that it will give my cousin Badgeley infinite pleasure to stand in where I may not. If only you had given me more notice…' he spread his hands apologetically.

His mother's expression became rigid. 'What sort of business can you possibly have that takes you out of Town just when I have need of you, Tristan?' she expostulated.

Tristan kept smiling, and replied sweetly, 'And what on earth made *you* think I have no business of my own, Mama?'

'Oh no, please, Lady Neville, it is of no consequence at all,' Miss Arabella soothed her hostess earnestly, admirably hiding her disappointment.

Tristan's heart went out to her. Before this mama could answer, he said contritely, 'I am desolated, Miss Montjoy, to be deprived of the pleasure of showing you all that Town has to offer. But I can at least offer you a ride in the Park, shall we say at 4:00? I have a lovely brown mare that I feel will suit you very well, and perhaps Mr. Badgeley and Miss Attenborough can make up a party.'

'Oh,' breathed Miss Montjoy in relief. 'I should like that of all things, sir!'

'Excellent,' he said, reaching for the bell pull. 'For now I must bid you good morning, and will come for you at the appointed hour. Ah. Caine. Lady Neville and Miss Montjoy are just leaving.'

He bowed them firmly out of the room over his mother's protests, and as soon as they had gone sat quickly at the small desk in the corner and dashed off a quick note that he folded, addressed, and gave to the footman to post immediately. Then, calling for Hubbard and for Sam Cutler, he outlined his plans to each, and left the house for an imposing office in the street where operated the firm in charge of the Neville family fortune.

An hour or so later he left in a state of sober thought, and revived himself with a solitary nuncheon at Brooks, observing as he partook of a rather nice roast, drank a glass of claret, and scanned the news of several journals, that this must be a pleasure no longer open to him if he were to continue his current cork-brained trajectory. He returned home in a brown study, changed into riding attire, and rode his chestnut the few blocks to Neville House, with Sam behind him sidesaddle on the brown mare.

He was able to avoid his mother by merit of Miss Montjoy's promptitude in meeting him at the top of the stairs. Sam gave her a leg up, and she and Tristan left him to amuse himself in the Neville kitchen for the next hour.

'You seem all too eager to leave the house,' teased Tristan.

'Oh, you have no idea,' she laughed. 'I am not at all suited for this city life, I believe, and have been longing for a ride. What a lovely mare this is,' she patted the brown mare's neck. 'Where did you find her?'

'At Tat's. She was a part of a sale there, and I could not quite bear to leave her to her fate. I hope you will use her while you are in Town, Miss Montjoy. She is entirely at your disposal.'

They passed the time pleasantly chatting, and duly met Badgeley and Miss Attenborough in the Park. Tristan had a deal to say to his cousin that wasn't fit for female ears, so confined his conversation to the ladies. Miss Arabella continued to show herself to be all that was amusing, relaxing to be with, and full of lively intelligence. Tristan thought that, had they met at the beginning of the Season, had she not been forced to miss it due to illness, he might have found her a perfectly acceptable and even enjoyable companion with whom to live a comfortable life of *noblesse oblige*, obligatory sex, and irritating children. Now it was too late. Accustomed to another voice in his ear, he found Miss

Arabella's cheerful acquiescence to his opinions tiresome, and her refreshing honesty ultimately predictable.

He hoped Miss Angel Hathaway might learn to enjoy the activity of riding. For come what may, he could not give up his horses.

After dropping Miss Arabella at Neville House, he left Sam to take the brown mare home and continued through the streets on his chestnut, stopping only to buy a bouquet of flowers from a seller on a corner. Failing to find Angel on the streets that led from the shop to her home, he stopped outside the house and, heart hammering, promised a coin to a young lad loitering in the square in return for holding his horse this quarter of an hour.

He loosened a neckcloth that suddenly seemed too tight. He strode forward, opened the gate, and knocked on the door of the Hathaway house.

His luck was in. Angel herself answered the door, polite curiosity giving way to round-eyed surprise. 'Mr... Mr. Neville! What on earth... to what do I owe... I have only just...'

He thrust the flowers toward her. 'I believe, Miss Hathaway, that you have been avoiding me.'

'Oh! How beautiful!' She took the flowers and inhaled their sweet scent, her face softening in pleasure, allowing herself a moment to sort through her own tangled emotions. 'Not... not precisely *avoiding* you sir. Only that...' She looked up at him with... yes. Longing. He saw it and his heart leapt. Then it was gone. 'There are things, you see. Regarding my family, that if you knew... could only cause you to hold me in disgust.'

'I could never hold you in disgust, Miss Hathaway.'

'You say that now. But somehow... like a worm... the knowledge of who I am, *what* I am must always eat away at you. And if we... if somehow...' she shook her head. 'I could not bear it, you see.'

'My dear Miss Hathaway,' he said, and took her hand. She tried to pull it away, but he held it firm. 'Miss Hathaway,' he repeated. 'Before we go further, I must ask of you two things.'

She glanced up at him. 'What two things, sir?'

'The first is this: does any man have a claim on your affections, Miss Hathaway, that you look toward with favor?'

Angel gasped, blushed, and glanced away. 'Mr. Neville, this is hardly the time… what I mean is, I cannot possibly entertain… No!' she exclaimed finally. 'That is, I… *no*.'

'Good,' he said, relief flooding him. 'Then the second question, perhaps more important.' He took her other hand, and would not let her pull them away. 'Could you… could you love *me*, Angel? Were I cut off from family and fortune, could you love me, the man, as I am?'

'I… O, Mr. Neville, please… I regard you in the light… you are most…' she looked wildly over her shoulder, as if for escape.

'The truth, Angel,' insisted Tristan. 'If the answer is no, I will not trouble you again, I promise. We will part, here and now, forever.'

'But I… you must…' tears started to her eyes. 'O Tristan, it is so very stupid to pretend! I loved you the very first time I saw you. I did not think it possible, but so it was.'

Tristan exhaled and smiled with a pleasure that filled his soul with inexpressible joy. He wanted to leap in the air. He wanted to wrap Angel in his arms and feel her warmth and… He cleared his throat and forced himself to breathe.

'But I would not… could not… be the wedge that drives you from your family and friends, Mr. Neville. Tristan,' Angel said, struggling to regain her poise. 'I had rather die alone.'

'Like Patience on her monument,' he murmured, smiling.

'I… yes. Like that. For if you knew the truth about my family….'

'Miss Hathaway… Angel… I do wish you will trust me with your confidence. Come. It cannot be so bad. Tell me.'

She did, leaving nothing out. He listened, made no comment, gave no show of horror or distress, even though it really was so bad, even though shock and revulsion contended with pity, love, rage, and several other emotions equally at odds with one another.

'And now you know,' Angel finished. 'The scandal. The…
infamy. Why I cannot ever…'

'I will think of a solution,' he said firmly. 'There is a way
forward.'

'And you are speaking from your vast experience?' she smiled
doubtfully.

'No,' he admitted with a lightness he was far from feeling.
'Merely from the great height of my position, which makes all
obstacles dissolve. A benefit of being nobly born.

'I must be away for a sennight, on some pressing business, my
dear,' he continued. 'When I return, I will call on you. And that
call will be of an official nature.' He smiled at her, kissed his
fingers, and rested them on her cheek. '*Au revoir*, beloved Patience.
Have faith.'

*****

In truth, Tristan Neville was rocked to the souls of his
feet by Angel Hathaway's revelations. To marry a *bourgeoisie*… sin
enough, in the eyes of the *ton*. To marry a woman whose father
was a mere nobody and whose mother the subject of one of the
greatest scandals of its day… unthinkable. Unconscionable.

His journey, conceived as an errand of hope, became a
needed distancing of himself from everything in the world he
knew. To think. To question. Perhaps even, to grieve. And then,
only then, to plan… whatever it was that needed planning.

By cock crow the following morning Tristan was on the road,
making his way south and west in a penetrating rain. He pushed
on through the weather seeking refuge in barns and sheds at need,
finally putting up at a wayside inn that was off the post road and
therefore unaccustomed to serving Gentlemen of Quality. After
making sure the chestnut was comfortably bedded down, rubbed
dry properly with a fat wisp of twisted straw, hayed, watered, and
fed a sustaining mash, he ate a supper of greasy meat washed
down with passable ale in the common room, but balked at

sharing a bed of doubtful cleanliness with two other men of rough habit and nonexistent hygiene; choosing instead to doss down in the straw under the manger of his horse's stall, wrapped in his greatcoat.

He set out the next morning somewhat the worse for wear. Fortunately the weather had cleared, so he passed the hours alternately admiring the green countryside as it grew hilly, and soberly contemplating a future likely to put an end to the luxuries and comforts he had taken for granted all his life so far. He ran figures in his head that covered every scenario and eventuality he could think of. They always came out with the same answer: that while he could absolutely live relatively comfortably and even support a thrifty wife on his personal income alone, he would have to give up certain things he had accepted as essential to his wellbeing. A good part of his domestic staff, for instance, not to mention his small house with its stylish address. The better part of his stable. His membership at Brooks. His subscriptions to various theaters and opera houses, most certainly. And his tailor? His boot maker? Oh, God. Surely he could keep them, a man had his standards. His conviction began to waver. The reality of living in straitened circumstances was far thornier in reality than it was in theory.

And then there was the question of Angel's birth; always it came down to the question of Angel's birth. Could it become a sore point for him, a source of disgust to others, were the truth about Seraphine Hathaway known? Was Angel correct in thinking him capable of holding her responsible for any slight he might suffer in society or occupation going forward? The lady herself… oh, unimpeachable. Perfect. But her background…

Tristan might despise much of his Society and all it stood for. But it is one thing to be a critic, and work glacially to change things from within. Quite another to flout everything his family stood for, everything they had attained, by what would be perceived as betrayal.

Tristan loved his comforts. He was not built to be a revolutionary.

But neither could he stomach the thought of a conventional life of boring verisimilitude.

He arrived early in the evening of the second day at the White Horse Inn several miles distant from Lady Temple's estate, tired and still damp. Having bespoken a private room for himself and comfortable stabling for his weary horse, he entered the inn with some relief to have a supper of hearty beef and thick bread washed down with ale at a table near the cheerful fire of the public room, followed by a ewer and basin of hot water in his chamber to wash the travel stains from his tired body. He left his clothing and his boots outside the door for cleaning, and fell immediately into bed and a deep sleep on reasonably clean sheets.

By morning he felt much restored. He shaved, washed, and dressed carefully for this meeting with his formidable great-aunt, who he hoped would remember him as one member of the family who cared nothing for her fortune. A look at his boots and the general set of his clothing elicited a brief pang of regret that he had left Town without the redoubtable Hubbard, whose extraordinary talents kept him groomed and clothed to a nicety. No. If he married Angel Hathaway, he must keep Hubbard. There were limits.

The chestnut horse looked well, at any rate. It had cleaned up its feed and been well groomed by an admiring ostler, who had also cleaned Tristan's tack until it gleamed. Tristan tipped the man handsomely and rode the short distance to his great-aunt's estate feeling in reasonable twig.

He met Lady Temple standing imperiously in the garden, dressed in dark lilac bombazine with oceans of lace in a style that had been current a generation ago, topped by an alarming wig that added a full foot to her already impressive height. She stared piercingly at him through her quizzing glass, taking in every particle of his dress and demeanor, as he bowed and stood at attention in front of her.

'You have arrived in haste, on horseback, and without your man,' she remarked with hauteur. 'Therefore you cannot want money. Nor are you pretending a social visit, you'd have appeared before me rather more *point de vice*. It must, then, be an unsuitable woman. Good God, Neville. What can you be thinking.'

'I did write,' said Tristan.

She harrumphed. 'Two brief missives, the first received a bare twenty-four hours before your hasty arrival, the other just hours ago. You should be ashamed, Neville, really you should.'

'I do deeply regret not having Hubbard with me. I'd no idea how difficult the simple acts of shaving and dressing oneself could be. I am, however, very glad to see you, Aunt, and delighted to find you in your usual robust health.'

She snorted. 'Humbugger. You and that odious uncle of yours. Have you eaten anything this morning? Of course not. Sit down.' She pointed to a chair. He sat. She gestured to some unseen person, then settled herself in a far more comfortable chair, which had cushions and a parasol to shade her, opposite him.

That he had not immediately been shown off the property by his great-aunt's gamekeeper and the business end of a blunderbuss, he considered a hopeful sign.

They spent a good half hour taking care of necessities. There was gossip from London that his aunt swore not to think about but was all agog to hear - the more salacious, the better - and as often as not featuring the misadventures of Badgeley. There was the satisfaction to be had in knowing she had outlived several more ladies of her generation, which allowed her to enumerate all the reasons for her continued health. There were recent political affairs to be commented on, and modern excesses of fashion and manners to disparage. When asked what sort of cattle Tristan kept in his stables these days, she professed horror that he, a gentleman, did not keep any sort of town equipage, but only riding horses. She refrained from asking about the family, most of whom she disliked on form; and finally, when Tristan had eaten, drunk, and talked his fill, fixed him with her unnerving blue stare and demanded to know what he wanted.

So he told her.

To her credit, Lady Temple was a keen listener, and maintained a scowling, attentive silence until he was finished.

'So the Finister chit has resurfaced. A bad business, that. Very bad. No chance it's a hoax?'

'It appears not, ma'am.'

'And Denham himself has returned.' She sighed. 'A terrible business, Tristan, terrible. How you could become embroiled in something like this…'

'But it doesn't touch Miss Hathaway, Aunt. I swear it does not.'

'And as for these Hathaways… I've crossed paths with one or two. Prissy non-conformists, the lot of them.' She eyed him with disfavor. 'I should speak with your uncle Neville. I expect he could enlighten me.'

'Nathaniel? What can he possibly add that I have not told you already? Besides, we've spoken already, and he has leant his support.'

'Has he. I wonder,' she grumped. Then lapsed into thoughtfulness for long minutes. Just as Tristan feared she had fallen asleep, she abruptly asked after his brother, the current Viscount Christopher Neville (whom she considered a dead bore), and his wife Lady Lydia (whom she disliked for the way she 'puffed off her consequence as if her family had half the antiquity of the Nevilles'). After being assured that the family title, honor, & inheritance were safe in the pair's astonishingly energetic procreative abilities, she grunted again. On being given a point-by-point recital of Neville's small personal fortune, 'for you will absolutely be disinherited by your odious mother,' she shook her head and remarked heavily that she hoped he knew what he was doing. And when her great-nephew promised that the Female in Question would neither arrive unattended nor prove to be a fortune-hunting doxy, she fixed him with a stern eye, and demanded to know why she should believe him.

'Because I give you my word as a gen…' Neville began, then stopped, and pressed his lips together. 'I was going to say that you have my word as a gentleman, Aunt,' he continued. 'But it has been bruited about in some circles that I am not a gentleman at all, merely a nobleman.'

'Merely a… *what*?' demanded Lady Georgina in horror. 'Who would have the audacity to say such a thing!'

'Miss Angel Hathaway herself, ma'am.'

Lady Temple surprised him with a bark of laughter. 'Well, I'll grant the chit has nerve,' she said. 'She'll need it, if she is to marry into the Nevilles. But if you dare to bring some little trollop…'

'Aunt, how can you believe I would!'

'Men are easily led by their cocks, my boy, and can be made to believe almost anything when following them,' she said crisply.

'You shock me, ma'am,' murmured Tristan. 'It's almost as from experience.' He crooked an eyebrow at her suggestively. Rumor amongst the family had it that Lady Temple's gamekeeper had been her petticoat pensioner for years.

'You keep a civil tongue in your head, young man,' she retorted with asperity. 'And for God's sake, bring your belongings back from that dreadful inn and let Noodle brush you up. If we are to have the Bishop here for our nuncheon tomorrow, you must look several notches better than Madman. But before I exert myself to work miracles on your behalf, you had best tell me outright this moment that you are bent on being leg-shackled to this Miss Angel Hathaway, you miserable cub.' She stared down her imperial nose with challenge.

Tristan drew a breath. Then paused, eyes full of uncertainty as he stared into an unknowable future far different from any he had imagined. The seconds ticked by. Lady temple's gaze never wavered. Then finally, another deep, steadying breath.

'I will marry Miss Angel Hathaway. I will spend the rest of my life with Miss Angel Hathaway.'

Lady Georgina nodded crisply. 'So be it. Now go away. You've given me a great deal to conjure from nothing, if you desire my help in this hare-brained venture. I do not want to see so much as a shadow of you before dinner. Country hours, mind.' She waved him away.

*****

Attenborough House was one of a number of grand dwellings on Cavendish Square, a leafy and beautiful aspect that did not fail to have an impact on Angel. The houses were well enough, of course, predictably vast and graciously proportioned, but the gardens in the square - O! The gardens! – *the fairest flowers o' th' season*, all colors of the rainbow, with roses of white, maroon, red, and even striped, with shrubs that drooped lilac, and with herbs and primroses and deep, glossy creepers that hid hellebores and bluebells in deep shade, some few of them still in bloom, that gave the whole a romantic and restful appearance that was wonderfully fragrant. Angel would have loved to spend an hour or two walking there, but suspected this was a treat reserved only for those who lived around it. Gardeners it had in plenty, and a few nannies with prams and small children running about. But the sweepers and coal carters and other varied personages that made sure the houses were well maintained, orderly, and stocked with all things essential to the life of an aristocrat, did not enter the gardens.

Madame and Angel were admitted via the service door, a young porter engaged for the day trudging along behind them with a large block of wrapped parcels just now unloaded from his wheeled cart. These he gratefully gave over to a very stuffy footman who felt himself far too grand to respond to the lad's cheerful, 'Glad to heave this lot over to you, mate. Right heavy it was,' and said rather sniffily that the Young Person might enter the kitchen where Cook would doubtless allow him a bit of refreshment. Madame and Angel were ushered upstairs to a spacious drawing room that had a bank of windows facing north.

Madame looked around the room with approval. '*Bien*,' she said in her best stage French accent, the better to impress the housemaid who showed them into the room. 'The light here will do very well.' The pair unpacked various parcels that contained the rough iterations of garments that would become the elegant draperies of a bride and her mama on the important event of her wedding to Edward Badgeley, heir to the Torrington fortune and titles, and laid them out carefully on a table and over the back of a velvet-covered sofa.

Henrietta arrived first, and seeing the layout of her dresses, clapped her hands with uncharacteristic delight - for who can resist luscious fabrics in the process of being turned into even more delicious clothing in honor of a life changing event? - and announced herself well pleased with everything. Her maid helped her strip down to a cambric chemise so that Madame and Angel could drape her in silk and tiffany and begin the painstaking measurements, pinnings, and critical adjustments that would be made to create exactly the right effect.

As they did this, Lady Abigail Attenborough breezed in with her own dresser, exclaimed in delight, and bustled around her daughter offering ideas, advice, and critical assessments about the process that she was sure would be well received because of her great expertise, but in fact put her very much in the way. Fortunately, as Madame had a mouthful of pins, busy hands, and eyes for nothing but the details of the delicate measures that she called out for Angel to write down and, when needed, sketch for clarity, no answer was required. She knew that if she merely nodded agreement with everything her clients said while doing exactly as she intended herself, the ladies would be well satisfied with the final product, certain that it was their very own design.

When the two dressmakers had done all they could to be satisfied with the delicate process of creating a better form for the very complicated garment that was to be a simple, graceful dress of ivory and deep rose, refreshments were brought in and the modistes invited to sit and rest themselves for a few moments while Lady Abigail regaled them with other details of the wedding that were keeping her extremely occupied. Attenborough, she assured them, was quite determined that his daughter should be handed off in the greatest of style in an intimate ceremony one hoped would be the talk of the season. Miss Henrietta smiled at this, knowing full well that her esteemed father had taken one look at his rib's plans, blanched, and retired to the quiet of his club.

Suitably refreshed, the dressmakers began to work on the capacious dimensions of milady's form, while milady chattered steadily about the reducing plan she had embarked upon that included a half glass of vinegar at every meal and a paltry number of biscuits that simply had to be anointed with cream and jam to make them palatable, then wondered if in fact she ought to have chosen the violet after all. In the middle of this the butler entered to announce the arrival of Lady Charlotte Torrington and the dowager Viscountess Letitia Neville, and was her ladyship receiving.

'Well of course I shall be delighted to see Lady Charlotte, for no one could be more obliging, and her eye for color is impeccable,' said Lady Abigail, with only the slightest hesitation and intake of breath. 'But I wonder that Lady Letitia...' her voice trailed off uncertainly, then she added with resolve, 'Show them in. And send up something suitable to offer them.'

Lady Abigail would have been an insensitive woman indeed not to know that Lady Letitia thought her quite beneath her touch. Lady Abigail may have drawn the attention of Lord Henry Attenborough in her first season on the Marriage Mart, but she knew very well that dazzling beauty had not been as large a factor in the attraction as her father's money; something that, despite their great name, the Attenboroughs had none of. And that money, everyone knew, had been made in rubbish.

Her hard and cunning grandfather swore there was gold to be found in rubbish for those not too proud to look, and he meant it literally. For in wading and combing through unnameable filth day after foul-smelling day, he found salable objects that appealed to all levels of his world, from ivory combs missing a single tooth, to scraps of cloth to be sold as rags, to lost rings and baubles of precious metal that could be melted down and made into something else. Eventually he had set up shop as a trader, then finally expanded into exports and imports. Abigail's father, better educated by far than his own had been, built on the success of his forbear and married the daughter of a wealthy ship owner. And Abigail had been raised, educated, and launched into Society as if she had been born to it.

She was proud of her family's progress. But the Lady Nevilles of the world would always find ways to remind her that money was not enough to make her One Of Them.

Lady Letitia was, of course, the mother of Tristan Neville. Who, one was lead to believe by one's sister-in-law Lady Torrington, via a daughter who had heard it from that ramshackle Edward Badgeley, had been seen in the company of a common dressmaker. Lady Letitia, had Lady Abigail known it, was here to spy out the little tart who was trying to steal her Tristan away. Never known for her tact, she now stared down her aquiline nose at Mme. Simard and her assistant with a supercilious expression that made her resemble one of the Cleveland Bay horses that pulled her barouche. As the dressmakers laid out and fitted lilac silk and ivory lace, she looked in vain for a girl she felt certain must be luscious and of melting looks, who would certainly have manners that pretended to be better than her birth, but whose coarse beauty would tell the true tale. In this, she was frustrated. Mme. Simard was much too old. The assistant, a pretty, quiet, dark-haired girl who smiled easily but did not speak unless spoken to and then with a well modulated voice that hinted of a genuine French background, did not fit the profile Lady Neville had imagined as a mantrap. And in this, Lady Neville proved that she had no knowledge at all of the tastes or even the interests of her younger son.

Meanwhile, Lady Charlotte Torrington fluttered over Henrietta fondly with a kiss on the cheek and a squeeze of her hands, then butterfly-like moved on to Lady Attenborough - currently swathed in an ocean of pale lilac - which Angel Hathaway was assiduously pinning to Madame Simard's exacting standards. While Lady Charlotte assured Lady Abigail that the lilac looked very well and that a very small piping of violet to set the lace edging off would be quite enough of such a strong color, Lady Letitia moved to Henrietta to wish her happy in a life that was soon to change drastically. 'I do hope Badgeley will thrive under your good sense, Henrietta,' she crooned. 'I feel he is very fortunate indeed to have found such a paragon to be what one feels must be his long suffering wife.'

'I thank you, ma'am', smiled Henrietta calmly. 'Mr. Badgeley and I have known one another nearly from the cradle. I believe that we shall deal famously together.'

Lady Neville patted her hands fondly. 'That's right,' she said approvingly. 'One must always keep the high road in these *affaires*. And after all, to be married to a Badgeley must always be seen as a great coup. Nearly as large an honor as bringing a Neville up to scratch. My eldest son, the current Viscount, you know, married Salisbury's daughter, and between them they have sired five brats. My daughters both married into very good families, and have produced another half dozen between them. It's a wonder they have time to accomplish anything else, with all that breeding going on, but the title is secure.'

'Letitia!' gasped Lady Charlotte. 'Please! I pray you, moderate your language in front of Henrietta!'

'Henrietta is no blushing miss, are you, my dear,' she tweaked Henrietta's cheek. Henrietta smiled wanly. One's duty to produce an heir was one thing. The act of... procreating... that many times... made her feel vaguely queasy. But she managed not to respond to the implied insult by so much as the flicker of an eyelid. Instead, she focused her attention on a strip of deep rose velvet that was to become a capelet, and asked sweetly, 'And has

Mr. Tristan Neville looked with favor on any such fortunate girl? For he is nearly thirty, is he not?'

'One hears,' Lady Charlotte tittered with a hint of malice in revenge for Lady Letitia's disparagement of her adored Ned, 'that he has not always been so particular in his attentions, and until recently kept a certain high flyer - who shall remain nameless - very well occupied indeed. As well as consorting with people of the lowest sort, nothing more than *trades* people.'

Anger flickered briefly across Lady Neville's face. She was still furious at her younger son's thoughtlessness in leaving Town when she had come up expressly to throw Arabella Montjoy at his head. A setback indeed, but not a complete loss in the war of good marriages.

'You may set your mind at rest on that account,' she purred smugly, quickly masking her emotion. 'Tristan knows his worth. Dally he may - what man does not? - But he will not marry beneath him.'

If Angel Hathaway's hand twitched involuntarily as she wrote down a measurement, no one noticed.

'On the contrary,' she continued, 'I have every expectation of news regarding Tristan, very shortly. I have just this week had the pleasure of receiving Lady Elizabeth Montjoy and her lovely daughter Arabella to stay. Montjoy is but a Baronet, of course, and Tristan may look as high as he pleases, but Lady Elizabeth has Royal connections, and Arabella comes with quite five thousand pounds. She and Tristan were inseparable when he was last in the country, indeed were quite in one another's pockets. And now, after squiring her on one of his own horses in the Park, he has put the animal at her complete disposal during his absence. Oh, yes,' her lips curved confidently, 'I quite think that we shall be hearing of a match, perhaps even upon his return.'

Angel uncharacteristically dropped her notebook and scrambled to collect it. 'Oh!' she said to Madame Simard. 'I am so very sorry, *madame,* so clumsy of me...' Madame Simard looked closely at her, and removed the pins from her mouth. '*Eh, bien*

Angel, no matter,' she said briskly. 'Do you help Miss Attenborough to change, and then see to the packing of her new garments, *s'il vous plait.*'

'*Oui, Madame,*' said Angel, eyes lowered.

Lady Letitia gazed at Angel through narrowed eyes, then turned to Lady Abigail's gown-in-the-making. 'This is very fine work indeed, Abigail,' she said approvingly. 'Is this the dressmaker you have been telling me so much about?'

'Indeed yes,' sad Lady Abigail, and introduced Madame Simard, who curtseyed deeply while saying she was *enchantée* to be in milady's presence. Lady Neville smiled down her long nose and turned again to Angel, who Lady Abigail now introduced, and who curtseyed punctiliously, eyes lowered, in her turn.

'Hathaway,' murmured the dowager silkily. 'Are you then related to the actress of The Swan Theatre?'

'I have the honor to be her daughter,' said Angel stiffly.

'If you call being the daughter of an *actress* an honor.' Lady Neville sniffed contemptuously, and turned away in time to miss the rage that flashed in Angel's eyes.

'Oh, Letitia,' admonished Lady Charlotte. '*Tout le monde* must like Mrs. Hathaway. Not only is she a very great light in the theatre, but her demeanor is faultless. She is frequently received by Hensleigh and his lady, you know."

'The bluestocking,' said Lady Letitia dismissively. 'One has heard. But the stage is hardly a profession one can accept as good *ton.*' She looked at Angel, whose back was to her, but whose figure was rigid in every aspect. 'Have I offended, you, Miss Hathaway? Surely you must be accustomed to it.'

Angel turned. '*Au contraire, Madame.* My mother is a woman of grace and manners, who has taught her children the value of work. Unlike some I could mention. *Maintenant, si vous m'excuse. Madame.*' She curtseyed to Henrietta Attenborough and Lady Attenborough. '*Merci mille fois, mesdames.* It is a great honor to dress two such ladies as yourselves.' And she gently gathered up the package containing Henrietta's dress and left the room.

'Oh, Letitia,' admonished Lady Charlotte. 'Now look what you've done. Miss Hathaway is a very pretty behaved young woman, and an excellent seamstress as well.'

'She is a dressmaker's assistant who must needs learn her place.'

'Well. You have certainly succeeded in reminding her of it,' remarked Lady Abigail with barely controlled anger. 'You will forgive me for saying that I cannot - I simply cannot - countenance your insulting people at your leisure in my own home, *Lady* Neville, and in front of my daughter too, especially in this time of joy. I had thought better of you, ma'am.'

Lady Neville stared at her hostess with icy hauteur. 'I understand you perfectly, madam,' she said coldly. 'I shall take my leave. Come along, Charlotte.'

Lady Charlotte was not a woman of strong character, but she knew where her allies were. 'I believe I shall stay, actually, Letitia,' she said gently. 'We shall no doubt meet at a later time.'

With a look of pure venom, Lady Neville turned on her heel as the butler opened the door for her, and departed.

'Henrietta,' said her mother into a fraught silence, 'please find Miss Hathaway before she leaves the house. Madame Simard will miss her assistance sorely.'

Henrietta nodded and quietly left the room.

'Oh, Abigail,' wailed Lady Charlotte. 'I am so very sorry. I could *sink*, positively I could! I know what she can be like, but I never thought... never dreamed... and in your own home...'

'My dear Charlotte, I do not blame you in the least. She is a rude, overbearing woman. But I am sorry for any ongoing unpleasantness this may engender between you and your sister-in-law.'

'*Et voila, madame*' announced the beleaguered Madame Simard, standing away from the dress now pinned to fit its future wearer to perfection. '*C'est belle, n'est-ce pas?*'

'Oh, yes,' breathed Lady Abigail, turning this way and that, the better to see herself in the long mirror that had been placed in the room. 'Charlotte, what do you think?'

Lady Charlotte studied the effect and nodded approval. 'Indeed, Abigail, it is very well. Very well indeed. Madame Simard, I think I must have a walking dress from you.'

'*Merci bien, madame*,' nodded the little modiste with a smile. 'It would be my honor.' She tweaked a fold of the dress, moved two pins infinitesimally to correct the shape, and announced herself satisfied. With Lady Abigail re-clothed in a gayly colored morning dress, and the ceremonial garment carefully wrapped up by Madame Simard, Henrietta returned, leading a subdued Angel.

'My dear, my dear,' Lady Abigail went to her with outstretched hands, 'I cannot express my horror at what you have had to endure and I am so very sorry.'

'And I also,' seconded Lady Charlotte. 'It was very ill done.' She fidgeted uncomfortably. 'Dear Abigail, I must now take my leave. Please do forgive me. Henrietta, my dear, a word in your ear ere I depart.' Henrietta withdrew with the agitated lady, followed by Madame Simard, who announced her intention to find a footman downstairs.

Angel accepted the proferred hands and bobbed a curtsey. 'It was not your fault, *madame, je vous assure*,' she said. 'You have shown Madame Simard and myself nothing but kindness.'

'Perhaps, but I feel I must apologize for Lady Neville.' She sighed. 'I cannot think what she was about, coming here, for she does not like me above half. And I certainly do not like her.'

'I think I have an idea,' said Angel. 'But it need not trouble you.'

Lady Abigail looked at her penetratingly and sighed. 'As you wish. You are a good girl, Angel. Your Madame Simard is very fortunate to have you at her side. None works harder than she, and her life has not been easy, I think. And I have great respect for your mama.'

'You are kind, *Madame*.'

'Not in the least. I am known to be a flighty and shallow chatterbox, and my breeding is of no account whatsoever.'

'I find that hard to believe, *Madame*.'

'Do you? And yet, my grandfather was used to travel this very street with his cart, and plotted how one day his family would live in one of these houses. And now we do. And my Henrietta is a member of the *ton*. Were he alive to see his granddaughter marry Edward Badgeley, my grandfather would burst with pride, though he would not himself even be admitted to the house. I, however, honor him. You see what I am telling you, dear girl, yes? At present, all must seem very ill to you indeed. Very unjust. But you must continue to strive for what is important to you. You must not give up. Do you understand? Is it well? Shall we go on?'

'Yes, of course, *madame*. Thank-you, *Madame*,' Angel bowed her head.

'Good. Then you may be on your way. But first, here,' she delved into a pocket and brought out a small purse that chinked when she folded Angel's fingers around it.

Angel's eyes widened. 'Oh no, please, *madame*, you must not… I cannot…'

'Nonsense, my girl. You can, and you will. Put it toward your dowry. Fare you well for now, Miss Hathaway.'

*****

The first accident that occurred on The Swan's stage could easily have passed as carelessness. A bag of tools left in an ill-lit cross-over behind the scenery that allowed actors to get from one side of the stage to the other without being seen tripped one of the dancers as she ran to make a rehearsal entrance, and sent her hurtling through the screen into a painted arbor. The dancer howled, Stephen and Marianne were sent for, the owner of the bag of tools was adamant in swearing that he wouldn't never have done such a chuckleheaded thing, the scene designer railed at the damage done to his very beautiful scenery that now must be repaired so that it could be used that night, the dancer was treated for minor cuts and bruises and pronounced fit to perform with her ankle wrapped tightly, and when Pearce and Hemmings questioned the owner of the bag of tools again, the carpenter remembered that he had in fact loaned the bag to a rigger earlier, young Tom 'twas, who'd had need of summat, he disremembered what. Of Tom the rigger there was conveniently no sign; he had gone home for his supper.

Hemings and Pearce, with their earlier suspicions of Tom now confirmed, agreed not to worry Mrs. Hathaway with news of the incident. By the time the curtain rang down on the cheers and shouts of an enthusiastic audience, the affair was all but forgotten.

Until several evenings later, when a lighting stand that had been set a safe distance from one of the legs of scenery masking the backstage area from the audience inexplicably set fire to that leg in the middle of one of Bridie's songs. River and Hemmings leapt into action to herd shrieking dancers offstage, River flung one hysterical dancer to the stage floor and rolled her in a bear hug to put out a smoldering costume, Pearce jumped to the stage and bellowed to an audience showing every sign of panic to remain calm, all would be well, and whirled his cloak from his shoulders just as Seraphine herself, thick blanket in her arms, began to beat the flames back before they could spread. Within moments, she and Pearce were gaining the upper hand, Hemings, River, Jeremy, and Jacob Freeman had formed a line that doused the scenery and the remnant of the smoldering leg with bucket after bucket of water, the bulk of the audience stayed in place to roar advice and approval, all the doors were thrown open to air out the smoke, Pearce announced that the performance would resume, the impromptu fire fighters took a bow to whistles, shouts, and applause, the dancers and musicians returned with Bridie, and the show, as it always must, went on.

It took hours longer for Seraphine to finish raging through the theatre, excoriating every member of the company together and separately; demanding answers, flaying Pearce and Hemmings for not having told her about the previous act of sabotage, threatening immediate dismissal of every single member of the company, yes, *tous ensemble*, immediately, if a story did not come to light of how this cowardly act that could have killed every one of them could possibly have occurred, and how would they all feel about coming back to work tomorrow knowing that somebody among them was willing to betray their trust and kill them, yes, all of them, *et porquoi, on se demande, pour quelle raison?* For were they not paid well, were they not respected, were they not all *comme une famille, alors?* Receiving no answer from the ashen-faced company that stood or sat uncertainly around her on the stage, she shook her head in disbelief, flung herself down the stairs, into the office, and slammed the door on Pearce's face as he trailed behind uttering disjointed admonishments.

A timid knock at the door was followed by the quaking figure of Doll Bridger, all bravado gone, tears staining her face. 'Please, ma'am, please don't let us go, please. We love The Swan and we don't none of us want to leave, and whatever would we do, ma'am...'

'Doll,' said Seraphine wearily. 'Do you have something to tell me?'

'Ay, ma'am,' she took a shaky breath and sat on the edge of a chair. 'It were Tom Fay did it, ma'am.'

'The rigger?'

'Ay, ma'am, the same. We saw him movin' of the lamp, and we said summing to him, see, but he told us to keep quiet, like, on account he had a big reason to teach... um... a certain party, I swear, ma'am, we din't know 'twas you he'd be talkin' of - and no one was goin' to be hurt, and it were a lot of money he'd be making', see. And if we... shut up and said nothin'... there'd be... summing in it for us, and oh ma'am,' she started to sob brokenly, 'We never meant it like that, never! And it were so... so scary... and then you and Mr. Pearce and Mr. Hemmings and and Mr. Freeman and Mr. River... was so heroic, like, and we seen how... how bad we'd been... and oh, ma'am please forgive us, please,' she looked pathetically at Seraphine, face washed in tears.

Seraphine handed her a handkerchief. 'There, Doll. I won't let you go, foolish girl. I'm glad you came forward. Where is Tom now?'

'Dunno, ma'am. We ain't seen him since... since he done it, I reckon.'

'He wasn't here tonight?'

'No, ma'am.'

'And you say he was working for someone else. Someone who paid him to set the fire.'

'Ay, ma'am. Din't say who. Just a flash cove with a load of ready, which Tom was in the way to gettin' some of.'

Seraphine nodded. 'Of course. He probably wasn't given a proper name.' She sighed. 'Get on with you now, Doll. Go home and get some sleep. You have someone to walk with you?'

'Yes, ma'am. Sophie and Lil, they're waitin' for us. And we'll wash your handkercher, ma'am, we will.'

An hour later, Stephen found her still seated and staring at the wall in deep thought, her lamp guttering beside her.

'They're almost finished onstage,' he said. 'T'was a near thing, *Maman.*'

'*Oui.* We were very fortunate.'

'I think we can all agree on who is behind it. And that this is not the end of it.'

'No,' she said wearily. 'It is not. It is rather a declaration of war.'

Madame Seraphine

IV.

"Nothing of him that doth fade,
But doth suffer a sea-change
Into something rich and strange."

- William Shakespeare, *The Tempest* I.2

Madame Seraphine

Tristan arrived home with a spring in his step, joy in his heart, and a special license in his pocket that would allow marriage with Angel Hathaway at their earliest convenience.

His first action was to run Badgeley and Kilronen to ground at their latest favorite gaming hell, where they formed part of an inebriated group shouting bets, side bets, and exhortations on the outcome of an intense game of hazard between two gentlemen whose bellicosity increased with their drunkenness. Tristan's friends hailed him in high good humor once he had managed to draw their attention from the play, which they invited him to join. 'It's famous sport, Tris!' slurred Badgeley merrily. 'Fairclough's having the devil's own luck, I've laid a pony Milton demands the dice be broken within the hour, and Fairclough to call him out for it!'

'Stake me a bullseye, old son, do,' begged Sir Robert. 'I've a notion I shall win handsomely tonight.'

Tristan pulled him aside. 'I'll give it to you outright, Robin, if you loan me your traveling chariot.'

'A yellow bounder would be far cheaper, me boyo, I assure you,' avowed Sir Robert, swaying gently. Then he looked at Neville suspiciously. 'You wouldn't be fleeing the country now, would you?'

'No. But when I need transport it will be quickly.'

Sir Robert whistled. 'An elopement, is it?'

'It is, but if you breathe one word to this lot...'

'Tell you something in your ear, Tris,' said Sir Robert with a hiccup, 'Badgeley's already put it about that you'll be disowned if you marry the dressmaker mort, and wagers are being laid.'

'*Damn* Badgeley. I never met such a rattle-pate.'

'Tris, do but think. Your family will never countenance it.'

'They have no say in the matter.'

'Except for cutting you off.'

'Except for that.'

'You are a better man than I, Neville. Either that, or you are a desperate lunatic. Can't...' he hiccuped softly, 'quite make out which 'tis.'

'It is only my pockets, Robin. Not my neck at risk.'

'Then,' Sir Robert said handsomely, 'you may have my chariot at your convenience, my dear. I wouldn't think of renting it to you, an you soon to have bellows to mend.' He attempted a bow, overbalanced, and was only saved from falling by Tristan's strong hand on his arm. He leaned into its support for a moment, inhaling the scent of the man. Tristan firmly placed him upright.

'Mind yourself, Robin,' he warned gently.

'I know, Tris. I know,' murmured Sir Robert. But,' he wheedled, 'if tonight you could just lend me, say, a monkey...'

'I'll stake you. I only hope that widow of yours comes up to scratch.'

'Oh, but me laddie,' said Sir Robert, fluttering his lashes and simpering. 'Have you not heard? Lady Hannah has consented to make me the happiest man alive. We shall be shackled quietly at my lady's estates in a month's time.'

Tristan grinned. 'I wish you happy, Robin.' He wrung his friend's hand. 'I hope you will both achieve the outcome you most desire. And I trust you will invite me for frequent hunting and racing weeks at your varying estates to relieve my incipient penury!'

He left with the satisfying sense that all was falling into place nicely.

But his happiness came crashing down around him the next day.

All attempts to see Angel and express both his undying admiration and his daring plan for their future proved futile. His jaunty appearance at *Chez Simard* was rebuffed with the news that Miss Hathaway was out upon an errand, no, they could not say where, sir, no, she was not expected back for at least an hour. After two hours pacing the streets and failing to find her anywhere, he presented himself at the shop once more, to be told that Miss Hathaway was occupied and could not be pulled away from her work at present. When he went by once more at the time she usually left work, he was greeted by Madame Simard herself, who set her small person directly in his path, fixed him with her terrifying steely gaze, and ordered him to, 'stop loitering about my shop, a-trying to see Miss Hathaway. It don't serve you, sir, and it's no good for her. You leave her be, sir, and don't come back here unless it be to buy summing for your high-born lady.'

'Pestering… loitering…my… what?' Tristan drew himself up and looked down his aristocratic nose at the diminutive draper. 'Madame, you know my regard for Miss Hathaway is of the highest degree,' he said haughtily. 'I merely wish…'

'*Just* what I would expect you to say, sir,' retorted the undaunted modiste with eyes blazing. 'But your mama has been singin' *quite* another tune, she has, and fair brought poor Miss Hathaway to her knees with her meanness and her humiliations. I'll not have my darling girl used so shabbily, do you hear me? So you just be off with you, sir. And save your attentions for your own sort.' She shoved him out the door and locked it firmly behind him.

Tristan was now alarmed. He traced Angel's accustomed route home quickly, hoping to overtake her, but found no sign of her anywhere along the road, or in the Park, or in any of her usual haunts. At last he stood in front of the narrow front of Hathaway house and stared at it, in a quandry. He had been gone for little over a sennight. What could have changed in that short period of time?

He knocked on the door. Jacob answered, his imposing frame filling the doorway. 'Good evening, Mr. Neville, sir,' he said formally before Tristan could speak. 'Miss Hathaway is not receiving. And 'tis best you do not stop here again, sir.'

'Not stop… but Mr. Freeman, what can be the trouble? What has happened that Miss Hathaway will not see me?'

'That is for you to understand, sir. You just go your way now gentleman-like, and do not come here again. An you do, it will go ill with you.'

'There's no need to threaten me, Jacob,' said Tristan, irritated. 'I'm not such a cawker as to try to mill you down. If I have done anything to offend…'

'It's all right, Jacob,' said a determined voice behind him. 'I will speak to the gentleman. It will not take long.'

'Miss Hathaway!' exclaimed Tristan in relief. 'Angel! Please explain to me...'

Jacob unwillingly stepped aside several paces. Angel came forward, but when Tristan made to come near her, she flinched away and held a resisting hand out to stop him. 'Mr. Neville,' she said formally, refusing to meet his eyes, 'although it has been gratifying in the extreme to... to... to have your acquaintance and... to accept your f..flattering... at...attention,' she took a deep breath before continuing, 'I feel it is necessary for me to stop seeing... for you to go... away... and... and to end this f...riend...ship that can only result...' she cleared her throat, 'in pain.' She backed up and made to turn away, but Tristan leapt forward and took her by the arm.

'But *why*?' he demanded. She tried to pull away. Tristan resisted. 'Angel...' Jacob moved forward. 'No, Mr. Freeman, please, I mean no harm,' he said. 'I just... how have I hurt you, Miss Hathaway? Please tell me,' he implored, and turned loose her arm.

She finally looked up at him, green eyes dark with misery and fury. 'Was it your idea, sir, to set your mother's scorn on me? Could you not have faced me with the truth? Am I worth so little?' she demanded.

He reeled back. 'My *mother*? What on earth...'

'In the week since you've been so *conveniently* away, I have endured the most excoriating humiliation at the hands of Lady Neville, sir, who has left no doubt in my mind of the distance between my station in life and yours, and that she expects *at any moment*, sir, to hear the news of your engagement to a *lady of impeccable breeding and title*. Her name, I believe, is Arabella Montjoy. Can you deny it?'

Tristan reeled back in disbelief. '*Arabella Montjoy*! Miss Hathaway, I barely know the girl! I mean, I have known her for years, but it isn't... it can't...'

Angel's lip curled in contempt. 'Lady Neville *crowed* over this, Mr. Neville, *in* my presence, and I'll swear she did it deliberately, because she *knew* of our... *friendship*. Oh yes, she knew. Your precious friend Badgeley blabbed it to his sister as a great jest, and of course she in turn delivered the story to her mama. I knew from the start, O I *knew* this would be a disaster for me. But you fooled me into thinking you were a different sort of man, Mr. Neville, and like a green girl, I *believed* you.' Angry tears started to her eyes and she dashed them away impatiently. 'My family tried to warn me, my friends tried to warn me, and I thought... I thought you would not betray me. But I was wrong. You have.'

Neville, white with shock, stood silent through her tirade and made no move to stop her or to deny his allegations. But before she could slam the door in his face he said quietly and firmly, 'Miss Hathaway, I am sorry you have suffered so at the hands of my family... and yours. It isn't true. Any of it.'

'And yet you rode out with her. You keep a horse for her private use.'

'I... it... it's no such thing! A mere act of politeness, nothing more, I swear! It is you that has my whole heart, Angel. There is none other. I will spend as long as it takes, my whole life, if needed, to prove my worth to you.'

Angel choked back a convulsive sob and the tears spilled from eyes to cheeks. 'No. it is no use. Goodbye, Mr. Neville,' and she closed the door against him.

Tristan stood for a long time, staring at darkness, mind reeling. Gradually the shock he suffered drained from his body, and as his mind began to work once more, misery was replaced by cold anger, and a decision. He set off grimly in the direction of Neville house, and there was ushered into the presence of Lady Letitia, who sat in a wing chair in the withdrawing room, with a fire crackling brightly at her feet and a pot of China tea on a small table by her side. He curled his lip at the charming sight, which once upon a time would have had a soothing effect on him and now seemed just one more layer of artifice. All it lacked was a fussy lapdog and the devout attention of a little African page to make it worthy of a portrait, which, Tristan thought, was exactly how his revered parent must have planned it.

'Tristan, my son!' she exclaimed, seeing him. 'What a delightful surprise to see you.' She held her hand out.

He bowed over it punctiliously. 'A surprise, mama? Surely you have been waiting to see me these three days and more, the better to gloat,' he said.

'I do not know what you mean,' she dissembled, and made to rise. He did not step back, but stood rather too close, with an expression that in truth made her just a little nervous. She let her gaze drop to his attire and retreated to cold and injured dignity.

'And this is how you attend your mother, Tristan?' she asked acidly. 'Still dressed for the road, disheveled and in your dirt?'

'I am not here to attend on you, mother,' he shot back. 'I am merely here to deliver a message.'

'Deliver... what can you mean?' she asked, growing angry. 'Have you lost your mind? I find your manners execrable, sir.'

'Do you, mother? Then I learned them from you. And you know very well what I mean.'

'How *dare* you!' She pushed him back, rose to her feet, and faced him, rage in her eyes. 'How *dare* you speak to me in this manner!'

'And how dare *you* use your power and your grandiose sense of your own importance to threaten and intimidate a young woman who has done you not one iota of harm!'

'That little fortune hunter is like all the rest of them and looking no farther than your money! Of course I sent her packing, I did it for you, to help you! *She is not our sort!*'

'You have helped indeed, mama! You have helped me to see how purile *our sort* is. And how much preferable I find the honest company of Angel Hathaway and those like her!'

'A *dressmaker's assistant?*'

'No, mama! An intelligent young woman with fortitude and skill, who is making her way in a world we created to exclude *her sort* unless we can use them to serve us. And I intend to marry her.'

'You cannot! I *forbid* it,' said his mother forcefully, with all the power of three hundred years of heritage behind her.

But rather than being cowed by the glare that had withered stronger men than he, Tristan merely smiled cynical approval in a way that was horridly reminiscent of his uncle Nathaniel. 'Oh well done, mother. You should have been on the stage. And may I remind you that you have no power either to direct my affairs or plan my marriage.'

She gasped. 'When your brother hears about this... this *extraordinary behavior*, he will...'

'Suddenly disappear to Scotland for a week's fishing, I imagine. Do not worry, mother. Our impeccable and ancient family is in the best of hands. Kit has been very busy, and has a whole nursery full of brats to ensure its august heritage.'

Lady Letitia, white with fury, turned jerkily from him and went to the window, where she stood rigidly staring out at nothing. 'Then you leave me no choice, Tristan,' she said in carefully measured tones. 'If you insist on making this... *dreadful* mess of your life and this grave insult to your history and your inheritance... there is no option, sir. You will be disinherited, and banned from the family.'

'As Kit is the head of the family, ma'am, this decision must rest with him.'

'Christopher will do as I bid him.'

'Then so be it, ma'am. I am sorry that it must be this way. I feel that you are the one to be making a very grave mistake, and one which you will live to bitterly regret. I, however, may rest content that there is nothing you can offer me that outweighs the possibility of a life well lived.'

Lady Letitia was badly shaken. She had never dreamed - no, not in her wildest dreams - that a son of hers, well born, carefully raised, fed daily on his worth, would turn on all that was important in Polite Society and give away the possibility of a fortune with such apparent ease. She could not know the soul-searching that had led to her son's decision. That a different word from her would have mended the whole. She dared not show weakness. She dared not turn to face him again - her handsome, beautiful, favored son - and have her deep distress show itself. 'We are finished here,' she said coldly to the window.

'Then', said Tristan, all anger drained away and only sorrow remaining, 'with great regret, I bid you adieu, mama.'

She had been certain he would relent at the last moment. See reason and come back to her, to the family, to the life he had been accustomed to from birth.

But when the door closed softly behind him, she knew he would not. Having finally met the limit of her power, she was left behind only with her august position and bitter tears.

She ran to the door, yanked it open, and called his name. But Tristan was gone.

He walked for many hours and many miles through the darkness of the city's streets, parks, and byways. Through gravel and mud, through cobble and sludge, past the grand squares of the rich, through empty construction sites that were building blocks of houses for the newly middle class or newly wealthy, even skirting meaner neighborhoods whose narrow streets reeked of danger and despair, making his hackles rise.

He hadn't intended to let the conversation go that far. But so it always had been between himself and his mother. Was he really ready to live without the comforts of his life, of his family's fortune? Would his brother really let their mother's plan go forward? Christopher, Lord Neville, was easygoing to a fault, but if something offended his notions of propriety or justice, he was the most stubborn man born. So it mattered very much whether the Earl was offended more by the indignity that must be suffered to one's standing in Society if one's brother formed what must be considered the worst sort of *mesalliance*, or by the injustice of spurning a respected and beloved member of a family so utterly when his only infraction was to offer love in the wrong quarter.

It was dawn, and the air was alive with birdsong and the musical calls of tradespeople with their carts when he returned to his house - oh God, would he really have to give up this house and its loyal staff? He stood on the doorstep transfixed by this thought and was found there by Caine, who had just stepped out to flag down the rag man and instead saw his master, covered in mud, disheveled in every point of dress and demeanor, his beautiful boots no doubt ruined. Caine uttered a squawk and with deep worry ushered Tristan into the hall, took his hat and coat, and delivered him into the hands of Hubbard. That gentleman took one look at his ravaged master and with quiet efficiency got him out of his ruined clothing and eventually into his bed. He would have guessed that Master Tristan had been dipped badly at cards and had drowned his sorrows while trying to reverse his luck. But there was no scent about him of smoke or club, no rancid stench of alcohol emanating from his skin. There was no race meet nearby, so he hadn't lost his fortune on a sure thing in the stakes. And there was no sign of bruises or blood, so there hadn't been a mill.

All that remained, Hubbard deduced, was that black-haired wench Angel Hathaway. He resolved to nose about and see what he could find in the rumor mill.

As he turned down the lamp and banked the fire, he heard Tristan groan. 'I'm ruined, Hubbard,' he said thickly.

'Yes sir,' said Hubbard soothingly. 'Best you sleep now, sir.' He let himself out of the room, and by sheer dint of exhaustion, Tristan did indeed fall into a deep sleep.

*****

The Swan's patrons, far from being repelled by the fire, buzzed for days with stories of the blaze and the stirring actions of the company's staff. As the story spread through the city, it grew in entertainment value, with the result that several performances of The Swan's unique approach to Shakespeare's

Much Ado About Nothing - including several musical interludes and an expansion of the clown elements - were packed to the walls, especially by those now kicking themselves for not being able to say they'd been there On The Night. The ladies applauded Madame Seraphine's spirited Beatrice as she raged '*O that I were a man! I would eat his heart in the marketplace!*' An equal number of slightly nervous men comforted themselves that a mere actress uttered this ferocity, and as in the end all villains were punished and all maids and gentleman properly married, Mr. Shakespeare - helped by the redoubtable Mr. Pearce - illustrated once more that *Jack shall have Jill, naught shall go ill, the man shall have his mare again, and all shall be well* in the God-granted Great Chain of Being. And most went away well satisfied.

Except for one: who simply smiled twistedly as he observed the action from beneath hooded eyes in the eyrie of his box.

And two others: one young and chestnut-haired, with an unobstructed view from behind the curtain, the other across the hall wearing the hard stare of experience - who observed the observer.

Of course Denham saw Seraphine's performance as a direct taunt, as her very survival was a taunt. How she had done it, he could not imagine. That she had done it at all; that the fire meant to intimidate had merely improved her business and popularity; elicited an overwhelming desire to prove to her that there was no world in which he could not crush her. The fire should have been larger. Should have created more damage. There should have been a stampede to get out of a burning building. There should have been injuries. There should have been no audience tonight. Bev's fault, all of it. It was time to raise the ante. The callow girl he had thought destroyed utterly had grown into power, and had friends. But she was still only a woman. She could be broken. His mouth twitched in anticipation. He rose to leave the theatre before the crush of odiferous humanity should make his progress unpleasant.

His watchers slipped unobtrusively from their posts and made their way to the front of the house to observe their target's exit; Stephen coming from around the building to fade into the deep shadows behind the pillared portico, Neville from behind the stairs that led up to the boxes. As Denham exited the front doors, Neville moved to follow, nearly colliding with young Hathaway, entering through the same doors. The men exclaimed and greeted one another other, then Stephen asked, 'What brings you to The Swan, sir? I was led to believe you hold the wicked stage in contempt.'

'Curiosity, Hathaway. One has heard so often of the excellence of Madame Seraphine's Beatrice that I thought it good to see for myself,' Neville said smoothly. 'Especially after her bravery in the recent mishap of the fire.'

'And were you satisfied?' asked Stephen, with a look that suggested he did not believe a word of what he had just heard.

'Hathaway, do not let us fence. You have been watching a certain older gentleman who has returned to England as recently as yourself.'

'I have, sir, been watching one Lord Denham. He just departed in a hackney. What is your interest in the fellow?'

'The same as yours, I imagine. I want to see your mother. There is a matter that must...'

'You need not mince words, sir. I am very aware of her past.'

'Indeed? Including the fact of...'

'My birth, sir,' Stephen finished for him. His jaw worked, but he did not glance away. 'I know I have the misfortune to be the blackguard's son.'

'In blood, yes. You owe him no other resemblance.'

'Then I must be grateful.'

A rare smile crossed Neville's face. 'Your family was right to send you to sea, Hathaway. I doubt not it was the making of you.'

'I do not see how this concerns you, sir.'

'No. But one thing concerns both of us.'

'Destroying Denham?'

'Bringing him to justice.'

'Earls do not face justice. Sir.'

'Justice has many faces, Hathaway.'

A burst of applause accompanied by whistles, shouts, and a great stomping of feet emanated from behind the doors that separated the house from the lobby.

'We are about to be inundated with people,' observed Stephen.

Neville nodded. 'We will speak further. In the meantime, if you would show me to the dressing rooms…'

'This way,' said Stephen. 'We'll go 'round the side.'

'*Oui, venez*.' Seraphine responded to a light rap on her door some moments later, and was shocked when Nathaniel Neville opened it. Seeing him reflected in her looking glass, elegant in a coat of mulberry superfine and nankeen knee britches that admirably set off a well-shaped leg, her mouth formed a startled O, while her hand, but recently involved in wiping makeup from her face with a cream-soaked cotton wad, stopped in mid swipe. '*Mon bon Dieu!*' she swore in alarm. She dropped the swab and made a wild grab for a wrapper that would cover those parts of her shoulders, arms, and breasts that were left all too visible when Madame had stripped her costume, corset, and petticoats down to a light linen shift in order to be cooler. '*M'sieu, s'il vous plait!*'

With an appreciative smile that, will he or nil he, warmed other parts of him, Neville reached the wrapper before she could, and draped it chivalrously around her shoulders, where she thrust her arms into the sleeves hurriedly and clutched it around her protectively.

'I am sorry, *Madame*,' said Neville, looking not at all contrite. 'I should have identified myself before entering. But then,' he smiled again, 'I would have been denied the very charming sight of the celebrated Madame Seraphine *en deshabileé*.

'Mr. Neville. You are… it is most…'

'Oh, come,' he chided. 'We two have too much experience of the world to be coy. I have no aspersions on your modesty.

Although I must say that my limited experiences with…
actresses… is that their dressing rooms are more notable for a
plethora of cicisbeos and swains than…' he looked with interest
around the small room, with its sofa covered in costume pieces,
hangers with dresses and undergarments, a counter covered with
hats, plumes, and pieces of paste jewelry, and a small shelf that
groaned with scripts, '…yours.'

'Your experiences with others of my trade do not define all of
us, sir.'

'So I see,' he acknowledged. He worked admirably to look
into her eyes rather than the parts now hidden tantalizingly under
the silk wrapper, adding more abruptly than he intended, 'I want
to speak with you about a matter of some importance.'

'And what can that be?'

'Denham.'

She flinched, but said firmly enough, 'I will be with you when
I am properly dressed, *M'sieu*, and not before.'

'Of course, *Madame*,' he bowed slightly, turning the handle of
the door. 'I await your pleasure.'

Half an hour later, properly armored against the world in a
plain gown of cinnamon-colored India muslin over a linen
chemise of the creamy hue called Isabella, with her hair caught in
its usual bandeau, she ushered Neville into the office. He had
already ordered a supper and some liquid refreshment to be
brought for them, which arrived from the kitchen shortly
thereafter.

'High-handed of you,' remarked Seraphine.

'I thought you would be hungry after a taxing performance,'
he responded.

'Will you not eat something yourself?'

'I dined earlier. But this is a very nice brandy.'

'Thank-you. Mr. Pearce has a very good palate, I believe. And
excellent connections.' She looked at him uncertainly. 'You are not
here in an official capacity, are you?'

'I know better than to question the provenance of such a distinguished beverage.' He sipped it appreciatively.

'Then… if it regards my daughter Angel…'

'Your daughter?' He frowned. 'What earthly reason have I to be in the least interested in your daughter, ma'am?'

'You know very well, sir,' Seraphine fiddled uncomfortably with a fork. 'She has been excessively foolish, and… and now, I fear… your nephew…'

Neville held his hand up. 'Mrs. Hathaway, I have not the remotest desire to know anything at all pertaining either to your daughter or any one of my several nephews.'

'Good', Seraphine said in relief, and tucked in to a supper of lamb with mint sauce and peas without further comment, all conversation ceasing while she ate. 'Thank-you for ordering champagne for me,' she said after a few minutes during which Neville had sipped his brandy and watched her in some amusement. 'I find bordeaux a trifle heavy at this hour and cannot abide ratafia.'

'I admit, I was on the verge of ordering Canary, but was very quickly set straight by Mrs. Freeman.'

'I am French, *m'sieu*. Not for me the swill that English ladies adore. And now tell me why are you so *convenable*. I am quite overcome with suspicion.'

'You cut me to the quick, *Madame*,' he said, hand on heart in feigned despair. 'Cannot I be allowed the pleasure of a beautiful woman's company…'

'Do not think you can… *qu'est-ce que le mot*… bamboozle, *n'est-ce pas*? You cannot *bamboozle* me, *m'sieu*,' she said sharply, pointing a fork at him. 'I may not know you well, but I know you better than that.'

He looked at her steadily, the hint of a smile playing about his mouth. 'As it happens, you know more of me than most, Mrs. Hathaway. And I in turn… know more of you. So let us no longer pretend that you are French.'

Seraphine put the fork down with a clatter and leaned back in her chair. 'Ah. And how long have you known?' She studied him carefully. 'I do not think... Did we meet... before?'

'No. And rest assured, *Madame*, even if we had, your remarkable... I can call it nothing else... rise from the ashes... is so extraordinary, and so complete, as to render you unrecognizable to even your own family.'

'But you recognised me.'

'It is my job, Mrs. Hathaway, to recognise people. And your elder brother and I were friends at Oxford. So I knew of the scandal.'

Her eyes widened. 'You cannot mean to unmask me, sir. I do not desire to be made known to a family of strangers who would almost certainly spurn me, nor do I wish to be made a mockery.'

'I have no such intention, Mrs. Hathaway.'

She sighed. 'So. There are no longer any secrets between us. I hold yours, and you hold mine. What a very odd position that puts us in.'

'Indeed.'

'What is your interest in Denham?'

'I told you once, Mrs. Hathaway, that I am interested in justice. Denham - an exile with several unexplained deaths to his account, and no personal responsibility that can be proved - must always be of interest. Especially now that he has returned to England.'

'Why would he return, do you think?'

'It's my belief that the death of his most recent wife has made even Europe too hot for him. Perhaps he thought England safe, after the passage of twenty-five years. Perhaps he was sent here by a power unfriendly to us. We do not know, yet. Seeing him, and then you, at The Swan on the same night, piqued my interest, and I remembered the old scandal. When I met your son Stephen, I knew. His resemblance to William Whateley cannot have escaped his brother.'

'William Whateley. The brother who died, *n'est-ce pas*? The heir.'

'It was said to be a regrettable hunting accident. But many believed - and I concur - that it was the first of Denham's murders. Your miraculous existence is a terrible threat to him. He may appear now as an elderly roué, nothing more than a court card. But he is very dangerous to you, *Madame*.'

'I know,' admitted Seraphine, wearily. She outlined the meetings with Denham - both hers and Pearce's - her encounter with the determined young men in the park, the random accident and injury around the theatre, including the fire - 'although none can be traced to him. We are taking every precaution that we can, but we cannot be everywhere at all times. I very much fear what will come next, sir.'

'Has he made demands?'

'He wants money, of course. For 'protection'.'

'Will you capitulate?'

'Never.'

'Then allow me to help you.'

'Why should you desire that, sir? Our affairs can mean nothing to you.'

'Bringing one who has destroyed innumerable lives to justice means everything to me. And also...' he struggled with himself for a moment. 'I owe you a life, ma'am.'

'I *beg* your pardon?' asked Seraphine, nonplussed.

'You saved my life, that night in Le Havre.'

'No such thing, sir! I merely called attention to you in the water, swimming for the ship. 'Twas Jacob saved you, and the sailors.'

'Others pulled me from the water, *Madame*, but had you not pointed me out and insisted on action being taken, I would certainly have died that night. I have said before, Mrs. Hathaway, I always despatch my debts.'

Seraphine colored. 'But sir... it was not altruism. Merely that I cannot bear to see needless suffering.'

'Yes,' he said, the expression in his eyes softening as he looked at her. 'I know that of you now. Mrs. Hathaway…'

A quick knock at the door was followed by Stephen, who carried a lantern.

'Are you quite finished, *Maman, M'sieu?* Jacob and Marianne await us, and Hemings would like to go home.'

'*Merde!*' exclaimed Seraphine. 'I had no notion of the time.'

'I shall leave you then,' said Neville, rising gracefully and bowing over Seraphine's hand. 'But I pray you remember that you have a friend, at need.' He nodded to Stephen, and departed.

'A friend at need? What does that fellow mean, *Maman?*'

'Where is our cousin Charles?' deflected Seraphine. 'Was it a race to the box office?'

'*Absolument pas.* I have the takings safe. He seems remarkably resigned to the new state of affairs, I must say.'

'Does he,' said Seraphine, frowning. 'That does not sound at all like Charles.'

'Perhaps his luck with cards has changed.'

'That *definitely* does not sound like Charles. Is Bridie ready?'

'Bridie has left with River,' Stephen said piously. 'They are… *comment ça s'appelle… On se marche…*' he frowned.

'Walking out?'

'*Oui, c'est ça.* Walking out.' He grinned.

'*J'aurais du savoir,*' she said, exasperated. 'I hope that idiot girl knows what she is about, this time.'

'Bridie may not. But River does, *je vous assure.* Now answer my question. What does Neville want with you?'

Seraphine rose, blew out the lamp on the desk, and reached for her cloak behind the door. 'He has guessed our story, Stephen.'

'*On le connais.* But what to think?'

'I think…' she thought for a moment. 'I think it is a relief. He wants Denham. And that must help us.'

'Can he be trusted?'

'*Je pense que oui.* Time will tell.'

Elsewhere in the city, a body was found washed against the pilings along Canary Pier when the tide went out. It was not identified, and no one claimed it, but it certainly resembled the rigger Tom Fay.

*****

'It's your own damned fault, Letty,' said Neville callously to his sister-in-law the following morning, after he had been accosted in the middle of his breakfast and forced to listen to a recital, uttered in dramatic accents that would have done a Cheltenham tragedy proud, of all the ills done her by her son Tristan. 'If you'd kept silent, my nephew may have come 'round to your way of thinking in his own time. Now you've successfully goaded him into making the very *mesalliance* you most abhor.'

'I merely wanted to make him understand the gravity of the situation.'

'You merely rode roughshod and flayed him with it. You're a fool, Letty. He has twice the spine of any of your other brats.'

'You live to cross me! If my dear William were alive…'

'He would have locked you in your bedchamber rather than allow you to make such a cake of yourself. You must own you've made a dreadful mistake.'

'Tristan is just a boy! He doesn't understand…'

'Tristan is past twenty-six, and cut his eyeteeth some years ago.'

'He doesn't know his own mind!'

'Doesn't know… Have you gone completely mad? I thought this whole damned farradiddle came about precisely because my nephew *does* know his own mind.'

'You know perfectly well what I mean, Nathaniel,' she said stiffly.

'I believe I do, ma'am. You mean that Tristan has refused to acknowledge the workings of *your* mind; even to the point of refusing to capitulate to your threats of disowning him.'

'The case was desperate. He had to be brought to understand.'

'Brought to heel, you mean, as if he were an errant spaniel. That worked so well that he now understands very clearly that his mother cares more for her title and position in Society than she does for her own son!'

Lady Neville gasped and reeled back as if he had slapped her. 'Nathaniel,' she breathed, 'how can you suggest... how can you even imagine...'

His eyes gleamed maliciously. 'Oh. Am I so wrong, Letty?' he taunted. 'Come, tell me. I am listening.'

'How... I...' Lady Neville struggled to find words, eyes glancing everywhere in the room as if the perfect retort might be hidden among the folds of the curtains, or in a book in the case beside the mantel. Failing, she turned back to her brother-in-law and fixed all her hurt and rage on him. '*Get. Out. Of my house,*' she commanded. '*Immediately.*'

'It is in fact *our* house, Letty, and I have the advantage of paying its taxes. But I leave you for the nonce, with the greatest pleasure in the world,' said Neville complacently. He swept her an ironic bow and left the room, stopping by the front door only long enough to be helped into his great coat and handed his hat and gloves before setting off on foot in the direction of his nephew's lodgings.

He found Tristan standing fully dressed and more *point device* than a broken-hearted lover had any right to be, staring moodily out his front window at the street below, a half-empty glass of claret in hand.

'Uncle,' he greeted Neville curtly. 'Come to gloat, or to add your voice to that of my esteemed Mama?'

'Neither. I have rather come to see how you are faring.' He eyed his nephew's punctilious dress through his quizzing glass. 'Do I take it that you are on the point of capitulation?'

'You do not,' said Tristan shortly. 'I have, in fact, just returned from a second informative meeting with my banker.'

Neville helped himself to a glass of the claret and made himself comfortable in a chair at the head of the table. 'You fascinate me,' he said, sipping the claret and lightly swinging his quizzing glass by its cord.

'I gather you have spoken with the dowager Lady Neville?'

'Indeed. I warned you, I think, how it would be.'

'You did. But as you no doubt know, matters escalated beyond my control while I was in Herefordshire with my great-aunt Lady Georgina. So you perceive me with good intentions in my heart, a special license in my pocket, a lady who feels betrayed and ill used and therefore will not speak to me, and a mother who has disowned me.'

'So… you went to see your banker prior to fleeing to Italy on the next packet, like any sensible man in your situation would do?'

In spite of himself, Tristan laughed, and sat opposite his uncle. 'Apparently I am not so sensible a man, Nat. I went to my banker to begin separating my finances from those of my family.'

'Even if the lady who has caused this turmoil refuses to marry you?'

'Even if.'

'If you marry as the family wishes, you will be very wealthy, Tris.'

'Yet I find myself content. There are some few things I admit I shall miss sorely, but I appear to have an easy enough competence.'

'Enough to stretch to married life?'

'That need not trouble me this present.'

Nathaniel smiled. 'I applaud you, sir.'

'Do you?' asked Tristan, surprised.

'Indeed, yes. I find you more like my late brother than I could have hoped. And on the strength of our last discussion, I have a proposition for you.'

'I'm all ears, sir.'

'As you know, I work for the Crown in a capacity that takes me out of the country quite often.'

'Something to do with trade agreements, one is led to believe.'

'A convenient title, which eliminates many awkward discussions,' his uncle agreed. 'Trade agreements being so eminently dull that nobody asks about them.'

Tristan laughed. 'And how is that to your benefit, sir?'

'Let me tell you,' said Neville, and proceeded to outline what it was that he actually did for the Crown, as well as what he did that the Crown knew nothing of.

When he had done, Tristan gave a low whistle. 'I'd no idea,' he said, observing his uncle with new respect. 'But it answers a good many questions I've had over the years.'

'You cannot repeat a word of this to anyone, Tristan.'

'Or you'll have to have me extirpated, sir?'

'I might just have you 'disappeared' to Canada. I am at least that fond of you.'

'Generous,' acknowledged Tristan. 'What must I do in your service?'

'The details remain to be seen, but I fancy you might begin as an able assistant to a man who is about to be made a political appointee whose affairs make his presence in certain capitals in Europe from time to time.'

'That man being you?'

'Of course. But in the meantime, there are certain other, shall we say, *internal* affairs to be settled that it might interest you to be a part of, which will enable you to see if another sort of work is to your liking. As it happens, it directly concerns your Miss Hathaway.'

'I... beg your pardon, sir?' asked Tristan, perplexed.

'I want you to follow her movements without being discovered.'

Tristan blushed fiery red. 'Follow Miss Hathaway? But sir, I...'

Nathaniel raised his eyebrows in mild surprise. 'Do you not like the task? I thought that, since you had already made a habit of it, it might be to your taste.'

'But that was different, sir. That was...'

'Neville, if you mean to tell me that spying in the name of love is fundamentally different than spying in the name of gathering information or offering protection, I wash my hands of you. In my employ, there will be many times when what you are asked to do will be far more repugnant to your ethics and sensibilities.'

'You ask me this because you think Miss Hathaway is in danger.'

'I do. Mind you have someone trustworthy beside you to act as a messenger at need.'

'What do you expect to happen, sir?'

'I do not know what, or when. I only know that it will.'

'And you, sir?'

'I find I have developed quite a passion for the theatre, Tristan,' he said with an odd smile. 'Remarkable, is it not.'

*****

A week of dawdling in doorways, loitering near alleys, and casually walking or riding the streets at hours when Angel might be walking between work and home or going out with friends left Tristan wondering if his uncle had overestimated a situation that had never been clear in the first place. The act of sneaking about, watching her lead a life that excluded him, caused him pain beyond bearing. It also, seeing her looking wan and disinterested in all that went on around her, kindled a certain degree of hope. Several times his attention on her nearly caused his discovery, and only by ducking quickly into a doorway or pulling his horse to the other side of a passing wagon saved his anonymity.

The weather grew thick, even by London standards. Elsewhere, daylight would be lengthening into beautiful twilight hours as the season stretched toward midsummer. But in London heavy air pressed the smoke of hundreds of thousands of coal fires in hundreds of thousands of chimneys to the ground, where it mingled with damp river mists and created a fug so murky that street lamps had to be lit before six in the evening and even then the light pooled and barely pushed the shadows back.

Thief weather, Jacob Freeman thought grimly as he walked Angel through crowded streets toward their home. Thug weather. His senses tingled, & he held a short and purposeful blackthorn cudgel ready in the folds of his coat, while foot travelers, carts, and carriage traffic appeared as ghostly ships on a grey and shapeless ocean, passed them by, and were swallowed just as mysteriously behind them.

They were only a few blocks from home when Brutus stopped suddenly and growled deep in his throat, hackles raised. It was that brief second that saved them from complete ambush. Instantly Jacob whipped the cudgel out and thrust Angel behind him as four closely jacketed assailants sprang out of the deep shadows and were on them, two attacking Jacob, two making a grab for Angel, who screamed and let the dog go. Brutus launched himself at one man with a roar and locked a wrist in powerful jaws with a sickening crunch. The owner screamed in pain and dropped to the ground. Angel whirled to face the other and with rage and terror let loose a hard kick to the crotch that would have disabled one less heavily protected by cloth but still caused the man to yell & redouble his efforts to grab her. Jacob used his huge form and powerful arms to level one man with a heavy blow to the side of the head, punching another in the stomach with a fist that knocked him back, but the man regained his balance and piled into Jacob. Brutus flung himself again at the flailing nemesis who finally reached his blade and slashed at the raging dog as Angel dodged, scratched, bit, kicked, and swore at the man who came after her over and over again. A thundering explosion and flash of a gun split the air, Jacob sagged, but with superhuman strength launched himself at Angel's assailant who he had by the neck and they both crashed to the ground. '*Brutus, Brutus, Brutus!!!*' Angel cried and ran to the dog that lay panting on the ground and with a nasty laugh the man with the knife came for Angel as the one Jacob had first knocked down staggered to his feet, bleeding and half blinded from the punishing blow. Jacob rose dizzily, cudgel back in hand, pulled Angel roughly to him and they backed against the stone of the building beside them while the two enraged thugs closed in on them with club and knife and then suddenly, impossibly, there were bellows from the end of the road and two bundled male shapes emerged out of the thick fog - one burly, one slender, both shouting *'Stop! Stop in the name of the Crown!'* - running to their aid with lanterns bobbing wildly. The two attackers backed away from their prey and looked for an exit. Jacob leapt forward and struck one with the full force of his body, grabbing and twisting the arm that held the knife until the arm cracked audibly under the strain and the man howled in agony. The other broke to get past the intruders, slashing a cudgel at the slender man who ran toward him, who ducked nimbly and with the business end of his cane struck a blow to the side of the rogue's head, sending him sprawling to the muddy street, where he lay still. The slender man kept running until he reached Angel's side. She screamed and put up her hands to scratch but he caught them saying *'Angel, Angel, Angel'* over and over again, *'Angel it is I. Tristan. It is done, Angel'* and she collapsed weeping on the ground and crawled to Brutus' side where she wept bitterly over her faithful dog, calling *Brutus, Brutus,* while tearing the flounce off her petticoat and ripping it into strips.

Sometimes the universe is kind. As she went on calling his name, stroking this ear, feeling for the wound, making strips of cloth into a pad and a bandage, the tip of the lurcher's tail twitched and then with a weak wag, he whimpered and tried to lick her face and she cradled him and wept and crooned to him. Tristan came and carefully, with lantern raised and gentle fingers, felt the giant dog's body. He found the slash, along the ribs, and blood pooling, and Angel put a pad on it and applied pressure, still crooning.

'He may live, Angel, an you can stop the bleeding,' he encouraged her. 'Ah, Brutus, you good, good dog. Best of dogs.' Then he rose and went to the other gentleman, one Billy Beggs, late of the Runners, currently one of London's very first police officers.

'You're a lucky one, and that's the truth', Beggs was saying to Freeman, who, slumped against the wall in exhaustion and pain, battered from head to toe, nursed a shoulder that bled sluggishly through his coat.

'If it hadn't been for you and Mr. Neville coming along as you did, it would have gone hard with us, sir,' he panted.

'Here, miss,' Beggs called to Angel. 'An you be done with that dog, yer man here could use some help.' Angel, nodded, but was loath to leave Brutus.

'Here, let me,' said Tristan, returning to her. 'Hold his mouth so he doesn't bite me.' And with difficulty, he moved the dog closer to Jacob.

'No, Angel,' Jacob protested weakly as she tenderly probed the seeping wound. ''Tis but a scratch.'

'This coat's ruint already,' said Beggs. 'Best to tear 'un off and be done.' Angel nodded, and with hands that seemed to operate separately from her frozen brain, ripped the sleeve and felt around the back of the shoulder while Jacob grunted and gritted his teeth, breath rapid.

'You've young Neville to thank for this,' said Beggs conversationally. 'He's been a followin' of you two this past sennight and told me what he was half expectin' to happen. I dint pay him no mind, on account of him bein' a young swell, half flash and half foolish, so I thought. But then I seen Micky Flynn and a coupla his boys in the neighborhood, which they ain't often in this part of town. And I reckon that there,' he nodded at the corpse of a man lying in the mud, his own knife buried in his throat, 'is Micky Flynn his own self. Looks like that dog done him a deal of damage afore you finished him off, big fella.'

He got to his feet and, looking deeply into the physical details of the chaotic scene, strolled to the sprawled form of the other man dispatched by Jacob, studying him with lantern raised for some minutes without speaking. 'Georgie Smythe,' he said dispassionately. 'With his neck broke.' He shook his head in wonder and looked sidelong at Jacob. 'I'm right glad you be on our side, and that's a fact.'

Jacob looked blearily at the scene, puzzled. 'There should be another,' he said. 'There were four.'

Beggs shone his lantern around the area. 'Damned if you ain't right. Right here's where young Neville laid him out. And look where he drug hisself back up to his feet and slipped away while we wasn't payin' no heed.' He followed the man's steps for a few yards, then returned, shaking his head. 'I coulda used that 'un, to split on the others, like. Well, mebbe we'll find 'un.'

'Beggs,' called Neville from the shadowy fog. 'This fellow's alive. Says his name's Ramage.'

Bev Ramage sat half-conscious, head sagged against his breast, cradling a mangled hand with the other, and moaning. 'Please, sirs,' he repeated over and again. 'Please sirs. I'll tell you all but please sirs. Do not let him think me alive. He'll take my family, oh sirs. Do not let him take me alive.'

'Musta took a heavy hit to the head,' remarked Beggs. 'Man's raving.'

'Who, Ramage?' asked Tristan. 'Who mustn't know you're alive?'

Ramage wept into the hands cradling his head. 'I wish I'd never,' he said brokenly. 'I wish I'd never.'

'Never what, man?' demanded Beggs. 'Out with it, you lobcock.'

Tristan leaned closer to the helpless man. 'Who do you speak of, Ramage? Is it Denham?'

Ramage flinched and sketched a nod. 'Mustn't know. Never let him know… I'll talk. I will. Just…'

Tristan took Beggs aside. 'We need to move, Beggs. I must get Miss Hathaway away, and Mr. Freeman to a doctor. This man Ramage needs immediate medical attention. Can you get me a hackney for my people? I'll tell you more later, but we cannot safely stay here longer. There may be others.'

'Right you are, sir. You just watch this lot a few tics more for me. I'll be back directly.'

Tristan moved toward Angel, Jacob, and Brutus. The bandaged Brutus alive but panting shallowly. Jacob near to fainting, grinding his teeth to keep from moaning as Angel packed his wound with the remains of her petticoat against further blood loss. Angel clearly in shock, hands doing what her mind could not comprehend to make all right. She rebuttoned the remains of Jacob's coat tightly. 'We'll get you home, Jacob,' she promised. 'Marianne will see you to rights. I promise. Please. Please, hold on a little longer. Please.' She sat next to him and pulled her dog's head into her lap, wrapping an arm through Jacob's good one, speaking softly to both while she watched Tristan in the bobbing light, as he grimly studied the retreating tracks of the escaped man, then the two corpses, before returning to Ramage, who had reached the end of caring and passed out. Tristan shook his head and sat by Jacob.

'You look like hell, my friend,' he remarked, holding the lamp up.

'Even so, sir. Angel's done wonders and saved us both, I shouldn't wonder, sir. You look to her, now.'

Tristan moved the lamp to Angel. 'You would make a worthy soldier's wife,' he said gently.

'Oh, no,' she said, wide eyes turned on him. 'No, I could not ever…'

'Angel, there is blood,' Tristan interrupted abruptly. 'Are you… were you…'

'The blood is not mine. Oh, Tristan', suddenly she began to shake, 'I am so frightened. I…'

Tristan put down the lantern, quickly stripped off his coat, detached her gently from Jacob, and put it around her shoulders, maneuvering around the dog to hold her to him. 'It's all right, my brave love,' he said gently. 'You have saved your friends.'

She choked back a sob and clung to him, shaking uncontrollably. He could hear her teeth chatter. 'But it's my fault. If not for me…'

The sound of wheels on cobbles, and lights shining. A wagon turned into the road and stopped fifty yards short of the scene of the adventure, then a form that became Nathaniel Neville improbably appeared out of the fog, inexplicably dressed in a frieze coat and leggings. 'Uncle?' called Tristan, and carefully rose to his feet. 'I was never so glad to see anyone.'

They clasped hands. 'Your Sam found me outside The Swan. I've just run into Beggs. He filled me in. Miss Hathaway?'

'Safe but very shaken. Jacob and the dog both injured. Two dead, one has managed to get away.'

'Beggs said there was one yet living?'

'A man called Ramage. Terrified of Denham. Keeps talking about something the villain has over his family. How he must be thought dead.' Tristan shone his light to where Ramage still slumped.

'Does he now,' said Neville. 'Beggs will take him. He'll be along directly, with a wagon and helpers. Let us get Miss Hathaway and Freeman home.'

'And the dog.'

'The dog?'

'Yes. A heroic dog, I must add.'

'It lives?'

'So far. And I can tell you with certainty that Miss Hathaway will not leave it.'

Neville sighed. 'Needs must. Come on.' He moved to the vehicle he had arrived in - a dogcart pulled by a stout cob with a pile of blankets heaped in the bed.

Tristan smiled briefly. 'I won't ask where you found this equipage. Or, 'he wrinkled his nose, 'that alarming coat.'

'Don't,' agreed Nathaniel. 'It's been a busy night. Help me get our passengers loaded.'

Angel rode in the back, in the blankets with the dog, having refused all efforts to get her on the seat next to Tristan's uncle. The semi-conscious Freeman was propped carefully on the bench instead, sagging heavily against him. Beggs arrived with a wagon, spoke to Tristan briefly, and set his men to their work with the corpses and the man called Ramage. Tristan climbed into the back of the cart beside Angel. And slowly, painfully, they rumbled their way to the Hathaway house.

'There'll be chaos when we arrive,' remarked Tristan.

'I hope not', said Neville. 'Sam's gone ahead to warn them.'

*****

Only Marianne was home to receive Sam's message. After a surge of shock that nearly paralyzed her with fear she galvanized herself, sent Sam to The Swan, cleared the kitchen table, scrubbed it, covered it with an old sheet, pushed the benches out of the way, built up the kitchen fire, and hung a filled kettle on the crane. She was just setting out ointments and tinctures and was in the process of brewing healing draughts when Stephen arrived out of breath with the news that Sam had stayed behind to inform Seraphine and bring her and Bridie home after the show. He set his instruments out on a bench while Marianne ripped an old shirt into strips, and the dogcart arrived to a rudimentary but efficient hospital. Stephen and Nathaniel unloaded Jacob, Marianne murmuring by his head, and laid him groaning on the table. Tristan and Angel lifted Brutus on his blankets and moved him to the hearth. Neville issued quiet orders to his nephew that elicited a nod and a spark of anticipation in the younger man's eyes, and as he turned to leave was met by Seraphine, who rushed with a sob to wrap Angel in her arms. Ignoring her daughter's protestations about staying with her dog, she bundled her up the stairs and went to work stripping her of her ruined clothes, ordering Bridie, who trailed behind with wide eyes, to bring hot water and a cloth. While Angel stood shivering, Seraphine worked carefully to clean her and catalogue any potential hurts. Fortunately, these comprised only of some bruises, rapidly turning purple, far from enough for Angel to accept a night dress and bed. Instead, she stubbornly insisted on a clean shift and old linen overdress long reduced to household chore wear, then returned downstairs in time to help hold Brutus still while Stephen worked to treat and close the deep wound across his ribs. Without her presence, the dog would have been impossible. She held his head firmly in one arm, the other hand closing his mouth against the instinct to bite, all the while crooning encouragement to him until the dog was attended to and returned to his spot on the blankets by the hearth.

'Jacob?' asked Angel anxiously when Brutus was settled again.

'He had lost a deal of blood,' said Stephen wearily. 'But the bullet went through the muscle, so it was a cleaner wound than I expected. We've put him to bed; Marianne is with him. You did good work, *ma soeur*,' he added. 'Without you the outcome might have been different.'

Angel nodded, her expression strained. 'Without him... and Brutus... oh, Stephen... they were so brave, but there were four, and I was not armed, I could do nothing but bite and scratch...' she rubbed her face with a shudder. 'I was sure we would die, but then Tristan came...' she turned to Tristan in wonder as he stood, weary from helping Stephen and Marianne by lifting, turning, handing needed articles, removing soaked and bloodied clothing. He was stripped to his shirt sleeves, rumpled and covered in grime. And she saw him for the first time as something human and vulnerable, yet enduring. And beautiful. Beyond thought, she moved to him with hands out. Unhesitating, he wrapped her in his arms and settled next to her on the bench that had been moved closer to the hearth. And there they stayed, leaning on one another, neither speaking.

Stephen observed them without remark, gathered up the last of the soiled linens and clothing, and motioned to Bridie to follow him to the fire pit at the foot of the garden with the detritus from cleaning the table so they could burn the lot. Seraphine came downstairs with Angel's ruined clothes. She hesitated when she saw her daughter nestled in Tristan Neville's arms, but closed her mouth in a tight line and followed the others to the garden.

By the time Nathaniel Neville returned, the kitchen was clean and orderly once more, and all except Jacob sat around the table, sipping a buttered toddy made by Seraphine. Stephen and Tristan had scrubbed off blood, sweat, and grime under the hand pump outside the kitchen door. Stephen had changed; Tristan gratefully accepted a package of clean linens dumped in front of him by his uncle, and at Bridie's direction disappeared to rid himself of his own stained and bloodied garments. Seraphine served another mug of toddy from the hearth.

'I believe we owe you more thanks than we can possibly repay, sir,' she said, giving it to him.

'And Freeman?' Neville asked, seating himself next to her when she had settled.

'Sleeping now,' said Marianne. 'Mercifully, he will live.'

'He's made of strong stuff, our Jacob,' approved Stephen. 'He'd taken the devil of a battering.'

Neville grunted. 'He inflicted far more damage than he sustained, I am happy to report. Three men down with nothing but a cudgel and his bare hands. With some help from a dog, of course,' he smiled briefly at Angel. 'And my poxy nephew.'

Marianne looked at him imploringly. 'They won't... the Runners, that is... won't arrest him for battery or...'

'They will not, Mrs. Freeman. They are more likely to issue a reward. But your troubles are far from over,' he added, addressing Seraphine as Tristan came back into the room and climbed into his seat beside Angel.

'Not over!' exclaimed Angel. 'But surely, sir, the third man... the one that... lived... will tell the officers that it was Denham that was behind this whole affair? That it was more than just an attack by ruffians?'

Neville sighed. 'He will if he awakens, Miss Hathaway. He is currently comatose.'

'But we *know*. We know who it is behind these attacks!' insisted Angel.

'Knowing is not proving,' said Seraphine.

'Where is the captive, Neville?' demanded Stephen. 'I should like to treat him myself. He must survive to incriminate the *voyou indicible* who engineered this piece of infamy.'

'I understand your desire to bring an unspeakable rogue to justice, Hathaway,' said Neville. 'But Ramage's whereabouts and condition are closely guarded. And you are only one of many who wish to question him.'

'This could take weeks, even months,' protested Seraphine. 'And we in danger the entire time while that man walks abroad.' She looked around the table. 'There's nothing for it,' she said firmly. 'Angel, we must arrange to send you away.'

'*Maman*! As if I would leave you here...'

'*Tu ne me comprends pas, ma chère.* As I understand the matter, Denham does not know he has failed in this attempt against you, *c'est vrai?*'

'Yes,' said Neville. 'Unless the man who escaped has gotten to him. Denham is being closely watched. We will know soon enough.'

'*Alors*, Angel must be made to disappear,' agreed Stephen. 'He must not know he has failed, *ma soeur*. So you must go away if we are to apprehend the man. But where?'

'I think that is where I may be of help,' said Tristan. 'My great-aunt, Lady Georgina Temple, lives near Faringdon. Angel would be made welcome there...'

'*Berkshire!*' exclaimed Seraphine. 'No, and no, and no! It is too far. Too dangerous. Who would be there to look out for her? This is trading one abduction for another!'

'No, *Maman*, it is not,' said Angel quietly. 'It is a kind offer, made by friends, and I am inclined to accept.'

'You cannot! I forbid t!'

'You forget, *Maman*. I am of age, and it is my decision,' said her daughter firmly. 'If I must be made to disappear for a time, then I will go to this Lady Temple. But,' she added, with a challenging glare at Tristan, 'I will not go without Brutus.'

'I'll go with you,' offered Bridie, looking suddenly cheerful. 'So as you won't be worried about no hanky-panky occurring on the road, Mrs. Hathaway, ma'am.'

'Bridie!' gasped Seraphine, scandalized, while Angel blushed furiously and the gentlemen, after a bare second of indecision where desperation and absurdity collided, laughed uproariously.

'Now that is something I would never have thought to hear from you,' managed Stephen through his mirth.

Bridie drew herself up haughtily and looked down her nose at the men. 'I am sure I do not know what you mean,' she said in the aristocratic drawl she'd been working on for weeks. 'I am become a respectable woman, you know.' And with that, she got to her feet, announced that she had packing to do, and swept from the room. The still-blushing Angel scurried after her. Marianne followed, 'to make sure they don't pack five handkerchiefs and no linens.'

'*Madame*,' said Neville, recovering faster than the others. 'You and Mr. Hathaway are correct; by maintaining ignorance over your daughter's whereabouts, we may draw Denham into the open. When he finds he has failed to take Miss Hathaway, be will be desperate. By holding Ramage's location and condition secret as well, he may think…' he considered, 'yes. That, perhaps Ramage has run off with her himself. It will serve. Do you not agree?'

'…Yes,' Seraphine agreed reluctantly. 'It will serve. But to banish my daughter to Berkshire…'

Neville took her hands gently. 'It is hardly banishment, ma'am. My aunt's estate affords every comfort, and is but ninety miles distant. I wish that you may learn to trust me. I promise you that no harm will come to Angel.'

'Now,' he let go of her hands and turned to the others briskly. 'I have arranged the use of Sir Robert Kilronan's chaise. The ladies will travel...'

'*Robin*'s chaise?' asked Tristan, confused. 'How...'

'He remembered your previous request, and I merely accepted on your behalf. The ladies will travel...'

'And the dog...' murmured Tristan.

'The ladies and... er... the dog... will travel in the chaise. You, nephew, will ride beside them. You will be further attended by Sam Cutler and the excellent Hubbard, both, I'm told, good men with... ah... barking pieces.'

'Neville, you are the most complete hand,' Tristan grinned wearily. 'You'd already planned the whole thing.'

'"Twas you had the plan. I only the execution. How you have earned the loyalty of two such doughty men as Cutler and Hubbard is beyond me,' Neville accorded his nephew the slightest of bows. 'You may change horses at the Red Lion on the Bath Road near Slough, and again at Newbury. Can that chestnut of yours go the distance?"'

'I expect so. We shall not be going at breakneck speed, after all.'

'Good man.'

'*Non!*' exclaimed the alarmed Seraphine. 'Mr. Neville, sir, you have treated my daughter with the utmost disregard. I will not allow...'

'I regard your daughter with the highest regard and respect,' countered Tristan. 'She will be safe with me, ma'am.'

'But for my daughter to be seen gallivanting about the countryside with...'

'You can hardly make an issue of impropriety, ma'am,' Neville interjected drily, 'when you regularly display your abundant charms on a stage in front of hundreds of people and took your daughter across the greater part of France in a vegetable cart, dressed as men.'

'*This is not at all the same...*' Seraphine sat down suddenly and put her head in her hands. '*Je pense que le monde est devenu fou,*' she uttered weakly, the fight suddenly drained out of her. 'I do not know what to think anymore.'

Neville dropped a reassuring hand to her shoulder. 'You are under a great deal of strain, *Madame*. Your fears for your daughter are understandable. But you may think, that this is not the sort of flight you have faced before. Your daughter will be everywhere surrounded by friends.'

'But what will this Lady… Temple, did you say… think when my daughter and Bridie and a large dog suddenly appear at her doorstep? *Mon bon Dieu*, it is a very great irregularity.'

'My aunt is well aware of the work I do,' said Neville. 'She will know precisely how to go on.'

'And if Denham searches the post roads?'

'We shall deal with that if it occurs. For the moment, at need, this is the best plan possible.'

Angel and Bridie reappeared, attired for travel, with cloaks over their arms and only a small portmanteau each. Marianne herded them from behind. Angel was pale but resolute; Bridie pink with excitement.

'In good time,' approved Neville. 'We must away. Sam has the chaise and the horses at the end of the street.'

'Already?' asked Seraphine in shock.

Angel took her mother's hands and pulled her to her feet. 'It is not for long, *Maman, je te promet*. You will Tell Madame Simard, *n'est-ce pas?*'

'Angel, my darling,' implored Seraphine.

'I am no longer a child, *maman*. This is my decision. Be safe. Find that man and bring him to justice. *A bientot, ma chere.*'

Seraphine hugged her daughter tightly and kissed her firmly on both cheeks. 'But Bridie,' she turned admonishingly to the dancer, 'I want no silliness from you, *ma fille, tu m'attend?* If you dawdle, you'll find Doll Bridger in your place onstage.'

'As if she could,' said Bridie scornfully. 'Stephen, tell Chance, will you, where I've gone. Dunno for how long, but he'd better not forget me.'

Tristan and Stephen carefully lifted Brutus on his blankets and led the way outside, with Marianne lighting their way and the two young ladies following.

'Neville,' said Stephen to Nathaniel when he returned, 'I do not know whether to thank you or call you out, sir.'

'Neither is required, Hathaway. I hope that we are reaching the conclusion of this ugly affair.' He took Seraphine's hands in his, turned them, and gently kissed the soft skin of her wrists. '*Au revoir, Madame.* It has been a difficult night. I will call on you betimes, when I hope to have more news.' And he disappeared into the fog of the waning night, leaving her rubbing her wrists lightly, her heart shredded with doubt.

*****

'This is a bit of all right,' grinned Bridie from her shadowed corner, nestled in the comfortable squabs of the seat while an upright postilion and elegant skewbald pair made their way through dirt and cobble side streets. Angel, from the opposite corner, her feet carefully positioned over the sleeping form of Brutus which took up most of the floor, studied the interior of the chaise, closed off from fog and weather, bumping and swaying gently through the night to the steady chink of harness and clop of hooves through fog and flickering light. Dense shadow interspersed with flashes of torch and lamp briefly illuminated predawn walkers and conveyances on unknowable errands before returning to darkness. The shape of the postilion in front of them on the near-side horse, the gleam of harness and parti-colored rumps lit by the carriage lamps, the knowledge of Sam and Hubbard in the footmans' seat behind them in the open air, the cloaked form of Tristan Neville on his horse jogging easily beside them, were dreamlike. In another world, at another time, she would have enjoyed this journey. Here, now, she was exhausted, afraid for her family, for her dog, for her future, afraid for Molly Boggs without her help in the shop, afraid of the deep abiding worry that had stalked her since before they had fled France, a world in chaos, her family scattered, the flight, the water, the new city, the new life. Her life. Just beginning to be settled and known. Until she had met Tristan Neville. Until she had learned of her father's death, her mother's past. Denham.

Her mother, she smiled, would tell her that it was not worth such turmoil. Her mother would have made a good pirate, a thing of challenge, and adventure. Angel... wanted security. Things known. Predictable.

And yet, here she was, having narrowly escaped death or abduction, responsible for the injuries sustained by a faithful dog and a man whose life she felt was now in her hands. Now being rescued herself - was this a rescue? It felt more like an orderly retreat - by the man she... the man she. Loved. Yes. The man she loved, who she had thought never to see again this side of the grave.

What should that mean? That he now jogged by her side. That he had been shadowing her all these days. That he had taken her under his wing so easily, as if... as if.

'T'is is too hard a knot for me t'untie,' she sighed to the air.

'That's Viola,' said Bridie sharply, yanking her gaze from the window and fixing Angel with a bright eye.

'It is.'

'D'you know it off by heart?'

Angel smiled. 'I should be a poor excuse for an actress' daughter an I did not.'

'Can you teach it me?'

'Seriously?'

'Ay. I'm thinking... maybe I could have a line of work, like as your Ma. I've a good memory. The words, they're like music, see. And I could always understand music. I been studying on your mam. I'll work, Angel, an you'll teach me.'

'Alright. I'll teach you how to read, and then you can learn anything you like.'

Bridie shook her head. 'The words is... are... no good, Angel. They just swim on the page and I can't make sense of them.'

Angel studied her with interest. 'Do they? Perhaps it will help if you look at the page while you say the words out loud. We can try it.'

Bridie smiled beatifically and leaned back against the squabs with a deep sigh of contentment. 'Right, then,' she said. 'Imagine me, a real actress.' And she fell promptly to sleep.

But Angel, the anesthetic effects of shock wearing off, began to shake from weariness and terror. She shook until her teeth chattered, and sobs rose. She wrapped herself more tightly in her cloak, stuffing a corner against her mouth, and curled herself as tightly as she could in her corner, shivering with fear, sobbing from loss, reliving landscapes of horror unending, visions that stretched for years. Until, exhausted from emotion and despair, she slept, too.

They reached the Red Lion by by sun-up, but it had started to rain. When Tristan opened the door of the chaise he found both ladies sleeping soundly, the great, groggy form of Brutus arrayed under their feet. He closed the door again and entered the inn, ordered refreshment for Sam, Hubbard, and the postilion, downed a flagon of ale, and dashed off a note to go back to London with the Mail while the ostlers in the courtyard took the tired Skewbalds to the stables, offered the chestnut horse a drink and a nibble of hay, and hooked up a fresh team of sturdy roans.

'My compliments to Sir Robert on the quality of his horses,' Tristan said to the postilion. 'And make sure they arrive home in good fettle.' He handed the man coin enough to go forward, remounted his horse, and set off in the rain with the chaise pulled by a new team and postboy.

By the time they reached the halfway mark of their journey, both ladies and dog had awakened, stiff, cramped, bladders bursting, and extremely hungry. The bladders were taken care of at a secluded lay-by, the ladies stepping behind a handy screen of trees while the gentlemen discreetly turned their backs and unloaded Brutus so he could make use of a chaise wheel. Their hunger had to wait until they arrived at the pleasantly half-timbered King's Head in Newbury. When the ladies appeared at the coffee room door - disheveled, uncertain, and with a staggering brindled lurcher at heel - the landlord frowned and began to tell them he would not have that brute in the house nor serve such as them, and made to shoo them off.

Then Tristan stepped out from behind them, and despite his covering of road dirt, rain, and an impressive bruise blooming dark purple along the left side of his face, and deployed his quizzing glass to deadly effect by gazing with disdain at the landlord, the bar, and a spotless paneled room that in fact looked extremely inviting. 'I had been led to believe that this... establishment... could offer a light repast and a private parlor,' he drawled. 'It seems I have been misinformed.'

This mastery of the situation by an obvious member of the *ton* threw the landlord - quickly followed by his wife - into a frenzy of apology and bustle at the end of which travelers and dog were situated comfortably at a table before a fire in a small parlor and faced with a satisfying variety of food and drink that all parties fell on as if they hadn't eaten in weeks.

Bridie chattered cheerfully throughout the meal, exclaiming on the countryside, the air that was so clear away from London, even in the rain, and went into gales of laughter over Tristan's hauteur 'like as if you was - were - a Duke, or somming', and when he said modestly that he was, after all, the son and brother of hereditary Earls, she added wisely that this would account for his ability to pass himself off as a nobleman.

'But I *am*... oh, never mind,' said her target.

Angel was shy around this new Tristan who, even stripped of the finery of a fashionable young man of the town, had the air of a man accustomed to being in charge while maintaining a politely cheerful demeanor that she knew must have been an effort. The lines on his bruised face showed deep weariness. The way he moved showed how much of him ached from lack of sleep, long riding, and the night's rough business. Indeed, the manhandling she had sustained herself left her bruised and sore in parts of her body that she couldn't even name, but she was spending the day in a carriage whose comfort outshone anything she had ever encountered before. She was not riding a horse through the rain, seeing to the comforts of others. She tried tentatively to thank him, she longed to kiss his bruises and feel his arms around her again, but he merely smiled absently and made some offhand answer to turn her thanks away.

In truth, Tristan wanted nothing more than to put up at this inn, sleep the remainder of the wet day and the entire night through, and rest both himself and his horse before continuing on.

The horse, at least, got its rest, after all. Sam discovered a loose shoe that must needs be tended to lest it be lost and the chestnut lamed on hard roads. So he stayed behind with assurances of an early arrival the following day, Tristan rode a bay hireling whose manners were nonexistent and whose paces were at best bone-jarring, and Hubbard, with a last longing look at the warm, dry taproom Sam was to continue enjoying, climbed onto his solitary perch and hunched himself into his greatcoat against the weather.

Fortunately, the rain let up and streaks of watery sun began to show in the west by the time they passed the final stage of the journey. Here and there along the green-edged road that wound up and down through rolling countryside, vistas offered glimpses of grazing sheep, cattle, and horses, and as the road turned, the ancient white horse etched into the chalk hills by some remote ancestral tribe showed itself in the distance. Twilight offered a first scattering of stars above the last sun-stained westerly clouds, and finally the chaise rolled through small village and up to the front entrance of Templeton.

With the cool efficiency of a field marshall, and showing no surprise at their arrival, Lady Georgina immediately consigned the care of horses and postilion to her own head groom, sent Hubbard and a footman up one set of stairs over Tristan's protestations of his intent to lodge elsewhere, and an upstairs maid and second footman in the other direction with the ladies' luggage. After Tristan made the proper introductions and the ladies had curtseyed and murmured the proper kinds of thanks, there was a minor setback when Lady Georgina realized that there was a large injured dog to contend with as well. While Angel stammered apologies and Tristan attempted explanations, his formidable great-aunt merely ordered the butler to get two of the gardeners out of their beds to help get the dog up the stairs and into Angel's bed chamber. While they awaited the gardeners she ordered Tristan to 'get the hairy brute to its feet and show it to a bush, for I won't have it pissing in the yellow room, which has only just been redecorated at vast expense', which sent Bridie into giggles and Angel into fresh paroxysms of embarrassment.

While Tristan dealt with the needs of the dog, Lady Georgina studied Angel covertly and wondered that her great-nephew should have fallen in love with such a pale and serious girl, whose haunted eyes seemed too large for her face, and were tear-stained and violet-rimmed from weariness. She had supposed the daughter of an actress would be showier, more along the lines of the pert young rogue who accompanied her. But, she would doubtless have time to discover more, since the missive she'd received not so many hours ago from Nathaniel Neville had warned that the young women were to be her guests for an undefined period while a dangerous situation in London was resolved. Since Lady Georgina thoroughly approved of her nephew's work, and was accustomed to receiving human 'packages' for various lengths of time while he sorted out papers and plans for passage to Canada, America, or the Antipodes, she had learned to be patient.

The gardeners appeared, bleary and half-dressed, hoisted Brutus in his blankets, and set off into the house. Lady Charlotte bustled the girls after them with promises of food and drink to be delivered on trays, ordering Tristan to stay behind with her for a few words and a glass of something sustaining. As Bridie and Angel curtseyed their thanks and moved to climb the wide, ancient oaken stairs, Tristan stopped Angel and took her hand.

'I know that there is a deal to say, Miss Hathaway, that must await another day,' he said. 'But know you are safe now. Sleep well, my dearest.' He kissed her palm lightly and turned away too quickly to see her press it to her face.

*****

Marianne had the small window of their bed chamber open to the air, which today was rain-sodden, but at least the rain had knocked some of the city's airborne soot and ash to the ground. Underneath the acrid stench was a greener smell from the small garden, of leaf, grass, and herb mingled with the astringency of the tinctures and salves now being applied to Jacob's injuries by Stephen. 'You're lucky the ruffian could not get a better shot in the fog,' Stephen remarked when the wound had been examined, treated, and re-bandaged. 'And luckier still the ball did not lodge in your arm.'

'I was always hard to kill, sir,' said Jacob. His voice was gravelly and his color greyer than Stephen liked.

'I am glad for it,' he said, 'and in your debt for saving my sister from... *Le bon Dieu le connait seulment.*'

'As your stepfather gave me a life I surely would have lost, it is a debt I gladly repay.'

'Yes,' frowned Stephen. 'But having done so, be not too quick about shuffling off this mortal coil, *non?* You have a deal of life yet to live, *mon ami.*'

The sound of the back gate creaking open and shut, then footsteps on gravel, brought the three friends to attention. Stephen quickly went to investigate. Marianne put a firm hand on Jacob's chest to prevent him rising. 'Do not you dare move, Jacob Freeman,' she warned him.

'But Marianne, I am feeling much better.'

'If you defy me, sir', she warned, finger raised in admonition, 'do not think I will not give you a draft will make you sleep three days. Best you listen.'

'Madam shrew, I will,' acquiesced Jacob gratefully, lying back against the pillows. There was no part of him that did not ache. He could tolerate a spell of wifely bullying.

Stephen reappeared in the doorway. 'I've brought you a visitor, Jacob,' he grinned, and stood aside to allow Nathaniel Neville to pass.

'No, do not rise, Freeman. I came merely to check on you. Your quack here assures me you will live. When you are able, the authorities most interested in last night's action would like to hear your account of the affair.'

Jacob's eyes widened. 'Sir, I dare not... I am a peace-loving man, sir. It was never my intent to kill. The threat to Miss Hathaway... the surprise... I did what I must, sir. But go to the authorities with the story... as an African man who...'

Neville put his hand up. 'Let me speak, Freeman. When first I saw you, I thought you familiar for reasons I could not call to mind. On a recent trip to France, I recognized the face I had seen

before, on a poster. It offered a substantial award for the capture
of a runaway slave guilty of murdering his master.'

'Sir, please. I...'

'Stop, Mr. Freeman.' He studied the enormous man for a
silent moment through his quizzing glass, during which eternity
Jacob wished himself invisible, wished he had died last night,
wished he were anywhere but here. 'Yes,' continued Neville finally,
lowering the glass. 'The resemblance is striking. But,' he said
carefully, pinning Jacob's eyes with his own, '...that fugitive - one
Japhet Wiley - met his end in the Terror. He is undeniably dead.'

Marianne stifled a sob. Jacob sighed as if all the air he had
stored in that spot in the body where fear lives had gone out of
him at once.

Neville played idly with the quizzing glass on its riband. 'I am
as you know no friend of human bondage, Mr. Freeman. When I
think of Japhet Wiley and those like him, I do not think of cold
blooded murder. I think rather of an accrual of unspeakable ills
that may bring a desperate man to kill. Although Japhet Wiley is
dead, I know without question that his death has not been in vain.'

'Then...' hesitated Jacob, 'the authorities who wish to speak
to me...'

'Are quite another matter,' said Neville, brightening. 'The two
men whose lives you put a period to last night were members of a
family whose career has been made through robbery, extortion,
and murder these past ten years and more. There is a handsome
reward for the apprehension of any of them. Those authorities I
am in touch with would like to give this to you personally, along
with their thanks. I will happily be your escort, sir, to collect your
reward. In case...' he stopped.

'...They will not think an African deserving of the full
reward,' finished Marianne flatly.

Neville looked uncomfortable. 'I wish I could say it were not
so.'

'And there are other members of the family, who will be
looking for me,' Jacob added.

'Unfortunately.'

'I can handle myself, sir. But I would not want to bring further
misfortune to this house.'

'Is it your desire to leave these shores? I can arrange it.'

'Nothing so drastic, sir. There is a community in London for us, and much to be done.'

'And employment?'

'A friend is looking for a partner at The Three Cocks on Bankside. With the reward added to what we have saved, we could thrive there, I believe.'

'But not this present, Jacob,' added Marianne. 'Not until current affairs are settled. In *every* way. *If* you understand me, sir.' She fixed Neville with a brown stare filled with meaning.

'I do not follow... Oh!' he reddened. 'Errm... yes. Yes... of course,' he stammered, and took his leave rapidly.

'What was that, Marianne?' asked Jacob, puzzled.

'Never you mind,' said Marianne. 'Would some ale and an egg go down well, my love?'

*****

'I am delighted to hear that', said Seraphine happily when Neville came to her with news of Jacob's reward. 'I cannot conceive of one more worthy. 'Nor,' she added wistfully, 'can I imagine a life that does not have Jacob and Marianne in it. We have been through so much together, you see.'

'Bankside is not so very far away, after all,' said Neville.

'No. No, of course. But...' she shook her head and sighed. '*Eh bien. Plus ça change. Je le connais bien, moi.* What do you hear of Angel?'

'A message came back from Slough that all was well to that point. They could not have arrived at Faringdon much before nightfall. I know you are anxious, but it is yourself I worry about at this juncture. The man Ramage, whom we apprehended, has not recovered consciousness. The doctors fear he may not. If he does, he will no doubt be anxious to lay the information required for the law to take Denham up. If not...' he frowned.

'Can Denham find him?'

'I think not. But there is the ruffian yet unaccounted for. When Denham discovers himself on the ropes, I doubt not he will lash out like any trapped animal.'

'*We have scotch'd the snake, not killed it,*' Seraphine murmured.

'Yes.'

'And I without Jacob.'

'You have Stephen, and Marianne. You have… you have me, Mrs. Hathaway. Are you needed at The Swan today?'

'Not onstage. Mr. Pearce must be told about the attempt against Angel, and that Bridie will be away this little time.'

'Both messages can be conveyed in writing.'

'He will want details.'

'Will you mention Denham?'

'No. My cousin has many qualities, but neither a subtle mind nor discretion are among them. He will be much too occupied with his own affairs to be overly troubled by ours. Tomorrow is to be my cousin's *Hamlet*, you see. Do not smirk, sir,' she admonished him. 'I am well aware that his age and girth must seem at odds with anyone's notion of a Prince of Denmark. But after all, our own Prince Regent…'

Neville put his hand up. 'I will not listen to treason, Mrs. Hathaway, even were I to agree with you. If you are not needed for a few days, it will be better for you to stay in, I think.'

'Like a frightened rabbit? That I will not, sir.'

'In that case, I shall escort you. Please, this once, do not argue, Mrs. Hathaway. It is imperative for your safety. I *will* escort you, if go to The Swan you must, today, tomorrow, and for the immediate future. Come. Can my company really be so repugnant? *A bientot, Madame.*' He bowed himself out with a smile.

He truly did have a warm and charming smile, when he chose to deploy it. Seraphine, momentarily at a loss for words, felt a tremor in her belly that had nothing to do with breakfast.

She gave herself a brisk mental shake and moved from paying some pernicious bills that seemed somehow to be higher than they ought, to inspecting a basket full of sheets and clothing upstairs that required decisions like 'could this much-worn skirt actually be repaired', or 'might that stained pinafore make another round'. Having decided in favor of the rag bag, she was startled by a distraught Marianne, announcing the arrival of Lord Denham.

'I tried to turn him away, Seraphine, but the man will not be put off.'

'Stephen?' asked Seraphine anxiously.

'Gone to see Molly Boggs and Chance River.'

'Jacob?'

'I gave him a draught for his pain only an hour since, and he is sleeping.'

'*D'accord.*' Seraphine thought quickly and took a deep breath. 'There is nothing for it. I must meet him. Please show him to the morning room, Marianne, and offer him refreshment. I shall be down directly. But first... try to get a message to Stephen?'

Marianne left with a nod. Seraphine dawdled as she changed her morning dress for the sober round gown of cinnamon, with a fichu tucked around the shoulders and neck to heighten its modesty. She covered most of her hair in a plain ivory cap, then made her way downstairs, pausing for another steadying breath before entering this new stage on her own terms.

Denham stood by the window, examining the small garden. On the table were set a plate of sweetmeats, a pitcher, and two mugs.

'Have you come to gloat, sir?' she asked acidly as he turned.

'To gloat, *Madame*?' he asked, all innocence. 'What have I to gloat about, pray? I came merely to offer my condolences. One has heard of last night's fracas. What a sorry affair,' he murmured, 'to lose your daughter as your mother lost hers, on a time.' He looked at her with an attempt at limpidity, but Seraphine saw the doubt underneath, and with a brief stab of joy realized that he did not yet know the outcome of the previous evening's adventures.

'One understands that dreadful event... so avoidable, had your father only seen sense and allowed us to marry those heavy years since... killed your poor mother.'

'I am made of sterner stuff, my lord,' she said coldly.

'Have you heard anything? From the... er... presumed kidnappers? A question of... ransom, perhaps?' he asked, casually helping himself to a sweetmeat.

'I assumed *you* were here for that purpose.'

'I?' he looked astonished, wiping his fingers fastidiously with a large handkerchief. 'But why should I, a man of my years, desire to harm the daughter of one who is, after all, only an *actress*?' With a simple inflection he made the word sound like *whore*. 'Really, Mrs... Hathaway... you do yourself a great wrong to be living in this hovel,' he gestured around the room and toward the garden with contempt, 'When you could have been so... much... more.'

'I will not be insulted in my own house, my lord. We are finished here.' She moved suggestively to the door.

'Not. Yet,' he murmured. He poured two tankards of ale and offered her one. 'You first,' he said.

'Afraid I'm going to poison you, sir?'

'One learns, when one has lived as long as I, to have a care about what one ingests.'

Seraphine smiled tightly. 'Oh, do not fear me. I would far rather see you swing.' She sipped.

He laughed, drank deeply, and put the tankard down with satisfaction. 'I fear you will be disappointed, *madame*. I was never born to be hanged.'

'What have you done with my daughter?'

'Nothing. But I can in all likelihood get her back for you.'

'I have no money to offer you.'

'Oh, but there I think you are wrong. You are, after all, a sharer in The Swan, a not inconsiderable little venture. And,' he said, beginning to advance on her, 'there are other means of payment.'

Seraphine deftly put the table between them. '*Je ne vous comprends, M'sieu.*'

'You little doxy. You know - precisely - what I mean.' He moved the table, trapping her behind it, then came toward her again. She dodged to the left and was blocked by the sudden presence of his cane. She feinted to the right and he was on her quickly, his hand surprisingly strong around her neck and squeezing. 'Do. Not. Struggle,' he ordered her, his eyes glittering with hatred. 'I will break your whore's neck.'

She went still.

'Now, Sarah Finister,' Denham continued, tightening his grip on her throat. Her breath came shallow and spots appeared before her eyes.

'Please,' she whispered with an effort and tried with weakening arms to push him off.

He laughed softly, and with his cane lifted her skirt. 'It will be such a pleasure to teach you...'

'*Maman!*' The door crashed open and Stephen charged across the room. Denham loosed his hold on Seraphine, who fell to the floor, retching. With a snarl Denham turned to meet the young man, who grabbed him forcefully with both hands and threw him against the wall. Denham crashed heavily, staggered, then regained his feet and with a swift motion, pulled the top of his cane to reveal the sword within. Stephen stood in front of his mother, grabbed a heavy candlestick from the table, and hissed, 'Sard off. This moment. Or I will kill you with the greatest pleasure, you contemptible cockchafer.'

Denham pulled himself up carefully, the sword pointed at Stephen's heart, and made a great show of dusting himself off with his handkerchief. 'With the greatest of pleasure... *my son,*' he said with a soft laugh. 'But I assure you, an you value your sister's life, we will meet again, and soon.' He took another sweetmeat off the tray, washed it down with the rest of the ale, and departed with insulting dignity. Stephen followed to the foot of the stairs to make sure of his exit. Marianne opened the front door stiffly, eyes cast down, then closed and bolted it as soon as Denham passed through.

'O Stephen,' croaked Seraphine as he and Marianne gently helped her to her feet. 'I was never... so happy to see... anyone! Are you... did he...'

Stephen shushed her gently. 'Do not speak, brave one. He is gone.' He righted a chair that had been turned over in the melee, settled her in it, and gently, carefully, placed long, cool fingers on her bruised neck. She flinched away. He shushed her & his light touch gradually relaxed her. 'See if you can steady your breathing,' he said. She coughed. 'No, not too deep yet. Take only as much as you can. Carefully. Again. Good.'

'Stephen,' she rasped between breaths. 'He does not know that Angel is safe.'

'And he has incriminated himself.'

'Has he hurt you badly, Seraphine?' Marianne asked in concern.

'My throat,' she croaked.

'But I think not permanently injured,' said Stephen in relief as he completed his gentle investigation.

Marianne nodded. 'I will bring you something will ease it.' On her way out she collected the destroyed contents of the table - the jug spilled, one tankard on the floor, sweetmeats scattered - and eventually returned with a soothing beef jelly for Seraphine to swallow, an unguent for her throat, and some sustaining bread, butter, and chicken for Stephen, who finished straightening the room and rolled up the soaked rug to be hung in the airing closet next to the chimney for drying and cleaning.

The unguent on her neck and the smooth, cool *consommé* sliding down her throat made Seraphine feel so much better that she hazarded a glass of madeira while Stephen attacked the chicken and Marianne nibbled bread and butter. She was very shaky, still. The glass wobbled as she raised it to her lips.

A sharp rap of the front door knocker sent Stephen downstairs to answer, poker in hand, but it was Nathaniel Neville at the door, who when briefed by Stephen, took the stairs two at time, sat himself next to Seraphine, took her hand protectively, and listened with troubled eyes and deep attention to the story told haltingly by Seraphine, supported and embroidered by the others.

'And how do you now, ma'am?' he asked Seraphine in concern. 'I would have expected to see you prostrate and in strong hysterics after such a misadventure, yet here you sit, coolly sipping madeira and eating a jelly.'

'I was... terrified when that... *thing*... got his hand about my throat,' she rasped. 'I thought... it was as if...' her eyes turned dark with remembered fear, 'but never mind. Stephen came to my rescue.' She shot her son a look of love and gratitude so shining that Neville was disturbed to find himself stabbed with a jolt of jealousy - 'and made an end of the affair. And now...' she looked warmly at them all, 'I know it seems odd,' she whispered hoarsely, 'but now I feel quite energized. Only... that my throat is so... so very sore.'

Neville's eyes warmed. 'You were born to be an adventurer, *madame*,' he said appreciatively.

'*C'est vrai*,' agreed her son. 'I believe her to be far braver than ever I was in the middle of a sea raid.'

'And so she was on our flight from France,' Marianne added.

'You are being kind,' rasped Seraphine, blushing deeply. 'Yet… there is something remarkably… invigorating… about fright,' she swallowed with difficulty and continued, 'once one has *lived*… through it. But… but… O,' she took another unsteady sip of madeira. 'I was so very frightened. Please,' she implored. 'Tell me of Angel? That must be why you are here. Please say that she is well?'

'I have just received notice of their safe arrival last night, and is being well cared for by my Aunt Georgina. I do wish you will consider staying in tonight.'

She shook her head carefully. 'I promised. Mr. Pearce.'

'Then I shall escort you, as promised.'

Seraphine blushed. 'I do not… need you, sir. Stephen…'

'As it happens, *Maman*,' said Stephen, 'I am engaged this evening, with Mr. McGrath. So if you wouldn't mind, sir,' he looked at Neville meaningfully.

'Come,' Neville grinned maliciously, 'Can the adventuress sail through death-defying escapades with a confirmed murderer, only to stumble at the offer of the companionship of a respectable gentleman for an evening of theatre?'

'I do not consider… you a respectable man,' she croaked, and pulled her hand away. 'Nor do I want…'

'The company of such a notorious boor as myself. I understand. You may consider me nothing more than a wooden soldier, silent at your side.'

Stephen laughed. 'A palpable hit, *Maman*,' he said. 'If to The Swan you must, I beg you will accept Mr. Neville's kind offer. But now you must needs rest. Please to keep your throat warm and well wrapped, *Maman*, for Marianne's salve to do its work. No more talking. We will be downstairs at need.'

Seraphine nodded gratefully, surprised to find herself weepy, and tired to the bone. She allowed her son to move her to the sofa in the withdrawing room, and after the others left her went almost instantly to sleep.

She awakened hours later feeling much restored, but unaccountably shaky from her encounter with Denham. Too like the past, too horrifyingly and bone-liquifyingly familiar…

No. To give in to fear, to shrink away from what might lie ahead, meant that Denham had won.

And Denham would. Not. Win.

Already his grip was looser: Not only was her daughter safe; but her own friends and family - indeed, her very accomplishments — armored herself and gave her strength. Seraphine Hathaway would not allow a bully this power, ever again. No.

She dressed carefully to disguise the lurid bruises now showing around her neck. Neville appeared punctually, and after a brief but bitter - and in her case, halting - altercation, over his desire that she ride in a chair when her preference was to walk, they set off to the theatre with the actress settled sulkily in a chair, while the gentleman strode beside her.

An otherwise uneventful evening was marred only by an imperious summons commanding Seraphine to present herself at Lady Augusta Hensleigh's box at the interval, where that lady looked at her severely and said without preamble, 'You have been very bad to me, you know.'

'But Lady Augusta,' croaked Seraphine in dismay, 'What can I... possibly have done to offend?'

'Can you not guess?' the lady looked at her narrowly. 'Be that as it may. I want three words with you, and they are of the utmost importance. Call upon me the day after tomorrow, not a moment after one o'clock. And by the bye, that cousin of yours has no business taking on the Dane at his age. He will do far more as Claudius. What on earth is wrong with your voice? Never mind. Ah, Lady Jersey,' she turned dismissively from Seraphine. 'Just the person I most desire to see.'

Troubled, Seraphine crept back downstairs and was met by the protective Neville, who fielded envious glances and rebuffed all efforts by several persistent admirers to relieve him of his charge as he escorted her to the back of the theatre. For once, Seraphine was grateful for his attention. She was nearly ill with exhaustion, and every part of her body ached. At the end of the evening, she excused herself from appearing at supper with her cousin, 'For it is your evening to shine, my dear.'

'It did go well, didn't it, Sera!' glowed Charles. 'I think perhaps we should make a run of it!' And then, looking at her pale face suspiciously, added, 'I say, you don't look at all the thing. Your voice...' And then, concern clouding his expression, 'It isn't Angel, is it? Is there anything...'

'No, no,' she assured him, her aching throat and throbbing head longing for silence. 'Angel is well, to my knowledge, and Bridie with her. I am merely... strained... from the alarums, Charles. I desire a good rest.'

'Mind you get it, then. We don't want our Beatrice sounding like an old hag, do we?' He patted her cheek and left her to meet his public.

Neville only smiled benignly when Seraphine mocked him as a watchdog worthy even of Brutus, and capitulated to her desire to walk. They strolled through roiling mist and dense, ash-heavy fog in comfortable silence, which Neville found extremely relaxing.

As for Seraphine, his presence next to her, the shape and make of him, his scent, the heat of his living self, warmed her in ways she found both compelling and confusing; she who had had so much of unwanted male company that she thought never to feel simple desire – or the slow blooming of love - in her life. She might resist it with every fiber of her being. She could not deny it.

When they reached her door, she unlocked it and turned to thank her escort. He bowed over her gloved hand, his breath on her bare wrist sent a jolt of heat through her, her scent made him a little giddy, and they parted in something that closely resembled panic.

*****

The day's events had taxed Denham almost beyond his endurance. Age robbed him of vigor and stamina, a state of being that enraged him. It limited his ability to turn fortune to his side as easily as had been his wont. It forced reliance on the abilities of expensive hirelings to bring about the completion of his plans. Those hirelings were coarse. They bungled. They overreacted. They lacked elegance. And they failed. Ramage had clearly managed to make off with the black-haired chit himself, and sequestered her in order to squeeze certain documents from his employer's grasp - what else could it have been? He had underestimated Ramage. But Ramage had grossly underestimated his master. His family would pay the price.

Rested and returned by Tibbs to proper order, he sallied forth to White's, glad his rooms were not far distant, for truth be known a chair represented an expense beyond his current means. He cursed the people who had brought him to this pass. He should have been living comfortably on the Finister fortunes. He might be - should be! - enjoying the full comfort of old age in a tidy villa in Italy. But Italy was now closed to him; his wrenched daughter-in-law had seen to that. And that damned property in the Cotswolds… Thwarted. He was everywhere thwarted of his rights. His needs. Someone must pay.

A pleasant hour in a comfortable chair with a decanter by his side brought him no closer to solving his current troubles. Still angry, he followed a liveried servant to the dining room and had just been seated in front of a fragrant roast, an attendant boat of gravy, dish of potatoes, and bottle of claret, when a waiter came to him bearing a small tray with a card on it.

'I am sorry to disturb my lord, but my lord's son reminds you of your kind invitation to dine, and waits upon your pleasure.'

Denham's brows snapped together. 'My son! I have n…' he took the card, read it, and covered smoothly, '…no notion that it was today. Send him up, and set another place.'

'*Father*,' Stephen Hathaway bowed punctiliously moments later with a mouth that smiled and eyes that were cold. 'So good of you to see me. May I?' Without waiting for a response, he sat opposite Denham in the place hastily laid for him, observed the food, and began helping himself generously. He quickly dispatched a full plate, chatting smoothly about this, that, and nothing at all, while Denham stared at him from hooded eyes that held extreme dislike. 'If you are looking for your sister, I cannot help you,' he interrupted.

Stephen hesitated in the process of smothering a second helping of beef and potatoes with more gravy. 'Cannot, or will not? Gravy?' he handed the boat across the table. Denham took it automatically and poured, eyes fixed on the man so like his brother - himself - that there could be no question of his getting.

Denham's guts twisted. He jerkily ate a few bites of his dinner and washed it down with claret, to settle his roiling system and create space for rapid thought.

'If the answer is that you *will* not,' continued Hathaway as he blotted his mouth on a snowy napkin, 'then I have a proposition for you.'

Denham took several more forkfuls of gravy-covered beef. Chewed slowly. Insolently. Took another pull of claret while looking at Hathaway with a hatred that discomfited the younger man not at all. Stephen sat in stillness, eyes steady, expression neutral, endlessly patient.

'And what sort of *proposition* could a person of your... background... possibly offer that would interest me?'

'A golden one, of course... *mon pere.*' Hathaway took a small purse from his pocket and set it beside Denham's plate with a heavy *chunk*.

Denham glanced at it and sneered. 'A purse of that size is your proposition? You must take me for a fool... *boy.*'

'You haven't looked at it yet.' Stephen drank off a glass of claret, eyes never leaving Denham's face.

Denham twitched the purse open with two fingers, then glanced suspiciously at Hathaway. 'Where did you get these?'

'When one is at sea, one may still find a great deal of old Spanish gold, if one knows where to look. A. Great. Deal.' Stephen leaned forward, elbows propped comfortably on the table, grinning like a shark.

'And for this... *great deal...* of gold...'

'You will return my sister. And then you will disappear. And never trouble my family again.'

'This amount...'

'Is a downpayment, pending the safe return of my sister.'

'That bitch you call...'

Hathaway leaned forward and clamped his hand over the hand that rested on the purse, eyes blazing. 'Think twice before completing that thought', he hissed quietly.

'Or what?' Denham taunted, though he had started back involuntarily and discovered the bones in his wrist perilously close to being painfully crushed.

'Or you will be dead before you have time to shout. Do not doubt me. Make. No. Sound.'

There was a metallic 'snick' under the table and Denham felt the sharp point of a knife pressing into the artery of his inner thigh. He looked wildly around him, but his desire to dine well away from others now worked against him and there was no one near enough to help. He looked back at Hathaway, his gaze irresistibly drawn into the hazel eyes that haunted his dreams, as if his brother had somehow inhabited the form of this horrifying young man and come back to enact his revenge. He nodded imperceptibly.

The sharp point of the knife retracted. The vise-like grip on his wrist drew back. Hathaway sat quietly again across from him, as if nothing out of the ordinary had occurred.

'I will await your message,' he said, and rose. 'Keep the purse.'

'And if I simply disappear, and leave your sister to her fate?' Denham spat.

'*Je n'ai pas peur de ca, m'sieu.* Revenge is not your dish to serve.' And with that cryptic statement, he turned on his heel and departed.

Denham sat for a few minutes, drinking claret to steady his nerves, his injured hand tucked protectively in the pocket of his coat. As he drank, he considered. He had suffered a shattering setback, yes. But he was still Somebody, unlike the ill-bred brat who had naively given his sire a gift of gold. The purse offered flexibility; badly needed currency to use against those who had done him harm, and still enough left to disappear from London. He would start with Ramage, and the girl.

Feeling far more cheerful, he finished the remains of his dinner - which was, after all, very good - and made his way rather unsteadily homeward.

Late in the night he awakened shivering, his bowels in an uproar. Too much wine, Tibbs reproved him. Too much rich food, 'and you know what the doctor said'. Denham roared and threw a paperweight at his man's head.

Toward morning, emptied of all that he had consumed, he finally slept peacefully again.

*****

Seraphine presented herself at Hensleigh House on the stroke
of one, dressed meticulously in her favorite bottle-green-and-
cream striped dress. A darker green spencer jacket over the top
covered the purpling bruises on her neck and a bonnet newly
freshened with silk flowers and ribbons befitted the season. Left
by Milady's very stuffy butler to kick her heels in a drawing room,
she sifted through her conscience and failed to find herself guilty
of any betrayal of a powerful friend's trust. At last the lady
entered, and Seraphine curtseyed deeply.

'Oh do stop, Seraphine,' Lady Augusta snapped. 'Are we not
accounted friends?'

'I thought so, ma'am,' admitted Seraphine. 'But it seems I
have offended you in some way, and I cannot think how.'

'Can you not?' asked the aggrieved lady. 'Was our friendship
worth so little that you could not confide to me - *I*, who could
help you - that you are, in fact the same Sarah Finister that
disappeared twenty-five years since?'

'How... *Madame*, it was not a secret I could safely divulge.
Nor do I know how you can have discovered it!'

'In London? How could I not! A whisper starts and grows to
a rumor. And where there is as rumor there are those who make it
their business to uncover the truth.'

'I have never added so much as a breath to any such
nonsense.'

'No. And had you lived quietly, as many of our better known
emigrés do, you might have remained anonymous. But the
mysterious Madame Seraphine of The Swan must be a source of
speculation, and eventually the truth. Do you deny it?'

'No, Lady Augusta. I do not.'

'Then why, Seraphine? Why not make the smallest push to
reach your family?'

'You know perfectly well, *Madame*', Seraphine said stiffly. 'I
need hardly describe to you, of all people, the reaction such an
action would elicit in the Polite World. I will not put myself or my
children through the humiliation that must needs follow.'

Lady Augusta had the grace to look away. 'I am sorry you think so ill of us, my dear. But,' she sighed, 'it is not without cause.' She indicated two richly embroidered chairs across from one another, and the ladies sat. 'Your family has suffered greatly, you know.'

'Not nearly as much as I, *Madame*.'

'Yet… given the opportunity… would you not regain your place in Society?'

'Lady Augusta, to my knowledge, my family made not the slightest attempt to find me. I have undergone much these twenty-five years, first merely to survive, then to make a life to sustain and content me and mine. And I have succeeded. I have a freedom undreamt of by most of our sex, I have a position in life that suits me, and children who give me pride. What more should I desire? If I have one regret,' she stopped suddenly, eyebrows drawn together in concern, 'it would be for my younger brother, Julian. He tried to save me, you know, but at the time of the… at the time, he was only twelve years of age or so. And Denham was….' she unconsciously put her fingers to her neck protectively… 'terrifying,' she finished.

Lady Augusta smiled as if the clouds had parted and showed her a heavenly choir. 'That, I believe, is where I can help,' she said, and rang a bell. 'Jenks,' she ordered the butler, 'have the tray brought in. And our guest.'

A moment later a portly figure punctiliously dressed in the sober garb of a wealthy country gentleman entered the room and made his bow with a slight creaking of the stays that supported his form. He then stood uncertainly, gaze flicking to Lady Augusta before settling hungrily on Seraphine.

'I am sorry,' Seraphine said hesitantly, with an uncommon clenching of her stomach. 'But…'

'Seraphine Hathaway,' said Lady Augusta, 'it gives me great pleasure to introduce you to Mr. Julian Finister.'

Seraphine gasped. '*Julian!*' she squeaked, and pressed her hands to her mouth.

'Good morning, Mrs…. Oh, confound it all,' he said, coloring. May I call you… *sister*… Sarah?' he approached her, hands out, and she rose and clasped them tightly, heart beating wildly. They said nothing more while the tray arrived with its abundance of refreshments, but stared and stared, speechless. Lady Augusta quietly followed the maid through the door and closed it behind her.

There was a great deal of awkwardness, and much that needed to be talked about, but refreshments and a decanter of claret - of which Seraphine partook sparingly and her brother heavily - eased some of the difficulties. They carefully navigated the gap in years and experiences. Tears were shed, guilt assuaged, forgiveness given, and questions laid to rest. And then there was nothing left to say. The high-spirited sister Julian remembered had become a woman of poise, beauty, but... he admitted... a certain *reputation*. The earnest and robust boy Seraphine remembered had become a pompous landowner of narrow views. In silence, each struggled to marry conflicting images of past, present, what was, and what could never be. At length, Seraphine broke a troubled silence.

'I am very glad we have met again, Julian, and to know that all is now well,' she said gently.

'Oh, yes!' he agreed. 'It has been... a pleasure... and a relief... and I must thank Neville for his good offices, for I would not have...'

'*Neville!*' said Seraphine, brows snapped together.

'Yes, of course Neville,' said her brother, perplexed. 'It was he arranged this meeting.'

'*Did* he!'

'Naturally. He is a family friend, and was an immense help after the... the sad event...'

'*Was* he!'

'Did you not know? But... without him there would be...' he took a breath. 'We owe him a great deal. But in the end, it didn't... we couldn't.... Well. It all came right, didn't it?' he smiled at her imploringly.

'Yes, Julian,' she said kindly. 'It has all come right. But I think you will agree... that it cannot go further, my dear.'

Her brother blinked.

'I am glad of this meeting, Julian, so very glad. But we have no claim on one another, you and I, and very different lives to live.'

'Yes... of course... that is...' he took a breath of palpable relief. 'It *would* be most awkward... But sister... I do want to help you. I thought, perhaps... to step away from what you have become. To live somewhat more quietly, away from Town...'

'And out of the way of awkward rumor and gossip?' finished Seraphine, with an ironic twist to her mouth.

'I see we understand one another. Will it serve, do you think? Of course I... the family, that is... would cover any expenses that a suitable lodging and your living might incur.'

'Such an arrangement would naturally make *your* life a deal more comfortable,' his sister agreed. 'But *mon frère*, no. My life contents me well.'

'Ah,' said Finister, crestfallen. 'Neville warned me you would say so. But my lady wife... thought...'

'Of course she did', soothed Seraphine. 'But this I promise your lady wife - and you: I will at no time lay a claim on you. And in return', she raised a finger warningly, 'I expect that you will not meddle with me or mine. I am firm on this, Julian, and will sign an affidavit to that effect, if it will make you more comfortable.'

Finister blinked rapidly, opened and shut his mouth several times, then expostulated, 'No, no. Of course that will not be necessary,' as though such a document had not been precisely what his wife had ordered him to prepare. Nervously, he took another long swallow of claret, and ate a comfit. 'Jolly good, these,' he said inconsequentially. 'Will you have another? Hensleigh keeps a good table, and an excellent cellar, I don't mind saying.' Then, with a sigh, added wistfully, 'It is so very good to see you, Sarah. I cannot begin to say.' They rose, and he took her hands affectionately. 'I suppose this must be goodbye, mustn't it?'

'Indeed, my dear,' she said gently.

'I shall look for news of you in the papers,' he smiled.

'And I of you.'

He laughed. 'Oh, I hope not! Unless it be news of my childrens' marriages, or God forbid, my death.' He patted her cheek lovingly, and departed.

'*Neville* suggested this meeting, ma'am?' demanded Seraphine incredulously as Lady Augusta when she re-entered the room. '*Why?*'

'I believe he thought it an obligation, as a family friend.'

'No friend of *mine*, however! I shall have a word or three to say to *him*! The audacity…'

' *Mrs.* Hathaway,' said Lady Augusta, eyes flashing. 'I wish you will disavow yourself of the notion that you are the sole aggrieved party in this *affaire*. You are most certainly *not*. Neville acted with the purest of motives, to allay the years of guilt and grief suffered by your family.'

'Without so much as consulting the object of that suffering, however! Only wait until…'

'Fortunately for the *gentleman*, a taste of your lamentable temper will have to wait. He is called quite suddenly to the continent for an undetermined period of time.'

In spite of herself, Seraphine paled. 'Gone…'

'Trade agreements, he said.' Lady Augusta gently rubbed her temple. 'It seemed such a good idea, when he suggested it. But when I saw your brother, how very *different*…'

'No, *Madame*, you were not wrong,' admitted Seraphine with a steadying breath. 'And you are very generous to have made such an awkward situation *convenable*.'

But she left her patroness with her thoughts in uncharacteristic turmoil. She knew what 'trade' meant to Neville. What danger his journeys put him in. And her last words to him, her last thoughts of him, had been argumentative.

Every step she took sounded suddenly hollow.

Had she but known it, her path took her past Denham's lodging, where that gentleman had awakened quite marvelously refreshed, rather as if the night's purge had cleansed his system. He lingered over his dressing while his mind went to work on the mystery of Ramage and the girl. He set several lackeys on several errands of discovery. And finally he sallied forth to White's to play a hand of piquet and pick up whatever gossip might be bruited about. Though his appetite hadn't fully recovered, he found a light repast acceptable, the madeira to his liking, and the cards favorable. He stayed through the evening, but heard no whisper that was of use to him.

Better news awaited at home, where Tibbs brought information from a certain tavern near the docks: that two bravos from a powerful family of professional criminals had been found dead in an alley, one from a heavy blow to the head, another with his neck plain broken; that rumor suggested a flash cove had hired them to do a rum scrap and the bravos, never before bested and promised an easy mark, were confronted with a black giant and a guard dog.

Denham's eyebrows snapped together. 'From whom had you this?'

'He wouldn't give me a name, my lord, but said his cousin came back from a rum job beaten all to pieces and bit all over by a big brindle cur. Just barely got away, he swore.'

'But what of Ramage? And where the devil is the girl?'

'He didn't say, my lord. Only but what the flash cove - that would be Ramage, sir, to my thinking - and the tib has disappeared, like. He also said as how another cove came upon the mill with what must have been a Runner. So he thought it likely the flash cove had sold them out. And the family of the dustmen, why they're on the lookout for any as know his whereabouts too, so's they can get their own back.'

Denham smiled. He resolved to add grease to the wheels of revenge, and let the ruffians do the work of discovery for him. He yawned, allowed Tibbs to prepare him for bed, eased himself into the sheets, and snuffed the candle. It was good to be holding strong cards at last.

It was a week later that the seizures began.

*****

Tristan stayed only one more night in the country before returning to London with Sir Robert's chaise, this time drawn by two of his great-aunt's lively Welsh-bred roadsters and her personal postilion for the first stage. Angel watched the equipage disappear around the bend of a tree-lined avenue with mingled panic and relief, her thoughts jumbled, her heart aching. She wanted Tristan Neville with a desperation that made her blood sing. She felt she was losing her dearest friend in the world. Yet when he was near, she became confused, unaccountably shy, and could not meet his eyes.

And Neville left downcast, believing that somehow he had missed his last best chance to earn Angel Hathaway's love.

But it was summer, roses bloomed in Lady Georgina's garden, and brambles full of fragrant early blackberries begged to be picked along lanes that led to pasture and village. Angel and Bridie spent several mornings strolling aimlessly through a green haze with Brutus haltingly at their sides, surrounded by the sounds of birds warbling, cattle lowing, sheep bleating, the clinking of harness and machinery in the fields while human voices called, laughed, shouted, as the first cut of sweet-smelling hay was stacked in the fields to dry. 'Like being in Paradise, so it is,' breathed Bridie. 'Only… there an't much to do-like, is there?'

Angel taught Bridie the words of *As You Like It* out of a collection of Shakespeare's plays borrowed from Lady Georgina's library. Bridie, as good as her vow, set about memorizing not only the character of Rosalind, but those of Celia and Phebe as well, 'for it can't hurt to know 'em all off, just in case.' Learning to read the same words was harder, but Angel was patient, and Bridie cheered to realize that she had learned more reading than she had thought as a child. She plodded along, a finger marking each word of each speech she had memorized so easily, making the print fit the sounds.

When their work was interrupted one day by their imperious hostess, Angel noticed a rip in the seam of the old fashioned but well-made gown the mistress wore. '*Oh mon Dieu, Madame,*' she cried out in consternation, *Je vous en pris,* allow me to mend that for you before it becomes far worse and ruins your pretty dress.'

Lady Georgina looked at her quizzically. 'Do you actually wish to do so?'

'But yes, of course,' said Angel, puzzled. 'I cannot be idle. Allow me to repay your kind hospitality, *s'il vous plait*. And while I repair the tear, *Madame*,' she suggested, eyeing the dress critically, 'perhaps you will permit - oh, just a very few changes. To bring the whole up to date.'

'No, you may *not*,' said *Madame* crossly. 'I don't care a fig for modern fashions, and am perfectly happy to go on as I have.'

'Of course', Angel smiled winningly. 'But only think how pleasant to have a dress that is not new, no, but *refreshed* a little and so very becoming to a lady of your stature. With not a *sous* spent.'

'Do you *dare* to call me a dowdy pinch-penny, miss?' Lady Georgina demanded, a dangerous edge to her voice.

At the library table, Bridie barely stifled a snort.

'*Jamais*,' swore Angel with a limpidity that made her hostess more rather than less suspicious. 'Only that perhaps the panniers on the dress as it exists now must be very clumsy for a lady as active as yourself, *n'est-ce pas?*'

Lady Georgina stared at her through narrowed eyes. Angel looked back earnestly.

'Oh damn you, girl!' she finally exploded. 'You should be a confounded politician! You may do what you like with the dratted gown.'

'It will be my pleasure. And yours, too, *je vous promet*.'

Once in Angel's hands, it was only a matter of days before the tear had been mended invisibly and the neck, sleeves, and skirt of the dress tweaked so that not only did it fit Lady Charlotte's majestic frame far better than the original, but made her look nearly elegant, as her lover the head gardner commented later with a broad, suggestive smile.

By watching Angel work, watching her sing as she did so, seeing her kindness to all creatures, Lady Georgina came to understand her nephew's emotions. Her mind made up, she set about taking matters in hand. When Angel and Bridie came in from their morning walk - Bridie twirling and dancing while she sang a silly song, Angel laughing and clapping time, the great brindled Brutus panting happily beside them - Lady Georgina demanded Angel's presence in the morning room. Bridie danced on to the library, leaving at least one footman dazzled by her voice and beauty. His employer sharply brought his attention back to his job and ordered refreshments to be brought up, leaving the poor besotted servant stammering his apologies to a closed door.

'The sooner that girl leaves, the better,' the dowager grumbled. 'She is nothing but trouble among the young men on the staff.'

'She has a sweetheart, ma'am,' said Angel doubtfully. 'I believe they are quite certain to be married.'

'Well, he'd better hurry,' Lady Georgina retorted. 'Sit. And you too, you hairy hound. No, do not drool on me sir. Sit,' she pointed imperiously to a chair and Angel and the dog sat, one in it, the other by its arm.

'What are your intentions regarding my great-nephew?' Lady Georgina asked bluntly.

Angel gasped, blushed, and blinked wildly. 'I have no... that is we never... What I mean is, I am very aware...'

'Good God, girl, don't be a fool. It's a simple question.'

Angel paled. '*Madame, je vous assure*, I have no intention of marrying him,' she said unsteadily.

'He means to have you, you know. It is the most dreadful *mesalliance*, and my nephew is well aware that the family will disown him...'

'I could not bear to be the cause of ...'

'Yes, yes, very noble,' remarked her hostess brusquely. Do you love him?'

'I... hold him in the greatest...'

'Stupid girl, do. You. Love. Him. And let me be clear. I mean the man. Not his position.'

'I... it... Yes. With all my heart,' she managed to gasp, hand clutched to her chest.

'I have it from his mother that Arabella Montjoy is expecting an offer from him at any moment. It would be a very good match, and he stands to inherit a great deal of money. If he marries you, he will no longer be a wealthy man.'

Angel brushed away the tears that threatened to overtake her. 'I understand that, *Madame*. I could not wish for him to suffer such a...'

'Oh, don't be a fool, girl. Look at me. This minute, miss. And dry your tears. I am prepared to support this marriage, Lord knows why. Tristan has been used to having every comfort his position affords, but he has shown himself willing to embrace quite another sort of life for you. You say you love him. Very well: do not keep him waiting longer, or you *will* lose him. Ah,' she added as the door opened to a maid with a tray of sweetmeats and a pitcher. 'May I offer you a glass of orgeat, Miss Hathaway?'

That evening, as if on cue, Tristan Neville rode up to the house tired and dusty from the road, on an equally tired brown mare, with Sam beside him on the ubiquitous chestnut. Bridie shrieked and danced out to meet them, demanding instantly to hear all the gossip from London. Tristan dismounted, answering her distractedly as he loosened the girths and patted the mare, then his heart gave a jolt when he saw Angel - healthy, vibrant, more beautiful than ever - approaching at a more sedate pace.

'Hello, Sam,' she said, then shyly turned to Tristan. 'I am very glad to see you, Mr. Neville.' She smiled up at him and cupped the mare's soft muzzle in her hands as if for security.

'And I you, Miss Hathaway. Oh, Bridie,' he brought a small packet out of his pocket. 'River bade me give this you. He says he will follow soon, and bids you behave yourself in the meanwhile.'

Bridie squeaked with delight, grabbed the packet, and danced away, leaving Tristan and Angel face to face and tongue-tied.

'I... er...' Tristan stammered and cleared his throat. 'Miss Hathaway... I... that is, it would be my... Angel...' he stared fixedly for a moment at the horizon, then, with a sudden change of tactic, asked, 'Do I recall you saying you saying you had a... erm... demon pony when you were young?'

'How odd you should remember that, sir,' said Angel, startled into a laugh.

'Did you?'

'I did. But why...'

'I just thought that since you are here... and I am here... with no particular business to attend at present... and knowing how fond you are of animals... I thought perhaps... I could teach you to... ride. Properly. If you like. And if... you might just accept the gift of this saintly mare.' He nervously straightened his cravat.

'I should be delighted to learn to ride properly,' Angel smiled warmly to put him out of his misery, 'And she is beautiful. Though perhaps this present she could use a feed and a rest, sir. She looks very tired.'

'Oh she will recover overnight,' Tristan grinned happily. He patted the mare affectionately and handed the reins to Sam, who had been standing woodenly looking at nothing in particular and was relieved to escape with the horses. Tentatively, Tristan reached out to Angel with both hands. Shyly, she clasped them warmly and with a jolt that shook her to the core, felt the warmth, the strength in those hands. Her eyes widened and her throat tightened as Tristan kissed one hand, then the other, then drew her toward him and put his arms around her. With a little gasp she returned his embrace as if clutching a dream, and mumbled something incomprehensible into his coat. 'What was that?' he asked, lifting her face. 'What's this? Tears? No, no. That won't do.' He gently kissed them away from her eyelids, tasted their saltiness, found her mouth and kissed her, drank in her scent, her warmth, felt her soft curves melting into him, the responding shudder of desire as she breathed in the heady scent of horses, sweat, and radiant sun that made up Tristan Neville. Their kisses, first tentative, grew to yearning, then yielded to a long, deep, wave of passion.

'Will you, Angel?' he breathed huskily into her neck. 'Will you be my wife?'

'Yes,' she murmured, choking back more tears. 'O yes. But O Tristan, let it be soon.' And they found their halting way back to the house still entwined like two vines, stopping every few steps to kiss, to touch, to breathe each other in.

'*Well*,' uttered Lady Temple with grim satisfaction from her vantage point by the parlour window. 'We'd best see *this* knot tied right smartly. Do you get a message to Parson, Chilham. I'll not risk having the next Neville born a bastard!'

Two days later Bridie wafted through the garden, speaking the words of Rosalind and adding the gestures and mannerisms that she had seen Madame Seraphine add to give the character life, when she spied a dusty figure trudging with a sailor's gait up the long drive in shirtsleeves and waistcoat, coat flung over his arm and carry bag on his shoulder. She shaded her eyes and squinted, her heart suddenly beating faster as she realized that however improbable it might be, it was Chance River, her very own Chance, come to find her. With an excited squeal she gathered up her skirts, sprinted out the garden gate, around the house, and stood to await him, trying to look like a fine lady, but dancing from foot to foot in anticipation. Chance looked up then, and saw her. With a broad grin he walked more quickly until they stood facing one another, delight reflected in his bronze face, in her rosy one. With a shout he dropped his bag and picked her up in a great bear hug and swung her around while she shrieked with pleasure, then set her down again.

'Well, Bridie,' he grinned at her when they were once more face to face.

'Well, Chance,' she grinned back. 'I'm right glad to see you.'

'Landed yourself in a sweet spot, lass,' he said with a rueful look at the gracious estate that was Templeton. 'Likely you won't never want to come back home again.'

Bridie laughed. ''Tis beautiful and green, and smells good, and I like it very well, I won't lie.' she conceded. 'But Chance, it's been right lonely here with just Angel to talk to, for the people as work in the house are that hoity-toity, and them as work in the garden are that thick, and now Tristan's here to distract Angel, well, I been left on me own quite a bit more than I like, I got to say, them being all lovey-dovey and like that.'

'Oho. So it's all sorted between them.'

'It is that, and now you're here, you can come to the wedding, which *if* you ask me is happening not a minute too soon,' she took him by the arm and made a dance step.

But he looked uncertain. 'Is your head all full of fancies then, lass? Might you be thinking I'm not good enough to be your man anymore?'

'What do you mean by that, you great ejit?' she demanded, hands on hips. 'Of course you're still me own man, Chance River, and I'm your own woman.' She held up her left hand to display the tiny ring that now glinted on it. 'An't that what this means?'

'It is,' he grinned and pulled her to him, breathing in the rich mass of her hair.

'But that don't mean I don't want to be married in our own little church in Covent Garden, wearin' a beautiful primrose dress made by your mam,' Bridie said, her voice muffled against his broad chest. 'Can we do that, Chance?'

He laughed. 'Happen we can, lass. You don't mind sharing space with me ma?'

'I don't. You don't mind me keeping to my line of work?'

'I don't. We can use it. But if I ever catch you with another man, Bridie Murphy, I'll break your pretty neck, so I will.'

'And if I ever catch you with another woman, Chance River, I'll have your balls for breakfast, so I will.' She kissed her lover long and deep, her hands mirroring his in provocative stroking and touching, and after awhile, said thickly, 'So do we have a deal struck, Chance River?'

'Aye, we do, Bridie Murphy,' said her lover, hot with passion. 'And I saw a sweet little nook tucked away right round the back of this here garden, enough to give a mort a green gown. So's we can celebrate proper.'

*****

Denham's corpse was discovered by the daily cleaning woman. After her initial shock on seeing the gentleman 'a layin' there so still and pale-like, with such a look of evil on his face, I screamed, yes so I did', as she testified later with a wide eyed shudder -- and before raising hue and cry - she did a quick reconnoiter of the room and found that the gentleman's great ruby ring, pocket watch, and other pieces of jewelry were missing, along with several very fine embroidered handkerchiefs, two good shirts, a handful of neckcloths, and a small strongbox where she knew he must have kept his money. This so incensed her that when the coroner, the surgeon Mr. McGrath, his handsome young assistant Stephen Hathaway, and the jurors arrived, she gave it as her opinion that 'that man, calls himself Tibbs and very niffy-naffy too', must have done for his ailing master and made off with what goods he could carry. There was no reason to doubt this, as it was not an uncommon event, and there was no sign of Tibbs himself; nor would there ever be. He had, after all, learned from a master.

The remains themselves bore such clear marks of decades of ruinous living that it was an easy task for the coroner to reach a verdict of Death By Natural Causes of one Richard Whately, fifth Earl Denham. Next of kin would be sought, remaining belongings sold to cover outstanding debts, and miscellaneous papers discovered in a locked drawer that did not directly pertain to legal matters burned.

As assistant to Mr. McGrath, it was not incumbent upon Hathaway to offer any sort of opinion. But as McGrath and the coroner studied the deceased's condition and discussed probable causes of death with the jurors, the younger man, feigning dispassionate study, stooped by the dead man's ear. '*Au revoir, mon pere,*' he murmured, in case the earl's hovering soul could still hear him. '*Ma vengeance est complet,*' The eyes of the son, which might have been expected to show some triumph, displayed only deep pity.

With McGrath's job done, Stephen made his thoughtful way to The Swan. Awaiting a break in rehearsal, he enjoyed watching his mother work through the actions of a role considered to be one of her best. When she-as-Rosalind cried out her heart's anguish, 'O coz coz coz, that thou didst know how many fathom deep I am in love! But it cannot be sounded; my affection hath an unknown bottom, like the Bay of Portugal,' he laughed immoderately.

'It is a great deal of nonsense, is it not?' she laughed back at him as they made their way to the office downstairs.

'Almost as if it was your own heart, *Maman*', he teased.

'I don't know what you mean,' she said with asperity.

'Do you not?'

'No,' she insisted, but colored to the roots of her hair, and he crooked a smile and raised a suggestive eyebrow.

When he broke his news to her, all laughter died. She turned white and sat abruptly on the cluttered sofa. 'But... how?' she asked, blankly.

'Does it matter? Be satisfied that you are free, *Maman*. And so are we all.'

'Yes, but Stephen... there must have been... he was so...'

'It was judged by Mr. McGrath to be natural causes, *ma chére*,' he said firmly, sitting beside her. 'Brought on by a long life of dissipation.'

'But... Stephen... was it not...'

He put a finger to her lips. 'Justice has been served, my dear. And there's an end. Come. Will you not dance in the street?'

She took his hand in both of hers and laid her face against it. 'No doubt dancing will come later,' she said shakily. 'At present...'

'Seraphine!' called Pearce from the stage. 'It is your entrance!'

'Anon!' she called back, and rose as if in a dream. '*Merci, mon fils,*' she said softly, and kissed him tenderly on both cheeks. *Je sais tout. Je connais tout. Tu est toujours mon ange.*'

Stephen looked after her, waiting until he heard her voice ring with Shakespeare's words again before he sought out Marianne. Together, they destroyed all traces of the powder, and kept no recipe for temptation.

Seraphine's distraction - the death of the monster whose shadow had haunted her life, her unaccountable distress over Neville's absence, her continued worry about Angel - worked in her favor for that night's performance as the hopelessly besotted Rosalind. She received not only a standing ovation, but no less than three proposals of marriage and one extremely improper suggestion that detailed what pleasures her legs might offer when wrapped around the naked body of a certain gentleman of wealth and breeding. To laugh about these with Marianne in the dressing room was an immense relief.

The next morning, she posted a letter to Angel, telling her that all was safe, and bidding her home.

In another part of Town, a weary Nathaniel Neville divested himself of the news and 'goods' eagerly expected by certain interested parties at the back door of a tavern tucked well away from Whitehall and its open ears. He looked forward gratefully to nothing more than a bath, clean small clothes, and the healing oblivion of sleep. He had been awake for days, his exhaustion compounded by all the marks of having had the worst of a brawl.

Any thought of a well-earned rest fled when his man - busy with making Neville look human again and tutting over the sad state of his ruined clothing - let drop an *on dit* regarding the death of that old *roué* the fifth Earl Denham. Neville, galvanized and instantly awake, changed course entirely and within an hour was seen outside on a mission a discovery. He ran Stephen Hathaway to earth in a favored coffee house, greeted the younger man as if by chance, and sat without invitation at the younger man's corner table.

'You look like hell, Neville,' observed Stephen critically. 'Difficult journey?'

'I made it out.'

'You should allow me to look to those bruises.'

'They will heal.'

'And how many more times do you think you will be so fortunate?'

'How did you do it, Hathaway?' Neville changed the subject harshly.

'*Comment?*' asked Stephen, after a pause.

'You know perfectly well what I mean. Denham.'

Stephen sipped his coffee and looked at Neville speculatively. 'What I know depends on what you speak of and your purpose in asking,' he said.

'I ask as a friend.'

'A friend… with legal connections?' He sipped again. Put the cup down.

'A friend… with an interest in seeing justice done.'

'I would have thought them to be congruent.'

'In this instance, no.'

'This instance being…'

'A debt settled. And a particular interest in your mother's continued wellbeing.'

'*En verité?* I have been led to believe you no friend to one such as my mother.'

'It is no secret that I have not regarded her trade as one seemly to an honest woman.'

Stephen regarded him coolly. 'Then how can her wellbeing possibly concern you, *m'sieu?*'

Neville colored. 'Damn you, Hathaway,' he said irritably. 'Your wretched mother has turned everything I ever thought I knew of women on its head. And that, I can tell you, has caused me no end of distress.'

'But your intentions…'

'Are nothing but honorable.'

'You relieve me. She was very angry at your brazen unmasking of our family's existence to her extremely proper brother, *tu connais*. He had the gall to suggest she give up her… unsuitable… occupation… and settle into dowdy obscurity. Paid for by his largesse, *bien sur*.'

'Did he! Perhaps I was not as forthright as I might have been,' Neville admitted with a grimace. 'She probably thought his idea mine. It was not. But for the rest, her family deserves the comfort of knowing her to be alive, after all this time. And, as it seems likely to have come to light at some point, I thought it best to act positively, and avoid unpleasant surprises later. I never thought her brother…' He grinned reluctantly. 'I'd have given a monkey to hear her response. But to our point, Hathaway! It had to be a poison. But what? And how?'

Stephen looked at the table and traced a design in its scratched surface. 'I cannot tell you that, sir,' he said. 'My employer Mr. McGrath, the coroner, and several officials, are of the combined opinion that the fifth Earl Denham - assuming it is he we speak of - died of fatal complications of a dissipated life. As Mr. McGrath's assistant, I have no reason to disagree. But,' he looked directly at Neville, 'in my capacity as a medical man… *if* there was indeed poison involved… I can attest that there are certain fungi known to those who study the nature of plants, that can be used to make a… substance, let us say… that, when ingested, will imitate a flux. But not immediately. An initial reaction is followed by quiescence, when the… target… feels well and continues his daily rounds unfettered. But the poison is still at work, in the organs and the nervous system. And in a week… two weeks, in a person with an iron constitution… fever and chills begin in earnest. And death must follow.'

'It leaves no trace?'

'None.'

'There is no cure?'

'If there is, I do not know it.'

'And McGrath…'

'Believes, as I said, that the man died of natural causes, resulting from a lifetime of loose living and drink.'

'Good God, Hathaway. If there had been a mistake!'

Hathaway looked down his aquiline nose with such hauteur that for an unnerving moment Neville thought he could be looking at the Third Earl Denham, back from the dead.

'What are you suggesting, sir?' asked Stephen quietly.

'You were seen at White's, dining with the gentleman.'

'I had business with him. As did, I am sure you know, several even less savory parties at a somewhat later date.'

'So you're saying any one of them could have got hold of this poison and used it.'

Hathaway shrugged.

'But how would it have been administered?'

'To a person of skill, it is an easy sleight of hand to top-dress a meal. While the subject is distracted, say, by a piece of information, or a document. A method no doubt you already know.'

'That assumes a great deal. For instance, that the target actually eats the tainted food or drink.'

'I find it is very hard to watch another man eat without indulging oneself as well,' Hathaway mused. 'It could have been anyone.'

'And what was your... business... with the Earl?'

'I offered him a large bribe to leave my family in peace. He accepted it. And now, regrettably, it is no doubt enriching Denham's clever manservant. Pity. It was all I had.'

Neville snorted, then shook his head in grudging appreciation. 'You're a cool hand, Hathaway. I could use a man like you, you know.'

'*Merci du compliment, m'sieu. Mais non.*'

'Why?'

Stephen smiled reflectively. 'In another country, in another language, in another existence, a wise woman told me that I had the capacity to choose the path of death, or the path of life. I might excel in one, at the cost of my soul. Or be ordinary in the other, and keep it. I choose the path of Life, Mr. Neville. I have seen too clearly what the other looks like.'

Then, as he rose, he grinned wolfishly. 'You really should seek medical attention for those bruises. I am happy to offer my services - to a new member of the family.' And he left chuckling.

Elsewhere in London, Beverly Ramage quietly died without ever regaining consciousness. His family surrounded him. Safe now, without ever knowing they had been in danger. And as if understanding this on some deep level, Ramage departed with only a sigh, finally free himself.

*****

Fueled by exhaustion and a creeping sense of loss that he couldn't quite identify, Nathaniel Neville found his mind straying into landscapes unfamiliar to him. Like how friendly his drawing room would look, graced by an elegant and companionable Mistress Neville... who in his imagination somehow took on the appearance of Seraphine Hathaway. The thought of having her by his side... her lovely body beside his in their bed, the awakening of a passion that he knew could exist if he were patient...

But then, senses returned, he knew any image of Madame Seraphine as an obedient and co-operative wife was pure fantasy.

That she would doubtless suggest getting a dog if loyal companionship was his aim.

And that distressed him deeply.

As he rounded the corner to the Swan's stage door, he all but collided with Charles Pearce, himself tottering away from it in a state of dishevelment that showed all the markings of having been bested in a bout of fisticuffs.

'Pearce!' he exclaimed, steadying the portly actor. 'What on earth has happened?'

Pearce detached himself and made an effort to stand straight. 'My dear sir,' he managed through a handkerchief pressed to his nose and mouth. 'My dear sir! The most dreadful occurrence!' He stared at Neville with wild eyes.

'Has there been a robbery?' demanded Neville. 'Are not Hemings or Freeman there? Is Sera... *the company*... safe? Spit it out, man! *What has happened?*'

'*Married!*' uttered Pearce dramatically, and sagged against the wall. 'She has become *married!*'

'I *beg* your... Seraph... *Mrs. Hathaway*... has not become married?'

'No, not her, sir! It's that poxy daughter of hers! Angel! She's run off and married that fly-by-night nephew of yours, if you please, and my cousin has flown into an apoplexy and near to taken the theatre to pieces over it! I believe I should call you out, sir! Were I not in the middle of an extremely taxing production of *Hamlet*...'

Neville looked from Pearce to the stage door. 'Right,' he said firmly. 'I'll go in.'

'If I were you, I'd come along to the Lamb and Flag for a stiffener first, Neville. She's popped my cork, sir! No telling what she'll do to *you*.'

Neville stifled a strong desire to laugh. 'I shall hazard it, however.'

'I don't like your chances.'

'A pony against.'

'Done.' They shook on it. Neville strode to the door, pounded with an authority he was far from feeling, and demanded that the reluctant Hemings let him in as a string of opera dancers issued forth, tittering and gossiping among themselves, nervously giving Pearce a wide berth.

He entered a theatre that had the indrawn sense of a battlefield in the aftermath of action. All sounds muted, all figures whispering wraithlike in and out of the lamplights, all quietly cleaning up the backstage, the edges of the stage itself, without the laughter and lighthearted conversation that usually accompanied the ending of a show. In the house, maids cleared away pamphlets, fans, gloves, handkerchiefs, even the odd hat, while casting anxious glances at the stage.

In the center of which, now pooled in light, now in semi-shadow, prowled Seraphine like a caged beast, muttering to herself and brandishing a letter. Neville stopped in the shadow of the proscenium and observed the reality of her: the flaws, the fury, the grace, the courage, the imperfections; all making up a being of a complexity and depth that his mind had never before allowed him to contemplate in Woman. This fierce being would never grace a drawing room with a bowl of roses in hand. This being would make a companion of fire and mettle, if a man could withstand it.

He watched, still and silent, as the stagehands completed their rounds and headed off to the local, the cleaners vacated the house, and the dressers shook, brushed, and hung every costume to air in the dressing rooms. The theatre closed in on itself, and settled into silence. Seraphine stopped pacing, stood alone on the edge of the stage, weeping quietly. Close around her Neville felt the dust, the life, the shades of laughter and tears, voices and groans and scents, ghosts of what had been and what might be and what had always been. Above her, beyond the proscenium arch, the balconies, the ceiling, the house itself, rose into darkness. Somewhere there was a thump. Somewhere a door opened and closed. Somewhere voices were swallowed by night. Somewhere a beam creaked and settled. It was, Neville thought, as if the theatre enfolded itself about Seraphine, she a part of it, it a part of herself.

She sensed, rather than heard, a shift in his stance that subtly altered the air. 'Mr. Hemings!' She rapped out. 'Am I keeping you?'

'You are keeping me indeed,' said Neville. 'But perhaps not in the way you meant.'

She turned to him, her eyes dark with misery and anger, and held the letter up to him accusingly. '*You*. I have *you* to thank for this, *you* who swore I could trust you, who swore to keep my daughter safe.'

'Is she then not safe?' he asked neutrally, unmoving.

She made a sound - half bitter laugh, half sob. 'Of course she is not safe. To have let her go off with that... that... elegant *swine*, all pleasing graces, all solicitation, to be *entrapped* into a relationship that *cannot* be allowed, *cannot* end in aught but heartbreak...'

'Entrapped?'

'*Of course* entrapped. How can she, a girl of her years...'

'Come now, *Madame*. Your daughter is fully of age. And certainly, if my experience of her serves, wise enough to know her own heart.'

'But *that man*...'

'If you are referring to my nephew Tristan Neville, I must inform you that far from entrapping your daughter, he has chosen to marry her despite being stripped of his own fortune. Come,' he coaxed. 'Seraphine. Nothing any of us has done availed to keep this pair apart. We must accept their nuptials and move forward. It is not so very bad, after all.'

'I wish - oh how I *wish* - that it could be stopped. If I had the means...'

'They are not yet wed?' he asked, surprised.

'Her letter says it is to be in three days. My daughter. My own sweet Angel.' Her shoulders slumped. He stepped out on to the stage and stood next to her, not so close as to cause more distress but close enough that she could feel his warmth, his solidity.

'She is still your own sweet Angel,' he said quietly. 'That will not change. But it is, after all, the way of the young through all time to form new couplings and new lives.'

She made no response, but wept in deep, shuddering waves. As she wept, she leaned nearer him. And as the minutes ticked on, her tears subsided, leaving her deeply weary. 'I have another bone to pick with you, sir,' she said finally. 'Regarding a meeting with my brother. But for the life of me, with all that has happened…' she sighed.

'It was time for Sarah Finister to return,' he said.

'Sarah Finister is dead.'

'No. Only transformed into a stronger, more beautiful version of herself. Seraphine Hathaway can now own her without fear.

'So this is your perspective,' he continued, gazing at the seats disappearing in ranks toward ceiling and darkness. 'I should be terrified.'

'You? With all your secret acts of derring-do and deeds accomplished in the night?' She searched her pockets for a handkerchief. He handed her his large one. She mopped her eyes and blew her nose. 'I was worried, you know.'

'Cloak and dagger stuff,' he said dismissively. 'I tell myself it must end. But then… a challenge beckons, and the danger makes me feel alive to my fingertips. Adventure is a drug as dangerous as opium or blue ruin, in its way.'

'As Theatre is.'

'Theatre!'

'Every evening I step onto this stage and take a great leap, knowing that every moment can either end in disaster or in a bliss greater than any I have known before. I exit in relief and swear I will never go back. And then I cannot wait for more.'

'We are more alike than we think.'

'Except that your form of excitement may lead to your death. Mine only to a dignified retirement when my audience no longer cheers me.'

'That's a sort of death.'

'Yes.'

'Marry me, Seraphine.'

'No. I should be the devil of a wife.' She gestured around her helplessly. 'I love this life too much, you see.'

'I believe that you are as much a part of The Swan's art and architecture as the bones of the building itself,' he agreed.

'I never took you for a romantic, Mr. Neville,' she said, and tentatively linked her arm through his. Feeling no resistance, she rested her head on his shoulder with a sigh.

'If that is your notion of romance, you are a very peculiar woman, Mrs. Hathaway.'

'No less peculiar than the man standing in this sleeping theatre, listening to the architecture and its human counterpart creaking into dust.'

He laughed. The sound rang out and then was absorbed into the air. 'We were not born under a wooing star, I fear.'

'Is this your idea of wooing?'

'Sadly, yes.'

They stood together, breathing each other in, gazing into the darkness.

'If I *were* to marry you…' she said musingly.

'Yes?'

'It would only be to save your life. For what use are you to Crown and Country if you insist on desperate acts that have mortal ends?'

'Very noble. And I, of course, offer for you only because I wish to take you to your daughter's wedding in my curricle and do not want twenty-four unchaperoned hours in your company to leave your reputation in tatters.'

'My reputation was in tatters long before I met you.'

'Then I suppose there's nothing for it. I must be dragged down to your level.'

'Why twenty-four hours? Surely Berkshire is not so far distant.'

'I intend to dawdle,' Neville said meaningfully, and gently gathered her closer.

'All right and tight, ma'am?' came Hemings' voice from the prompt corner.

'*Mon dieu*, Mr. Hemings!' she started guiltily. '*Desolée*. You'll be wanting to be away. I'll do the locking up.'

'Shall I get a chair for you, ma'am?'

'It won't be necessary, Hemings,' said Neville.

'Right, then. Goodnight, ma'am. Sir.' His footsteps faded away, and the stage door thudded closed behind him.

'I can perfectly well get a chair.'

'No.'

'Will you really take me to Angel?'

'Yes. But first - and always - I will see you safe home, Seraphine.'